Cowboy Country

JUDITH BOWEN
The Man from Blue River

He needed a companion...
she wanted to be his wife

RENEE ROSZEL
To Lasso a Lady

She was gorgeous and ready
to get married. But her future stepson
had something to say about that!

Relive the romance...
Two complete novels
by two of your favorite authors!

JUDITH BOWEN

was born in Edmonton, Alberta, and grew up in a logging camp in the Rocky Mountain foothills. She had many friends who lived on farms and ranches, a fact to which she attributes her love of the outdoors, not to mention her fascination with cowboys. Judith currently lives in British Columbia with her own hero and their three children.

RENEE ROSZEL

With over 8.5 million book sales worldwide, Renee Roszel has been writing for Harlequin and Silhouette since 1983. She has over thirty published novels to her credit and her writing honors include the Oklahoma Writer of the Year Award, presented in 1991, a finalist berth for the prestigious Romance Writers of America RITA Award, and multiple nominations by *Romantic Times Magazine.* She keeps her stories humorous and light, and her heroes gorgeous, sexy and bigger than life. After all, she asks, "Why not spend your days and nights with the very best?"

JUDITH BOWEN
RENEE ROSZEL

Cowboy
Country

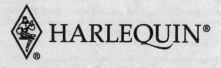

HARLEQUIN®

TORONTO • NEW YORK • LONDON
AMSTERDAM • PARIS • SYDNEY • HAMBURG
STOCKHOLM • ATHENS • TOKYO • MILAN • MADRID
PRAGUE • WARSAW • BUDAPEST • AUCKLAND

HARLEQUIN BOOKS

by Request—COWBOY COUNTRY

Copyright © 2002 by Harlequin Books S.A.

ISBN 0-373-21726-9

The publisher acknowledges the copyright holders
of the individual works as follows:
THE MAN FROM BLUE RIVER
Copyright © 1996 by Judith Bowen
TO LASSO A LADY
Copyright © 1996 by Renee Roszel Wilson

This edition published by arrangement with Harlequin Books S.A.

Visit us at www.eHarlequin.com

Printed in U.S.A.

CONTENTS

THE MAN FROM BLUE RIVER
Judith Bowen

CHAPTER ONE

AN UNDERDONE BURGER with a heap of greasy fries on the side, a limp pickle, maybe some half-cooked onions stuck to the top of the bun. That bright yellow ballpark mustard for sure. You'd expect something like that from a diner called Mom's.

But change a person's life forever?

Okay, maybe she shouldn't have pulled off the interstate just then. It was early, not quite five o'clock. Maybe she should've gone on to Rock Springs, checked in at a Howard Johnson's, found a Denny's. At least she'd heard of Rock Springs.

But she was hungry now. And her shoulders felt cramped from driving for so long and hanging on to the wheel so hard. She didn't mean to; it was just that after a while, she'd notice her fingers were tight on the wheel, her knuckles white with the strain of it, her shoulders all hunched up and watchful. Then she'd let go. But pretty soon, it'd happen all over again.

Still…what had she heard so many times? Never play poker with a man called Ace, never eat at a place called Mom's—and what was that last piece of homely advice Uncle Nate used to drum into the cousins? She couldn't remember. At least she could still smile. That was something.

So she pulled into the parking lot of the diner called Mom's and got out of the car and stretched. The air was country-clean and thick with the smell of desert and cold dried-up riverbeds and maybe, way, way in the distance, snow. Part of the Continental Divide wound through here, she knew. The Wind River Mountains. She'd driven through the Rattlesnakes and the Green Mountains already today. Tomorrow she'd tackle the Wind Rivers. Maybe.

And the diner? Well, it was exactly what she expected. A little run-down, a little cramped, the typed menu blurred under its plastic cover. Most of the prices had been crossed out and updated with ballpoint pen. There was no sign of "Mom," which Martha considered a good sign. A middle-aged man in a stained shirt, with a fairly clean white apron around his paunch, acknowledged her from behind the counter.

"What can I get ya, hon?"

She smiled, taking no offense at the familiarity, that was just how they talked out West. She'd already discovered that. "Grilled cheese on brown and a vanilla milk shake. Thanks."

What could go wrong with grilled cheese?

Two men in baseball caps and cowboy boots drank beer from cans at the back of the diner. They looked as though they'd been there for a while. Both turned to give her long, level, mildly curious stares before settling onto their elbows again, bellies shoved up against the scarred Formica counter, full male attention centered on the television set in the corner. The Kings were playing the Sabres.

Martha Thomas wasn't used to being ignored. It took real effort sometimes to realize *that* part of her life was over. She didn't have a column in a city daily twice a week anymore, she no longer co-hosted KBRT's celebrity food show, she was no longer a busy woman with a solid professional past, a history, a reputation—a woman who commanded and received respect. All of it gone. Vanished. Because of the kind of bottom-line mentality she'd never thought they'd see on the *Post*. But then, she'd never thought the old man would sell out, either.

At thirty-five, she was out of a job. No sense crying over what couldn't be changed. That wasn't the way the Thomases did things. Opportunity. She had to see this time in the wilderness as an opportunity, she told herself determinedly for the millionth time. Nothing but genuine gold-plated opportunity.

She picked up the ink-smudged weekly someone had abandoned on the vinyl bench seat and spread it before her on the tabletop, scanning the headlines quickly, professionally: Water Table Record Low. Library Hosts Laramie Author.

"Here ya go, miss."

She smiled up at the man who brought her meal. "Thanks." He must be combination cook and waiter.

"Passing through?"

It was harmless enough, but she felt her insides tense. Why was she so jumpy these days? With an effort, she relaxed.

"Yes." She nodded and reached for her sandwich. "Hey, this looks good." She decided to ignore the fact that it was on sliced white, not brown as she'd ordered. And the milk shake was served, old-fashion style, right in the stainless steel container in which it had been made. She took a sip. Mmm, thick and cold and creamy, just as she'd hoped. A place like Mom's probably didn't stock brown bread. No call for it.

The man stood there, waiting for her to elaborate on her answer. Just friendly, that was all.

"I thought I'd go on through to Tewson tonight. Do you know if there are any hotels there? Motels?" She was too tired to think of driving on to the next decent-size place on the map. It was Thursday and she'd been on the road ten days already. No one expected her. No one expected her anywhere on God's green earth. She chewed her sandwich slowly—pretty good, really, with the kind of sticky orange processed cheese she'd always secretly liked.

The man nodded, then moved back behind the counter. "Older hotel there, but clean enough. The Tewson Arms. Ma Jamieson runs it. Just past the lights, you can't miss it. And you won't need no reservation." He grinned, and she smiled back. "Least not until the rodeo comes to town, and that ain't till the end of next July."

Martha took another bite. Even on sliced white, the sandwich tasted delicious. She hadn't realized until now that, except for a handful of peanuts and some juice, she hadn't eaten since breakfast. And that had been where? Sheridan? Gillette? Her mind was beginning to play games.

Thirteen years at the *Post* and then—bam!—out the door. New owners, new bottom line, new management. New broom. Instead of the mid-career promotion she'd expected, they'd handed her a buyout. "Take a long holiday, you owe it to yourself," her producer at the television station had said. "There'll be work for you when you're ready to come back."

Yes, she'd left town with her head held high, her apartment sublet. But maybe she'd been hasty. What was she going to do for the next couple of months? Wander around and see the West? Be a tourist? Head for Palm Springs for a long-overdue visit, as her mother had suggested when Martha called to give her the bad news about the *Post?*

"Piece of pie, miss? Lemon, apple, blueberry, pumpkin?"

"No, thanks." Pumpkin? Gosh, she could just imagine. Sometimes the instinctive reactions of a food critic were a nuisance. "Too full. The sandwich is very good."

The man shrugged and swiped at the counter with his none-too-clean rag. Martha glanced again at the weekly in front of her as she finished her shake. She turned a page, saw a story about some midnight vandal who'd let all the dogs out of the local pound. That made her smile. She noticed the recipe column, a syndicated piece she'd seen before, then let her gaze fall idly to the want ads. She ran her eye down them quickly—half-ton for sale, low mileage, no rust; estate items, best offer; wanted, dry firewood…

Then her throat seemed to close up, and she could hardly swallow the last bite of her sandwich. There it was, in bold black and white:

WANTED: Lady companion for two girls. Remote location. No cooking/housekeeping re-

quired. Suitable applicants apply in own
handwriting to Box G, c/o Tewson Times, Tewson, Wyoming, or see Mrs. Violet Jamieson…

That would be Ma Jamieson. *Lady companion.*
Martha felt the blood rush to her face, but she didn't
glance up at the man who ran Mom's. She didn't think
she needed to draw attention to her sudden interest in
the classified section of the *Tewson Times.* Interviews
were Saturday, two days from now. *Remote, a job
anybody could do, even me, something to keep me
occupied for a few months, while I lick my wounds,
while I make plans…* This was the kind of coincidence you couldn't get away with in fiction, yet in
real life it happened all the time.

Martha paid for her meal and left, taking the newspaper with her. She didn't realize until she got outside
that her hands were shaking.

She looked around. Not a living thing moved in the
vast open landscape. Rolling hills, sagebrush, dark
forbidding mountains in the distance. A deep blue sky
shot with the gold of the lowering sun. Not a sound,
either, beyond the tinny distant roar of the hockey
crowd from the television set in Mom's.

And the wind. Wind that tugged at her hair, at her
newspaper, at the edges of her jacket. Did it ever stop?
The low moan made her bones ache. Martha hugged
herself and shivered.

Gorgeous, yes. Wyoming was gorgeous. But was it
the sort of place *anybody* could call home? Even for
a few short months?

SATURDAY DAWNED bright and blue.

Martha stopped at the door of the hotel room she'd been directed to and took a deep breath. How did she look? She'd tied her hair back neatly with a scarf. Glancing down, she bent to rub her palm over the stubborn wrinkles that had remained in her linen skirt even after hanging in the bathroom overnight. The matching cardigan and a turquoise silk shell, also slightly creased, would have to do.

Modesty, that was the ticket, she'd decided Thursday night when she'd found the Tewson Arms and checked in. After all, anybody who'd place an ad for a "lady companion" in this day and age had to be a pretty old-fashioned kind of person.

Man? Woman? She had no idea.

She hadn't dreamed she'd be applying for a job. Yet even casually dressed and somewhat rumpled as she was, she knew she was probably overdressed by local standards. Society events in Tewson apparently ran to the type of boisterous party that had echoed throughout the hotel the night before. A stag party, a proud Ma Jamieson had informed her, for Judd Barker's oldest boy, who was getting married next month over in Rock Springs.

Martha had smiled. Most hotel owners, she was sure, would have been ticked off to find such a rough-and-tumble party in progress on their premises. Maybe would even have called the sheriff. Not Ma Jamieson. But then, this was Tewson, Wyoming. Heck, in Tewson, Wyoming, the sheriff was probably at the party.

Martha straightened, took another deep calming

breath, then rapped briskly. A small girl of perhaps eight opened the door.

She stared at Martha.

Martha smiled. "May I come in? I've got an appointment for ten o'clock."

"Oh!" The girl flung the door open wide. "Come right in, ma'am." An even smaller pajama-clad girl sat on a sofa in front of a blaring television set, thumb in mouth, bedraggled toy kangaroo drawn up against her side. She held her thumb aloft for a couple of seconds, gave Martha a shy smile, then popped it back in and returned her attention to "Mr. Rogers' Neighborhood." This child was blond. The girl who'd let her in had dark hair that stuck out wildly around her small, heart-shaped face. Her eyes were black as midnight.

"I told you to turn off that TV, Daisy," the older girl hissed suddenly. "And you better get dressed. See who's here?" She sent her sister a deeply significant look.

"Ma'am, please sit down." Martha took the chair that the older girl rather grandly indicated, one of three drawn up to a wooden table in an alcove of the old-fashioned room. The girl hooked her thin legs around the rungs of the opposite chair and leaned forward on her elbows.

The room was a little larger than the one she'd been assigned on the third floor, Martha noted, high-ceilinged and with a connecting door in one wall. Similar decor. Pre-Reno wild West. Old ceilings tin-stamped and painted. The door no doubt led to another room such as this, a common arrangement in older hotels. It was probably locked.

Who was taking care of these children? There was no evidence of an adult's presence in the room, not even a suitcase that looked like it might belong to some grown-up. Two soft-sided nylon bags, one bright red, one bright blue, sagged on the floor by the bed, spilling forth clothing and toys. The girl staring at her remained silent. It was most disconcerting.

Martha cleared her throat. "I'm Martha Thomas," she said, thinking she might as well take the bull by the horns. "Er, *Mrs*. Martha Thomas." That was the lie she'd put on her application at the last moment, but Martha had thought it wouldn't matter for the short while she'd have the job and the "Mrs." might sound more mature and trustworthy to a prospective employer. Especially one looking for a "lady" companion.

"What's your name, dear?" The "dear" might have been a mistake. The girl's eyes darkened ominously.

"Anne. That's Anne with an *e*." Something rang faintly in Martha's memory. What was it?

"Is not," came a small voice from the sofa. The thumb was again suspended. "Is not Anne—"

"Is, too!" was the fierce response. The blond girl replaced the thumb and stared at the screen, apparently losing interest.

"It's Blossom *Anne* Langston." The girl held Martha's gaze defiantly, chin up, as if daring her to comment. "And that there's my *baby* sister, Daisy Langston."

"I'm very pleased to meet you, Anne. I suppose you know why I'm here?" The girl nodded. "Is your mommy or your daddy here to meet me? Or whoever's taking care of you?" Perhaps they were orphans.

"Our ma's dead."

"Is not," came the small voice again.

"She is too dead, Daisy! Don't say she ain't."

"Just gone away. That's what Fraser says." The thumb disappeared, then emerged again, its owner apparently thinking of something to add. "She's gonna come back and surprise us and bring us lotsa presents like she always does."

"Daisy, you don't know nothin'!" Her sister scowled fiercely. "And Fraser don't know nothin', either. He just wants us to think that, that's all. You better hurry and get dressed, before Fraser catches you or you're gonna be in *big* trouble."

She turned back to Martha. "My ma's dead," she repeated. The flat hopelessness of the statement caught at Martha's heart. Poor motherless child!

Who—and where—was this Fraser person? She needed to change the subject. "How old are you, Anne?" In her experience, which she had to admit was pretty limited, kids never seemed to mind nosy questions.

"Ten goin' on 'leven," she said promptly, adding matter-of-factly, "I'm kinda small for my age."

Martha smiled. Anne leaned toward her and whispered loudly, "Daisy's only just turned five. That's why she don't know nothin'."

"Do too! Do too!"

Anne ignored her sister. She continued to stare at Martha, who was beginning to feel as Alice might have felt after she'd tumbled into Wonderland. Nothing quite made sense.

"And who's Fraser?"

Anne glanced at her sister, who was absorbed again in Mr. Rogers's monologue and still showed no signs of getting dressed. "He's our dad," she whispered. "But we call him Fraser. It's more modern, don't you think? Like on TV." She seemed pleased. "Fraser McKenna. You know, one of the Blue River Mc-Kennas?"

Martha first nodded, then shook her head uncertainly. The Blue River McKennas? *Should* she have heard of this man?

"We got our ma's last name," Anne explained quickly, still whispering. "Langston. But, anyway, she's dead, just like I told you." She studied Martha for a few seconds, then added, "Fell down a hole and got ate up by a grizzly bear." She gave Martha a triumphant look.

Martha felt her head begin to spin. Should she point out that, to her almost certain knowledge, there were no grizzly bears left in Wyoming? But why extend this odd discussion? Presumably this Fraser McKenna, the father, was the one who would be interviewing her.

She checked her watch. Where was he? She'd made the appointment with Mrs. Jamieson, who'd handed her a slip of paper with the time and a room number yesterday afternoon. Maybe there'd been some kind of mix-up, some misunderstanding.... "Where exactly *is* your dad, Anne? It's already past ten and—"

"Oh, he ain't doing this, ma'am. He said since we were the ones getting the lady companion—" she said the words with pride, almost with capital letters "—we oughtta be the ones to pick her."

"*You're* interviewing for the job?"

"Me'n Daisy." She frowned at her sister. "Only Daisy won't help."

"Will too." The younger girl turned and gave Martha a sweet smile. "I want her, Bloss." She pointed at Martha. "Don't want Katie Barker. And I hate Mrs. Mills!"

"Heck, I told you you don't know nothin', Daisy," said her sister in annoyance. "This one's only been here a little while and you ain't even talked to her yet or had a real good look at her. How do you figure she's the right one?"

Daisy flexed her damp thumb and examined it carefully for a second or two. "Just know," she said flatly, and popped it back in again with a contented sigh.

"Well, it's true," Anne said grudgingly. "You are the best so far. You're pretty, and you don't seem *too* terrible old, and that's something—"

"But you know nothing about me!" Martha was finally shocked into deciding that she had to take charge. "Where *is* your father, Anne? I need to see him."

Anne ignored her. "Katie Barker just wants to trick Fraser into marrying her—now that our ma's dead, that is," she added hastily. "That's all she wants. She doesn't care about us one little bit. And Mrs. Mills is a mean old witch. We ain't having her, that's for sure!''

She smiled, just the shadow of a smile, but the first Martha had seen. ''We'll run away, Daisy and me, if he gets Mrs. Mills, and Fraser knows it. That just leaves you, 'cause we're going home today, Fraser says, after lunch, and if we don't get nobody we'll just have to stick another ad in the paper and go to all this trouble again and—''

''Anne, dear,'' Martha said gently, leaning forward and covering the girl's thin hand with her own. The girl froze. *''Where is your father?''*

There was a muffled curse and a yelp from the room next door, followed by a loud thump and another curse, as if a man had stumbled over a dog. *A dog?* Anne's eyes slid sideways, toward the connecting door. Martha could feel the girl's hand tense under hers.

''Bloss? Daisy?''

The connecting door burst open and a small grayish brown bundle of fur shot into the room and hopped onto the sofa beside Daisy, whimpering. Daisy giggled and put her arm around the dog. The dog licked her face. Martha stared at the half-dressed man who'd appeared in the open doorway, one large hand braced on each side of the frame.

Dear Lord.

Was this the father? The man's hair was awry, his face unshaven, his chest bare. He had on jeans but that was all. He took a step toward them, then winced and put his weight down gingerly on his bare left foot. ''Damn dog! You girls up already?''

He saw her and straightened, head up. Alert. Then he muttered something that sounded an awful lot like a string of curses and wiped vigorously at his unshaven face. He blinked hard once or twice. Even from where she sat, Martha could see that his eyes were bloodshot. Suddenly she put two and two together....

"You're drunk!" Martha stood up, outraged. To her horror, she felt her protective instincts quiver. Just what kind of father was this?

"Nope." The man held his head with both hands. "Hung over," he said simply, frowning. He shrugged a couple of times and shook his head gently, as though testing the density of the air around him.

"Boozing and chasing women," Anne chimed in, shaking her head in a brisk mime of adult disapproval. "Auntie Vi says it ain't good, ain't good at all."

Martha stared at the girl. *Boozing and chasing women?* And he was in charge—apparently—of these two dear sweet innocent souls?

"Hell's bells," the man said flatly, ignoring his daughter to stare at Martha. "Vi Jamieson doesn't know homegrown from steel-cut. Never did."

She held her shoulders straight. Drunk, hung over— they amounted to much the same thing, didn't they?

"This isn't what it looks like," he said.

"You're not nursing a hangover?" she asked, unable to keep the sarcasm from her voice. "You weren't whooping and hollering through the hotel, along with just about everybody else in this town last night? Mrs. Jamieson tells me it was quite the stag party."

"Uh-huh. Ted Barker's."

"So I understand."

"Yeah," he admitted after a pause, "I was there." Then he winced as if even the recollection was painful, and raised one shoulder. One tanned solidly muscled shoulder. She tried not to gaze at that shoulder, at his upper arm, his bare broad chest, lean and solid. There wasn't an ounce of extra flesh on this man. Not an ounce of softness.

Next thing he'd be telling her he hadn't wanted to go to the party....

"It wasn't my idea. I'm not much of a drinking man, believe it or not." His eyes, hard and none too apologetic, held hers. "Couple of buddies of mine dragged me in."

"Uh-huh."

Suddenly his face darkened. "Look, just who the hell are you, anyway?"

"This here's Mrs. Martha Thomas," Anne said, withdrawing her hand from Martha's and taking a step forward. "You better be polite to her, Fraser. And no cussin'. She's gonna be our lady companion," she added proudly, looking up at Martha.

"But I thought..." The man stared first at the girl, then at her, accusingly. Martha felt those eyes like the chill of midnight on bare skin. Midnight, with no moon rising. She bristled at the challenge, feeling herself take the girl's side automatically.

"She *is?*" he said. "Who the hell *is* she? What happened to Mrs. Mills? What about Katie?"

"We ain't having them," Anne returned sturdily, chin up. "We made up our minds, me 'n' Daisy. You said we could. Auntie Vi told us about this one last night when she was baby-sittin' us, and we didn't tell you. Auntie Vi said not to bother. You'd just scare her off, prob'ly."

He stared at Martha for a few more seconds—it felt like forever—then shook his head, as though to clear it.

"C'mon, Daisy. Get dressed, darlin'," he said quietly, hardly demonstrating the *big* trouble Anne had said her sister would be in if their father caught her still in her pajamas. Daisy obediently got up and shut off the television. She began rummaging in the clothing half-spilled from the blue bag.

"Martha Thomas?" The man repeated her name slowly and frowned. His voice was deep and slightly hoarse. "*Mrs.,* you say?"

Martha nodded and took a quick breath. "That's right."

The man shook his head again in apparent disbelief. "You—uh, Bloss here says you answered the ad in the paper?" He sounded incredulous.

"I did." She didn't see the point in offering more information. If he hadn't expected anyone to answer his ad, why had he placed it? She wasn't sure she was still interested, anyway. The open road was looking more attractive by the minute.

"You from around here?"

"No." She shook her head, hesitated, then said, "Wisconsin."

"Wisconsin," he muttered, straightening. "Okay, let me think." He frowned, eyes closed, and ran his hands through his shaggy black hair several times, the action throwing all the hard muscles of his chest and upper arms into relief. Martha couldn't help being impressed. He was a very fine-looking man, even if he needed a shave and a haircut. And a shirt.

"Listen." He exhaled loudly and opened his eyes. "I'm sorry about this." He waved a hand impatiently. "We're a little, uh, disorganized this morning."

She shrugged slightly and held his gaze willingly, fully, for the first time. He raised one eyebrow, the smallest gesture of appeal. "Can we talk?"

His eyes were very dark, like Anne's. His face looked drawn, as though he hadn't slept well, or much. There was a grimness about his jaw and something hidden in his face, something elusive that seemed to separate him from her, even in these admittedly ridiculous circumstances. Something that kept him distant from the world. Or the world from him.

She nodded, surprising herself. "I suppose we'd better."

"Have you had breakfast? Hell, of course you've had breakfast," he muttered, not waiting for her answer. He dug deep into the front pocket of his jeans. "Damn!" He glanced at the watch he'd retrieved, then absently strapped it to his wrist. "Coffee? How about I meet you in the café downstairs in, oh, say, twenty minutes, half an hour?"

Martha barely hesitated, again surprising herself. "That would be fine." She bit back the acid comment she'd been about to add—that, yes, he clearly would benefit from some coffee, the stronger the better. It was none of her business. None of this was any of her business. She stood stiffly and smoothed the fabric of her skirt, an automatic gesture.

Anne smiled at her then, a shy radiant smile, the first real smile Martha had seen since she'd entered the room. She felt her heart tighten until it hurt. *This child needed her.* She could feel it. And the other one, Daisy, who by now had managed to wriggle herself into some pants and was in the process of putting on a T-shirt, inside out—she needed her, too. No mother. And no prize for a father, either, by the look of it.

Martha took a deep painful breath. Long ago she had stopped allowing herself to dream of having children. It was too late; she'd waited too long. She'd be thirty-six next spring, and the prospect of a family and children was as remote as it had ever been, only now it mattered more. Back then, when she'd been in her twenties, other dreams had owned her—her career, travel, a series of very nice but ultimately unsuitable men, one or two could-have-been-serious affairs.

What were the odds that her dream would come true now? No job, and the prospect of having to start over somewhere new. No particular man on the horizon. Soon she'd be too old even to think about having a baby. No point in fooling herself: it wasn't going to happen. *That* was the reality.

Martha walked to the door, shoulders squared. She smiled at the two girls and nodded coolly at their father.

"Twenty minutes."

CHAPTER TWO

IN FACT, IT WASN'T even twenty minutes. She'd just finished her first cup of coffee, racking her brain desperately for what to say to this prospective employer, when she saw him making his way through the hotel dining room. Eyes followed him, both male and female, and she could understand why. He wasn't exceptionally tall, perhaps six feet or just over, but he had the kind of physical male presence that had nothing to do with size.

The girls trailed behind, and Martha watched as he settled them at a table and stopped to speak to the waitress for a few moments. Then he continued toward her, his expression determined. He carried a mug in his hand. Coffee, probably, black and hot.

The slight delay gave her a chance to still her churning insides. From his frown she judged that Fraser McKenna wasn't altogether pleased about this meeting either, but at the same time he looked like a man who knew he had a job to do and who intended to get that job done.

She had to admire him—he wasted no words.

"You still interested in looking after those two?" He nodded toward the girls. He'd taken the chair opposite Martha. "After...uh, you know?" He made a vague gesture toward the upper floor. He didn't seem all that embarrassed about the circumstances of their earlier meeting. Nor did he apologize.

"I—I'm not sure," she said truthfully, staring down at her cup. Finally she looked up. He was watching her.

"Why's that?" was his blunt reply. He reached for the sugar.

The arrival of a waitress with more coffee gave her a chance to collect herself. "Well, let's just say this seems to be kind of an odd situation."

"Odd?"

Martha raised her cup to be refilled; she didn't miss the doe eyes the waitress had for her companion. Fraser appeared not to notice. His gaze never left Martha's face.

"Yes, odd. For some reason, you don't seem all that keen on hiring me, period. And I've never been interviewed by a couple of kids for a job or—"

"They're the ones who'll be spending time with you," he interrupted quietly. "Not me." He nodded his thanks to the waitress, and she beamed before moving off with the coffeepot. "Makes sense to me to see if they like you."

"Mmm." She had to admit that it did. "And basically, well, I just decided to apply for the job on an impulse. Maybe the whole thing's not such a great idea, after all...." She was beginning to wonder what crazy notion had made her apply in the first place.

His question, when it came, startled her.

"Do you believe in fate, Mrs. Thomas?" His eyes held a peculiar intensity.

She felt completely rattled now and carefully set down her cup before replying. "Is that a serious question, Mr. McKenna?"

"Fraser," he said, and studied the spoon he'd just used. He turned it over several times, frowning. "Yes. It's a serious question." He regarded her intently again, adding, "Truth is, I never thought anybody'd answer that ad."

"Well, no, Mr.—uh, Fraser," Martha said firmly. "I don't believe in fate. I believe people are responsible for their own futures. They control their own fates." Wasn't that why, deep down, she hadn't regarded what had happened at the *Post* as a complete and total disaster, as many of her friends and colleagues had? Wasn't the buyout a perfect opportunity to start something new?

He sighed, stared at her a moment longer, then nodded slowly. "So do I."

For a long moment he said nothing more. He simply continued to frown at the pattern his spoon was making on the tabletop, distracted, clearly thinking about something altogether different. Something else, maybe someone else. Martha studied her own cup. *This was a job interview?*

"All right." He cleared his throat. He seemed to rouse himself with some effort. "Look, is there a Mr. Thomas somewhere in the picture?"

Thoroughly disconcerted now, Martha cast about wildly for his meaning. *Her father?* Then she remembered her lie.

"No. I mean, he's no problem," she added hastily.

"Separated? Divorced? Dead?"

"Dead," Martha snapped back. Well, that was true at least—her father *was* dead. Her mother had moved to California a year after he'd died. She hadn't seen her in nearly three years. She regretted that; it was something she intended to change.

She noticed that Fraser McKenna must have taken the time to have a quick shower, although he hadn't shaved. The trace of a beard gave him a dark look, a dangerous and mysterious look, although his words couldn't have been more direct. Tact did not seem to be his long suit.

"I'm sorry. About your husband, that is," he said wearily, running his hand through unruly dark hair, then hunching forward to stir his coffee. "Maybe you think it's none of my business." His eyes looked bleak for a second or two. Or had she imagined it?

"Generally speaking, I wouldn't ask," he went on. "It's just that my ranch is a long way from what some might call civilization, and I don't want to take on any more complications than I need to. I've got no interest in getting mixed up in some, well, awkward domestic situation. Do you understand my meaning?"

Did she? She met his eyes gamely.

"To be frank," he went on, "I'd prefer to hire a widow over a divorced woman. Or over one who's left her husband for one reason or another and might want to go back in a couple of weeks."

"I understand."

"It's been known to happen, that kind of thing."

She nodded. His eyes were stone-hard. Obviously this man had been hurt by a woman. The girls' mother, from the sounds of it.

"The fact is, it's time I got some help with the girls," he began again. His voice was rough. "Bloss and Daisy need a woman around. I've looked after them by myself for—" He stopped abruptly, then as quickly went on, "Well, for quite a while. But I'm just too busy. Daisy's home, but Blossom's in school. They need someone who'll be there for them when I can't be, to answer questions, show them things." He paused. "Woman things."

Woman things. The words brushed her skin, butterfly-soft. She felt the blood rush to her throat and tremble there.

"It doesn't make sense to drag them all over the ranch with me anymore. I've got a business to run, and winter's coming on." He paused again, then continued—a little hesitantly, she thought. "And they seem to like you fine. That's good enough for me."

His eyes held hers. "They're growing up, Mrs. Thomas. They need a woman around."

"A lady companion?" she ventured, her voice sounding softer than she'd planned.

"Yeah," he said, almost as softly. "A lady companion. A woman like you."

Martha saw something flare in his dark gaze for a second or two, just a flash and then it was gone, but it told her that beneath the grim exterior was a man who cared very much for the well-being of his daughters. He took a big swallow of his coffee.

"B-but this is crazy." She managed a shaky laugh.

"Crazy?"

"Crazy. You really don't know anything about me, for starters."

"Ah, hell." He waved one hand dismissively. "I talked to Vi—she likes you. Bloss showed me your application. You've got decent handwriting. Strong. Honest. Straightforward."

If only he knew!

He drained his mug. "That counts for something. I expect people to be honest with me. Or, if they're not, I expect them to have a damn good reason to lie. Either way's fine with me." He set down his cup. "And you're a widow, to boot. Just what I'm looking for, although I have to say I'd've preferred someone a little older."

Widow? Straightforward? Dear God, everything she'd told him so far was a lie!

"How much are you offering?" she asked. This was a business proposition, after all. His remark about her age, well, she'd let that pass. How old was he? Thirty-five? Forty? Forty-five? Hard to tell with these tanned outdoor types.

He named a salary, not a lot, but of course room and board was part of the bargain, and it wasn't the money she cared about, anyway.

"No cooking?" She was only teasing, only echoing the ad.

"Nope. I'm a fairly decent cook myself and so is Bloss, believe it or not. She's had to be, poor kid." He frowned, shrugged, didn't explain. "A neighbor a few miles down the road comes in to keep house for us once a week."

He stared at his hands, spread wide and flat in front of him on the table. They were work-hardened hands, the backs tanned and scarred, the fingers long, strong, capable. Martha could feel the tension in his posture, could feel the answering tension in her own body. It couldn't be easy for such a man to admit to a stranger what he'd just admitted—that he needed help. He'd said the girls needed a woman in their lives, and no doubt they did, but she knew, too, that it was his way of saying he couldn't cope on his own any longer.

"Sounds all right to me," she said finally, to her own astonishment. What in heaven's name was she doing? And a few months was all she could give this odd little family. What then?

"Fine." His expression, when he glanced up to catch her gaze, held grim triumph. Another man might have smiled. "When can you start, Mrs. Thomas?"

"This afternoon."

THINGS HAPPENED FAST. Maybe too fast.

A few hours after she'd agreed to look after Fraser McKenna's two little girls, her belongings had been packed up and transferred to McKenna's red Ford Bronco, stenciled on both doors with what she assumed was the name of his ranch—Westbank Rambouillets. Her hotel bill had been paid, and with Fraser and his daughters following in the Bronco she'd driven her rental car to the agency in Rock Springs. She'd wondered, as she drove, if she was doing the smart thing.

What *was* the smart thing, anyway? All her life she'd done the smart thing, and where had she ended up? Just one more casualty in the downsizing operation of a big media conglomerate, that was where.

Maybe this was the time to do something crazy for a change, now when it didn't really count.

That something crazy had put her in the passenger seat of a stranger's dusty vehicle heading north, God only knew how far. Maybe she should have asked.

"How did the dog…get hurt?" She'd already found out it wasn't easy making conversation with this man.

"Spook?" Fraser glanced at her, then frowned back at the empty road, which had begun to wind up into rugged hills. They hadn't seen another car in half an hour. Martha saw a sign that read: Pine Ridge, 102 miles.

The mangy three-legged mutt growled softly from the floor behind her. He lay at the feet of the two girls, who were both sound asleep in the back seat in a tangle of hair and knees and elbows and potato-chip crumbs and comic books and stuffed toys. The dog's name was Spook, Daisy had told her.

Well named, Martha thought. The mutt didn't like her much; that was clear. The feeling was mutual. He'd growled almost constantly from the moment she climbed into the vehicle in Rock Springs.

"Got him from a fellow two winters ago who found him wandering down at Big Sandy," Fraser said finally. "He'd been abandoned, the fellow figured, and had pretty bad frostbite. Vet had to amputate his back leg."

"Poor dog!" Martha couldn't help a twinge of sympathy, despite her opinion of Spook. "How could anyone do that—just leave a helpless animal on its own to starve?"

Fraser looked directly at her, then back at the road.

Martha thought his look suggested more than his words indicated. "Maybe it was an accident. Maybe the dog ran off when his people stopped for gas or something." He shrugged. "Who knows? Anything could've happened."

Yes—and who knows why the rescuer had brought the maimed animal to Fraser McKenna?

The man beside her shrugged again, winced and swore sharply under his breath, his shoulders tensed. His head must be killing him. Maybe that was why he was so quiet.

"Anyway, you might have noticed he's not too friendly. But the girls like him fine. And he won't let me go anywhere without him." He gave Martha the shadow of a smile.

He must have really tied one on last night, she thought. Still, even scowling and unshaven and not much more than surly, he was a pretty attractive man. Physically, anyway. She could see why the unknown Katie Barker took such an interest. A boozer and a woman-chaser, Anne had said bluntly, reporting Mrs. Jamieson's opinion. On the other hand, Martha supposed there weren't too many eligible men in this part of the country, even if this particular one came with two children attached. Perhaps Miss Barker couldn't afford to be that choosy.

My new boss.

Martha turned toward the window, trying to ignore the dog's faint menacing growl from behind her. Well, she'd taken on the job with both eyes open. At least until she made up her mind what she was going to do when she went back home. *If* she went back home.

But whatever she ended up deciding, she'd only be at this ranch for a few short months. Unless, of course, this Katie Barker or some other Wyoming lass managed to drag her employer to the altar before then.

Wild Wyoming man or not, Fraser McKenna didn't worry her. Not on a personal level. Sure, he seemed a little unfinished around the edges, a little abrupt, a little blunt. Sure, he was handsome as the devil himself, if you liked the type, all big and rough and brooding. But he was polite enough in a rather charming old-fashioned way, and he wasn't the first good-looking man she'd seen up close. She could handle that. He'd been truthful with her back at the hotel. Honest, straightforward—which was more than *she'd* been. She liked that about him. Mostly, it was clear to her that he loved his daughters deeply. That one simple fact outweighed everything else.

And—who was she kidding?—deep down, Martha felt excited as heck about the turn of events. How often did a city woman like her, who'd grown up with pavement and dancing lessons and summers at the lake, have the chance to spend time on a genuine Western ranch? This was an adventure. This was a bonus. This was serendipity. This was Lady Luck. And it wasn't as though she'd committed her entire *life* to anything.

''What are rambouillets?'' She was pretty sure she'd mangled the pronunciation, but at least he'd probably talk about whatever kind of beasts he raised. Most of what she knew about ranching she'd gotten from the movies.

''Ram-bo-lays,'' he enunciated slowly. At least he

didn't seem to mind her occasional pesky questions. "They're sheep. I run about—"

"Sheep!"

"Yeah. Sheep." She heard the faint smile in his voice. "I run a couple of thousand head on my high range in the summer. Wool and meat, mostly wool. I have a smaller year-round operation down at the main ranch—purebreds and breeding stock. So, yes, sheep," he repeated. "That surprise you?"

"I guess it does. I thought a rambouillet was some kind of fancy cow. I had no idea there was anything but cattle out here in Wyoming."

"Cattle, sheep, hay—whatever pays the bills. I've got a neighbor who raises ostriches." He turned, and she couldn't be sure if the gleam in his eye meant he was kidding. Ostriches! He had to be. "I've had cattle for years, and I've still got some. Whitefaces. But I prefer the sheep."

"How many staff?"

"Two pretty regular. Tom's my top hand, and his cousin Alfred's on the payroll. Then I've got a couple of part-timers, depending on the work. More during lambing and branding."

"You mentioned someone comes in to do some work in the house. Does she live far away?" Even if the ranches out here were few and far between, it'd be nice to have another woman to talk to occasionally.

"Couple of miles."

Martha waited, and when there was no more information forthcoming, she continued, "Young? Old? Married? Children?"

He smiled slightly, but said nothing.

"Does she do a good job? Do the girls like her? Does she have a *name?*" Martha finished in frustration.

"Name's Birdie. Birdie LeBlanc. Yeah, she's married." He shrugged. "Husband's name is Hugh. He works for me off and on. You'll meet her soon enough." The subject clearly held no interest for him.

Martha gave up. She leaned her head against the vinyl headrest and closed her eyes. She envied Anne and Daisy the health and youth to be able to fall asleep so easily. Sleep was something that had too often eluded her these past few weeks. Maybe it would be different up at Fraser McKenna's ranch.

She opened her eyes a sliver to glance at him. He was frowning again, driving a little too fast over what must be familiar terrain. Occasionally he swerved to avoid potholes. He leaned against the driver's door, relaxed, slouched away from her. One hand on the wheel, eyes intent on the road. Preoccupied. Distant. Once more she felt that sense of buried power—physical, vital, tautly controlled. Secrets. A sense, too, of his separateness. A deliberate separateness. A feeling that some faint chord sounded inside him, music only he could hear.

Utter fancy.

Martha wrenched her eyes away and closed them again—ah, the bliss of sleep, of not remembering. She yawned, remembering to yawn delicately, simply by widening her nostrils, ladylike, the way Gran Thomas had taught her. As if this man would care if she showed all her fillings.

Then, suddenly, she felt a tiny giggle rising to the

surface. Of course he'd care—she was the Lady Companion. She was supposed to be setting a good example.

Somehow the impossible happened. She slept. The next thing Martha knew, she was waking up, cold, uncomfortable, scrunched up against the passenger door. Her mouth felt full of cotton wool, and she heard the whimpered protests of the girls waking in the seat behind her, the deep soothing tones of their father and, outside, dogs barking. A door slammed, Fraser's door. It was dark, very dark, except for a few yard lights, and she could see a thick blanket of stars in the sky. She'd never seen so many stars; hadn't known there *were* so many.

"Hey!" She nearly fell into his arms as he opened her door. Her legs were cramped and numb. "Ouch."

"You okay?" It wasn't much in the way of comfort.

She grimaced. "Sure. I'm fine." Martha cracked a tiny smile to herself. The overhead light was bright in her eyes, and she wondered how she must look, stupid with sleep, eyes blinking, neck cricked and stiff from her awkward position. She swung her legs toward the open door and stumbled out.

"Ouch!"

"Hold on." He put his arm around her shoulder and held her firmly against his side as her left leg gave way. Martha could feel the pins and needles in her knee and calf. It was nothing to the sudden pounding of blood in her brain. Fraser McKenna hadn't touched her until now, hadn't even shaken her hand when they met. Even now, he acted as though he couldn't bear

to be near her, stepping back awkwardly the instant
she put her weight on her lame leg.

"I'm fine," she said, but she knew her voice was
unsteady. "Just give me a minute. I—I guess my leg
went to sleep." She took a couple of deep breaths and
limped away from the truck. The air was cold and
sweet. She could smell dead grass and leaves and the
bark of trees, and felt frost crunch under her thin soles.
A couple of ghostlike black-and-white farm dogs kept
a respectful distance. She shivered. "This is your
ranch?"

"Westbank Ranch. West of the Blue."

"The Blue?"

"The Blue River."

She heard the quiet pride in his voice, felt the
knowledge in her bones that this man was home, that
he knew he was home, and that the place he called
home meant a great deal to him.

"I'll get the girls out," he said gruffly, and moved
away into the darkness. The farm dogs followed him,
tails wagging. Spook leapt about, his missing leg apparently little handicap. He snuffled through the frost-
rimmed grass, relieved himself against a nearby bush,
then trotted back to deliver a last threatening growl at
her.

"Beat it," she said halfheartedly. He raced around
to the other side of the vehicle, to where Fraser had
managed to bundle Daisy against his shoulder and lift
her clear. Martha followed. Anne had already climbed
out, her hair awry, her face creased with sleep. She
scowled as Martha reached out to give her a hand.
My, my, Martha thought. Independent. Like father,

like daughter. But she let Anne shake off her offer of help and watched as the girl trailed across the ghostly grass after her father, Spook trotting importantly, if awkwardly, at her side. They walked toward the dark bulk that must be the ranch house. Daisy's bedraggled kangaroo dangled from one small hand, the other hand tucked near her mouth on Fraser's shoulder. Martha knew where her thumb would be. The farm dogs had bounded ahead and disappeared into the darkness. No one looked back. No one seemed too concerned about waiting for the Lady Companion.

Martha grabbed two of her bags from the back of the Bronco and followed.

FIFTEEN MINUTES LATER, the girls were tucked in their beds, pajama-less, but at least Martha and Fraser had managed to get jeans and socks off before allowing them to curl up under the quilts in their T-shirts and underwear. Martha walked toward the door. There were toys everywhere, and clothes. But something about the room struck her as unusual. What was it?

She turned as she reached the door, felt her heart twist as she saw Fraser lay one large hand lightly, briefly, on top of each sleepy head. No doubt he'd bend down to kiss them if he was alone.

Martha looked away quickly and stepped into the hall. This was a private moment between the man and his children. His gesture spoke of deep and tender feelings, feelings impossible to share with a stranger. It made something inside her hurt unbearably to face the hard truth once again—she would never touch the sleep-sweaty brow of a child of her own.

She shivered. Fraser had turned up the heat when they'd first come in, but the house was still cold. Cold and silent. She felt as if the very walls were watching her, as if they disapproved of her.

Where had he put her bags? Martha looked around, taking in the rough-hewn structure of the building, log beams exposed, walls thick with many years of paint and wallpaper. An old-fashioned dark wood wainscoting ran at waist-height along the hall. It was a plain house, what she'd seen of it so far, plain and substantial. Like the man who lived in it.

"I put you down here." The man in question emerged from the bedroom, turning off the light behind him and leaving the door ajar. "This way."

He set off down the hall and Martha followed. She'd been put in the room at the end of the hall, opposite the girls' room and beside another bedroom. His? The bathroom—she peeked in quickly as she went by—was next to the girls' room.

"I hope this suits you," Fraser said gruffly, standing aside to let her enter. Martha went forward quickly. Her bags were at the foot of a high white-painted iron bedstead, the mattress covered in another quilt, this one faded with time and many launderings. There was a dresser, walnut, from another time, and a chest with drawers, also dark polished walnut. A painted door led, presumably, to a closet. The floor was bare. It struck her, then, what had seemed so odd a moment ago—everything in the girls' room looked new. Brand-new.

"This'll be just fine," Martha said. Somehow she knew he'd been waiting for her reply, because she

heard him let his breath out slowly. Relief? "I'll want
a reading lamp of some kind for the bedside table,"
she added. "And maybe a chair."

"I'll fix you up tomorrow." He didn't move, and
she glanced up at him uncertainly. Did he want to say
something more? She hoped not. Lord, she was
tired.... "That all right?"

"Fine."

"Bathroom's across the hall," he said, leading the
way again. "Sorry, but we have to share it. There's
another one off the kitchen."

Martha nodded. "That's fine." Then she laughed
weakly, an afterthought. "Look, I don't want you to
think I'm terribly fussy about my arrangements. I'm
not. Maybe in the morning we can go over what you
expect from me—my duties, that sort of thing...."

"You want a hot drink or anything now?" he
asked. "Coffee? Tea?"

She didn't, but she could tell it was a formal gesture
of hospitality on his part, an effort to make her feel
welcome. She supposed she could manage to keep her
eyes open for another ten minutes or so.

"That would be lovely. Maybe some hot chocolate." She smiled again, and this time saw a flicker of
response in his eyes.

In the kitchen, she sat at the scrubbed wooden table
as he prepared their drinks.

"How's your head?" she asked tentatively.

He gave her a rueful smile. "A lot better." He
plugged in the kettle, then began to rummage through
a cupboard.

"Despite what Bloss may have said, I'm not much

of a boozer,'' he commented dryly, pushing aside a box to reach into the back of the cupboard. He seemed more relaxed here in his own house than he'd been all day. ''Never could handle my liquor, even as a young fellow. That's why I generally stay away from it. I always pay for it when I don't.''

He shut the cupboard door, box of cocoa in his hand. ''Like today.'' He smiled again, no more than a faint friendly smile, but Martha felt a response right down to her toes. So—what about chasing women? Was that just so much talk, too? She didn't dare ask.

He measured the cocoa powder into two mugs, adding sugar and mixing the blend carefully with a tiny amount of evaporated milk. She knew he was doing this to prevent lumps in the cocoa.

Her heart swelled at the memory. She hadn't had hot chocolate made with hot water and evaporated milk since her summer with Gran Thomas in Michigan all those years ago. She'd completely forgotten, but now it came back to her in a flood. A plain kitchen, something like this, with an old-fashioned oil range in the middle. Painted cupboards and evidence of Gran's industry everywhere, from the crocheted tea cozy to the cross-stitch on the tea towels. What she'd always called ''fancy work.'' Chintz curtains, starched monthly, Martha recalled, at the windows. Why, it was—it must be at least twenty-five years ago! Yet watching Fraser measure out the ingredients had brought it back to her, every detail sharp and intense.

''Thanks.'' She took the mug from him, realizing she'd been careful to make sure their fingers didn't touch. Why was that? She inhaled deeply of the sweet steam. "Smells wonderful." She took a sip. "My grandmother used to make hot chocolate just like this."

"She did?" He arched one dark eyebrow and raised his mug in a brief salute. He hadn't joined her at the table but, instead, stood facing her a few feet away, leaning against the counter, watching her. She suddenly felt self-conscious. Young, warm-cheeked, as though she really were that girl of ten again.

"Yes." Martha took another sip. "Mmm." She curled her fingers around the mug and smiled. "I guess your daughters like hot chocolate like this, too."

He frowned down into the contents of his cup. Then he looked at her for a long moment, half-speculatively, a moment in which Martha began to retrace her thoughts, wondering what she'd said, if she'd made some terrible blunder—

"I've got something to tell you that maybe I should have mentioned before, Mrs. Thomas," he said finally.

Something to tell her? "What's that?"

"Those two girls asleep up there are not my daughters."

CHAPTER THREE

"WHAT DO YOU MEAN—they're not your daughters?"

"Just what I said." He set his mug down heavily on the counter. "They're not my children. I'm not their father."

"B-but Anne looks just like you!" It was a stupid comment, but...*not his children!*

He scowled. "Nevertheless, I'm not her father. I'm not her stepfather. As a matter of fact, I don't know for sure who her father is." He ran one hand through his hair in a weary gesture and muttered, "I don't think Brenda did, either. Look, maybe we should talk about this in the morning—"

"You can't just...just drop a bombshell like that and expect me to forget all about it and go to sleep!" Martha felt outrage mounting beneath her shock. "And who the heck's Brenda? I took on this job expecting to be looking after your daughters—"

"Brenda's their mother." His tone was level. "She's away. I never told you they were my daughters. The ad in the paper didn't say they were my daughters."

"No, maybe it didn't." Martha's mind was racing, skittering, trying to remember just what it *had* said. "But I certainly assumed they were your children, and you said nothing to encourage me to think differently.''

"Okay, okay," he said, spreading his hands wide, palms up. "I didn't, no. I take full responsibility for that."

He had the nerve to sound irritated!

"But the truth is," he continued, "I hedged because I wasn't sure you'd take the job if I told you straight out. It's complicated. The point is, I had to hire somebody." She almost flinched at the indifference in his voice. He wasn't a bit apologetic. He'd had to hire *somebody*.

He frowned. "Hell, I don't see what difference it makes, anyway, exactly what the situation is, whose kids they are. Either way, it's my problem, not yours. The job's the same."

She stood, then sat back down again. Just what *was* the situation? She was furious with this man. And to think she'd been complimenting herself on what a good judge of character she was, knowing an honest man when she saw one, blah, blah, blah. Still, she had options. "What makes you so sure I'm going to take the job now?"

"Nothing." He continued to regard her levelly and steadily. "Except we're a long way from nowhere up here. Not that I wouldn't take you back if you wanted. Hell, if you want to go, go." He shrugged. "But I still think you're the right woman for the job."

Oh, sure, she felt like saying. How many choices had he had? And what would he know, anyway? He didn't know *her* at all. Not that there was much sense in pointing that out again. Martha kneaded the tight muscles at the base of her neck. It had been a very long day. She was exhausted. All she wanted was her bed and the oblivion of sleep.

"Look, maybe this wasn't the best way to have handled it, Mrs. Thomas, but I felt—"

"You can quit calling me Mrs. Thomas," she snapped. "My name's Martha." He had a surprise or two coming himself, when she told him there was no Mr. Thomas, dead or otherwise.

"All right. Martha." He said her name in a low tone that had her glancing up at him. He'd made the plain and ordinary syllables sound somehow dark and mysterious, almost exotic. He was still standing, still looking at her hard, hands buried in his back pockets.

"Maybe we'll have a chance to talk about this tomorrow, Martha. You'll understand when I tell you that I don't care to discuss it in front of the girls."

"Is this—" Her voice came out weaker than she'd intended, and she stopped to clear her throat before going on. She stood abruptly and carried her mug to the sink, then looked up at him again, trying to gather her nerve. She had a horrible feeling in her stomach. Her knees felt shaky. "Is…is this at least legal?" she managed. "Whatever's going on around here? Brenda? The girls? You?"

He stared at her so long, his eyes dark and somber and searching, that Martha felt she'd have to look away—or scream—if he didn't answer her.

"I don't know," he said to her horror. Then he sighed, deeply, heavily. "I wish I could tell you one way or the other. But I just don't know."

A LIE FOR A LIE.

Anne had said Fraser was their father; Martha had said she was a widow. She might as well set them straight on that soon. Mind you, last night, tossing and turning on the too-soft mattress, she'd made up her mind to leave. It was the rational thing to do. Go on to California, as she'd originally planned, spend some time with her mother, perhaps head to the Baja for the rest of the winter.

The last thing she needed was to get mixed up in some highly dubious, possibly illegal scheme looking after two girls. It was just a question of informing Fraser as soon as she had a chance and making the arrangements. *Brrr,* it was cold! Martha dug her hands deeper into the silk-lined pockets of her leather jacket. She didn't have the wardrobe for a winter here, either.

"Let's go over to the barn now," Daisy said, interrupting her musings. "I want to show you my pony and the kittens that just got borned and—"

"Slow down, young lady." Martha laughed and let the five-year-old pull her in the direction of the barn. The girl had one mittened hand in Martha's; the other clutched the toy kangaroo. Daisy had already shown her the entire ranch house, from the cellar, lined with empty wooden shelves where ranch women of the past—perhaps Fraser's mother or grandmother—had put up stores for the winter, to a sectioned-off part of the attic, where Fraser had set up a playroom. She knew now why everything in the girls' room looked new—everything *was* new.

Daisy had led her into Fraser's bedroom, too, before Martha had realized it and hurried the girl out. But not before she'd taken in the plain wooden furniture, of a similar era to the furnishings of her own room, the big bed, competently if roughly made, the faded denim jacket thrown over a wooden chair. Other than the farm magazines piled on a low table beside the bed, there was only one personal note in the room— a silver picture frame that stood on a tall dresser. But the frame faced away from her, and Martha hadn't had the nerve to walk over and look at it closely. It was an intrusion, being in his room at all.

Anne had stayed behind to wash the breakfast dishes. Fraser, apparently, had gone out earlier, and Martha was waiting for him to come back so she could tell him what she'd decided to do. Martha had noticed how grown-up and important it made Anne feel to fix the French toast and ham for their breakfast. Martha suspected that she would have liked to come with them, that she was as eager as Daisy to show her the ranch. But Anne had scoffed when Martha suggested leaving the cleanup until later, letting on that she was far too grown-up for such childish enthusiasms.

Martha had the feeling that anyone Fraser ended up hiring would have to tread carefully with that one; Anne didn't wear her heart on her sleeve quite the way her sister did. Why did the thought of another woman looking after the girls suddenly hurt a little? She hadn't spent enough time with them yet to care.

"Daisy, sweetheart?"

"Uh-huh?" The girl looked up at her, face trusting and bright with pleasure and the late-October cold. "Tell me why you call your sister Blossom." Martha felt a tiny bit guilty. It wasn't fair to ask the child questions, but…

"Oh, she just likes to be called Anne. She says she made it up all by herself, but I know she got it out of a storybook. She told me'n' Fraser she wants us to call her that from now on, ever since our mama went away." Daisy skipped a couple of steps beside her and Martha smiled. "Anne with an *e*," Daisy half sang, and again Martha had an odd sense of déjà vu. "But me'n' Fraser keep forgetting. That makes her real mad."

Martha smiled again. "Well, Blossom *is* kind of an unusual name."

"Our mama gave us flower names," Daisy said simply. She looked up at Martha, suddenly serious. "She likes flowers. Daisy of the field—that's what Fraser calls me. Fraser says our names are special because everybody knows flowers are the beautiful-est things in the whole wide world."

Martha squeezed the child's hand. "Fraser is right," she whispered. "But I think I'll call your sister Anne, if that's what she prefers."

"Okay. C'mon." Daisy tugged at the barn door, and Martha stepped up and pushed it open for her.

After the crisp cold outside, the cavernous interior was dim and fragrant with hay and the scent of animals. And here, out of the wind, Martha felt a lot warmer. From somewhere she heard the friendly nicker of a horse. Another answered, then a third.

"This is where the baby lambs stay when their mamas can't feed them, and Fraser and Tom and Birdie's Hugh have to look after them." Daisy had climbed onto the bars of an empty pen. "Sometimes mamas can't look after their babies even if they want to—that's what Fraser says—and then people have to do it for them. And over there's where Fraser keeps all the medicine stuff they need for the lambs, and—"

"Hold on, hold on." Martha laughed. *Fraser this, Fraser that.* "How do you expect me to remember all this, sweetie? I don't know anything about sheep. Or cows or—"

"Don't worry. Me'n' Bloss will show you everything," Daisy promised, her eyes big and blue. "C'mon. There's way more."

"I know." Martha patted her shoulder. "But don't forget I'm just a visitor here. I can't see everything in one day." How was she to gently let the girl know that she wouldn't be staying? That they'd have to find another Lady Companion?

Martha followed the girl to one of the empty pens. Daisy quickly scrambled between the bars and ran to the corner. Martha looked around. There appeared to be no one else in the barn. Gingerly she put one foot on the lower rail, then eased herself over the top. Her feet sank into the deep straw bedding in the pen as she moved toward the girl.

"Oh, my! Kittens!" Delighted, Martha dropped to her knees in the dark far corner of the pen and reached for a mewing, blinking ball of fur. "Daisy, aren't they adorable?"

The girl had already picked up two kittens, one gray, one orange, and was cuddling them to her chest. The mother cat leapt away lightly and sat on a nearby straw bale licking her fur. From time to time, she mewed silently, showing her pink gums and tongue and sharp white teeth, but other than that, she didn't seem worried about her family.

"Oh, look, this one's got its eyes open," Daisy said, turning and holding up the orange kitten. Martha could just see milky blue slits, whereas the kitten she held still had tightly closed eyes.

"Fraser says I can have one when they're big enough to leave their mama," Daisy said, holding first one kitten, then the other to her nose and kissing the tops of their tiny furry heads. "He says I can have one kitten to live in the house with us, or I can have as many kittens as I want if they live down at the barn."

Daisy screwed up her face, obviously considering her options for the umpteenth time.

As many as she wanted at the barn.

Fraser McKenna sounded like a very wise man. It was a fleeting thought, and it gave Martha a little extra comfort to think that she was leaving the girls with a man of character. Boozing, womanizing, whatever— the boozing had already turned out to be a rumor, apparently—all her instincts told her the girls were safe with Fraser. There probably wasn't a place anywhere in the world that was safer. Oddly she'd felt safe with him, too. At first. Not that it mattered all that much. By tomorrow or the next day, or whenever it was convenient for him, she'd be on her way.

"Aren't you sweet?" She raised the kitten she held and laughed aloud as she felt its drum-tight belly. "Ouch!" Each of the kitten's four little legs were spread wide, needle-sharp claws extended. One had snagged her thumb. She perched the kitten on her shoulder and nuzzled the warm fur. The kitten dug its claws into the leather of her coat, holding on for dear life.

Suddenly the mother cat drew herself up and hissed. Martha heard a familiar growl and looked over her shoulder. Spook stood at the railing, his nose poked into the pen, the rest of him well away from the mother cat.

"Morning, ladies."

"Oh...good morning," Martha returned.

"I see you've found the kittens."

"Yes." Martha put the kitten down and scrambled to her feet. "Daisy brought me." She felt a warm flush rise into her cheeks. Thank goodness for the relative dimness of the barn. "W-we didn't know you were here."

Fraser stood with one boot on the lowest rail, shoulders hunched forward over the top rail. He wore a sheepskin vest and jeans and a plaid shirt, sleeves rolled up to just below his elbows. His hat was dusty. Spook kept up a low growl at his feet. "Just came in. I had to check on one of my rams."

"There're sheep in here?" Martha looked around. She'd thought the barn was nearly empty.

"I've got a couple of pens on the other side where I keep animals that need special attention," he said, but she could see that his eyes were on Daisy and the kitten, not on her. He smiled slightly.

Then he looked at her, Martha, and the smile faded to a wariness she'd seen before. "One of my yearling rams had a run-in with a varmint of some kind last week and needed a few stitches.''

"Oh." *Oh. Is that all you can think of to say, Martha Thomas?* It was. Clearly she was doing the smart thing by leaving. She didn't feel comfortable with this man anymore. Partly because of his revelation last night, partly because of the annoying way her body insisted on responding to him, the nagging attraction she felt—purely physical of course—which he clearly didn't return in the slightest. Not that she'd want him to, ever! She'd analyzed her reactions while she'd tossed and turned during the sleepless night, and had decided it was not only sophomoric but downright embarrassing.

The sooner she was gone, the better. How had she ever thought she could stay here and work with him? Share meals? Live in the same house? Even applying for this ridiculous job had been thoroughly out of character. Now, in the hard light of day, she wondered what in the world had gotten into her.

"Look at this one, Fraser." Daisy ran over to the railing with the orange kitten. Fraser took the kitten from her gently and held it in one large hand. "Isn't he just the sweetest little guy? I think I want him for my very own."

Daisy looked back at the rest of the litter doubtfully. By now several of the kittens had strayed from their nest and their mother was fretfully calling them back. "Or maybe that little black one..."

Fraser smiled, and his eyes inadvertently met Martha's. The smile faded in a flash, but in that split second, before he'd hidden it from her, she'd seen such love in his eyes, such affection for this child. Such understanding. She suddenly knew it didn't matter that he wasn't Daisy's father. He cared for the girl—cared for her and her sister—as perhaps their own father never had. Martha instantly knew it for the truth it was. For that split second, she'd seen into Fraser McKenna's soul. It shook her.

"Why don't you take that little fella up to show Bloss?"

"Oh, can I?" Daisy beamed, and reached up to take the kitten carefully from Fraser. "Can I really, Fraser?" He leaned over and lifted her to his side of the railing.

"Sure. I don't think his mama will miss him for a little while. Do you?"

He was asking her—Martha. Martha mumbled something in agreement and awkwardly put her leg through the space between the rails. She hoped he wasn't watching.

"Careful. Don't bump your head—"

"Ouch!" She stood and rubbed the back of her head where it had connected with the upper rail. "Too late." She grinned, feeling like an idiot, and this time, when she caught his glimmer of a smile, she felt something weary and worn and cautious loosen its hold on her heart, something she hadn't even known was there.

She followed Fraser and Daisy out of the barn into the sunshine. The Wind River Mountains loomed brilliant in the distance, snowcapped and glorious and utterly uncompromising. No doubt about it, this was wild and beautiful country. God's country. Daisy had run on ahead, cradling the kitten in her jacket. Spook followed closely behind.

Fraser stopped by the barnyard gate and rested one hand on the top bar. In a far field Martha saw some sheep she hadn't noticed when she and Daisy left the house. She heard faint baa-ing sounds, far-off and thin. The animals were surprisingly white against the dull October brown of the pasture, and larger than she'd expected. *Ram-bo-lays,* she repeated mentally, mimicking Fraser's pronunciation. *Sheep, for Pete's sake.*

Why had he stopped? She glanced at him quickly. He was frowning and seemed in no hurry to open the gate. Shivering, she squeezed her fingers together in her pockets and dug her hands in deeper.

From this vantage point, the house, set on a slight natural rise, looked sprawling and comfortable, set away as it was from the series of weathered corrals and sheds laid out around the barn. Martha realized she hadn't really examined it before, not closely. It was constructed mainly of logs, she saw now, with additions here and there framed in lumber. Those additions were wood-shingled, their paint faded. The house looked solid and unpretentious and very much as though it belonged exactly where it stood.

"We need to talk," Fraser said.

She looked up at him again. In the sunshine she saw the lines of weariness she'd noticed when she first met him. Responsibility. Care. He looked like a man with a past. A man who, some days, carried the world on his shoulders.

"Yes."

"Here?" He raised one eyebrow. "I've got an office back in the barn. Or do you want to come up to the house for coffee?"

Martha shivered violently—couldn't help herself—and watched his quick look of concern turn to indifference as he gave her a lightning once-over. Well, of course she wasn't dressed warmly enough, but what did it matter? She'd be gone just as soon as she could get away.

"C-coffee, I think. Maybe we shouldn't leave the girls...."

"Let's go up to the house, then," he said. He took her elbow and escorted her through the gate, then pulled his hand abruptly away. He latched the gate and strode toward the ranch house.

He couldn't bear to touch her. Why?

Martha hurried to catch up, then fell in beside him, taking three steps to his two, determined not to lag behind. She dug her hands even deeper into her jacket pockets and fought back another attack of shivers.

Yes, they needed to talk. She knew he wouldn't be pleased when he heard what she had to say.

CHAPTER FOUR

MARTHA MADE the coffee while Fraser went to the sink just inside the kitchen door. From the corner of her eye, she watched him flex the muscles of his back and shoulders, then reach over to hang his hat on one of the wooden pegs near the door. Other hats hung there, and some outdoor jackets. He ran his fingers through his hair quickly and shrugged several more times, as though loosening tightness in his shoulders.

She looked away, busying herself with the coffee machine. Then she heard water running and looked toward him again as he bent to sluice water from the faucet onto his face. He washed his hands thoroughly and methodically with the bar of hard yellow soap Martha had noticed there earlier. He straightened and turned to grab a towel.

Their eyes met.

"Sugar bowl up here?" Martha reached blindly into a cupboard. What had she seen in that brief second or two before she'd wrenched her gaze away? Deep thought, yes. Speculation? Guarded interest? *In her?* Heavens, no—he was probably mustering arguments designed to convince her to stay, just as she was wildly racking her brain for all the reasons she should leave.

It had seemed so clear this morning. Leaving was definitely the smartest idea. Yet she found herself increasingly curious about the secrets held within these walls. Who was Brenda? And why did he care so much about her children if he wasn't their father? She thought of that split second in the barn, that one blinding flash of insight when she'd seen the way he looked at Daisy.

Well. She *had* been hoping for adventure, hadn't she?

"Sugar's next door over." He finished drying his face and hands, not hurrying, then walked over to the cupboard by the stove and pulled down an opened package of store-bought cookies, which he tossed onto the table. The machine spat out the last of the freshly brewed coffee.

"I'll check on the girls." He paused at the door that led to the hall and raised an eyebrow. "That kitten will give them something to do for a few minutes so we can have our coffee."

And our talk. Martha got down two thick mugs decorated with the faded crest of some Montana Hereford association. She heard his footsteps echo in the hall. There was no other sound except the distant bawl of a cow and the thin tick-tick-tick of a clock somewhere in the kitchen. The calm domesticity of the scene unsettled her. Everything in this house, on this ranch— almost everything that had happened since she'd left Tewson—was not as it seemed. Those were the facts. Yet, strangely, this kitchen said otherwise.

"The girls are fine. They're in their room," Fraser said when he returned. He pulled out a chair and sat down, then picked up a spoon and the sugar bowl. "All right," he said calmly. "Let me fill you in on—"

"Hold on." Why put it off? "I might as well tell you I've thought things over since last night, and I've decided—" Martha caught his glance and her throat dried "—uh, I don't think I'll stay. Considering."

He stirred his coffee slowly. "I see." His eyes showed no emotion. No surprise. No disappointment. It was as though he'd expected as much. "So you don't want to hear the whole story?"

She knew if she said she didn't, he'd just walk away from it. Shrug, finish his coffee, then get on the phone and round up someone else. He wasn't going to beg.

She swallowed. Darn it, she was too curious to just let it go like that. "Tell me, anyway."

He raised his mug and met her eyes. "Okay," he began slowly and deliberately. "These two girls were dumped on me. It's happened before and it'll happen again. Only, Brenda's taking her damn sweet time coming back, and so I've decided to look after things myself." He took a long swallow of the hot coffee.

"Who's Brenda?"

"A neighbor," he replied flatly, as if that explained everything.

"I see," Martha murmured, bewildered. She picked up her own mug. Neighbors. Okay, she could guess what that kind of connection meant in this part of the country. As thick as blood anywhere else. But what kind of woman dropped two kids on a rancher's doorstep, neighbor or not, then took off?

"Brenda's ten or twelve years younger than me, but

basically we grew up together. She and her sister, me and my brothers. The Langstons own the spread just north of here.'' He waved his spoon in the general direction.

He gave Martha a hard look, a direct look. "Have you ever met a woman who'd have been better off if she'd never had kids?"

Martha nodded uncertainly. She hadn't met a woman like that personally, but she knew such women existed. Men, too.

"Well, that's Brenda. She's not cut out for motherhood. If this were the sixties, she'd be a hippy. She's flaky as hell, always has been. Oh, she cares for Bloss and Daisy, no question of that. But she's not what you'd call a real down-to-earth responsible kind of person. She's—" He shrugged, hesitated as though he meant to add something more, then changed his mind.

"As I said last night, I have no idea who Blossom's father is," he continued bluntly, "although she looks a little like a cowboy I had around here the year before she was born..."

"Some drifter?"

"You could say that." He took another swallow of coffee. "Half-Indian, he was. Shoshone. Damn good wrangler, as I recall. Only stayed for one season." He reached for a cookie and pushed the bag toward her.

Martha shivered. She couldn't help herself. "What about Daisy? Who's *her* father?"

"I have no idea."

"Didn't her mother...didn't Brenda ever say?" Martha was horrified. She didn't regard herself as any kind of prude, in fact rather prided herself on her liberal views about most things. Still, for a woman to have children willy-nilly like that with any man who happened to pass through her life…

"Nope." He gave her another hard look. "And nobody ever asked. Nobody's business but hers, we all figured." He frowned and studied the coffee in his raised mug. "The Langstons generally kept to themselves."

"How does she manage? Does she have a job?"

"Brenda's run wild ever since she was a girl. She lives in an old trailer on her folks' place now, about a mile from here." He shrugged. "The rest of the family wasn't much better. The sister ran off years ago. Old Man Langston was no rancher. Always working on some invention or other, letting his land run to weed. There's a couple sheds full of stuff up there, contraptions that never worked."

He shrugged again. "I paid him rent for years to run my cattle on his land. Maybe they had something coming in from somewhere else. Maybe not. I never asked."

He wouldn't. *Nobody's business.* "But I still don't get it. Why did the girls end up here at your place?"

"Brenda dropped them off one day, like she always does. No warning." He got up and poured himself another cup of coffee. Martha studied the muscled width of his back, the trace of sweat down the center, the way his shirt fit him, rumpled-looking, definitely not ironed, but just about perfect. He turned and leaned back against the counter, facing her. "I came down from fixing fence one day and there they were."

"That's incredible!"

"As I said, it's happened before. I've known Bloss and Daisy since they were born. Every so often, maybe two or three times a year, Brenda gets itchy and brings the girls down here and takes off. That's just Brenda. Hell." He lifted one shoulder slightly. "We're used to it around here. Most times she shows up in a week or two. It's never been a problem really."

"And now it is."

He gave her a narrow look. "Still not really a problem," he said slowly. He walked back to the table. "Except she's never been gone this long before. The LeBlancs help out, Hugh and Birdie. They always do. But I got a business to run, and Birdie's not as young as she used to be. That's why I decided to hire someone to help out this time." He smiled wryly. "Brenda'll show up one of these days."

You hope, she thought. Martha found it hard to believe what she was hearing. "Why doesn't she leave them with her parents?"

"I guess you could say Brenda figures she can count on me." Her voice was level. "She trusts me. I've known her all her life. That's the way it works in this valley. Neighbors look out for each other." A flash of pain swept over his face, just a matter of a second or two, but Martha felt it in her gut. His eyes were expressionless when they met hers.

Trust. Trust was a very big word.

"Fact is, her parents weren't the most reliable sort, either. Seems to run in the family. Besides—" he ran his hand through his hair impatiently, and the heel of his boot scraped harshly on the floor "—her ma died a couple years ago, cancer, and her old man drank himself to death six months later. Brenda's been on her own for a while. It's been tough on her.''

"How long have the girls been living here?"

He hesitated. "Going on three months."

"Three months!"

He nodded.

The wall phone, just behind his head, rang. He reached for it, his eyes still on hers, still wary, still searching. For what? What did he want from her?

"Westbank Ranch. McKenna here," was his gruff greeting. He frowned. "Uh-huh, late last night."

Martha got up, taking her mug to the sink. Her head was spinning. This man had been looking after two children who weren't his for nearly three months! This was mid-October; he must have had them since just after school got out. She'd never heard of such a thing. Weren't there relatives somewhere? What about the sister? Where were the authorities? Three months! Where in heaven's name *was* the mother, and when was she coming back?

Gradually some of what he was saying on the phone penetrated.

"Can't say just yet, Katie." Had he shot a quick speculative glance at her? "Sure, the girls want to go to Ted's wedding, but I don't think it's a good idea." He paused. "We'll see." He listened again. "I don't know. Things are still, uh, a little unsettled around here."

He caught Martha's eye briefly, then listened again, somewhat impatiently, she thought with an unexpected sense of satisfaction once she realized who was on the other end of the line.

"Yeah, too bad. It was the girls' decision." He glanced at Martha again, and she looked away. "I appreciate that, Katie. I'll keep it in mind if I'm stuck." *The girls had decided they wanted her,* she remembered. Not Fraser.

"Katie, I can't talk now. I'll call you later, all right?" He listened a few seconds longer, then hung up. His eyes held hers. "Sorry about that."

"No problem." She couldn't help asking, "Katie Barker?"

His look of surprise pleased her. "You know Katie?"

"No, but the girls filled me in."

He raised one eyebrow. "They did?"

"Oh, how she'd been trying to drag you to the altar." Martha barely hid her amusement.

"Oh, hell." Was he blushing? He actually looked embarrassed. "Vi Jamieson putting ideas into their heads, that's all. Woman doesn't have enough to do in the off-season."

"I see." Martha got up and went to the counter. "More coffee?"

"No, thanks." He didn't return her smile. "So, anything I say change your mind?"

"I—I don't know." She rubbed the toe of one sneaker against the back of the other. "I'd made up my mind to leave this morning. Now...now, I just don't know."

"You got something else to go to?"

"No. Nothing important." She sat down again, one

foot tucked under her. She fiddled with the spoon on the table, reluctant to meet his eyes. "I just don't know what to do," she said helplessly.

"You've got to make up your mind." His voice was rough. "If you're staying, I want a commitment. These girls have been through enough, and I don't want them getting attached to you, and then you walking out the first time something doesn't suit you."

She looked up, angry. "I wouldn't walk out. I wouldn't do that."

"Maybe you wouldn't. A lot would. I don't intend to take any chances, that's all."

"That's ridiculous and you know it!"

His eyes blazed for a second, but she knew she had to say what was on her mind. "If I stayed, it'd be because I *wanted* to stay, not because of some promise you'd managed to drag out of me. And I need a few more answers before I can make up my mind."

"Fire away," he said grimly.

"Okay. Why do you still have the girls? Why haven't you turned them over to the authorities?"

"Dammit, woman!" Fraser exploded. He got up from the table and walked to the window, every inch of his body signaling anger. Anger and frustration. He wheeled. "You just don't get it, do you? What am I supposed to do—stick 'em in some city orphanage? Turn them over to a bunch of strangers? Some overworked social worker? I don't know what happens where you come from, but up here folks stick together. Brenda left her girls with *me*. I intend to take care of them until she gets back."

It was the first time she'd seen his anger, although

she'd sensed something volatile, something big and unnamed just under the surface of the man, from the instant she'd met him. Passions deeply felt and tightly reined. Still, his outburst didn't frighten her. If anything, this evidence of his true feelings exhilarated her. She felt the excitement of a new challenge.

"Okay, what about Brenda anyway? Where is she? You must have some idea."

"I wish I did." He shook his head wearily and leaned against the counter. "I set a private investigator on her two months ago, but he didn't turn up much. Trail too cold by then, I guess."

"Do the authorities know? School?"

"No." He hesitated. "At least I hope not. Daisy's at home and Bloss just started back in September. I take her to the bus and pick her up. So far, there's been no trouble. She never mentions Brenda."

"Oh, yes, she does," Martha said softly. "She told me her mother was dead." The black look on Fraser's face shocked her, but she continued. "Back at the hotel. And she told me you were her father. She said she called you Fraser, instead of Dad, because it was more modern."

"She told you that?"

"Yes."

He turned toward the window again, and Martha could read the tension in the rigid line of his shoulders. After a minute or so, he turned back, his face set. He didn't say anything. She knew he wouldn't. And the silence nearly suffocated her.

"So this whole situation is more or less illegal, isn't it?" she managed finally.

He nodded.

"The mother's never been reported missing or any of that, and now you want me to help you out? Help you look after these kids, help you keep them hidden until the mother returns? Help you keep them safe? Is that it?"

He stared at her a long time, his eyes darker than she'd ever seen them before, the shuttered look almost impenetrable. "Yes." He held her astonished gaze until her stomach quivered. "That's exactly what I want you to do."

"Wh-what if she doesn't come back?" Martha barely dared to voice the unthinkable. "Ever?"

"I don't know." His voice was harsh. "I'll just have to face that possibility when the time comes, won't I? *If* it comes."

But she knew exactly what he would do. He wouldn't give them up. He'd fight to keep them, to honor his promise to their mother. He was that kind of man. She felt something deep and primitive stir inside her. She shivered, suddenly cold, although the kitchen was very warm.

There was another long silence. Martha could hear the girls' distant laughter. She heard the clock over the kitchen stove tick busily. *You'll be thirty-six in April, Martha Virginia,* the clock sang—tick, tick, tick. *A woman in her thirty-seventh year on this earth—what's stopping you?*

She took a deep shaky breath and found herself nodding. "I'll think it over. That's all I can promise."

"Let me know as soon as you can," he said quietly. "Otherwise I'm going to have to get someone else."

"I understand."

Martha felt herself tremble as she held his gaze. A tiny light flickered deep in his eyes—a challenge?—and it didn't help her equanimity at all. "I'll let you know for sure by...well, how about this evening?"

"That'd be fine." He stood and walked toward the door and reached for his hat.

"Oh...by the way." Martha's heart hammered against her ribs. *In for a penny...* "I'm not a widow. I've never been married. I—I just told you I was because I thought it might help me get this job."

He didn't say anything. The fire in his eyes, the blackness, seemed to draw her in until she swore she could feel the hard shape of him against her skin, could feel the heat of his body on hers, could feel the muscles of his chest under the tips of her fingers, the flat of her hand.

She sucked in her breath sharply. Illusion. Her mind playing tricks. He jammed on his hat and pushed open the door without saying a word. Not even a nod. The door slammed behind him.

That was that. Martha ran to the window and watched him stride to the barn. He didn't look back.

Not once.

DAMN! EVEN NOW, a week later, he could still feel those big eyes of hers burning into his back. He tossed a bale of hay over the side of the truck. He was up with Tom and some of the crew throwing out feed for the cattle they'd left in one of the high pastures.

When he'd reached the safety of the barn that day—the day they'd talked in the kitchen—he'd let out a victory yell that had scared the horses half to death. Then he'd had to go around with a handful of oats for each by way of compensation.

You don't tip your hand in a game of stud and you don't beg a woman to stick around. He'd learned that long ago. Nor had he allowed himself to appeal outright to her emotions, desperate though he was to have her stay.

It hadn't been necessary. He'd seen the softness in her eyes when she looked at Daisy, when she held the kitten in her hands. When she smiled. She was a tenderhearted woman. Give her time, a little time, and her heart would do the job for him.

Maybe he ought to feel guilty, but he didn't. He hadn't lied. No one had to make the Langston story sadder than it already was. And she was an adult; she'd made up her own mind. Until February was all she'd promised. Well, they'd see....

Surely to God Brenda'd be back long before then. Before Christmas. Hell, before Thanksgiving. Then he'd pay Miss Martha Thomas out and send her on her way. Back to Wisconsin. Back to her city life. There was no question in his mind, although she hadn't said as much, that she was a city woman through and through.

Miss Thomas! What a laugh.

Fraser bent down and wrestled another bale of hay from the bed of the pickup. He grunted slightly as he heaved it over the side.

Whew! Hot work, and the day just above freezing. He took off his hat and wiped the sweat from his forehead with the sleeve of his jacket, then resettled

his hat firmly on his head. He glanced up at the Wind
Rivers. There was plenty of fresh snow up there; you
could taste it in the air. Almost the end of October,
and he'd seen snow to stay in this country by the end
of September.

So she wasn't married.

Now *that* had been unexpected. Not that it made a
bit of difference, her being a hot-blooded widow or a
vestal virgin. What was she doing single, anyway, a
woman like her at her age? He frowned. Didn't say a
hell of a lot for those Wisconsin lumberjacks.

Still, having an unmarried woman in his household
might be a problem. It might have a bearing on his
keeping the girls if the authorities found out. Single
woman, living in his house—damn!

It gave him an odd feeling. There was someone else
under his roof now. Someone else to look out for. And
only three short months ago, it had been just him.

He remembered that evening last week. Those big
blue eyes of hers, more gray than blue in the lamp-
light, had held his steadily as she'd told him she'd
changed her mind. If he'd leaned forward, just six
inches or so…

But he hadn't.

He'd deliberately looked away, at the wall calendar,
at an open cupboard door…

He couldn't figure this woman. Something about
her unsettled him. Something about her teased at his
senses. Something about her told him to keep well
clear.

He wished he knew what it was. He sometimes felt
that way when a woman turned him on, when he was

sexually attracted. But that wasn't the case here. At least he didn't think so. She wasn't his type, although…

Just what is your type these days, McKenna?

She was definitely attractive enough, in a plain sort of way that could grow on a man. She wore no makeup, but he liked that. She was average height, maybe a little taller. Medium build, strong-looking, a bit thin, maybe, but womanly enough in all the right places. Light brown hair, blue eyes, smooth pale skin. Calm. Sensible. She struck him as having a great deal of calmness to her spirit. She'd be good with the girls. He'd felt that instinctively the day he'd met her.

There was nothing coquettish about her, and maybe that was why he felt a little awkward around her. Martha seemed, well…proper. In his experience, most women liked to flirt a little. Enjoyed it. He could handle a flirt. There was nothing of the flirt in Martha Thomas. She was as straightforward as any man. Even the way she'd told him she wasn't a widow.

"I've never been married," she'd said simply. A faint flush had crept over the creamy skin of her throat that day in the kitchen, and he'd had an odd sensation of wanting to touch her.

Hell, he thought as he viciously heaved the last bale over the side of the pickup, there were worse things in life than telling stupid little lies to get a dumb job like the one he had to offer.

Fraser wiped his upper lip with his sleeve and straightened. He looked at his watch uneasily, just as he did most days about this time. Just after three. The school bus came at four o'clock. He still wasn't used to not meeting it twice a day.

In a way, he missed those trips. He missed Daisy asking a million questions on the short ride to meet her sister, and he missed the way Bloss's face lit up when she got off the bus and saw them. Poor kid. Brenda had a lot to answer for as a mother, in his opinion.

He frowned and jumped down from the bed of the pickup. Every time he thought of what might have happened to the girls' mother, he got a sick feeling in the pit of his stomach. He just wasn't cut out to take care of two kids like this for so long. Brenda knew that. He wasn't cut out to be a father. He wished to hell Brenda would get back, and soon.

The vague unease he felt flickered into fear. Just for a second or two. What if Martha forgot about picking up Bloss today? What if she and Daisy got busy with something and simply forgot what time it was? It hadn't happened yet, not once. But it could happen. Sometimes he'd been busy with something and damn near forgotten to pick up Bloss, and he'd had more practice than Martha.

He climbed into his pickup. "See you in about an hour or so, Tom," he called to his foreman as he backed out the truck and turned onto the narrow dirt road, his fear growing. Why? Deep down, did he really trust her? Was *that* it? He didn't know her. She was an outsider, an unknown quantity.

Quite a few neighbors knew he had the girls, but he could depend on them. This business with Daisy and Bloss the last couple of months had put him on edge. Had dragged the past right back in his face, strong and vivid. Damn Brenda, anyway, for leaving her two kids with him again. She knew how he felt about taking on that kind of responsibility.

And this Lady Companion he'd hired. Come right down to it, he didn't feel a hundred percent about her. She'd been altogether too damn nosy about why he had the girls in the first place. She asked too damn many questions, period.

The instant he drove into the yard, he knew she wasn't there. He knew Daisy was gone, too. His gut didn't lie.

He leapt out of the truck, leaving the door open and the engine running. Panic rolled through him, thick and dense and heavy, squeezing his heart.

"Martha!" He ran from room to room like a madman. No one was there. Birdie'd been there earlier—everything was neat and tidy—but the house had the kind of cold feeling that told him it had been empty for a while. "Daisy!"

Fraser...please, help me.... Echoes, dream voices from long ago, mocked him, whispered his name. He cursed them.

"Martha, damn you, where are you?"

He ran back to the open kitchen door, looked toward the shed where he kept the Bronco. Gone. He looked at the kitchen clock. Nearly half an hour before the school bus was due. They wouldn't have left to meet it yet, she and Daisy; it was just a five-minute drive.

She'd taken Daisy away. She was picking up Bloss from the bus and she was taking the girls away with her. "Handing them over to the proper authorities," as she'd put it so prissily last week. Maybe she'd already taken them. Maybe she'd taken them and gone away this morning. Maybe...

No. That was crazy. *Slow down, McKenna. Get hold of yourself. Think.*

Cursing the day he'd met her, cursing the dreams that had fed his soul with unbearable fear for nearly four years now—cursing everything but the girls—he jumped back into his pickup and slammed it into gear.

He'd be there when the bus came. He'd find out if Bloss was on that bus. He'd find out what the hell was going on. Miss Martha Thomas wasn't going to get away with this, by God.

Not if he could help it.

CHAPTER FIVE

MARTHA GEARED DOWN for the long hill ahead and glanced out the side window of the Bronco at the Wind Rivers. All that snow up on the mountains made her cold.

Good thing she'd decided to go into Pine Ridge for some warm clothes this morning after dropping Anne off at the bus. Winter boots. Wool socks. Flannel pajamas. She'd managed to find them all in the aging Pine Ridge Mall. And some things for the girls.

She glanced at Daisy, strapped into the seat belt beside her, clutching her tattered kangaroo. Would she ever get the toy away from the girl long enough to wash it? Laundry. Was that her responsibility now?

All Fraser had said was that she'd be looking after the children. He seemed to assume she'd know what that entailed. Why would she? A single woman who didn't even have any nieces or nephews. But then, what would he, a bachelor, know about looking after kids, either? Mind you, she reminded herself, he'd already had some practice. *Three months since their mother had disappeared.*

"What's your favorite color, sweetheart?"

"Purple."

"Purple, huh? What's Anne's favorite color?"

Daisy put her head to one side and considered. "Blue, I think. I don't know. Anne likes green, too."

The girl turned to face Martha gravely, eyes huge. Martha had finally convinced Daisy to call her sister by the name she preferred. "Don't ever give her nothin' pink. Uh-uh." She shook her head solemnly. "She *hates* pink. Aunty Vi gave us pink teddy bears once, and Anne threw hers out the hayloft window. The top one."

Angry little girl, Martha thought, frowning slightly as she geared down for another hill. Poor Anne. Martha had the feeling that the child missed her mother desperately, yet was too proud to admit it. "What happened to the teddy?"

"Got busted. But I fixed it. I put Band-Aids all over his legs—Birdie helped me—and now they're all better. Birdie's a nurse, y'know. A *real* nurse," Daisy confided with a shining innocent smile that never failed to warm Martha's heart. "Now I got two teddies, 'stead of one, 'cause Anne said I could keep hers forever and ever."

"That's nice." Martha smiled back at her.

Daisy bit her lip. "So don't ever give Anne stuff that's pink."

"I'll remember that."

Lesson learned. In the past week she'd learned a lot about the girls, what they liked and what they didn't like, but not much about their guardian. Fraser was usually gone before she took Anne to the school bus, and very often she didn't see him until nearly dinnertime, when he'd come into the house, grab something from the freezer and toss it in the microwave.

She was going to have a chat with him about that. Sure, she'd been told that cooking wasn't part of her job, but there was a limit to how much processed microwavable food anyone could be expected to eat. She'd be glad to take over the cooking if he was agreeable.

All he'd said when she told him she'd stay was a terse "I appreciate that." She'd decided it was the nearest he could come to saying thank-you. He was a fiercely independent man. It riled him that he had to get help to look after the girls, it riled him that she hadn't immediately promised to stay and it riled him that she wouldn't make a commitment beyond February. Good heavens, what did he expect? That she'd stay forever? What if the girls' mother never came back?

Not a problem. According to him, Brenda would be back any day now. Martha hoped he was right. But she wondered how he could be so sure about someone who'd abandon her children like that. Who could tell what she'd do?

"I decided I want to be a bumblebee, after all, Martha. Bumblebees like flowers."

Bumblebee? Martha frowned. Then she remembered—they'd talked about Halloween costumes on the way to town. Martha had been shocked to realize the girls had no plans for trick-or-treating. She'd loved Halloween when she was a child. Without consulting Anne, Martha and Daisy had gone ahead and picked out costumes at a store in the mall.

"Anne's gonna love the princess stuff," Daisy said dreamily.

"I hope you're right," Martha replied, gazing into the distance. Somehow, she couldn't see Anne as a princess. But then again...

Was that the school bus ahead? Martha stepped on the accelerator slightly. She wanted to be there when the bus stopped at the side road that led to Westbank Ranch. She didn't want to be late picking up Anne and taking her home.

Home. Was the ranch—and Fraser McKenna and a three-legged dog named Spook—what the girls now regarded as home?

The shopping trip this morning had been an impulse. When Fraser's housekeeper, Birdie LeBlanc, arrived before they left for the school bus, Martha had thought it might be best to stay out of her way. She hadn't left a note, thinking they'd be back long before this. But she wasn't too concerned. She didn't think Fraser expected to be informed of every little detail. He'd told her clearly that she was in charge of the girls. And he'd invited her to use the Bronco whenever she wanted.

She'd enjoyed the new experience of shopping with a child and had bought the girls all kinds of little presents. Coloring books for Daisy, a new school-book bag for Anne, push-out paper dolls for both of them. New hair ribbons. Crowing with delight, Daisy'd even picked out an enormous rawhide bone for Spook.

Everything had seemed new and exciting to the girl, which had warmed Martha's heart and turned the usual drudgery of shopping into a pleasure. She had the definite impression that the girls—Daisy, at least—hadn't spent much time in town, shopping or otherwise. Somehow she couldn't see Fraser taking them. Was this the "woman stuff" he'd talked about?

She and Daisy had had lunch together at the Pine Ridge Inn, and now it looked as though they'd be right on target to meet Anne at the bus. An altogether enjoyable day.

Actually Martha was starting to feel that taking care of Daisy and Anne was going to be more fun than work. It just required a little organization.

"Look!" Daisy shouted, and pointed ahead.

"There's the school bus." Martha winked at Daisy and the girl smiled back. Then she flicked on the radio, and they both began singing along to a Garth Brooks song.

"Hey, Martha!"

"What?" Martha stopped behind the bus, her mind only half on Daisy's exclamation. The warning lights on the bus were flashing red as the door opened and Anne stepped out. Martha touched the horn, waving madly through the windshield. The bus began to pull away, and Anne walked toward them, a smile lighting up her rather pinched features.

"There's Fraser, too!" Daisy shouted. "Over there."

Martha swung around. Yes, there was Fraser's dark green pickup parked on the road that led to the ranch. "What's he doing here?"

She frowned, thinking, then smiled as Anne opened the back door of the Bronco. "Hop in, Anne."

Martha turned to help Anne move some packages and didn't notice right away that Daisy had unsnapped her seat belt. The next instant the child had opened the door and climbed out of the Bronco.

"Oh, dear God!" Martha felt her heart slam against her ribs. Helpless, she watched Daisy dash across the road and open the passenger door of Fraser's pickup. Thank goodness there was no other traffic. Still, she should have anticipated...

Heart thumping, she put the Bronco in gear and eased it across the highway, turning onto the ranch road. She stopped opposite Fraser's truck. Why wasn't he getting out?

Something was wrong. She had an uneasy feeling in the pit of her stomach. She put on the emergency brake and got out, leaving Anne busily peering into the bags and parcels on the back seat.

"Hi!" She walked toward the pickup, conscious that her smile felt a little forced. "Didn't expect to see you here." She hesitated. "Everything all right?"

He didn't reply immediately, and Martha was shocked at his expression. Jaw grim, eyes blacker than midnight...

Spook barked energetically from his position on the seat between Fraser and Daisy, and she dimly registered Daisy's chatter, telling the dog everything that had happened since breakfast. Fraser muttered something—a curse, she had no doubt—and got out of the truck in one smooth fluid motion. She could feel the energy in his body, ruthless, taut, barely controlled. Her first instinct was to step back, but she held her ground. He slammed the door and leaned back against it, looking down at her. She saw a muscle jump in the side of his jaw.

"Where the hell were you?" he bit out finally.

"We...we went to town." Stunned, Martha waved one hand vaguely toward the Bronco. "Daisy and I. What do you mean, where were we?"

"You took Daisy to Pine Ridge?" His tone was incredulous, his expression black. "When? This morning?"

"Yes." Why was he so angry? "This morning, right after we dropped Anne off. I needed to buy some clothes and I thought I'd pick up a few things for the girls and—"

"You could have asked me," he broke in. "I could've gotten someone I know in town to pick up whatever the kids need. You could've ordered stuff out of the catalog—"

"I guess you forgot to tell me we were prisoners out here when you gave me my job description," she snapped. The nerve! He obviously expected her to read his mind, to figure out every little angle he'd cooked up to keep the girls hidden and safe at his ranch.

He stared at her a long moment, long enough for Martha to become aware of the thump-thump of her heart, the shakiness of her knees, the deep burning enigma in his eyes.

"You're not prisoners," he growled, then turned to order Spook to silence. The dog stopped barking instantly and began to lick Daisy's face with enthusiasm.

With a sinking feeling, Martha suddenly understood what he was saying. What he was *really* saying. He'd been worried someone in Pine Ridge would recognize

Daisy, perhaps ask questions she, Martha, wouldn't be able to answer. She was a stranger; it made sense the locals would notice her. In fact, now that she thought about it, the waitress at the restaurant had seemed to know Daisy. At the time she'd thought it was just normal small-town friendliness. Fraser faced the very real danger of more and more people finding out about Daisy and Anne the longer their mother stayed away.

Maybe she *should* have mentioned that she might go shopping this morning.

"Look." She touched his arm in an instinctive gesture. He didn't pull away, not immediately, but she felt his muscles tense, iron-hard under the thin cloth of his shirt. "I'm sorry. I just didn't realize—"

"Forget it." He pulled away from her hand then, his voice gruff. This time she glimpsed some emotion beneath the grim facade he presented to her. She saw a man in pain, a man with a whole hell behind his eyes, a hell he shared with no one. The girls were part of it; she knew that but wasn't sure why. *She* was part of it. And there was something else, something secret, unnamed, that was part of it.

Part of what? There was so much she didn't understand. Would she ever understand? Did she want to? Suddenly she felt weary. She pushed her hair from her eyes with both hands and took a deep calming breath. *Forget it, Martha Thomas, this is just a job. A short-term job. It was supposed to be fun, remember? A challenge? Something different.*

"You going to give Daisy a lift back to the ranch then?" she asked in as light a tone as she could manage.

He nodded, his eyes unreadable. "I'll drop her off at the house." Anger, worry, pain—she could tell he'd stuffed everything back inside him.

"Fine." She turned to head for the Bronco.

"Martha. Wait."

She stopped.

"I've got some work I have to do this afternoon. I might be late." She nodded. *Yes, boss.* "I need to talk to you tonight."

"Sure." She shrugged and continued toward the Bronco, excruciatingly aware of her too-tight designer jeans, her too-thin city jacket. Her hair that was a windblown mess. Above all, she was aware of his eyes on her retreat from across the road. She held her chin firm, her shoulders infinitesimally higher.

But when she got to the Bronco and dared to glance back, it was to see that he was already in his pickup and letting the clutch out to turn around.

Who was she kidding? Fraser McKenna hadn't given her a second glance.

FRASER GRIPPED the wheel until his hands hurt as the pickup pitched over the rocky track. *You damn near lost it back there this afternoon, buddy. You damn near lost it good.*

But he hadn't…he hadn't. Fraser relaxed his hands on the wheel. He took a deep breath. Then he gunned the engine and slipped the clutch. The pickup's wheels spun out on ice, then caught and the vehicle lurched forward. Upward. Where was he going, anyway?

He knew.

After he'd dropped off Daisy, he'd gone back to the

high pasture and pitched hay in a frenzy of physical exertion that had finally banished most of his demons. He could've gone back to the ranch house hours ago. He *didn't* have work to do that would take him much past suppertime.

That had been a lie, an excuse not to have to sit around the kitchen table with Martha and the girls talking about nothing. Smiling, pretending. At least when it'd been just him and the girls, they hadn't had to pretend. He'd been Fraser McKenna, the neighbor they'd known all their lives, and they'd been Brenda's two girls, whom he was keeping an eye on for a while.

Martha Thomas. She was the wild card. She was the one who'd turned those silent straightforward meals into something he didn't trust. Already, in less than a week, things had changed. Damn her, anyway, her and all her talk about how their days had been and what Anne had done at school and how Daisy and she had made cookies or some damn thing and what the kittens were doing now. Barn cats, for God's sake!

The pickup's engine growled as it climbed the frozen track. This was all so familiar. Back then, when the memories were razor-fresh, he'd come up here nearly every day. He'd had to come. Later he'd stopped. Had tried to forget, tried to push it all out of his mind. It had eased the pain to throw himself into hard physical work and stay away from this place of remembering.

He frowned. Come to think of it, he hadn't been up here for months, since way before Brenda had left. Maybe that was a good sign. Maybe he really was starting to forget, to put the past in the past where it belonged.

So what was he doing here now?

Snow blew across the narrow track in front of him. The wind was up. He couldn't stay long, didn't dare. Yet somehow he just wanted to come here. To think. To be alone with the rocks and the wind and the stones that marked her ashes. He remembered the day he'd brought them here. Buried them both. Charlotte's ashes mingled with the ashes of the child-that-never-was. *A handful, not more than one small handful.* Even in his dreams, even in his nightmares, he'd never given the child a name.

He maneuvered the truck around at the end of the track, then stopped and killed the engine. Suddenly it was silent, too silent. He opened the door, and an icy blast of wind swept into the cab, laden with flinty snow. He banged the door shut again with a curse. He peered through the thickening light. He could just make out the cairn he'd built, gray and faint. And cold. The stones looked so goddamned cold.

With another curse, he started the truck. What kind of sentimental fool was he? She was dead. He slammed the truck into gear. *Leave it be, McKenna. Nothing will bring her back. Ever. Nothing will bring you back, either—the man you were then. Life goes on, that's what everyone said. It must be true.*

And it *was* true, dammit. Life did go on. He'd struggled, brought Westbank Ranch back from the near disaster he'd caused. He'd neglected the ranch for nearly two years while he wrestled with his grief. Now he was in the black again, keeping other men employed, other families fed. Bloss and Daisy were under his roof now—they needed him. Until their mother got back anyway.

And this Martha Thomas—she was under his roof, too.

As he drove, Fraser looked down to where he knew the ranch buildings were situated. He could just make out a glow, probably the yard lights. He knew there'd be lights on in the house. He couldn't deny the good feeling that gave him, just thinking about it. The kind of feeling he'd had as a boy, coming home. First it'd been just him and Weston, then the twins when they got a little older, riding their ponies home after a long day in the hills, chasing down strays. Lazy talk, laughter over the sly jokes of boys, promises made and dreams of what the future might hold....

Wes and the twins had left Blue River long ago. Charlotte had been dead nearly four years. He'd been coming home to a cold dark house for too long. Maybe there were some advantages, after all, to hiring a Lady Companion for the girls. *Keep the home fires burning.* He smiled to himself in the darkness of the cab, the heater blasting hot air around his feet, the wipers slapping rhythmically against the snow. It was coming down now, really coming down.

Fraser changed gears, slowing for an icy turn. *Yeah, you nearly lost it this afternoon, McKenna.* The memory of those last few minutes back at the road with Martha still burned red-hot in his mind.

Against the rhythm of the slapping wipers, he saw her walk away from him after they'd talked, that chin of hers up in the air. He'd wanted nothing so much as to jump out of his truck, go after her, wheel her around to face him, then... *Then what, McKenna? Then what?*

Be honest. Pull her into your arms. Kiss her the way you've wanted to from the moment she laughed and said you were a crazy man back in Vi's hotel. He couldn't deny the heat he'd felt when she'd touched his arm today, when she'd swung away and marched across the road, spine starched and straight, all that glossy hair flying...

Damn! Why her? Every male fiber in his being had leapt at the challenge. Every cell in his body had urged him to chase her down when she'd turned and walked away from him. What was it about the woman that sent his blood rushing? Why after all this time? Not many women affected him that way. Why in hell had he had the bad luck to hire one who did?

Because you were stuck. Face it. Because nobody else answered your ad, that's why, he told himself cynically. Katie Barker would have taken the job, yes. But the girls had said they wouldn't have her, and he wasn't sure he wanted to cope with all the extra womanly attention Katie was bound to give him. Katie'd want marriage eventually—deserved it—and the last thing on his mind was marriage. At least Martha Thomas was a stranger, someone who'd be gone in a few months. Someone they'd never see again.

And the girls were happy. Wasn't that what mattered? Daisy'd chattered happily all the way back to the ranch that afternoon.

Brenda's youngest had a special place in his heart. She was tender and sweet and trusting, and he knew he'd die before he let anything hurt her or her sister again. Lately, once or twice, he'd felt rough surges of that fierce protective feeling he remembered so well, and it had scared the hell out of him. These two girls weren't his to love and protect. He could protect them, yes. Brenda expected him to do just that. He couldn't love them, though. There was no love left in him to give. He'd used it all up a long time ago.

The sooner Brenda got back, the better.

It had to work out. If he could just get through the next few weeks without becoming more attached to the girls than he already was. If he could just keep his hands off the Lady Companion. Which he would, definitely. Besides, he reminded himself, rubbing his jaw with one hand, Brenda was bound to show up soon, and then he'd be able to get back to the plain solitary life he'd carved out for himself in the past couple of years.

It was starting to sound like a mantra, he thought. *Brenda's coming back soon, Brenda'll be back soon...* But he had to believe that, didn't he?

THE LIGHTS of a vehicle swept into the yard, and Martha ran to the window. The snow was coming down thick and furious, lashed by the wind. The hammering of the pulse in her throat came from relief, pure relief, she told herself as she saw Fraser's tall form emerge from the pickup. She heard the truck door slam dully. She wouldn't want anyone, not even her worst enemy, out in a storm like this.

She dropped the edge of the curtain and ran to the door, then stopped herself. What was she doing now?

She couldn't run to the door, wringing her hands like some frantic wife. She'd make coffee, that was what she'd do, black and sweet. Surely he'd want something hot on a night like this. There was his dinner, too, leftovers, ready to be heated in the microwave. The girls were in bed, had been asleep for the past hour or so. Still, fingers shaking as she closed the cupboard, she couldn't help wheeling the instant she heard the door open.

He brought the storm with him. Frigid air swept into the kitchen as he stepped in, and the wind sucked at the curtains. Quickly he shut the door and leaned back against it, as though to keep the storm outside. Martha saw snow on his shoulders, snow dusting his hat, which he slowly raised one hand to remove, his eyes never leaving hers.

"Looks like winter's here," she said brightly, hoping the inane comment would break the spell that seemed to hold them both.

He nodded, placed his hat on the peg near the door and shrugged off his sheepskin jacket. He hung the jacket on another peg and turned to her again, this time his eyes carefully screened, as they hadn't been when he'd entered.

"Northeaster." He nodded again. "Always brings weather. Snow probably won't let up till morning. The girls in bed?"

"Yes."

He glanced at the kitchen clock. She knew it was already half-past nine.

"I've saved some supper for you. It'll just take a minute to warm up," she began, angry with herself

because her voice sounded so breathless, so...
relieved. "And there's coffee almost ready. Want a
cup?"

He looked at her for a long time, with the kind of
look she'd seen before but knew she'd never get used
to. "Sure."

No thank-you, no yes-please. He sat down on a
kitchen chair and pulled off his boots. Spook came
out from under the old-fashioned kitchen range to nuz-
zle his hand. Fraser reached over and ruffled the little
dog's ears and said something to him, something
rough and low and indistinct. Martha couldn't hear the
words, but she could feel them, could feel the affection and warmth in his voice.

"Thanks." He took the coffee mug she handed
him, curling his fingers around the mug.

"Shall I put your plate in the microwave?"

"Any time." He took a sip of the coffee and met
her questioning glance. "I appreciate you keeping
some for me."

"Oh, it's no problem," she replied, feeling her
cheeks warm. "Just some boring old leftover stew."

Martha's nerves were screaming. She wished she'd
thought earlier of putting on the radio, anything to
break up the thick silence, the careful words, that lay
between them. It was too late to turn it on now; he'd
know exactly why she was doing it. No, she had to
sit here quietly, let him be the one to take the initia-
tive. He'd said he wanted to talk to her. *So talk, darn
it.*

He ate his meal in silence. Martha fiddled with her

own coffee cup, one slippered foot tucked up under
her on the chair.

"Pretty good stew," he said finally, looking up.
"For old and boring, anyway." There was a glimmer
of amusement in his eyes.

Martha smiled, annoyed that his compliment had
made her feel so good. "I enjoy cooking."

"You're good at it." Again his comment made her
cheeks glow.

"I'd be happy to take it over while I'm here. If you
want me to,'' she quickly added. "I know you didn't
hire me as a cook, but I'm around, anyway, and—"

"Consider yourself hired." He smiled, faintly, but
still a smile. "I know I'll never take any prizes as a
cook. And I'm sure the girls would be pleased."

Martha smiled back, her heart unaccountably giddy.
"It's a deal." Then she wished she hadn't said that,
for fear he'd extend his hand in jest, as people often
did. She didn't want to touch him. She didn't know
why; she just didn't want to touch him.

She needn't have worried. He made no move to
shake her hand, simply stood and took his dishes to
the dishwasher, bending to put his plate and fork and
knife in the rack. Then he added detergent, twisted the
dial and started the machine.

The energetic hum of the dishwasher filled the too-
silent kitchen. Thank goodness!

Fraser turned toward her and began to speak in his
typically direct fashion. "I'm sorry about this afternoon. Out at the road. I was out of line."

"I should've told you," Martha began hesitantly.
"I should've told you I might go to town. Or at least

left you a note. You're right about me being a stranger around here—about people noticing. I just didn't think—''

"No," he interrupted. "It was my fault. Mine. I should've made it clear to you at the beginning."

He walked to the window, stared for a long moment into the blizzard—he could see the snow driven into the black glass by the wind—then walked back. "Maybe you don't realize just what kind of hornets' nest you've stepped into, and that's my fault, too.

"The first night you were here you asked if what I was doing was legal. I said I didn't know." His bleak gaze caught hers. "That's true. I don't know, but I'm damn sure I could get into trouble if the law found out I had these two girls here and their mother had disappeared." He raised one eyebrow, as though to ask whether she agreed.

He continued, "I mean, where the hell *is* Brenda? They could think I might've something to do with her disappearing, too...." He ran his hands through his hair, a gesture of exasperation. "The point is, I don't give a damn about any of that, except I want to stay clear of it. *I* know Brenda's just gone somewhere for a little excitement—it's happened before and it's going to happen again. I just need to buy a little more time until she gets back and takes her kids off my hands."

He moved to the window again, and Martha could see his frown reflected in the glass as he added, "That's all. That's why I hired you."

Still facing the window, he said, "And whatever it takes to make sure they stay safe with me until their mother gets back is what's going to happen," he said, his words measured and blunt. There was no mistaking his meaning.

Martha felt her patience thin at his tone. What did he take her for? "They're safe with me, too," she began stiffly. "I'll admit I was wrong to take Daisy to Pine Ridge without checking with you. I won't do it again. I think that should be the end of it."

When he said nothing, her patience snapped. "You're making far too big a deal of this." He turned slowly toward her, and she met his gaze, chin up. She felt distinctly annoyed at the implication that she'd jeopardize the safety of the girls in her charge. She made an abrupt sound, a half laugh of disbelief. "For Pete's sake, you'd think I was trying to kidnap them or something!"

He looked away, but not quickly enough. Martha was out of her chair in a flash. She grabbed his sleeve.

"You did, didn't you?" she cried. She hauled on his arm with one hand when he refused to look at her. He gazed stonily out the window, still refusing to meet her eyes, but she could feel his muscles tense, hard as steel, under her grip. "You thought I was going to take them away, turn them over to some government agency..."

He turned. Her voice died at the look in his eye.

"You did, didn't you?" she whispered. *"You really did."*

He was so close to her, so large, his presence so male and so overwhelming that, instinctively, she wanted to step back. To protect herself. *From what?*

But she didn't. She wanted to take her hand away

from his arm but discovered she couldn't. She felt numb, frozen. A doe in the headlights of a car at midnight, stunned and waiting for something terrible to happen.

His face was poker straight. He nodded ever so slightly. "You're right. I did."

"How could you?" Her voice was no more than a cracked whisper. "How could you even dream I'd do such a thing?" Her hand tightened on his arm, and she felt him stiffen. But he didn't pull away. "Don't you know I *care* about those two kids? I *believe* you're doing the right thing by keeping them here or I never would've stayed. I've seen you with them. I know how much *you* care about them. I don't want to see them hurt any more than you do."

"You've only been here a week—how could you care that much?" he said harshly, breaking away from her grip. He stepped back and turned to face her completely. "And don't get any wrong ideas here. They're not mine. They're my neighbor's kids. Of course I care for them—I'm responsible for them, aren't I? But that's all."

Martha stepped closer and looked up at him. She put her hand back on his arm, ignoring the way he stiffened, ignoring the hurt she felt in her heart that he should be so repelled by her. It didn't matter; she had something she needed to say to him.

"Listen here, Fraser McKenna," she said, her voice low. "You're wrong. You don't just *care* about those girls, you *love* them as if they were your own daughters, your own family—"

"What in hell are you talking about?" he growled, his eyes flashing fire.

"You say you don't really care, you tell yourself you're just doing this for Brenda," Martha went on, "but you're not. You're doing this for you. For Fraser McKenna. This means life and death to you for some godforsaken reason I don't understand, maybe *you* don't even underst—"

"You don't know what you're talking about!"

"Maybe not," Martha said softly, steeling herself not to flinch as he grabbed her shoulders. "But I know I'm right. And so do you."

His grip was hard; it hurt her, but she didn't lower her gaze for an instant, didn't dare. His eyes darkened; she saw the glow of anger in them, the slight flare of his nostrils as he took a deep breath. Her legs felt weak. If he hadn't held her she'd have fallen right there at his feet.

Suddenly his hands were on her face, one on each side of her head, his long fingers buried deep in her hair, trapping her, his thumbs near her mouth. His body was up against hers, hard and hot and lean. She felt the drumming of—what?—his heart, against the thunder of hers. She gasped. His face was close, so close she couldn't get her breath and when she did, her lungs filled with the scent of him. *Cold, snow, wood smoke, leather.* She saw the glint of perspiration on his top lip, unshaven and rough, a tiny scar she hadn't noticed before at the bridge of his nose. He moved one thumb slowly, ever so slowly, so that it grazed her lips, and she felt a shiver rack her body from her crown to her toes. The other thumb lightly stroked the skin of her throat, just at the line of her jaw. Just beneath the bone.

His eyes, black and fathomless and burning, followed the movement of his thumb, and she saw his lashes descend to shadow his tanned unshaven cheek. He seemed in the grip of some emotion he could barely control, and Martha felt every tremor of his body as her own. A tide of longing rose in her veins, beat against her eardrums.

"I don't pay you to care, Martha Thomas," he whispered, his voice harsh, his breath hot. "I pay you to get the job done. I pay you to leave me the hell out of it."

In another instant he would have kissed her. Would have torn the clothes from her and taken her right there on the floor of the kitchen. She knew it in her bones, in her skin, in the relentless rush of her blood.

But in the same instant he lowered his hard mouth to hers, he cursed savagely and twisted his head and pushed her away. Two strides and he'd ripped his jacket from its peg and slammed open the door. The chill of the storm and a few flakes of snow melting on her skin told her he'd gone.

She was left in the warmth of his kitchen, arms wrapped around herself, thinking she'd never felt colder.

CHAPTER SIX

HAD SHE IMAGINED everything?

Fraser made no reference to what had—or hadn't—happened between them the night of the storm. Martha didn't dare even think about it.

If anything, he was more remote than ever. More polite. More silent, if that was possible. Sometimes, though, during meals, or in the morning as she passed him in the hall, or in the evening as he read aloud to Daisy, and Martha helped Anne with her homework, or they played a simple board game with the girls, Martha would catch him looking at her.

He'd instantly look away; so would she. But she knew he hadn't forgotten, either. What had happened in the kitchen hadn't been a figment of her imagination. He knew, as did she, that if he'd made angry passionate love to her right there on the kitchen floor she wouldn't have stopped him, wouldn't even have tried.

If he was wary of her, the knowledge of what might have happened made her even warier of him.

And what did it mean, anyway? Unknowingly, she seemed to have stepped into some darkness, some mystery, that involved her employer, the girls, this very house they all lived in. It was as though the four walls around her harbored some other element, the missing piece to a puzzle, if she could only see it. All she'd done that night ten days ago—all she *thought* she'd done—was point out that perhaps Fraser wasn't as indifferent to the girls as he seemed to think.

Hadn't she?

THE FOLLOWING FRIDAY was Halloween. Birdie LeBlanc arrived in the morning to help Martha and Daisy get the costumes ready. Martha had taken an instant liking to the spare bright-eyed housekeeper, her busy person an apt reflection of her name. It was really Alberta, she'd confided to Martha the first time they met, the day Martha and Daisy had gone to Pine Ridge. Alberta Bernice. But no one had ever called her anything but Birdie.

Yes, she was a registered nurse, she told Martha. But no, she hadn't worked full-time since the boys took over the ranch. She and Hugh had stayed on in their place, semiretired, while the boys built two more houses on the property. Now Hugh occasionally gave his three sons a hand on the Triple V or, more often, worked for wages for Fraser. And Birdie, apart from her weekly housekeeping at Fraser's, did the occasional private-nursing job, but mostly filled in at the Pine Ridge Hospital when needed.

Martha had realized the second time she'd met the woman—when a dozen half-completed projects for her upcoming Christmas church bazaar had spilled from her large canvas carryall—that Birdie LeBlanc wasn't a woman to waste time.

She hadn't wasted any with Martha, either. Martha

had soon found herself telling the older woman all about her former life, why she'd left Wisconsin, and why she'd taken the job with Fraser McKenna. Birdie had reciprocated, filling Martha in on the identities of all the neighbors, tipping her off about the best deals to be had in Pine Ridge, and giving her the calendar of upcoming events at the local community hall.

Birdie hadn't been nearly as forthcoming about Martha's employer, though. The few questions Martha had ventured to ask had been met with a speculative look, and Birdie had seemed to consider her answers carefully. Then she'd invariably changed the direction of the conversation, pursing her lips, saying only, ''He's a good man, Fraser McKenna is. Don't you forget it, Martha, no matter what you hear. A good man.''

Which had only made Martha more curious. One particular mystery that had begun to plague her was the identity of the young woman in the silver frame Fraser kept on his dresser. Once, heart thumping and feeling guilty as heck, Martha had stolen into his room when Anne was at school and Daisy was out in the barn with Fraser and studied the photograph. It showed a young, pretty woman in her late twenties or so, jet black hair aswirl, dark eyes flashing, smiling impishly as she peered around the trunk of a birch tree. His sister? A girlfriend? Fraser had never said anything about his personal life or his family, if, indeed, he even had family still living. She hadn't dared come right out and ask Birdie. Somehow, as his employee, she felt it wasn't her place.

''Bet you're wishing you'd kept right on track to

California,'' Birdie said when she came in that morning, stamping the snow from her boots and bearing a large box that Martha and Daisy were delighted to find was filled with fresh molasses cookies. ''Ain't this weather aggravating?''

''Mmm, these are delicious,'' Martha mumbled through cookie crumbs. She gestured mutely to the window, where the brilliance of the morning sun was magnified a thousand times by the winter wonderland they'd found themselves in after the blizzard a week and a half ago. Temperatures had remained very low, and the foot of fresh snow had stayed. Winter was definitely here.

''No way. I wouldn't have missed this for anything,'' she continued, after swallowing. She smiled at the older woman. ''Have you ever seen anything more glorious?''

The Wind River Mountains rose stark and hard and white against the fresh blue Wyoming sky. Martha thought Fraser's ranch had about the most perfect setting she could ever have imagined.

''No need to tell me, Martha,'' Birdie replied. ''Lived here all my life and never got tired of it yet. Don't suppose I will now. The boys thought us old folks would head for warmer parts once we retired. Arizona, maybe. Huh!'' She laughed. ''Feet first, that's the only way we'll be leaving, I told 'em.'' She turned to Daisy. ''All right, young lady, hold still now and let's try these wings on.''

Daisy giggled as Birdie eased the bumblebee wings she'd contrived out of gauze and wire coat hangers over her head and fastened the elastic strips that anchored the contraption securely around her small chest.

"There. How's that?" Birdie adjusted one of the wings by squeezing and reshaping it, then stepped back, hands on hips to admire her work.

Martha clapped her hands, delighted. "Oh, Birdie, it's perfect! Wait'll your sister sees you, Daisy."

School let out early today, and the girls planned to spend the afternoon getting themselves ready for trick-or-treating. Daisy had promised to wait until Anne got home before painting black bumblebee legs on her yellow tights if Anne would agree to let her try on the princess outfit.

MARTHA HAD DECIDED the trick-or-treating should start before it grew too dark. Fraser, to her surprise, had offered to take the children around to the various neighboring ranches, while she stayed home to answer the door to any little goblins who ventured up the long road to the McKenna ranch.

By midafternoon, Birdie had gone home, and Anne and Daisy had tried on their costumes so many times Martha had lost count. Fraser came by briefly to fill his thermos with hot coffee, promising to be back by half-past four for an early meal. Martha put a casserole of lasagna in the oven and set the girls to stuffing "goodie bags" for the children who might arrive at their door that night. Into the brown paper sacks went popcorn balls tied up in plastic wrap—Daisy and Martha had made a big batch the previous day—some of Birdie's molasses cookies and a handful of candy. Anne wrote the name of the ranch and the phone number on the outside of each bag, so that careful parents would know where the homemade candy had come from.

By the time Fraser walked in at twenty past four, Martha felt nearly as excited as the girls.

"Look at me! Look at me!" Daisy twirled for Fraser's appraisal.

"Very scary," Fraser said good-humoredly when Daisy ran at him with her fingers pinching the air, her version of a bumblebee about to sting. Anne curtsied and he smiled, his eyes warm. "You look beautiful, Anne. Just like a real princess."

To Martha's amazement, Anne burst into tears, which only lasted a few seconds before she scrubbed them away in an agony of embarrassment. She ran to Fraser and threw her arms around his neck, burying her face in his shirt. Martha heard her whisper something to him. He nodded, glanced quickly at Martha and patted the girl's back in an awkward gesture of comfort. He put his other arm around her and hugged her tight, then released her.

"Come on now, darlin'," he said gruffly. "Let's eat."

"Yes. Supper's ready," Martha said, turning to pull the casserole out of the oven. Poor Anne! She'd probably never been told she looked like a princess before. Or that she was beautiful. Martha had to admit that with Anne's flyaway black hair and too-often angry face, her scrawny arms and legs usually sporting T-shirt and scruffy jeans, she hadn't glimpsed the princess inside, either. But Fraser had. He'd touched Anne's heart. A proud father's comment, for a girl who'd never known a father. Martha felt her own heart brim with emotion.

In no time the meal was over, and the girls were putting final touches on their costumes—lipstick for Anne, black stripes on cheeks and forehead for Daisy, as well as precariously poised coat-hanger antennae for her head. The children didn't seem to notice—neither Fraser nor Martha pointed it out—that the dazzling costumes were nearly hidden beneath their bulky winter coats.

"Whoopee!" Anne and Daisy raced out the door, accompanied by the madly barking Spook. What would Halloween be without a genuine honest-to-goodness Spook? Martha smiled to herself.

"What's that all about?"

Fraser's voice broke into her reverie. He'd found his gloves and was putting them on, his eyes steady on Martha.

"What's what about?"

"The smile."

"Oh." She laughed and made a faint gesture with her hand. "Just thinking about Spook. You know, the Halloween dog."

"Listen, Martha." Fraser's voice turned gruff. "I want you to know I appreciate what you're doing with the girls." He cleared his throat. "All this Halloween stuff. They're having a good time."

"I hope so," Martha said dreamily, thinking of many happy Halloweens in her own life. "It's fun for me, too."

He reached for the doorknob. "We'll be back in a couple of hours. You probably won't get too many kids at the door. Too far for them to come all the way down to the end of the road here.''

The horn of the pickup sounded then, obviously one of the girls trying to hurry him along. Martha smiled again and went to the window as he left in a swirl of cold air.

A stranger dropping by would have viewed this as just one more happy-family scene, she thought. One in a long series of such scenes between the birth of a child and leaving home. But it wasn't what it seemed to be, not at all—she and Fraser weren't husband and wife, never mind mother and father to these children. These children had been abandoned by their natural mother. They'd never known a father.

Martha's heart contracted painfully and she let the curtain drop. She began to gather up the supper dishes. All the more reason to make the most of every day spent here in Wyoming. It wouldn't last, but it was hers to cherish now. Lay down some happy memories, for the girls and for herself. Do the best she possibly could for these two motherless children who needed her—and Fraser—so much. Play her part in this pretend family, this charade of the real family she'd wanted for so long.

The ranch house felt lonely without the girls or Fraser around. The wind howled. Martha shivered as the old house creaked and groaned. A dog barked somewhere in the distance. Probably one of the sheepdogs Tom kept down at the bunkhouse. She was being silly. After all, there were several hands in the bunkhouse, only steps away. It wasn't as though there was any danger being alone in the house.

Just that she wasn't used to it anymore. She'd lived alone for many years in one apartment or another. Once she'd rented a house for a while with another single woman, a friend she'd made at the television station where she'd done her celebrity food show. Afternoon programing, lots of chat, some cooking, a few recipes from the rich and famous, local variety. The show had been fun.

Martha let her mind drift. She waited for the familiar sense of loss and longing to settle on her. For her part-time television job, for her newspaper column. It didn't happen. She realized that she didn't miss her former life much. In fact, she barely thought about it anymore. Strange as her new life was, her days at Westbank Ranch felt more real, than the past she remembered. All she missed was her old cat, Mr. Herbert, whom she'd left with a friend. She wondered how he was making out. Probably already had all the toms in his new neighborhood terrorized.

Martha gave a start when she saw headlight beams sweep into the yard. Could they possibly be back already?

"Trick or treat, trick or treat! Give us something good to eat!"

Martha laughed and swung the door wide. "Come in, come in." She gestured to the two little witches and the diminutive cowboy complete with toy six-guns and neckerchief.

"Howdy." Behind them came a tall mustachioed man in a ball cap. The father, no doubt.

"Hello," Martha said, offering her hand. "I'm Martha Thomas."

"Brett Sommers." The man gave her a friendly grin and shook her hand. "Rocking Bar J," he said, as though the name of the ranch explained everything. He nodded. "We're a coupla miles down the road from here."

Martha quickly handed round treat bags and listened to the chorus of thank-yous from the children. Then, laughing, she shepherded them outdoors again.

She'd no sooner closed the door than another group drove up, two pickups full of children. After that came a station wagon, loaded with two families of children, several more pickups and a battered utility van, equally stuffed with kids.

So much for Fraser's prediction. An hour and a half later, Martha frantically pawed through the dwindling supplies, making up new goodie bags and thinking she'd have a few things to say to Fraser when he got back. Tom, from down at the bunkhouse, had come up and apologetically asked if she had any spare candy, and she'd given him the bag of lollipops. It seemed many of the children were also stopping in at the bunkhouse for treats, getting in the way of the nightly card game and, jeez, he'd been winning, too, he told her. Martha didn't think Tom really minded. At least, he'd complained with a smile.

She glanced at the clock. Nearly seven. Fraser would be back with the girls any minute. Was that his truck now? Martha went to the window as a pickup pulled into the yard.

Yet another group of little goblins trooped in, followed by a woman. A few mothers had come out this evening; Martha had met several.

"Oh!" The woman stopped as she entered the bright kitchen and put her hand to her mouth. "You gave me quite a turn there for a moment!"

"I did?" Martha was handing out bags to the children and only paying half attention to the woman.

"You surely did. Why, for a moment there, I thought I saw a ghost through the window. Charlotte, clear as day," she said, still waving one hand weakly in the region of her heart.

"Oh?" Martha pushed a damp strand of hair from her forehead and faced the woman, brow furrowed. *Charlotte?*

"She's been gone these past four years, and I don't know for the life of me why I didn't think of that right off, but seeing you there, looking out the kitchen window, it surprised me so I... "

Martha frowned, tuning out the clamoring children, knowing somehow that this was important, whatever it was this woman was saying. *Charlotte? Gone these past four years?*

She hesitated, then smiled and held out her hand. "I'm Martha. I'm new here, working for Mr. Mc- Kenna. Martha Thomas."

"Oh, heavens yes, I know. We've heard, we surely have, most of us neighbors, and we've been dying to meet you, ma'am."

She could have guessed that, Martha thought wryly, judging from the numbers of friendly but definitely curious neighbors who'd came into the kitchen that evening with their children.

"Oh, and I'm Elsie Higson. When I said that about Charlotte, I—"

"Charlotte?" Martha broke in gently. "I don't believe I know who you mean."

"Why, Charlotte McKenna," the woman said, her bright eyes riveted on Martha's face. "Fraser McKenna's wife."

CHAPTER SEVEN

"HELP ME!"

His voice tangled in his throat and he couldn't answer. Branches clawed. His hands were slick and bloodied from sliding on the rocks. Lungs on fire.

"Fraser..." Still she called to him, fainter, farther.

Then the water reared up with a million knowing eyes and he leapt in, lashed out against the deep current that grabbed at his feet, pulled at his hair. Kept him from her. He choked and gasped and spat, water now cold and green and thick with ice, now warm and sweet as blood.

Dream rocks teased on shore, fading, wavering, ever just beyond his strength, beyond his reach. One more stroke, then another...

"Fraser!"

Blinded by the wet, confused by her voice, which seemed to come from over his shoulder, he shook webs of blackness from his eyes. The iciness swept him away from her. Downstream. Powerless. To the sea he'd never seen....

Again he struggled to answer her, and this time his voice burst from his chest, a great choked and desperate cry that woke him up, sick with fear. Panting.

He waited for the echo in the dark. There was no sound at all. Nothing.

A dream cry.

Thank God for that. Half in bed, half out, heart hammering, sheets twisted. Where was he?

Home. Moon charging the room with silver, on sweat, on skin.

Naked and alone.

With a great effort, he lay back. Breathed deeply. Felt oxygen strike his blood, slice through his veins. Felt old grief rise hot and heavy in his throat, fresh as a bee sting.

He hadn't reached her. He would not reach her. Not ever.

He raised his head again. Slow, cautious, confused. Where was the silvery frame, square, gleaming? Where were her smiling paper eyes? Ah, yes. Where she'd stood for so long, to remind him of what a man could never forget.

He sat up, shivering, pulled on his jeans and shirt. Picked up his boots, then set them down gently. Why wake the girls? Why wake the woman sleeping down the hall? The stranger. The woman whose hair smelled of sunshine and rain and someone else's memories. The woman from away, who'd brought these dreams with her. Brought them to haunt his nights again. Brought them with her as surely as she'd brought softness and sweetness and gentle womanly ways.

Outside, frost glimmered. November, cold as a witch's kiss. Cold as his heart.

He walked to the barn, snow crunching beneath his boots. He had some work he could do. He thought of the girls asleep in their beds, under his roof. Safe. Warm. Innocent as new lambs in their pens.

The woman was right; they were his family now, those two girls, like it or not.

Guard them, McKenna. His heart beat warm and strong and heavy. *Keep them safe.*

He swore, then, to the gods of the Wind Rivers, to the glittering stars in the blackness above, that he would. That nothing would bring them harm while they were in his care.

He'd watch over them, yes. But they needed more than that. They needed what he couldn't give them.

What he couldn't give anyone.

AT FIRST Martha thought she'd just ask him. Just come out one day when the girls were occupied elsewhere and ask Fraser why he hadn't told her about his wife.

But either he wasn't alone, such as when he'd appear in the kitchen with one of the hands or one of the girls. Or he made a point of staying away, as Martha suspected over the next day or two, when he spent long hours out of the house, even missing meals with them. Or, the rare time he did happen to come into the kitchen alone, Martha simply found herself unable to broach the subject.

It's none of your business, she told herself severely. *If he wanted to tell you, he would.* She was just curious. It wasn't as though it mattered one way or the other.

But still, what was the big secret?

Then one day while she was helping Birdie, she

noticed that the older woman had seen her sneaking a peek at the photograph in the silver frame. Martha decided to take the plunge.

"Who's this, Birdie?" she asked offhandedly, gesturing toward the young woman's picture.

"Ah." Birdie took the framed photograph in one hand and ran her dusting cloth over it slowly, lovingly. Her face twisted with some strong emotion. Pain? Sorrow? Regret?

"That Fraser's wife?" Martha ventured cautiously. She'd never been able to figure out Birdie's attitude to their employer. She seemed fiercely loyal, yet at the same time oddly defensive. As though Fraser was one of her own sons, in need of her protection.

Birdie set the frame down. "Who told you about Fraser's wife?" she asked.

"One of the moms who came around Halloween night. Elsie, she said her name was. She said I'd given her a turn when she saw me in the window, said I'd reminded her of Fraser's wife." Martha paused, trying to judge Birdie's reaction. The older woman said nothing.

"I didn't even know he had a wife!" Martha went on with a small laugh that sounded contrived to her own ears. After all, she really shouldn't be asking Birdie questions about Fraser behind his back. Nervously she swiped at a bookshelf with her cloth, then the beveled mirror that stood behind the door.

"Well, he did have a wife," Birdie said with a sigh. "Charlotte Mae. A lovely girl. Such a sad story in the end, my dear." She paused. "I'm surprised that Fraser keeps her picture here. He's gotten rid of everything else.''

"Sad?"

"Fraser hasn't told you anything?" Birdie asked sharply.

"No."

"Well, I guess he wouldn't." Birdie shook her head. "Humph. He's tried to put it out of his mind, I suppose. A man's way. Can't be done, that's the trouble. I've told him that myself many a time."

"Put what out of his mind?" Martha was more curious than ever. "Were they divorced?"

"Lord, no!" Birdie flipped out a clean sheet from the basket beside her and gestured for Martha to take one end. "Fraser McKenna lived for Charlotte Mae Racey, always had. So did Wes," she said with a quick look at Martha. "Weston's a year older than Fraser, and the twins, Cullen and Jack, are seven years younger. Maybe you knew that...."

Martha shook her head.

"Anyway, Charlotte Mae went off to San Francisco, and nobody ever thought she'd come back. But one day, back she came and Fraser married her. Just a few weeks later, as I recall. Wes was away at the time. Overseas," Birdie mused, a far-off, remembering light in her eye. Then she shook her head briskly. "Fraser was more in love with that woman than a man ought to be."

Birdie bit her lower lip and bent to the task at hand. Martha felt an excruciating pain just below her midriff. *In love with her, in love with her...*

But why shouldn't he be in love with his wife? "What happened, Birdie?"

Birdie looked grim. "She died. A terrible tragedy." She shook her head again. "Shouldn't have happened, but it did. Over three years ago now, nearly four. Fraser's never gotten over it."

She sighed deeply. "I've probably gone and said more than I should've. Fraser'd be wild if he knew. But I've told him many a time there's no point in pretending nothing happened. He can wipe out every trace that she ever lived here, I guess, try to forget— just like he's done. But he can't cut her out of his heart. Truth is, men can be so aggravatin' sometimes."

Martha felt stunned. She wanted to ask Birdie for more details, but knew she shouldn't. Birdie had already said that Fraser wouldn't be happy if he knew. How had Charlotte died? What kind of tragedy? Why was Fraser so determined to erase every trace of her presence from this home they'd once shared, every reminder that she'd lived here? Every reminder except one—the photograph in his room.

More in love with that woman than a man ought to be. Again Martha felt pain beneath her ribs as she drew in a shaky breath and realized her heart was pounding. But that was crazy! What did she care, except that it was a romantic story, with what sounded like a tragic ending? Shakespearean. And of course she'd feel sorry for any man who'd suffered as Fraser had—and still was, apparently. Who wouldn't?

Birdie's information explained a lot. Perhaps it explained why Fraser seemed so reluctant to come near her—except for that one crazy time in the kitchen, which Martha was doing her level best to forget. Maybe he preferred to avoid all women, not just her. She felt vaguely comforted, and not sure why it mattered.

Then she immediately discarded that theory. A man like Fraser McKenna drew women like bees to honey, no doubt always had, and if Vi Jamieson's comment back at the hotel meant anything, he carried a sizable reputation in that department. It must be based on *something*.

But the fact that he'd had a beautiful young wife who'd died tragically might explain why he'd been so angry that night in the kitchen. The night she'd told him the girls were his family now, or as good as, whether he wanted to admit it or not.

Martha was sorry she'd opened her mouth. It must have rubbed salt in open wounds, even after all this time—

"Going to the Barker wedding?"

Birdie's question brought her back to the present.

"Oh…" Martha hesitated. She had no desire to go to any kind of social gathering, certainly not a wedding. "I don't think so."

"The girls want to go, I'm sure. They're second cousins once removed to Mary Jane Hastings, the bride." Birdie made a face. "'Course Fraser might prefer to leave 'em at home. No sense askin' for trouble," she said darkly. "There'll be enough of that when Brenda gets back."

Martha knew what she meant. The fewer people who knew he had the girls in his care, the better. By this time, well over three months since Brenda had taken off, even the locals Fraser trusted must be asking questions. A wedding. It was the last thing she wanted to go to, even though she was dying to know what this Katie Barker was like, sister to the groom. The one who apparently had her eye on Fraser. Pure, natural curiosity, she told herself.

Martha had a sudden image of a dark and handsome Fraser McKenna with a beautiful woman in his arms, dancing, smiling, holding her close. The woman wore blue, but in her mind's eye, Martha couldn't quite see her face, and she felt that annoying pain again just under her ribs. She must be hungry. She glanced at her watch and saw it was nearly noon.

"Did you say something?" Martha realized the housekeeper was muttering as she turned off the vacuum.

"That Elsie Higson oughtta get some new glasses," she snorted. "Charlotte Mae was way shorter than you, couple inches, I'd guess. And the loveliest hair she had, black as coal. Great big brown eyes that'd melt your heart.

"Why, she didn't look a bit like you, Martha. Not a bit!"

FRASER WAS THINKING of china blue eyes and hair the color of honey. Buckwheat honey. His feeling that it was best to leave Martha and the girls at the ranch, away from prying eyes and nosy questions, was all mixed up with wishing he'd brought them. He missed them. He missed the girls. And, irritating as it was to admit, he missed the Lady Companion. Damned if he could figure out why.

"Come on, Fraser, darlin'. Cheer up. You're supposed to be happy at weddings, don't you know that?"

He looked down at the woman in his arms and smiled, a smile he knew rarely reached his eyes these days. He just plain didn't feel like socializing, even if Ted Barker was one of his oldest friends and even if, as best man, he'd had no choice but to come to Rock Springs for the wedding. Ted and Mary Jane. He glanced over at the bride and groom, dancing on the other side of the hall. Ted was grinning at something Mary Jane had said. They had eyes for no one but each other.

Fraser felt a pang in his chest. But it wasn't the ache of love he felt, not what Ted and his bride must be feeling. What he felt was the ache of loss—and he'd felt it more in the three weeks since the Lady Companion had arrived than he had in a long time. Somehow she brought back everything he thought he'd buried for good.

Now, even when he tried just for the hell of it, he couldn't pretend he had Charlotte Mae in his arms, rather than Katie Barker. Sometimes he thought if he didn't have that picture propped up in his room, she'd just fade away from his mind. From his memory.

He set his jaw. Charlotte deserved more. She deserved better than that from him.

Still, the traitorous thought lingered. If he'd brought the girls, he'd have had an excuse to bring Martha, too. And if he'd brought Martha, he'd have had an excuse to be dancing with her right now, not Katie Barker.

He wondered what she'd feel like in his arms, if she'd feel soft and womanly, if he'd be able to look deep into those big blue eyes without giving in to the need to kiss her, to gather her close to him, as he'd often thought he'd like to do. It was just fantasy, harmless enough. His womanizing days were over—

"Hear anything from Brenda yet?" Katie smiled at him. He liked Katie, respected her, wished the best for her. It wasn't fair to be fantasizing about some other woman when he was dancing with her.

"Nope. Not a damn word."

"How are the girls taking it?"

He wondered how much of her concern was genuine, then felt disloyal to his old friend's baby sister; Katie had offered to help look after the girls when he was in a bind, before he'd hired Martha. "Oh, they're making out all right. They like the woman I hired."

"Hmm." Katie sniffed and looked away for an instant. When she looked back her green eyes were sharp, her voice a little harder. "To tell you the truth, darlin', I'm surprised you hired a woman like her."

He frowned. "Why's that?"

"She's not one of us, Fraser." Katie's eyes narrowed, but her smile never faltered. "Millie—who manages the café down at Vi's hotel? She told me she saw her. City woman, she said, from a mile off."

"Can't see why that's a problem." In his opinion, hiring someone from somewhere else was a plus—she wouldn't be part of the local scene. She wouldn't be around to gossip or to pop up later, once Brenda was back. Though he couldn't imagine Martha gone, just him and the girls alone again.

A chill gripped his heart, and he stepped into a turn, concentrating on the feel of Katie's weight on his arm as she turned expertly with him. Brenda would be back then, he reminded himself firmly. Everything was going to work out fine.

"Just a little surprised you'd trust her, that's all," Katie said. The band finished the set, and she smiled as he offered her his arm to escort her to the head table. Katie was one of Mary Jane's maids of honor.

Trust Martha? He recalled the day he thought she'd taken the girls and turned them over to some social agency. He hadn't trusted her then, that was for damn sure. But now? His gut told him he could trust her. That when he got back to the ranch, she'd be there. That she'd watch over the girls, keep them safe, just as he would've done.

Some feeling, vaguely like disloyalty, told him he didn't care to discuss the situation any further with Katie. It told him he wanted to protect Martha from the kind of gossip he knew had been generated the moment he'd hired her.

Ted and Mary Jane were making the rounds, greeting guests.

"Look at old Ted," he said, nudging Katie and smiling broadly. "Ever think that rascal'd end up married?"

Katie laughed. "Thought you'd get married again before Teddy ever took the plunge." She squeezed his arm. "Any time you think about changing your mind,

Fraser..." She paused, looked up at him. "You know that."

He smiled, embarrassed. "I appreciate that, Katie." He put his arm around her shoulder in a brotherly gesture and pulled her close for a moment. "But it's not that way between you and me, Katie, and you know it. Let's stay friends."

She nodded, but he could tell it cost her and that made him feel even worse. After all, once, briefly, they'd been more than friends. Back when he'd tried to find a woman who could take the pain away. But that was over, had been over for a long time. "Besides, you know I've got no interest in marrying again."

Katie nodded again, but her smile was shaky. Then she seemed to gather herself together and, with a genuine squeal of delight, accepted the invitation of Adam Barker, another of her brothers, to a dance.

Fraser tugged at his formal tie, loosening it a bit. Damn these rented monkey suits, anyway! He'd give anything to be back at the ranch. He wasn't cut out for small talk and dancing. He'd arrived yesterday for a quick walk-through rehearsal and wasn't planning to leave until the morning.

Over the next hour, Fraser figured he'd danced with nearly every woman in the room, all the ones he knew and a few he didn't. Ted Barker had been a popular buckaroo on several Wind River ranches before taking his rodeo winnings and savings last year and leaving the high country to buy himself a ranch near Tewson. Mary Jane Hastings was the cause of all that—the

Rock Springs elementary-school teacher Ted had met while buying nails in the local hardware store.

"Whiskey, boy?" Judd Barker, the patriarch of the large and extended Barker family, handed him a glass. Forty on his next birthday, Fraser didn't feel much like a boy, but that was what Judd called anyone younger than his own seventy-odd years.

"Thanks, Judd." Fraser took a sip, grimaced and set the glass down on a table beside him. Bourbon wasn't his drink at the best of times. A couple of beers now and again, sure, but what he'd told Martha was true—he wasn't much for liquor. The wiry old rancher gave him a sharp look from under grizzled brows.

"Not drinkin', boy? What's the matter with ya?"

"Nothing." There was a long moment's comfortable silence, the mark of friendship and respect among ranching men, then Fraser surprised himself by saying, "I'm going to head out soon, Judd. Weather's turning." Not that it mattered, but now he'd mentioned it, he suddenly felt an urgency he hadn't felt before. "Fine wedding. I look forward to another one when you get Katie married off."

Judd Barker chuckled. "Maybe not as best man, boy. She 'pears to have you staked out."

"Heck, I don't know about that," Fraser replied lazily, watching Katie dance by with one of the top hands on her father's ranch. Katie was blushing and laughing at something the cowboy had said. That was a good sign, as far as Fraser was concerned. Katie's natural high spirits had returned. "Looks like Farley Bell's got his eye on her."

The older rancher just grunted.

Fraser thought about what he'd said a moment earlier. Why *not* head back tonight? He hadn't had much to drink, and he was sick and tired of dancing and answering sideways questions about Brenda and about the woman he'd hired to look after the girls. He'd had it with fending off the flirtatious younger sisters and Rock Springs divorcées so-called friends kept bringing over. He was tired of people assuming Katie Barker had some claim on him, unwarranted as he knew it was—and Katie knew it was.

And he wanted to get out of this damn tuxedo.

Making up his mind, he strode over to find Ted.

"I'm heading out, buddy. Back up to Blue River," he said to his friend. He bent down to kiss the bride.

"So soon?" Mary Jane said with a small frown. "Why, I don't believe you've met my cousin, Moyra yet, come up all the way from Cheyenne—"

"Maybe another time," Fraser said hastily.

"Got to get back to that there nanny you hired, huh?" his friend drawled with a broad wink. Fraser felt like slugging him. "I hear she ain't too hard on the eyes, either."

Fraser ignored him. "I hate to leave the girls too long. You know how it is."

"Sure," Ted agreed with a sly grin. "I know how it is."

Twenty minutes later, Fraser was in the cab of his pickup, maneuvering out of the parking lot. It was snowing lightly, but he'd just caught the weather report and didn't think he'd have any trouble getting back. He looked at the dimly lit clock on the dash— almost midnight. He'd be home in a couple of hours.

He felt a kind of excitement grip him as he turned onto the highway and headed north. It wasn't that he had to get back to the girls, the excuse he'd given Ted. Martha would take good care of them, he knew that.

It just felt right to be heading home.

Home. The word made him feel good inside. Home was where he wanted to be.

MARTHA AWOKE with a start. Or had she even been asleep?

She listened. It was quiet, absolutely quiet in the old house. And she could hear no car engine outside. That wasn't what had wakened her.

Martha felt for her slippers beside the bed. *Brr!* She tiptoed to the window, not wanting to interrupt the silence of the house. Outside, snowflakes drifted lazily from a dark sky to land softly on the hard-crusted snow. The moon was full, which made the scene before her even more magical and glorious.

What a beautiful place. What a beautiful winter night. Martha turned her head, listening. One of the girls?

She tiptoed down the hall and pushed open the door to the girls room. She winced as it creaked on its old hinges. But the sound didn't disturb their dreams. Daisy was curled on her side, cuddling her kangaroo, a dozen other stuffed toys holding vigil on her pillow and quilt. Anne lay flat on her back, hair wild and black against the white of the pillow slip, arms flung wide, legs sprawled. Martha gently pulled up her quilt and tucked it in. She stood for a moment as the feelings welled in her heart.

She cared for these motherless girls; she cared too much.

She tiptoed out of their room, pulling the door closed behind her, and returned to her own room. There was something wonderful about watching the sleep of innocent children. So much peace in the room, such warmth of cozy bodies relaxed in sleep, such a tangle of emotions at rest. Such trust.

But she missed Fraser. He was at the Barker wedding and wouldn't be back until tomorrow. His absence was the one wrong note in the ageless silent song of the old house.

That, and the letter on the kitchen table.

The letter had come Friday after Fraser had left for Rock Springs. Registered. The letter carrier had made the long trip up the drive, instead of leaving it in the mailbox. Martha had signed for it, her heart leaping when she'd seen the return address—no name, but a box number in Alabama. The detective Fraser had told her he'd hired? Brenda? Could she be writing after all this time to the man she'd left in charge of her children?

Martha told herself she hoped it was a letter from Brenda. A letter telling Fraser she'd be back soon, apologizing for having left him with the children for so long. Or perhaps she'd want the children sent to her. She just hoped Brenda had one heck of a good excuse for what she'd done.

And then she, Martha, could make her plans. Funny, but she didn't feel much like leaving anymore.

She'd become used to the place, to the laughter of the children, to kissing their bruises and reading them bedtime stories. Driving Anne to the bus every morning and picking her up every afternoon. There was a pleasant measured rhythm to her days that she'd never experienced—or appreciated—until now.

Still…she'd always known this job was just temporary. And she'd been here less than a month. There was danger in growing to love children she could never call her own. She thought of Daisy's shy trusting smile and Anne's squeal of triumph when she bested Martha at a board game, and she wondered if perhaps it wasn't already too late.

Martha stepped back to the window. She was sure she'd just heard a car's engine. But that was impossible. It was well past midnight. She picked up the small alarm clock on her bedside table and saw that it was, in fact, ten past two. But that was definitely the sound of a vehicle coming up the road.

Heart hammering, she looked out the window again. She'd never really felt frightened being alone, and there was no point in worrying now. Tom was in the bunkhouse, only a short phone call away if she needed him. But the dogs didn't bark, and that was what made Martha finally realize it wasn't a stranger driving up to the house.

It was Fraser.

He had returned. A stupid giddiness made her smile in the darkness, hug herself in the chill near the window.

She watched as he drove up to the house, instead of the garage where he usually parked. The few seconds she spent waiting for him to get out of the truck seemed to last a very long time. And when he did, slowly, stiffly, stretching hugely before bending down for a quick pat to the leaping, frisking dogs, her heart bumped again.

She was just relieved he was safely back. That was all. Martha watched him walk the few steps toward the house in his shirtsleeves, jacket hooked over his shoulder.

Then she remembered the letter.

She hurried to her bed and grabbed her robe, which she'd thrown over the footboard, and pulled it on. It wasn't particularly warm—embroidered Shanghai silk wasn't meant to be—but at least it covered her. Not that the opaque protection of a floor-length long-sleeved cotton flannel nightgown needed any further enhancement.

At the door she paused. Perhaps she should wait until morning to find out what was in that letter. Fraser would be tired, and maybe he wouldn't even want to open it now.

But then she pushed that thought aside. She couldn't wait. She wouldn't sleep a wink, wondering. She rushed down the hall as quietly as possible, careful not to disturb the girls.

When she reached the kitchen, she stopped. Fraser was in the kitchen, white dress shirt rumpled, no sign of a tie, jacket tossed onto a chair. But he hadn't moved beyond the outer door. He leaned against the frame, his eyes on the letter on the table. Spook whined at his feet.

He raised his eyes as she entered the room, and she

felt herself flush in the semidarkness. She didn't need to see his eyes clearly to know he was looking at her, all of her, from her sheepskin-slippered toes to the top of her head. She knew one of her braids had come undone and she must look a mess. She reached for the switch on the wall but didn't flick it.

"Y-you're back early." Could she possibly come up with anything more inane?

"Yes."

She waited, but he said nothing more. "Shall I turn on the light?"

"If you want. Did I wake you?"

"No. I couldn't sleep."

She turned on the light and squeezed her eyes in the sudden brightness. "You got a letter," she burst out. "It came after you left yesterday."

"I see that," he said quietly, his eyes never leaving hers. She felt flustered all of a sudden, exposed, and wished she hadn't left the sanctuary of her room. This was silly. Absolutely silly. Why was she here?

"Maybe it's from Brenda," she said.

"Maybe."

Martha was surprised. If she'd been in his place, she'd have grabbed the letter immediately and torn it open. After all, he'd been waiting months to hear news of the girls' mother. "Aren't you going to open it?"

He moved away from the door and reached for the letter. He turned it over, studied the postmark, the return address, then opened it slowly. There was a single sheet of paper inside, and Martha watched him as he read it.

His jaw tightened, his nostrils flared, and for one

tense incredible second, he closed his eyes and took a sharp breath. Martha almost felt him take a step backward, but he didn't actually move.

"What is it?" she whispered. "Is it from Brenda?"

"It's from her sister, Louise," he said, his voice flat. "Brenda's dead."

CHAPTER EIGHT

"DEAD!"

"Car accident three weeks ago." Fraser threw the letter and envelope onto the table, and the single sheet of paper fluttered to the floor. "Read it for yourself." He moved to stand in front of the window.

Martha scrabbled for the paper under the chair. "Omigod, omigod," she muttered. "I can't believe it." She barely realized she was speaking. "Those poor, poor girls." She felt like crying. Not for Brenda, although God knew the woman could use some of the sympathy in death that she'd so obviously needed in life.

But she'd never met Brenda and couldn't grieve for her. In fact, suddenly she was angry with her, so angry she couldn't believe the violence of her reaction. To leave those two little girls as Brenda had done—to abandon them! When there were people in the world who would've happily taken them in, adopted them, given them a home. *And now this...*

Then she felt terrible. After all, Brenda was dead.

She stood, the paper in her trembling hand. "Oh, Fraser, what are we going to do? What are we going to tell Anne and Daisy?"

He said nothing, didn't even turn to look at her, and

at the time Martha didn't think it strange that she'd included herself.

She smoothed the paper and tried to read it. The letter wasn't long, although the writing was cramped:

Dear Fraser,

Brenda died October 20 in a crash just west of Smoky Hills, maybe you heard. She had my address, how she got it I have no idea, she was hitching, that's how the cops got hold of me. As you may or may not know, I have left my past life behind me, I'm not proud of it, and I'm married now to a fine man, better than I deserve, and want nothing to do with this. He would leave me if he knew what kind of scum I was related to. Did Brenda sell the place? I want my share if she did. I heard she had a kid too, a while back. There was no kid killed with her, maybe it died before. I want nothing to do with any brat of hers, dead or alive. If you don't mind I'll send the ashes and maybe you could put them in the ground up there with Ma and Pa. I suppose that's the least I can do, she was my sister.

The signature was illegible.

Martha raised her face, aghast. Fraser swung to meet her gaze.

"Dear God in heaven," she whispered. "What kind of people *are* these?"

A muscle in his jaw tightened. "Brenda wasn't scum," he said bleakly. "She was a mixed-up kid who never really grew up. Or maybe she grew up too fast, I don't know. She never should've had kids of her own.''

"Except—" Martha checked the thought that had nearly tumbled out.

"Except then, we'd never have known Bloss and Daisy," he finished for her. His voice was quiet. His eyes were as black as she'd ever seen them.

He walked toward her, regarded her silently for a long moment in a way that made her knees tremble, and when he spoke his voice was gentle. She heard bone-deep weariness, too. "You'd better get some sleep. We'll deal with this in the morning."

She touched his sleeve. This time, for whatever reason, he didn't pull back. "What are we going to do, Fraser?" she whispered. "About the girls?"

She felt cold suddenly, icy cold, and wanted nothing more than the freedom to put her arms around him, to have him hold her, keep her from the chill, from the gloom of death that hung there in the kitchen with them. To have to tell her it wasn't true that the girls' mother was gone, smashed and broken in a car accident. She wanted nothing more than to feel his living warmth beneath her cheek and the thud of his heart, strong and steady next to hers.

He looked down at her for another endless moment. "I'll tell the girls. I'll have to notify the authorities now, I guess." He shrugged, but Martha could see the pain beneath the careless gesture. "It's not really your problem, Martha. I'll handle it."

He paused, then went on gruffly, "You can think about making some plans of your own now."

"It's over, then?" Her mouth felt dry. She made a

weak gesture to him, to herself, to the four walls that surrounded them. "You and...and the girls' living here, it's all over?" *And me.*

"Yes," he said.

SHE'D NEVER FORGET what she saw in Fraser's eyes that night. There was fire and there was hurt, a pain too deep to share. Loss, regret. The ache of loneliness. The fire behind the hurt was what drew her, though, what made the next few days bearable. She knew the truth in her heart—he was not going to give up.

The next afternoon, Martha and Fraser told Daisy and Anne that their mother was never coming back.

"B-but I want my mama," Daisy said, her small voice quavering. "I want to see her right now." She clutched her kangaroo tightly in both hands. Her lower lip trembled and she looked away from them.

Anne said nothing. In fact, beyond interrupting her play with building blocks for a few seconds, Anne didn't react. Martha wasn't even sure she understood what Fraser had said. If she had, her response was ominous.

Martha felt helpless. She'd never been through anything like this before; she had no idea what to say or do. She glanced at Fraser. His face was grim, although his voice, as he told the girls what had happened, was heartbreakingly gentle.

"What happened to her?" Anne asked bluntly. Her face was a mask of indifference, but Martha could see emotion struggling beneath the surface.

"She died in a car accident," Fraser said. "A long way from here. In another state."

"What state?"

"Alabama."

"Oh." Anne went back to her blocks, and Martha looked at Fraser in astonishment.

Daisy wailed and ran to Martha and buried her face in her lap. Martha hugged her tight, praying for control, praying she wouldn't break down just when the girls needed her to be calm. The Lady Companion.

She wasn't what they wanted. They wanted their mother, their own flesh and blood. Hopeless as she'd apparently been, Brenda was still their mother. Why did these innocent girls have to suffer so? No father, now no mother, no family of any kind except, from the sound of it, one horrible money-grubbing aunt they didn't even know existed. Thank goodness. Martha shuddered and gathered Daisy closer. None of this was their fault. None of this was of their making. It just wasn't fair.

Fraser's eyes, when their gazes met across the top of Daisy's blond tousled head, were agonized. Had his wife died in a car crash, too? Was this even worse for him than she'd realized?

Suddenly Anne erupted.

"I told you!" she screamed. She scrambled to her feet, kicked over her blocks, then ran to attack Fraser, both arms flailing blindly. "I told you my mother was dead! Didn't I tell you she was never coming back again?"

Fraser grabbed her but she wriggled out of his grasp. She doubled over and clutched her stomach in agony. "I hate her! I hate my mama! I'm glad she's dead!" The tears came then, in floods, and Fraser picked her up and walked with her to the window. Anne struggled, but Fraser was far stronger, and finally Anne collapsed against his chest, sobbing as though she'd never stop.

Spook alternately whined in sympathy and barked in helpless defiance at Martha's feet. Martha's own face was wet with tears. Daisy, fortunately, had gotten over the initial shock and was now gently weeping in Martha's arms. She finally raised her tearstained face. "If she didn't get deaded way far away, she'd come back, wouldn't she, Martha?"

"Yes, darling." She kissed the girl's damp cheek. "Of course she'd come back to you. She loved you very much."

Lies, lies, lies. What did it matter now? And who knew what had been in Brenda's mind? None of it mattered now, except that Brenda's daughters needed reassurance, needed to know they were indeed loved.

"What's going to happen to us now? Me 'n' my sister?"

"Don't worry, sweetie," Martha said, pushing back the child's curls. "You're safe here with us. Fraser's looking after you. I'm here. We're grown-ups. We'll take care of you. You don't have to worry."

Was she lying to the child? She didn't know. What were Fraser's intentions? Still, she meant it with all her heart; she wouldn't desert these children until their future with someone, somewhere, was assured. Until they were settled, until they were safe.

Again, a painful emotion squeezed her heart. She didn't want to give them up. She didn't want to say goodbye. She rested her cheek against the top of Daisy's head and took a deep shaky breath, breathing in Daisy's warm little-girl smell. Her action felt so familiar, so natural. She didn't think she'd ever forget the sensation of holding these children in her arms, so sturdy and warm, so real.

The physical comfort she received reminded her of something else, something less comfortable. Fraser. The man-scent, uniquely his, dangerous, vital, that she'd become so aware of in the past few weeks—as they'd shared meals, when she'd accidentally touched him, as they'd lived their lives under the same roof. The crazy feelings she'd had in the kitchen that night weeks ago swam back into her mind, and she opened her eyes over Daisy's fair crown, feeling a little dizzy.

Fraser was staring at her as though she was a stranger. As though he'd never seen her before. The look in his eyes, the fierceness and heat, consumed her. Startled, Martha raised her head and Fraser glanced away. He murmured something to the now quiet Anne, and she mumbled something back. He walked across the room with her, back and forth, still holding her.

They were a pair, Martha thought. They could well be father and daughter, both with that black hair, those dark eyes. Anne's came from her Indian heritage, if Fraser's theory about her wrangler father was correct, Fraser's from his Scottish—or was it Irish?—ancestry.

Both were fighters. Anne with her reluctance to trust, her scrappy determination to stand on her own feet and do everything herself—the opposite of her sister, who trusted everyone. Fraser was a fighter, too. Martha didn't know exactly why she believed that to be true; she just knew it was. A man who'd never let you down. Who'd never give up. A man you could depend on, absolutely and without question. She felt fleeting irony; at least Brenda'd gotten one thing right when she'd trusted Fraser McKenna to take care of her children.

Still, what were they to do now?

With a huge shaky breath, Anne asked Fraser to let her go, which he did. She walked back to the blocks she'd been working with, and without another word sank down to begin building again.

Daisy stayed in Martha's arms. Fraser came toward them. He nodded slightly at Anne. "I think things will go all right now."

"Yes," Martha said. She wasn't as sure. Anne's feelings ran deeper than she'd ever been able to fathom. But perhaps Fraser knew her better—they were two of a kind, after all.

Daisy climbed down from Martha's lap and sat on the floor down to watch her sister, thumb in her mouth, Spook nestled close to her side. Fraser motioned to Martha, and she got up to follow him out of the room.

"Look," he said, turning to her as soon as they were in the kitchen with the door closed, "I know it's a lot to ask, but would you consider staying on for maybe a week or so, until—"

"Of course I'll stay on!" Martha interrupted in a fierce whisper, not wanting the girls to hear from their side of the door. "For Pete's sake, what do you take me for?"

"You're free to leave here. I told you this was my problem."

"Well, it's my problem, too. Don't you see that? I care about those girls, I want to see that they're taken care of properly. I—"

"That's exactly why you've got to leave," Fraser broke in tersely. "Soon. They're getting too damn attached to you as it is."

Martha stared at him in dismay, her eyes widening as she understood his meaning. "Y-you mean you think I might be causing even more problems by staying on?"

He nodded. "You saw the way Daisy ran to you for comfort. They've just had one hell of a shock, and that's why I've asked you to stay for a short while. Until I get them settled. But it isn't going to do them any good to get even more attached to you and then have you take off, too."

Just like their mother. He didn't say it; he didn't have to say it.

Martha felt torn in two. Of course she understood what he was saying, but at the same time she wanted to stay and help the girls. Protect them. Comfort them. Her long-suppressed motherly instincts had sprung up fully fledged these past few weeks. What a mess!

"I'm sorry," she said simply, closing her eyes briefly and running her hands through her hair. How could loving these children be so wrong? "I—I understand about the girls. You're right. It's hard on them. I won't stay any longer than you think I should."

Fraser gave her a searching look, then crossed the

kitchen to the outside door and began to put on his boots and coat. Martha suddenly realized she hadn't slept more than an hour or two. She'd been through an emotional wringer with Fraser last night, and then today, breaking the bad news to the girls. Right now, all she wanted was a nice hot cup of tea and a few minutes alone. Perhaps Fraser felt the same.

"I'll be out in the barn if you need me," he said, settling his hat firmly on his head. He held her gaze. Martha looked straight at him—the same way he'd looked at her in the other room—as if she'd never seen him before. The too-long black hair under that familiar broad-brimmed hat, the lines of weariness and care etched in the handsome face, the rugged sheepskin jacket he wore, the usual jeans and scuffed boots, the dark eyes that banked a fire she'd only glimpsed once or twice. Solid, reliable—*sexy*.

She swallowed and willed the sudden flutter of her pulse to stillness. "Fine. If I need you, I'll let you know," she said, noticing only when he left that her words had been two-edged. Not that Fraser would have taken them any other way, of course. He knew she was talking about the girls.

If I need you, I'll let you know. If only she could, Martha thought sadly, reaching for the teapot. If only she could.

FRASER LEANED on the top rail of the pen and watched this year's big ram lambs jostle each other for the grain Tom had just poured into their feeders. He had some dandy young rams in this crop, and it wasn't going to be too hard to pick out the dozen he'd promised Dave Blackwell, a friend and colleague who was in the sheep business in Utah.

Besides the commercial flock Fraser ran on the higher pastures of his ranch in the summer, down to about twelve hundred ewes after the lambs were sold in the fall, he also ran a small but vigorous breeding program and regularly sold purebred breeding stock to other sheep producers. His rams were particularly sought after, had been ever since they'd started taking top prizes at the breeders' fairs five or six years ago.

Fraser much preferred sheep to cattle. He liked their comparative quietness, he liked their attention to business, grazing and putting on the most weight with the least amount of expensive finishing, and he liked their loyalty. Sheep stuck together.

Mind you, he'd had some mothering problems lately, with one particular line he was developing from stock he'd brought in from Idaho. In fact—he cast an experienced eye on one of the lambs he was thinking of taking to Blackwell and mentally crossed it off his list—a couple of the lambs in this very pen had been orphaned by mothers who had rejected them.

No one knew why that sort of thing happened, but it did from time to time. Sometimes one of a set of twins was rejected by the ewe. Sometimes it was a healthy big single. Poor mothering quality was not a desirable trait to keep in a line of breeding stock.

Luckily, if he or Tom or one of the shepherds were on hand and able to size up the situation right away, they could sometimes get another ewe to accept an orphan. Occasionally, a ewe with one of her own would take on a second. Every shepherd had his own bag of tricks for coping with the problem. If it happened here in the Westbank Ranch lambing pens, they could put the orphan onto a milk-replacement bar right away and raise it without a mother.

But those lambs never did as well. And they ended up going to market. Fraser never kept them to breed.

He sighed heavily. Blossom and Daisy. Another couple of orphans. What was he going to do with them?

He had to let the county authorities know. He knew they were going to take the girls away. No question. Why would they leave them with him now? A man with a business to run that took him away from home a lot of the time? A man on his own? Hired nanny or no hired nanny, they weren't going to look on his situation favorably. And that wasn't taking into account the fact, which was going to come out now, that he'd been harboring them for almost four months.

Somehow he'd get out of that one. Explain that Brenda had left before and had always come back. Play dumb. Birdie would put in a word for him. He wasn't too worried about that part. After all, he'd done what he set out to do.

But he'd never thought Brenda might not come back. What a shocker. Fraser felt the old grief rise in his chest. Charlotte Mae, beautiful, laughing, only thirty-one, gone with the child-that-never-was. Now Brenda, neighbor, friend, an innocent despite her twenty-nine years and two children. It didn't make sense. None of it.

Still, he had to keep his focus on the matter at hand.

Brenda's girls. With an effort, Fraser fought back the grief. He needed his energy for the battle ahead.

Even if he said he'd keep the girls with him, the authorities weren't going to approve of a series of hired nannies looking after them. Now that Brenda wasn't coming back, no one—certainly not a city woman like Martha Thomas—was going to stay on forever doing this kind of job. People had lives of their own.

Slowly, carefully, the way a person might probe a sore tooth, Fraser tested the emotions that had run through him earlier when he'd seen Daisy in Martha's arms. He'd been stunned. Bowled over. Swept away by the rightness of what he'd seen, the picture they'd made, mother and child. And he'd been shocked by the strength of emotion he'd felt for Daisy. Fierce. Protective. He'd never seen the girl in Brenda's arms just that way, her own mother, and yet here was a woman who'd known the child less than a month, able to do exactly the right thing. To give exactly the comfort the child needed.

Daisy had run to Martha, not to him. He'd been a little surprised. But at the same time, he realized he was in trouble. Big trouble. The girls, Daisy especially, were already deeply attached to the woman he'd hired to look after them. The Lady Companion. Things were only going to get worse. She had to go.

He shifted and reached down to scratch the woolly head of a curious lamb that had come over to investigate. *Martha gone.* He couldn't imagine it. Even the thought of her absence made him feel empty inside.

Already it seemed as though she'd been here forever. But there was no doubt she'd be relieved at this final outcome. Not at Brenda's death, not that, but at the prospect of being free to leave. The chance to get on with her life. He couldn't blame her. He knew he wasn't the easiest man to get along with—hell, Birdie'd told him that many a time. So had his brothers. Even Charlotte had teased him about being stand-offish and stubborn.

Maybe he was. One thing he did know, though, and it killed him to have to admit it—he didn't want those girls to disappear from his life. To be placed in the homes of strangers. They'd brought him something he thought he'd lost forever these past few bitter years.

Fraser forced his thoughts to a halt. But it was true; there was no denying it. They'd brought him a feeling of hope. A feeling that he could look forward to something, that there *was* something to look forward to—that things would get better.

They needed him; he needed them. It was as simple as that. But how could he possibly keep them? Legally? Forever? Until they grew up and moved away and didn't need him anymore?

Adopt them. You could adopt them, McKenna. Legally. Then no one could take them from you. Brenda left them with you—she trusted you. They're part of this valley, part of Blue River, same way she was. She'd want you to raise them here.

Fraser froze, stunned. Why hadn't he thought of that before? They were orphans, they had no one in the whole world but Brenda's useless sister, and she sure as hell didn't want them. That was clear enough. Even the letter she'd sent had to be clear evidence to the authorities that their own flesh and blood didn't want them.

But who in hell was going to let him, Fraser Mc-Kenna, a widower damn near forty years old, adopt two young girls? It was crazy. No judge was going to go for that. People around here, they'd say he was a boozer or a womanizer. His reputation wasn't great, he knew that, even if it *was* yesterday's news. And he'd had a woman with him, they'd say, unmarried, living under the same roof. Was that any kind of example, they'd ask, for a couple of innocent young girls?

Funny. They'd be wrong, of course. Yet no one would ever know how many times he'd thought of going down that long dark hall to Martha's bed. Of course, he hadn't done it. He hadn't even touched her, except that one time in the kitchen. She'd never mentioned it; neither had he. If he'd been able to find the words or the occasion, he might have told her he was sorry.

He wasn't, though. All he was sorry for was that he hadn't kissed her when he'd had the chance. Damn, something about that woman just wouldn't leave him alone. Yeah, the sooner she left, the better for them all.

Fraser stared at the lambs for a while, aware that an idea, a crazy idea, had began to grow in him. Unseeing, he made his way over to the small office he kept in one corner of the barn. He walked in, flicked on the propane heater in the corner and threw himself down on the battered wooden swivel chair behind the desk.

There *was* one way to accomplish what he had in mind. But could he pull it off in the time he had? And fundamentally, he hated the idea. Much as he hated it, though, the more he thought about it, the more he realized it was his one best chance. Maybe his only chance.

He wanted to adopt Blossom and Daisy? He'd never get to first base as a single man, a bachelor rancher way to hell and gone in the middle of nowhere.

But he could solve that problem. He could find himself a wife.

CHAPTER NINE

MARTHA FELT the skin on her nose and cheekbones and forehead tighten. It was the strangest sensation. It made her feel very vulnerable. Fraser's voice seemed far away. She felt as if someone had slapped her, slapped her hard.

With the greatest effort, she spoke, desperate to reveal none of what she felt in her voice. "So what you're saying now is you want me to stay until you get married?"

"Something like that." Fraser stopped abruptly and looked at her. She raised her chin slightly. She wished she hadn't sat down. He'd been pacing back and forth until she thought he'd wear a path in the living room carpet. Now he'd stopped in front of her, and she didn't like having to look up at him. She'd have preferred to stand.

She couldn't believe her ears, not after what Birdie had told her. *Married?* Her heart felt as though it had turned to stone and was sinking, sinking, sinking through the layers of flesh and bones in her body. But why should it feel that way? What could it mean to her? Being told her services were no longer required at the *Post* was far worse. That had been a career; this was just a temporary job. But she didn't remember feeling half as bad then.

She'd thought he had something against marriage, and if he didn't, why hadn't he gotten married in the first place and saved everyone a lot of trouble?

Now, four days after they'd told the girls their mother was dead *he was getting married?* She'd never have guessed. He'd wanted to tell her—that was why he'd been so determined to take Daisy over to the LeBlancs himself to play with their granddaughter, when Martha could have taken her and stayed and visited with Birdie. It was why he'd insisted on returning to the ranch house and talking to her when they were alone. Anne was at school; she'd missed the Monday after learning of her mother's death. Martha had thought she needed some extra time to begin to adjust to her loss, and Fraser had agreed. They'd had a quiet day together. Martha had believed the girls needed to have as little change as possible in their daily routines. Fraser had agreed.

Monday afternoon, while Fraser took the girls riding for an hour, Martha had decided to tidy up their room. That was when she found the book under Anne's pillow, an old paperback copy of *Anne of Green Gables,* by Lucy Maude Montgomery. Martha had paused, hand on the worn cover, and realized suddenly why Anne's words had sounded so familiar when she'd first told her that her name was Anne, not Blossom—Anne with an *e.* Anne Shirley, the orphan girl mistakenly sent to a Prince Edward Island farm when they'd wanted a boy to help with the work, had chosen to spell her name with an *e.* Anne Shirley, the girl no one had wanted, who'd found happiness with a crusty spinster and her elderly brother. Anne Shirley, the orphan who had found a true family at last.

Family. Martha had felt the tears swim and, annoyed, had blown her nose and tucked the book back under Anne's pillow. She'd wept a lot lately, with the girls and alone in her own bed. She was not normally a weeper, or a moaner, or a complainer. She wondered what Fraser must have thought when he'd seen her red-eyed much of the time during the past couple of days.

"I appreciate the job you've done here, Martha." Martha's attention centered again on the man in front of her. "But now you'll be able to leave. Ever since we heard about Brenda, I've been thinking about what's going to happen with the girls, and I've decided the best thing to do is adopt them—"

"Adopt them!"

"Yes, legally adopt them." He continued to pace. "I believe that would be best. It's the only way they can stay here with me. I'd hate to see them go to a foster home somewhere, which is what would probably happen. That or some group home—"

"No!" It came out more vehemently than Martha had intended. She shuddered. A foster home or a home with the horrible aunt. She prayed it wouldn't come to that. *How could she bear it? How could she bear to let them go? How could Fraser send her away like this?*

"Look, I realize this is none of my business," Martha said, "but I can't quite see what adopting the girls has to do with you getting married."

"It has everything to do with it," he said tensely. "Everything. How likely is it I can get guardianship or adopt them? A single man living up here alone. Come on, the judge would laugh me out of court."

He had a point. This was getting curiouser and curiouser. Fascinated, Martha watched him walk back and forth. Something prickled under her skin. His hair was disheveled, as though he'd run his hands through it many times today. His shirtsleeves were rolled up, exposing strongly muscled forearms, lightly dusted with dark hair and still tanned, even now in November. He thrust his fists violently into the back pockets of his jeans. She sensed a tremendous pent-up energy in him, a pure masculine energy she felt ought to frighten her but didn't. His back was broad and strong as he walked away from her, his shoulders straight. His legs were long and lean and powerful as he walked toward her again.

For a few seconds Martha wondered who the lucky woman might be, then frowned at the errant thought. "I see your point," she said. "I think." She still felt confused.

He stopped in front of her. "A man with a wife would have a lot better chance of adopting two girls like Blossom and Daisy," he said slowly. "*Now* do you understand?"

Martha's heart flipped over. "Y-you don't mean to tell me you're just going to marry someone so some…some child-welfare authority will consider you a better prospective parent?"

"That's exactly what I mean."

"Why, that's terrible! How could you do something

like that?'' She'd never, not in her wildest dreams, have thought Fraser capable of such a thing. "How could you marry someone you weren't in love with?''

His harsh laugh silenced her. "Don't be naive. I'm not looking for love, Miss Martha Thomas,'' he said. "I'm looking for a wife.''

Had he emphasized the *Miss?* That was unfair. She managed a humorless laugh herself. "That's preposterous! Who'd marry you? And I presume you're in a big hurry, too.'' Then she wished she hadn't laughed; she remembered Katie Barker.

Scowling, he ran his hands through his hair again. "I've got one or two prospects,'' he muttered, but he didn't look all that confident.

"Well, I've never met Miss Katie Barker,'' Martha said tartly, "but I can't say I envy her landing in this. According to the girls, the poor woman's in love with you.'' She stopped, wondered why her heart was beating so rapidly.

"I haven't asked her,'' he snapped with a fierce look that should have silenced her, but didn't.

Yet, Martha thought grimly. "Doesn't seem like a very honorable thing to me, you marrying her so you can adopt the girls. Apparently the girls don't even like her,'' Martha added, remembering with horror Anne's promise that if he'd hired Katie Barker, they'd have run away.

"Dammit, woman! I haven't asked her.'' He added irritably, "Hell. Couples have started out under worse circumstances—''

"Not much.''

"—and if things don't work out, well, we'll get a

divorce. People do get divorced in this country, you know." He glared at her. "Every day."

"I'm well aware of that," Martha said quietly. "And wouldn't that be a wonderful experience for the girls, too?" she couldn't help saying, then wished she'd bitten her tongue.

"Well, if you've got any better ideas, I'd like to hear them," he growled. He sounded frustrated. He stopped in front of her. "Look. I could use some coffee. You want a cup?"

She nodded and he escaped to the kitchen. Martha sat there for a moment, gradually becoming aware that her fingers were trembling. The room was unnaturally quiet. At the far end were the children's things. Daisy's purple-and-yellow lamb, which Martha had bought her in the hopes of weaning her from the kangaroo. Anne's new fleece jacket flung over a chair.

Suddenly the room swam. She bent her head and squeezed her eyes. What a mess! Where would she find the strength to walk away from them, the way Fraser expected? In just a month, they'd become an inextricable part of her life. How could she leave them to the likes of Katie Barker, who was probably a very nice woman but not someone they wanted as a stepmother? And just how badly would Katie Barker want him if the girls were part of the package? She might turn him down. Who else was on Fraser's list?

She knew her accusations had struck their mark. Fraser obviously wasn't entirely comfortable with his scheme, even though he appeared determined to follow through with it. He wasn't at all convinced it was the right thing to do, but he was going to do it, anyway, because he believed it was his best chance to get what he wanted. To adopt the girls. That, after all, was his main objective. She didn't doubt for a moment that he meant what he said. Or that he usually got what he wanted.

And he was an honorable man. It had been a low blow on her part to say he wasn't. Loveless marriage or not, she knew in her heart that he'd do his best to make it succeed. And he was right—many marriages had been founded on less. If Katie Barker loved him enough, perhaps in time he'd grow to love her, and it would all work out in the end.

Martha felt her heart sink. She felt terrible. The very thought of Katie Barker and Fraser McKenna together, sharing meals, raising the girls—*sharing a bed,* her mind shrieked at her. *That's what you really mean, Martha Virginia Thomas.*

Of course she didn't. That was utter nonsense. Martha sat straighter and laced her fingers together in a brief futile effort to hide the tremors. Giving up, she got to her feet.

Fraser came back with the coffee. He handed her a mug. She was reminded of the first night she'd arrived. Then, when he'd handed her the mug of hot chocolate, she'd been careful not to touch him. Now, it seemed he was as careful as she. What did it all mean?

She sipped at the hot liquid, hands locked around the warm ceramic. She tried not to look at Fraser. In fact, she looked everywhere but at him. She couldn't bear to look at him.

"I'm sorry you think it's such a rotten thing to do,"

he said roughly. Her gaze flew to his. "There's no other choice, or you can be sure I'd never do something like this."

When she didn't say anything, he went on. "Not that I'd ever do it for love, either." Again there was that humorless bitter sound. "Don't get me wrong. I have no interest in marriage at all."

He looked at her over his mug, brows drawn, eyes fierce. "Damn trouble with women is they all think like you," he growled. "They think they've got to be in love. Love, hell! What's wrong with security, a good roof over your head, sex when you want it, ordinary decent respect for each other, getting along as a couple of people with the same goals? What's so damn great about love?"

"I..." Martha barely trusted her voice. She cleared her throat and tried again. "So I suppose your next step is convincing some woman that you *are* in love with her so she'll marry you."

He glowered at her and said nothing. She was right. Convincing some woman he loved her when he didn't went completely against his principles, not to mention stuck in his craw but good.

"And you don't have a heck of a lot of time to do it in, do you?"

Still he said nothing. Emboldened, she plunged ahead. "So I guess you'll want me to stay on—what?—two, three weeks? Until you've got this all, uh—" she cleared her throat again "—arranged?" She should walk out right now, not be party to such a ridiculous plan. But she knew she couldn't do it, couldn't leave the girls to another temporary care giver.

"Something like that," he muttered, and turned away from her.

For a few moments Martha sat there, absorbing every aspect of the proposition Fraser was about to put to some unsuspecting woman. Then lightning struck. It started in her toes, and with the speed of real electricity ran up her body until every muscle tensed, every nerve jumped. Her heart literally stopped, then started again in triple time. Fortunately Fraser was at the other end of the room, head down, and he couldn't have heard her gasp.

Quickly, afraid she'd lose her nerve, she walked toward him, so that when he turned, he was facing her. He stopped abruptly. Martha wasn't sure she'd be able to speak. The idea had struck her so suddenly and so unexpectedly that she didn't know if she could trust her voice.

The idea was perfect. It would solve his problem without his having to sacrifice principles he'd no doubt deny he had. It would solve problems for her, too, not only her reluctance to walk away from the girls she'd grown to love, but the dreams she'd had when she was young and foolish. Dreams that love would find her one day, and then everything else, the rest of her life, would fall into place. It hadn't happened like that. It wasn't *going* to happen like that. And now she was neither young nor foolish. There were other ways besides waiting patiently for love to come along, better ways to make your dreams happen.

"Martha?" His voice sounded uncertain, as uncertain as she felt. Yet at the same time she'd never been so sure of anything in her life.

"You asked me if I had any better ideas?"

He nodded. "I did."

"You could marry me."

Martha immediately wished she could take back her words. She watched his face, cringing inwardly at every emotion she saw there. Surprise, disbelief, shock—then skepticism and a canniness that made her heart weep and her spirit shudder. Was it really so difficult for him to imagine being married to her? Was it really so impossible even to consider?

His eyes never left hers, but it must have been a full minute before he spoke. "What the hell are you talking about?"

"Why not?" Martha said, wishing her voice didn't sound so insubstantial, so…frightened. Was she really afraid of him? Or afraid he'd turn her down flat? "After all, you wouldn't have to try and convince anyone you're in love with her—" she couldn't bear to say *me* "—and as I told you before, I've come to realize in the last couple of weeks just how much the girls mean to me, too."

She felt the blood rush under her skin as he slowly, lazily surveyed her face, her jaw, her throat. "I've been realizing how much I hate the thought of leaving them now that I've…grown so used to them."

"Haven't you got a life somewhere else, Martha Thomas?"

"Wh-what?" She hadn't expected him to say that.

"Haven't you got somewhere to go? Somewhere you'd rather be?" His voice was deadly soft.

"No." She shook her head, knowing it for the awful truth. *There was nowhere in the world she'd rather be than right here.* "I was fired from my job in Wisconsin. I've sublet my apartment and found a place for my cat to stay. My furniture's in storage. My friends are, well…" She shrugged. Martha suddenly realized in how few painful words a person's life could be summed up.

"You'd marry me so that I could adopt Bloss and Daisy?" he continued, his voice still soft. There was a strange light in his eyes, something she'd never seen before.

"So that *we* could adopt Anne and Daisy," she corrected firmly. "Together."

He stared at her. "I wouldn't have to pretend I loved you and you wouldn't pretend you loved me?"

"That's right." God, how that hurt! But it was no lie—she knew he didn't love her. And, of course, she didn't love him. Liked him, sure, found him physically attractive, a sexy outdoorsy kind of guy. But love, no. Whatever love was. Deep down, she knew Fraser McKenna was a good man. That mattered. Tortured in some mysterious way, but fundamentally a good caring man.

She could do worse. Martha felt a chill drift across her overheated skin. Perhaps there were some women for whom love was not meant. The love of children, friends, animals, yes, but the kind of love she'd once thought possible between her and one special man, maybe not. She could accept that, if it was true, however much it hurt. She could build a life without that kind of love. There were other things just as important—honesty, kindness, good humor, a certain generosity of spirit. Loyalty.

Fraser stepped back from her, and Martha let her breath out slowly, a breath she hadn't been aware she was holding. "What's in it for you, Martha?" he asked, eyes narrowed. "I can't believe you'd do this just to help me out. A beautiful woman like you who's got her whole life ahead of her somewhere else, married to a man who loves you the way you deserve to be loved…" His voice trailed off.

"What's in it for you?" he repeated bluntly, eyes suddenly hard.

Martha took a deep shaky breath. *The truth. Only the truth was good enough.* "I'm nearly thirty-six years old, Fraser. Next spring. I can't wait for the fairy tale you're talking about to happen to me. I want a family. I want a child—"

"What are you saying?" he broke in, his voice rough.

"I want a baby of my own."

His face had gone white. His expression—of fury, of disbelief, of utter shock—frightened her. He turned abruptly and went to stand by the window. Behind him, Martha saw the Wind Rivers rise over the ranch in the distance, brilliant in the winter sunshine. The line of Fraser's shoulders was just as rigid and unmoving. After an eternity, he turned back.

"I won't do it. I'll never father another child. Not for you, not for any woman."

"*Another* child?" Martha breathed. "What do you mean?"

"I was married once—maybe you heard," he began, his voice utterly devoid of emotion. "My wife is dead."

Martha nodded.

He went on bitterly. "I might've known someone would be eager to fill you in. It doesn't matter. It's no secret."

"Birdie told me your wife died," Martha ventured as gently as she could.

"Yes." Fraser looked out the window again, and Martha could see a muscle working in his jaw. "I killed her."

"*What?*"

"I killed her." He turned toward her, his face a mask of pain. "She died having my baby."

"But...but that isn't the same." Martha shook her head, bewildered. "It happens sometimes, the doctors must have told you..."

"Yes. They did. But it comes down to the same thing. She went into labor too early because she was pregnant with my child, and she bled to death because I couldn't get her to a hospital in time to save her."

"My God, Fraser, you can't blame yourself!"

"Who else is to blame?" he bit out. "If I hadn't made her pregnant, if I'd managed to get her to the hospital, she'd be here today."

And Martha Thomas wouldn't be. None of this would have been necessary. The thought hung unspoken between them.

"Blame no one." Martha took a few steps toward him, her heart sick with the pain she felt for him. She wanted to touch him but didn't dare. "It could have happened to...to anyone, Fraser. You have to put it behind you. Go on with your life. I—I'm sure your wife would have wanted you to.''

"I wish I could, Martha," he said wearily. "I wish I could forget. But I dream of it, especially since you've come to live here. It's come back to me, like it was just yesterday.''

She'd never dreamed Fraser was carrying around this kind of burden. She hadn't known his wife had died in childbirth. Why hadn't Birdie told her? Martha swallowed uncomfortably. Of course, Birdie wouldn't. Fraser had wanted to forget it, Birdie had said. Birdie had warned her that it wasn't her place to tell Martha even the little she had.

But still, no matter how horrifying the memory, couldn't Fraser understand that it had been simply a freak thing? That his wife had just had the bad luck to be the one in how many thousands to die in a complication of pregnancy? Women had often died giving birth in the past, true—but in this day and age? Martha felt a sudden panic, as if her own dream was being consumed by something terrible beyond her control. She couldn't let that happen.

"I want a child, Fraser," she said quietly. He stared straight at her, and his eyes burned into hers. "I've always wanted a family and a child of my own, and it's—well, it's never happened. I'd never dreamed I'd be standing here offering to marry you if you'd give me the baby I want, but..." She looked down, couldn't bear any longer to meet the fire in his eyes. "When you brought this whole thing up, especially the part about not marrying for love, about just wanting to give Brenda's girls a real home, I—I guess I just realized that maybe this was my chance.'' She looked up at him and swallowed. ''I might never get another.''

Fraser walked toward her and took the coffee mug from her nerveless fingers. ''Sit down,'' he said gently, putting his hands on her shoulders. She sank onto the sofa, grateful that he didn't sit beside her.

He stood, hands in his pockets. ''I'm going to tell you what happened that night, Martha, and I want you to know that I've never told another soul what I'm going to tell you now. Not all of it, anyway.'' He stopped and was silent for so long that Martha thought he'd changed his mind.

''I want to tell you because I want you to understand why I've sworn I'd never...'' He paused, then went on gruffly, ''Well, never do what you want from me.''

He stared down at the floor for a minute or two, then raised his head. ''I didn't think much about having children one way or the other before I got married. I suppose a lot of men don't. I'd been in love with Charlotte since I was a kid. So had my brother Weston. We fought over her, but in the end I married her. She was pregnant when we got married, not with my child, but I didn't care.''

Martha couldn't believe what she was hearing. Or the matter-of-fact way he was telling her.

''I was crazy about her, always had been, and when she said she'd marry me, I was happier than I'd ever thought I could be. Then she lost the baby. A common enough thing, the doctors said. She was less than three months pregnant. A miscarriage. They said it happens all the time. But Charlotte wanted a baby. She never got over the miscarriage. A couple of years later she got pregnant again.''

Fraser ran a hand over his face, and Martha could see what this was costing him, despite the flat way he was telling her about his life, his deepest intimacies, things between husband and wife she had no business knowing.

"Everything went fine until she was about six months along. One day I'd been up with the sheep, and all the other hands were out. Just a freak situation. Birdie wasn't around—she was off on a private job.'' He took a deep breath. "Anyway, I came home late and found her lying on the kitchen floor in a pool of blood.''

Martha tried to stifle her gasp.

"She'd had the...the child. It was dead. Charlotte wasn't dead, not yet. When I tried to pick her up to take her to the car, she wouldn't let go of it.'' Again he paused. Martha's eyes were swimming.

"She wouldn't let go,'' he repeated heavily. "I had to carry them both to the car, and then I drove like a maniac, but it wasn't any use. She died before we got to Pine Ridge. When I...when I tried to lift her out of the car—I thought they could do something, bring her back somehow—she still wouldn't let go of the baby. It was dead. It was cold already. She was dead. There was nothing anybody could do.''

"Oh, Fraser—"

"Don't say anything, Martha.'' His voice was hard as ice. "I can't stand sympathy, not from anyone. I can't stand kind words. I just wanted you to know why I can't do what you want me to do." He walked toward the door.

Martha didn't say anything; she couldn't. She heard him walk through the kitchen, the small familiar sounds as he pulled on his coat and hat, the whine of the dog, the slam of the door, and then silence.

CHAPTER TEN

MARTHA DROVE to meet the school bus, her mind whirling, her body numb. Had she really just asked a man to marry her? Had she really just asked a man, practically a stranger, to father her baby? Dear God— she felt one burning cheek with an icy palm—what would Gran Thomas think if she were still alive?

Martha had been raised a lady, in an old-fashioned home. And ladies didn't ask near strangers to marry them. They certainly didn't ask near-strangers to father their children, although Martha was pretty sure the topic hadn't been covered all that thoroughly in the usual society bibles. She wanted to giggle, but recognized the urge as a crazy reaction to the events of the past hour.

That sobered her. She blinked rapidly to clear sudden tears. What hell had Fraser been living all this time? How long? Three years, had Birdie said, since his wife had died? Four? Too long to go on blaming himself for something he couldn't have prevented. Of course, Fraser would say he *could* have prevented it— if Charlotte hadn't become pregnant, if his ranch wasn't so remote, if he'd made sure one of the hands was always around when he couldn't be there. But as

Gran Thomas would have said, "If ifs and ands were pots and pans, there'd be no work for tinkers."

Who would have planned so meticulously for disaster? No one. No one would expect such a tragedy and then make complicated plans to avoid it. As Fraser had pointed out himself, the fact that Birdie, a trained nurse, wasn't home, and that all the hands happened to be away, was just a freak situation.

Did he intend to go on blaming himself forever? She had to convince him that he *wasn't* to blame. Her entire happiness depended on it.

And so did his.

Martha frowned. Where had *that* thought come from?

She saw the school bus just coming around the bend. At least she wasn't late. She pulled to a stop at the side of the Westbank Ranch road and switched off the ignition.

But then, considering what he'd just told her, she didn't think it was very likely he'd change his mind. Still, he might.

No, she thought with a sigh and a glance at her reflection in the rearview mirror to make sure she didn't look too disheveled. If things didn't work out here, she'd just go on, as Fraser had suggested and as she'd known she must one day. She dug in her bag and pulled out a brush, quickly tugging it through her hair.

She'd never been an unhappy person—that wouldn't change. If she didn't end up married, with children of her own, one day fairly soon, well, she'd just throw herself back into her work. She'd always enjoyed that. There was always work for a clever writer. Perhaps she'd go back to the television people and relaunch her food show, or go into business for herself doing something exciting. There were a million things to do if a person had a bit of imagination and some energy.

It was a lie, every word. All she wanted now was Fraser's baby growing inside her, the feel of his hands on her body, the knowledge that she could heal his spirit and help him forget. All she wanted was to gather these two orphans close to her, protect and nurture them, never let this cobbled-together family go again.

"Hi, honey. How was school?" Martha helped Anne toss her book bag onto the back seat. Anne looked tired and sad and even smaller today than she usually did.

"Okay, I guess." Then Anne smiled hopefully. "You bring any cookies today? Where's Daisy?"

"Starved, huh?" Martha reached into the back seat for the bag of cookies she'd brought and the flask of hot chocolate. "Daisy's at Birdie's. I thought we might take a little drive for a change, instead of going straight home."

"Where?" Anne's eyes flickered with interest. She thrust a hand into the bag and pulled out two chocolate-chip cookies.

Martha reversed the Bronco and glanced at the girl. "Where do you want to go? I thought we'd just drive around some of the roads here on the ranch. There are a lot of places I haven't been yet, and I thought you might like to show them to me."

"Okay." Anne munched in silence for a few moments as Martha drove. "I want to go to my mama's place if that's all right with you," she said quietly. "Up where Gram and Gramps used to live."

Martha hadn't expected that. She felt her heart lurch. "Where's that, honey?"

"I can show you. Its this next turn here to the right." Anne took another bite of her cookie.

"I guess you miss your mom a lot, don't you?" Martha ventured. Maybe now Anne would talk. She'd been concerned about the child's lack of emotion. Except for her outburst the day they told her Brenda was dead, she'd hardly said anything.

"Not really."

Martha slowed to take the corner Anne had pointed out. She waited. Anne was silent.

Martha tried again. "I guess you miss the place where you and Daisy grew up."

"Sometimes." Anne shrugged. Then she turned and looked directly at Martha. "You don't have to worry about me, Martha. I'm already used to my mama bein' dead. I told you she was dead, didn't I? I don't know how I knew exactly. I just did." The huge sigh that followed nearly broke Martha's heart.

She clung to the wheel hard as the rough track tossed the Bronco from side to side. *It was so darned unfair!*

"Anyways," the girl continued in a small voice, "I ain't worried. Fraser'll take care of us. He said he would and Fraser ain't never told me'n' Daisy somethin' he didn't do."

Martha shot the girl a swift look, stifling the urge

to correct her *ain't*s and her *ain't never*s. Anne's face was calm as she brushed the cookie crumbs from her hands, slowly, methodically, then wiped her palms on her jeans. Horror struck Martha's heart—what if Fraser's plan didn't work out? What if he couldn't adopt these children? What if he had to turn them over to the authorities?

That must not happen. Somehow Martha had to convince him either to marry her or go ahead with his original plan to marry someone else and adopt the children. Katie Barker. Her heart sank. Either way, the girls' needs had to come first. Fraser was prepared for that. Was she?

"There it is, Martha!" Anne slid to the front of the seat, as far as her seat belt would permit, and peered ahead. "Behind those trees."

Martha made the turn and geared down. The Bronco growled over the unplowed road with very little difficulty. Thank goodness. And she had four-wheel drive if she needed it.

The trailer where the girls had grown up was a sad-looking affair. It was old, its roof patched many times with sheet metal and tar, its wooden stoop sagging. There were faded curtains at the window, and Martha could see a blackened metal chimney sticking through the roof, probably for a wood-burning stove, judging by the stack of neatly piled wood at the side of the trailer.

No doubt the snow hid a multitude of sins, Martha thought. She shivered. She couldn't imagine a greater contrast than between this forsaken place and the trim two-story mock Colonial where she'd grown up in one of the immaculate well-treed and green-lawned Madison suburbs. There, the fireplace and chimney had been used mainly by Santa Claus; here, the wood stove no doubt heated the entire place.

"Careful!" Martha picked her way through the snow behind the running, leaping, laughing Anne. Anne scooped up a handful of snow and pitched it at Martha, just missing her. She shrieked with delight.

Martha was surprised. She'd thought Anne might be sad when they came here, to the place she'd been born.

"C'mere, Martha!" Anne was squinting through one of the windows. She'd already tried the door, but it was locked. Martha had to admit she was relieved. To see the remnants of Brenda's life here, her clothes, the cupboards no doubt containing foodstuffs—stale breakfast cereal, half-empty pots of jam, mismatched crockery—would be depressing. She didn't think Anne was ready to face that, despite her apparent high spirits. The truth simply hadn't had a chance to sink in yet, no matter what the child said.

Martha stepped up beside Anne, wiped the frost off the window and peered in. She was right; it was un-utterably depressing.

"Look, there's Daisy's old slippers." Martha saw a small worn pair of beaded moccasins on the floor by the ancient fridge. "They used to be mine, and then they got too small and I gave them to Daisy. And there's the fairy-tale book Gram gave me! Darn, I wish I could get in there and get it."

Anne pointed to a shelf by the television set where Martha could see several books on their sides.

"We'll come back sometime with the key," Martha said. "Fraser's probably got one."

"C'mon!" Anne grabbed Martha's hand and, laughing, pulled her away from the trailer and around the back. They took big steps through the snow, which was nearly as high as the tops of Martha's boots. "Let's make angels and— Hey, look! There's our old swing."

Martha saw two rope swings and a tire dangling from a crossbar lashed between two trees. At least Brenda had made an effort to make life happy for her children. She'd had no money to spare, but Anne obviously didn't have sad memories of this place. On the contrary...

"Okay." Martha flopped down in the snow. "Bet I can make a better angel than you can."

"Bigger maybe," Anne shouted, flopping down near her, "but not better!" She industriously began waving her arms and legs to form the angel's skirt and wings. When they both stood up again, Anne remembered to take a big step away from her angel, leaving the image clear and crisp, while Martha forgot and stepped all over her angel's skirt.

Anne crowed with delight, and Martha laughed until her stomach hurt. "Another one. Make another one, Martha," Anne begged, and skipped away to find a fresh expanse of snow. They made half a dozen more angels, then Anne got on the swing and began to pump, higher and higher, singing at the top of her lungs. Martha lay in the snow. She had rarely heard Anne sing. She felt terrific. She hadn't felt this good for a long time. She'd forgotten how much fun it was to play in the snow. Even a grieving child still had a child's heart for play.

Martha stared up at the wide blue sky. She could see forever. Dear Lord. How in heaven's name had she ended up in Wyoming? She smiled and closed her eyes for a few seconds, relishing the thin November sun on her face. This was so pleasant, so peaceful. All the tension she'd been feeling seemed to have drained away.

She couldn't hear a thing for the racket Anne was making and the added racket from a flock of curious crows that had settled in the cottonwoods around them. So it was with utter shock that Martha suddenly realized a dog had appeared out of nowhere. Spook.

Dazed, Martha watched Daisy run past her to jump onto the other swing, shouting with excitement. That must mean...

"Cold?" Fraser stood for a few seconds, looking down at her from very high up, his face dark against the bright sky. Then he hunkered down beside her, and Martha could see the teasing light in his eyes. In the brightness, his eyes, which she always thought so dark, were shot with gold.

"Not very." She smiled in response to his sudden grin and felt a rush of joy sweep through her entire body. Every nerve sang, and her inner pandemonium blended with the cries of the girls, the excited barking of the dog and the relentless censure of the crows. "I'm going to be a little wet when I get up, though. I'm not exactly dressed for this."

He surveyed her jacket and jeans, his eyes warm.

But he said nothing. Martha felt her cheeks burn. "H-how'd you know we were here?"

"I picked up Daisy at Birdie's, and then on the way back I saw your tracks head off the road." He frowned briefly, then looked at her and smiled again. "I figured I'd better see what you two were up to."

"Anne wanted to come here."

Fraser nodded, eyes serious.

"You don't think I did the wrong thing to bring her, do you?" All at once Martha was worried he might not approve.

He shook his head. "No. I've been wondering when they'd ask to come back for a visit. This is the first time. I think Anne was afraid to while there was a chance her mother'd come back. Now—" he shrugged "—I don't know. I'm no shrink. I guess maybe she can handle it now she knows she's not coming back here to live ever again."

"But she seems to like it well enough."

He shrugged again. "I think they both did. And heck, Brenda was just like a kid herself most of the time. Sure, they had fun."

Martha studied him as he watched the girls. Here they were, the two of them, having an important conversation, with her flat on her back in a foot of snow as though it was the most ordinary thing in the world. She struggled up on one elbow and he quickly offered his hand. She took it, warm and hard in hers, and sat up. Then, without his assistance, she got to her feet.

"Here. Let me help you." Fraser brushed the snow from the back of her jacket, and she twisted around to brush it from her backside and jeans. How could anything as absolutely boring and unsexy as a man brushing snow from a two-inch-thick down jacket make her feel so…so jumpy.

''Thanks.'' Martha quickly straightened and stepped back a foot or two. She shook herself. Fraser seemed not to notice her discomfiture. He was still watching the girls on the swing, eyes narrowed, brows slightly drawn. The silence between them stretched and stretched. Martha wondered if he was thinking about what had happened back at the house….

''I've thought about your suggestion since we talked, Martha,'' he said seriously. He'd been thinking *exactly* what she'd been thinking. He cleared his throat. ''I realized maybe I was wrong not to give it a little more consideration. I have to say, uh, that I like your idea in general, more than my original idea. And I want you to know I appreciate your offer to help me out, but—'' he paused and her cheeks burned and her stomach turned over at the *but* ''—I hope you'll understand why I can't accept your terms.''

His eyes, tortured, met hers. She flinched at the raw emotion she saw there. She nodded. ''I understand,'' she said quietly.

She didn't understand at all!

So that was that. She hadn't expected him to change his mind. Still, she felt a powerful sensation of loss, and she clenched her hands in the pockets of her jacket, desperate to keep her composure. Couldn't he see for himself that it was silly to expect the same thing to happen to her as had happened to his first wife? Couldn't he see that his wife's death had been one chance in…in ten thousand?

But, no, she kept forgetting that to him it hadn't been one chance in ten thousand. It had happened to *him,* not to someone else, some stranger. It had been his wife. And his child. They were both dead. And no matter what the facts were, what reason said, deep down he believed he'd been responsible. She couldn't argue with that. If he couldn't recognize the facts for himself…well, she was too proud to beg.

But after all, it was her dream, too, that had just crumbled. Sure, she'd believed she'd come to grips with the fact that it was extremely unlikely now, at thirty-five, that she'd marry and have children. But when the opportunity had presented itself that very day, fully fledged, completely unexpected, in the midst of Fraser's dilemma, her heart had leapt and grabbed at the chance. It was the future she still so desperately wanted. It was the dream she'd never really given up—a home, children to love, a decent man to share her life with. Maybe even a baby tugging at her breast one day, her own flesh and blood. *And Fraser's.*

Was she so different from other women? Were her terms really so unreasonable? Wouldn't another woman, wouldn't Katie Barker, for instance, want a child of her own? If he didn't care who he married, if it didn't matter to him, why wouldn't he marry her so that at least one of *her* dreams could come true? She could live with a man who didn't love her, but why should she be denied the experience of being a mother, of giving birth to her own child?

He'd said no; he'd turned her down flat.

Her cheeks burned, but her jaw was firm. She

wouldn't say another word about it ever. Not another
word.

HE HADN'T REALLY UNDERSTOOD what her offer had
cost her. Not until he saw her face go white. Then,
moments later, she'd turned away from him, eyes
overbright, cheeks red. Something kicked him in the
gut with the force of a half-broke mule—she was embarrassed. He'd hurt her feelings terribly by telling her
he wouldn't marry her, not on her terms.

After all, she'd had the courage to make the offer
in the first place.

And still, three days later, he'd settled nothing.
He'd phoned the county office and told them what had
happened and that the mother had appointed him
guardian—not quite a lie—and that everything was
okay. That wouldn't last. Someone would be out soon
to see what was going on. Maybe take the girls.

He waited in the barn, with a growing sense of irritation, for the feed truck he'd been expecting all
morning. He had some accounts to go over and calls
to make so he could organize the trip to Blackwell's
to take him the rams he'd promised. The trip would
give him time to think.

But he had to settle this marriage thing first. Sure,
it might have been simpler just to drive down to the
Barker ranch and ask Katie if she'd marry him. She'd
do it. At least he knew Katie pretty well, knew he
could probably get along with her all right. Physically,
well...he wasn't worried about pleasing her in bed.
But something Martha had said stuck with him and

stopped him from jumping in his pickup and going down to ask Katie.

Martha had said Katie was in love with him. Was she? Her father had seemed to think so at the wedding. And if Katie really was in love with him, or thought she was, it made him damned uncomfortable, because there was no way he was in love with her. Not only that, he figured there was no way he ever would be. It'd be a low-down miserable trick to pretend he was. He wouldn't lie to her. Katie deserved better.

Nor, he recollected, frowning, did the girls particularly like Katie. He considered a couple of other women he'd taken out from time to time since he'd been on his own. Halfhearted affairs that had gone nowhere. Was there any sense in pursuing that line of thought? He could be going from the frying pan into the fire if he didn't watch it.

And where did Martha fit into this? For a few seconds Fraser felt thoroughly fed up with Martha Thomas. Everything about the woman seemed to aggravate him. He—and everybody else—would be a lot better off when she finally left Blue River.

Then Fraser allowed his thoughts to drift. He saw her stretched out there in the snow. Relaxed, smiling. He felt again the impulse that had made him hunker down beside her, had made him want to reach out to touch the curve of her cheek. He'd barely stopped himself from stretching out beside her in the snow as if Spook and the girls weren't there at all. He'd wanted to bend down and kiss that wondrously kissable mouth. Full and soft and vulnerable. The brightness of the winter sun had picked out a few freckles on her nose he hadn't known she had. A few tiny lines at the corners of her eyes. Lines of laughter.

For a woman of nearly thirty-six, she had somehow retained an innocence, a freshness that was a powerful draw for him. Something about her scared him silly. He'd been aware of it since the day he'd met her. He had to watch himself. There was no one more cynical, more worn-out with the ups and downs of loving too much than Fraser James McKenna. No one knew that better than he did.

But she'd made her offer clear. It was plain, simple, straightforward. He wouldn't have to go through any hoops with her. He wouldn't have to pretend with her as he'd have to with another woman, even Katie to some degree. Martha didn't love him and he didn't love her. They'd be starting square and straight. What they did share was worth building on—they both loved the girls. Fraser hadn't admitted it to himself until that very instant, but it was true; somehow those two girls had weaseled their way into his heart. And dammit, whether he wanted to face it or not, nothing was ever going to be the same again.

The regret he felt because he couldn't go back to the solitary existence he'd carved out for himself in the past couple of years was mixed with the hope and pleasure he felt at the amazing unexpected prospect of the girls' becoming a real part of his life. And the life of the woman who would share his, he reminded himself. That was the trouble with love—you couldn't go back on it. Once you found yourself loving someone, you couldn't stop just because you'd made up your mind it was no good for you.

Charlotte Mae. She'd been too full of life; he'd loved her too much. So had Weston, and his relationship with his brother had never been the same after his marriage. Weston had wanted her, too. But if she'd wanted to marry Wes, she would have. She'd chosen him, Fraser.

His chest hurt just thinking about it. All those feelings when Charlotte came back from San Francisco—disbelief, triumph, a shattering of the limits he'd put on what he'd allowed himself to feel until then. Charlotte had come back and she'd wanted to marry him.

He hadn't cared whose child she brought in her belly. He hadn't wanted to know. He'd been happy. What he'd told Martha was true—it hadn't mattered to him. If the child had brought her back to him, if she'd needed him to give the child a name, he was happy to do it. He wanted them both. Then she'd lost it, and some spark in her had dimmed, some secret happiness had been lost. Until, nearly four years later, she'd become pregnant again.

And then he'd lost them both.

Fraser swore angrily and thoroughly.

The grain truck finally arrived, and he heard the blast from its horn with relief.

He'd never forget the horror of that night. He'd never forget the sight of all that blood, so red, so much—the smell of it. Two weeks later he'd burned the very clothes he'd worn, crusted with her blood, dried and hard in the folds. No, he'd never forget how she'd died, or why, or how much it had hurt him.

And now Martha Thomas wanted a child, too.

As he signed for the completed grain delivery an

hour later, he glanced toward the ranch house. Martha wasn't back yet from picking up Anne. She'd taken Daisy with her and had told him before she left that they'd probably go on to Birdie's for an hour or two so the girls could toboggan with Birdie's granddaughter, Jenny, who was visiting.

He pulled down his hat and squinted against the bright sun. Who the hell was that driving up to the house? Two of the sheepdogs were making a hell of a racket. Fraser felt a foreboding that had nothing to do with the fear he'd felt for months about the authorities finding out he had the girls. It was no secret now; the facts were out.

Lord. His heart slammed in his chest. *Surely to God that damn sister of hers wasn't coming back for them.*

But, no, the car had Wyoming plates. Fraser walked toward the house. He took a deep breath and squared his shoulders unconsciously. Government plates. Looked like the social-worker lady he'd been expecting all this time had arrived.

CHAPTER ELEVEN

"WELL, THAT JUST ABOUT wraps it up, Mr. Mc-Kenna." The social worker glanced up with a smile and gathered the papers spread on the table in front of her. "I've got everything I need to make my report. I wouldn't say no to that second cup of coffee now."

"Sure." Fraser picked up the coffeepot and brought it to the table.

He wasn't sure what he thought of the last half hour. Certainly Rose Pivnicki had been more understanding than he'd expected, in a cool bureaucratic kind of way. But he could see that she didn't approve of him keeping the girls and he knew she definitely wasn't thrilled that he'd already had them for almost four months.

"Thanks." She looked up at him, and he eased himself into the chair opposite her. Forcing her to look up put him in a dominant position, and he didn't want anything—not even accidental body language—to get this woman's back up.

"After I talk to my supervisor, I'll call you about keeping the girls temporarily. I can tell you, if our situation with foster parents wasn't so desperate at this particular time, there'd be no question about—"

"No question?"

"I'd be taking them back with me right now," she said, pressing her lips together firmly. "Until, well, we could make a more permanent arrangement."

Fraser saw red for a second or two and fought to control his response. Measured, reasonable, conciliatory—mustn't get her angry with him. "I appreciate that, ma'am. Blossom and Daisy have known me all their lives, and they're comfortable here. In fact—" he took a deep breath and plunged ahead "—my situation will be changing shortly. I'm hoping to—"

"Changing?" She studied him over the top of her cup.

"Yes. I'm getting married soon and, uh, I'd like to initiate steps to adopt the girls legally if I could." He held his breath. What had he said? He was committed now either way....

Rose Pivnicki stared at him, a speculative look that had him squirming inside. Could she see through his scheme with those large-framed innocent-looking bifocals of hers?

"That's very interesting, Mr. McKenna," she said slowly. "I had no idea you'd considered pursuing adoption. I must say your marriage would make it a lot easier for the department to support such an application. Hmm."

She continued to stare at him, then raised her eyebrows. "Frankly you wouldn't stand much chance adopting them on your own, you know. As a single man." She shook her head. "And the girls will be difficult to place permanently elsewhere, considering their ages. Most people want to adopt an infant. Then, well, there's the two of them."

He nodded politely. "I understand that."

Rose Pivnicki got to her feet and stuffed her papers into a bulging black nylon briefcase. "Well, I've got to be on my way," she said. "I'm sorry I missed meeting the girls, but I'll be back soon."

She'd be back soon. Fraser stood at the window and watched the social worker drive slowly away from the house, carefully negotiating the frozen ruts. He stood there for a long time, ignoring the soft whimpers of the dog at his feet. Then suddenly, ears perked, Spook barked sharply and rushed to stand by the kitchen door, wriggling with anticipation.

Sure enough, a minute later, Fraser saw the Bronco come around the bend in the road toward the house, Martha driving over the frozen track just as carefully as the social worker had. He watched her pull to a halt outside the house, felt his heart squeeze as Daisy opened the rear door and tumbled out, Anne right behind her. Then he saw Martha, laughing, get out on the driver's side, her arms full of packages, her hair tangled by the wind.

An enormous feeling of loss came over Fraser, then anger followed. Why couldn't he protect these girls and this woman under his care? Why couldn't he make things right for them? He felt frustrated. He felt angry. He felt he'd failed as a man. A real man would take action. A real man would make sure no harm came to those he cared about, would risk everything to protect the ones who'd put their faith in him. Their *trust.*

Brenda, God forgive her, had put her trust in him; these girls trusted him to take care of them, to do the right thing; even this woman he'd hired, this stranger, had trusted him enough to reveal her innermost dreams to him.

Why couldn't he take the risk? Why couldn't he trust himself?

The door flew open. "Fraser!" Daisy threw herself into his arms, the action signifying more strongly than words ever could her relationship with him. Her *trust*.

"Look what we made with Jenny." Daisy rooted around in the bag she carried and pulled out a rumpled piece of paper with a crayoned drawing. "A turkey! We're gonna hang it on the fridge, Martha says. For Thanksgiving."

Thanksgiving. A couple of days away. Did they have much to be thankful for?

"Looks good, darlin'." Fraser smiled at her.

Anne burst in the door. "Hi!" He'd rarely seen her in such a good mood. Spook barked and Anne scooped him up, laughing.

Martha followed Anne into the kitchen, her cheeks red, her eyes shining. Fraser caught her questioning glance—she'd obviously passed the social worker's car on the ranch road. Their gazes held for only a second or two, but to Fraser it seemed an eternity. The sounds of the children, the dog yelping—all of it faded to a muffled roar inside his head. The light in the kitchen seemed bent and distorted, as though he were underwater, warm water. Dream water, deep water, sweeping him away, leaving him weak as a kitten, powerless. He breathed deeply, sharply, to quell the dizziness.

"Where's some tape?" he heard Daisy ask Anne. "I need some tape to put up my turkey."

He gestured to Martha. "I need to see you, Martha. Alone."

Something about his expression must have told her not to ask any questions, not now, because she immediately followed him down the hall. The door to his office was open. He turned into it and shut the door behind Martha after she entered. He leaned against it, breathing hard. In the distance he could hear Anne and Daisy arguing good-naturedly over the tape, and Spook still whining with excitement.

"What is it, Fraser?" Martha's eyes were wide and blue.

"I'll marry you," he said roughly, cursing himself for breaking it to her like that. But if he didn't tell her now... "On your conditions. That's if you still want to...to go ahead with it."

She stared at him. "I do," she finally whispered, her face pale. Then, with a weak gesture, "Why... what made you change your mind?"

"I don't know," he said brusquely, turning away from her, thrusting his hands into his pockets. "Maybe it's because I finally figured you were right. You're right, Birdie's right, the doctors are right about...this thing..." He froze, couldn't get the rest of it out for a second or two. "This thing about Charlotte. It was a freak chance. It's not the sort of thing that happens too often. Those are the facts. And that's what I've got to make up my mind on. Facts."

It was true, but the truth didn't make it any easier. Nor did the truth change the fear, the near-panic that had gripped him tighter and tighter since he'd made his decision, standing there by the kitchen window, cursing himself for a coward and a fool.

He knew he'd made the right decision—by the girls, by Brenda, by Martha Thomas.

But that didn't mean he had to like it.

SHE WAS MARRYING a man she'd never even kissed.

The brief words of the scaled-down civil ceremony floated in her head.

This wasn't a dream. She was marrying Fraser Mc-Kenna, after all. He had changed his mind and agreed to her terms, for reasons she still didn't fully understand. This man who stood beside her tall and strong, dressed unfamiliarly in suit and tie—where were the jeans and sheepskin vest?—this man was about to become her husband, with the official consent of the state of Wyoming. And in the eyes of God.

Martha's heart beat so quickly she thought she'd faint. She heard Daisy giggle somewhere behind her and heard Birdie's "Shh!" At least they were pleased. The girls had been so keyed up they'd barely slept the past couple of days, and the LeBlancs had been shocked—impossible to miss that—but at the same time absolutely delighted at the news. It was hard not to feel that Fraser's neighbors had expected it all along. Probably half of them thought she was already pregnant, thus the haste. Even Tom, the dour foreman, had shaken her hand warmly, then winked broadly at Fraser and thumped him on the shoulder and called him a sly old son of a gun.

It was so hot in here, and there was such a buzz in

her head! She wished now, stupidly, that she'd bought the green dress she'd tried on in Pine Ridge's only decent clothing shop the day before, not the blue.

Pay attention, she told herself, panicking. *How can you worry about the color of your dress when you're in the middle of one of the most important ceremonies of your life? You're marrying this man beside you, a man you hardly know, for better and for worse.* No matter where this marriage went in the future, even if it ended one day, every vow she uttered this hour, this minute, came straight from her heart.

She heard the magistrate ask if she accepted this man, Fraser James, as her lawful husband. She heard her own voice answer, "I will." She heard the magistrate ask Fraser if he took this woman, Martha Virginia, as his lawful wife. She heard his voice, deep and strong and steady. "I will."

She closed her eyes. The deed was done. She heard the magistrate invite the man beside her to kiss his bride. There was a murmur from the guests assembled behind them. Martha's eyes flew open and she looked up. *She was his wife.*

Fraser's face was impassive. Their eyes met, his dark and tormented. He'd been through this before—was he thinking of that first time? Of another woman? A woman he'd loved?

She tilted her face up, offered herself in obedience to the magistrate's words, feeling like a complete fool. Fraser placed his palms on her cheeks, warm, dry, one on either side of her face, and covered her mouth with his. His lips were cool and firm, his kiss brief, but she felt the quick intake of his breath as their mouths met. Her own skin prickled and her eyes filled.

She was glad she'd closed her eyes. She was glad she hadn't seen his face.

She was marrying a man who'd shown no indication that he even particularly liked her. Yet she wanted him to father her child, dreamed of his hands touching her face, her breasts, his naked body against hers, the scent of his skin and she felt utter humiliation. He so clearly wanted none of that.

Or at least not with her.

Martha couldn't have said what she ate at the hastily arranged luncheon that followed the brief ceremony. Afterward, she accepted the congratulations of the few guests, neighbors mostly—her mother hadn't been able to come at such short notice and none of Fraser's family was there—kissed the girls, resplendent in new dresses, and allowed Fraser to escort her outside to the Bronco. Birdie had insisted on keeping the girls while Fraser took his bride on a weekend honeymoon.

Honeymoon! What a joke. But Fraser had told her that although he wasn't any crazier about the idea than she was, it made sense to go through with at least the appearance of normal wedded bliss at this stage of their marriage. He wanted nothing to jeopardize the adoption application he planned to make as soon as they got back.

The trip to Jackson was as silent as any other she'd made with Fraser. Only this time he was her husband. They had suitcases in the back seat, ski clothes, hers newly purchased. They were going to share a room when they got to where they were going. *They were going to share a bed.*

Martha didn't think her heart had slowed once since he'd changed his mind about marrying her just over a week ago. But he was still the stranger he'd always been. At least to her. Would that ever change? She scratched at a wedge of frost on the window with her fingernail. *What had she done?*

"Martha?" She turned and caught his quick look of concern. "You okay?"

"I'm fine." She'd never been further from fine in her life. "How about you?"

"Oh, I'll make it." He gave her a wry smile. "Look, is there anything you want to talk about? Anything you want to say about what we should do when we get back to the ranch? How we should, uh, handle things?"

Things. He meant the marriage, he meant their lives together, he meant their new roles with the girls. She shook her head. He was trying—she had to give him that. She ought to try, too. It was just that she couldn't think of a thing to say. It wasn't every day a person got married to someone who needed a wife so he could adopt someone else's kids.

"I think we should do everything we can to look on the bright side of this situation." His voice was stern. "Don't you?"

"Yes."

Martha glanced at him, and his eyes burned into hers, putting the lie to the indifference of his words. The Bronco slowed. Then, his jaw grim, Fraser pulled over to the side of the road and stopped the vehicle with a jerk. He turned toward her, one arm along the back of the seat, the other resting on the steering wheel.

"You're probably regretting this already, aren't you, Martha?"

"No." She shook her head. "I'm not." That at least was the honest truth.

"Okay." He looked ahead at the pavement, at the snow that blinded her on both sides of the road, then back at her. He seemed to have come to some kind of decision. "Look, I know this isn't exactly a match made in heaven, you and me. And that's probably putting it mildly. But we went into this with no illusions, both of us."

She smiled a little. He took a deep breath and went on, "What I am is a hard-scrabble sheep rancher who prefers his own company, always has. You're a city woman used to, I don't know—" he shrugged "—whatever people do in the city. You're used to apartment living, all the amenities. People around, excitement, fancy stores."

Martha smiled again. He made it sound a lot better than she remembered.

"It's always tough to make changes. Especially changes like this. I know we haven't had much time to get to know each other. But even if we don't have a lot in common, I'm giving you my word that I'm going to do my damnedest to make this work. I hope you are, too."

Martha swallowed, unable to take her eyes from his. She nodded slowly. "Yes, I am." Her lips felt dry. "I—I just need to get used to the idea, that's all."

"Good."

"Did you stop just to tell me that?" she asked faintly, wanting to inject a lighter tone into the suddenly too-serious conversation.

"Yes." He leaned toward her and captured her face in his hands. His eyes had a strange light in them she'd only glimpsed once before. That day in the snow... "And to do this."

His mouth covered hers, warm, seeking, tentative. Then, as she made a small startled noise in her throat, he shifted to put one arm around her and pull her hard against him. His other hand gripped her head tightly, his fingers wound into the back of her hair, holding her steady for his deepening kiss, his relentlessly questing mouth.

It wasn't necessary for him to hold her still. She wanted to kiss him. She welcomed his kiss. She'd waited so long for this. She'd prayed for the day he'd kiss her like this—freely, because he wanted to. She reached up and touched his hair as she'd longed to do. It felt warm and silky, and his scent, masculine and unique to him, to who he was, was so strong and rich in her lungs, so surprising and yet so expected, that she felt herself begin to tremble violently, uncontrollably...deliciously.

"God, Martha."

His voice was as shaky as her knees, and she didn't answer, just struggled to free her other hand, which had somehow been trapped between their pounding hearts. She wanted to pull him to her again, and she did, burying her fingers deep in his hair. She wanted to stretch and to press fully against him, feel her breasts flatten against the hard plane of his chest, the muscle and bone. She wanted nothing between them, not her jacket, not his shirt.

This was crazy!

Desperately she tried to control her spinning senses, but as she managed to whisper a tentative no—only a reaction, only what she thought she ought to do, not what she wanted—his answer was to growl a fierce *yes*. He claimed her mouth fully, thrusting deep, deeper, until the heat of his tongue, twined with hers, made her crazy, humming with need. Sudden, hot, insistent. *She wanted him. Right here, right now.*

She felt his hand on her breast, under her jacket, on the silk of her dress, searching for the tiny buttons that kept him from her. Then she felt him abandon his search and wrap both arms around her, iron-hard, and pull her tight, tighter, against him, his mouth clamped on hers, until the sudden jab of the gearshift in her thigh made her draw back with a cry of pain.

"*Hell!*" Abruptly Fraser released her. But his eyes held hers, and their breaths mingled as one cloud in the rapidly chilling air inside the vehicle. "You okay?"

She nodded, panting. "Just my leg. It got stuck." For one hysterical second she wanted to laugh.

One thumb traced her lower lip roughly. She shivered, unable to look away. "We may not have much in common," he said softly, "you and me. But I've got a feeling there's one place where that's not going to matter a whole lot."

She blushed. She actually blushed, and she a woman of some experience and in her thirty-sixth year.

CHAPTER TWELVE

JACKSON, WYOMING, was a town of several thousand and an entry point to the Grand Tetons. It was also God's country to the nation's skiers. Fraser liked to ski and he loved the Tetons, but it wasn't a place he would ordinarily have picked for a honeymoon. Too many diversions.

On the other hand, this was no ordinary honeymoon. He should be grateful that Martha—his wife now, he reminded himself—could ski. And a few diversions were probably in order, considering.

He was married. Mrs. Martha Virginia McKenna. And she was no virgin, despite her name. He felt the heat rise in his veins just at the thought of what had happened when he'd stopped the Bronco twenty miles back and kissed her. She wanted him. She wanted him damn near as much as he wanted her. And it scared him to realize just how much he *did* want her.

Maybe if he'd faced that fact before now, their wedding wouldn't have been the hurry-up shotgun affair it was. Maybe they could've had a chance to get to know each other, the way other couples did.

Only trouble was, he wanted her on his terms. Not hers.

Right now he didn't want to think about her terms.

She wanted a child. It had taken three long years for him to give Charlotte the baby she wanted. It had occurred to him—and made him feel sneaky and guilty as hell about keeping it to himself—that it might have been his fault. Maybe Martha wouldn't get pregnant right away, either, and maybe by then, all this marriage and adoption business would have worked itself out, one way or another. Maybe she never would get pregnant. It happened. He hated himself for the secret hope he felt.

Should he have told her? Was it fair, when the woman so desperately wanted a baby, not to tell her that she might stand a better chance with someone else? Still, she could have put two and two together herself; she knew how long he and Charlotte had been together. Fraser didn't like the feeling all of this was giving him, or the surge he felt at the thought of just how they were going to find out if he was right or not. This thinking about Martha's getting pregnant with his baby and exactly how she was going to conceive, if she was—in the usual garden-variety, time-tested way—was driving him crazy.

Would she have left if he'd told her? He didn't think so. She was just the type to dig in her heels and hang tight to what chance she had. In case he was wrong. She was a believer. And baby or no baby, she had said she wanted to be a mother to the girls. Perhaps that was enough, or would be in the end.

A bird in the hand...

Hell.

Fraser pulled into the parking lot of the hotel. Martha hadn't said a word since he'd kissed her. The afternoon light was already fading. That meant no skiing this afternoon, which meant...

All he could see ahead of him was a couple of nerve-racking hours to kill and then a big white rumpled-up honeymoon bed.

Then, suddenly, they were registered and in their room, and the bellboy was adjusting curtains and turning up the thermostat and flicking on lights. There was no honeymoon bed. Just two perfectly straightforward queen-size beds, copies of a million others in a million other hotel rooms. He hadn't been idiot enough to reserve a honeymoon suite. It would only have embarrassed them both.

The bellboy whistled tunelessly and gave him an odd look.

Damn! Fraser dug in his pocket and found a bill for the kid. He felt like a teenager himself.

And Martha. How did she feel? He glanced at her and was surprised to see how pale she was.

"Martha?"

She turned toward him and her eyes looked bigger and bluer than ever in her pale face. "Yes?"

The boy had left. Fraser put one hand on her shoulder gently, surprised—and hurt—to feel the tiny way she shrank from him. Was she frightened? Shy?

"Listen, maybe you want to take a rest or something. I'll go down and, uh—" he cast about wildly "—organize some rentals for tomorrow."

Her eyes clouded and she glanced away for an instant. Then she looked back at him and her eyes were clear. "Thanks," she said simply. "I guess I am a little tired after...after everything."

"I'll make dinner reservations, too."

"Sure."

"Seven o'clock, all right? Downstairs?"

She nodded.

"Okay." He frowned, not sure if there was something else he should be doing, should be thinking of. "Maybe you'd rather eat someplace else?"

"Downstairs is fine." He felt her hand on his sleeve. "Fraser? Don't worry about me. I'm a big girl. I'll be fine."

Their eyes held for a few seconds. There was some feeling inside him that swelled and swelled. Then it broke and, panicking, he turned away.

"Okay." Somehow he managed a smile. "See you later."

He organized the rentals and bought lift tickets for the next day and stopped in at the dining room to make the reservation for dinner. Then he still had an hour and a half to kill, so he went for a walk and came back to have a beer in the hotel bar. Just one. He'd used booze before to kill the pain, but this one was for courage. And to waste another half hour.

The hotel wasn't busy, nor were the slopes. It was the slow season before Christmas. Fraser wished the place was busier. He'd have preferred the bar full of noisy skiers, the dining room crowded, people waiting in the lobby. The last thing he wanted to face right now was being virtually alone with Martha. Being alone meant intimacy. Intimacy meant talking, meant maintaining a conversation over dinner, all the while thinking about that empty bed upstairs.

Having dinner with her meant putting in the hours

until the usual time people went to bed, trying to pretend it didn't matter one way or the other. It was going to kill him. He almost wished he'd stayed upstairs and made love to her right away. Gotten it over with, put that first time behind them. Maybe then they could relax, both of them.

Just the thought of her lying there naked and warm and willing made him hard. He'd dreamed of it a thousand times since she'd arrived and now it was for real, something he had to face in a couple of hours. She was his wife. They had a deal—she expected him to make love to her. He shifted uncomfortably on the bar stool, oblivious to the looks he'd been receiving from a table of women nearby.

God. He wanted Martha Thomas more than he could remember wanting a woman in years. So much it hurt. Then why, dammit, did he feel like a man on death row who had a date with the executioner in the morning?

Why couldn't life be simple? Straightforward and simple?

He drained his glass and stood up suddenly, tossing some bills onto the polished surface of the bar. Time to head upstairs.

HE COULDN'T BELIEVE IT. Here she was in his arms, dancing. Here was the top of her head, not six inches in front of him, shining in the light from the stage where the band, a bunch of guys in bow ties, played golden oldies. He could bend down and kiss the top of her head without the slightest effort.

And that dress. The color of her eyes, the color of

the big Wyoming sky he loved so much. The dress she'd been married in. Married *him* in. It was silky and soft, and he could feel the warm firmness of her skin beneath his hand on her waist. He moved his hand slightly, just to feel the smoothness of her body under the fabric, and felt her fingers tighten fractionally in his left hand.

Then she raised her head. Her eyes were smoky and liquid and filled with dreams. He felt an overwhelming urge to kiss her, to pull her closer. Somehow, under the guise of avoiding another couple on the dance floor, he managed to drag his gaze from hers. Still, he knew what he wanted. And she knew, too.

Neither spoke. They hadn't said a word since he'd asked her to dance fifteen minutes before. Even that had been unplanned, an impulse to escape the intimacy of talking—and to deny himself the unexpected pleasure of watching the play of light on her hair and in her eyes, the sparkle of her champagne glass as she lifted it to her mouth, the sound of her laughter, which sent pure electricity down his spine.

It hadn't worked. He'd gone from the frying pan straight into the fire.

Fraser took a deep breath and straightened. He had to get a hold of himself. This was crazier than crazy. He felt like some sex-starved teenager. He had to remember what this marriage was, why they'd married at all. *Whoa, boy. Slow down. Don't forget what she wants from you, McKenna. What she could get from any man, if he was willing.*

And what man wouldn't be? Fraser took another deep breath and moved past the bandstand into the relative darkness at the side of the room. When Martha stumbled slightly, he caught her. She murmured something and he bent his head to catch what she said, and the instant she turned her face toward his, so close, he kissed her.

Her mouth tasted of champagne and the particular sweetness of Martha. He'd tasted it once before and knew he'd never get enough of it. His blood heated and surged as he felt her body imprint his, soft and yielding, her hands wind round his neck, the eagerness of her tongue meeting his.

He was lost. He explored the amazing sweetness of her mouth again and again, his heart hammering until he thought it would burst. He shifted and pulled her against him discreetly—although there were no other couples near them on this side of the room—so that she could feel just how much he wanted her. Her soft gasp utterly snapped any control he still had.

"Let's go upstairs," he whispered, barely able to tear his mouth from hers. He buried his face in her hair, filling his lungs with her scent, waiting.

"Yes," she whispered finally, her voice soft and as shaky as his.

He took her hand and they left the room. Two other couples waited at the elevator, and he didn't dare look at her until they were alone. Both couples got off on the floor below theirs, chattering about the snow conditions and the weather forecast and where they planned to ski the next day. To Fraser, they might have been on another planet.

Then they were in their room, the door shut behind them. And she was in his arms again, her head thrown back, his mouth on her throat. The softness, the scent, the vulnerable gesture sent his blood boiling. He felt the pulse beating in her neck, fast, faster. Desire, yes, and fear, too, he realized when he lifted his head to look into her eyes.

His mouth met hers, lightly at first, then deeply as he braced himself against the door, cradling her hips against his. He felt her pull back a tiny bit, just a reaction, he thought—perhaps she'd been off-balance?—but then he remembered the faint shadow of fear he'd seen in her eyes before he kissed her, and he held her close and rested his head on the door, leaning back, remembering. She didn't resist, but she didn't kiss him either. She was quiet, like a bird trapped in the cage of his arms.

In a moment she raised her head, looked at him. He saw the conviction, the firmness of purpose. *She knew what she wanted; she was determined to see it through.* It hurt his heart to see it.

"You use the bathroom first," he said, amazed that he could even speak, that his words made any sense. "Go ahead."

She nodded, swallowed, then spoke. "All right." She crossed to the side of the room where they'd put the suitcases and began to rummage in one of them. He closed his eyes, listened to the slowing thunder of his heart, felt something deep and vital clutch at his throat.

Then he allowed himself to remember again exactly why she wanted him—to give her a baby. She required him the way any rancher required a good stallion for his mares or a sound herd bull to serve his heifers. Thick as nausea, the nightmare rose before him, and his muscles clenched as he felt again the revulsion, the horror, when he'd tried to pry the tiny dead child from Charlotte's arms. Her weak pleading, the mewl of a dying broken creature. *Please, don't take it from me,* she begged. *Not this one, too.*

Fraser took a deep shuddering breath, forcing back the forbidden. And now this woman wanted the same from him. A child. That was their bargain. That was their understanding, what he'd said he'd do. Those were her terms.

He heard the bathroom door click softly shut and then, as softly, the unmistakable sound of the lock being gently eased into place.

Nausea rose again. Blindly Fraser grabbed for the jacket he'd thrown over a chair earlier. Then he left the room, slamming the door behind him.

MARTHA HEARD the door slam. She knew he was gone. She sat down on the closed seat of the toilet and burst into tears.

This wasn't going to work. This was never going to work.

Here she was, a woman of nearly thirty-six and with two or three lovers in her fairly ordinary past, shaking like a leaf at the thought of going to bed with the man she'd legally married. Her husband, for Pete's sake!

Not a *real* husband, said a nasty voice inside. *You asked him; you made him marry you on your terms. What choice did he have? He doesn't even like you all that much.*

"Oh, go away," Martha sobbed. "Damn, damn, double damn!"

She stood up and washed her face with cold water. Methodically, she brushed her teeth, took down her hair and stepped into the shower. Five minutes and she was out, wearing the new nightie she'd bought in Pine Ridge for the big night. Forty percent polyester. You couldn't even get one hundred percent cotton in Pine Ridge.

Martha damp-dried her hair—she didn't have the energy to bother drying it completely—and gathered up her various toilet articles and put them back into her case. She zipped it shut.

Maybe he'd be back. Maybe he'd forgotten something down in the dining room. Or remembered he'd wanted to buy a newspaper. They'd been having a good time, hadn't they? They'd laughed a few times over dinner, they'd talked about the girls, she'd almost felt she was getting to know him. And then he'd asked her to dance....

Martha shivered and turned on the bathroom fan to get rid of the steam from her shower. She could still feel his arms around her, still hear his voice, rough and urgent when he'd asked if she wanted to go upstairs.

She had. She wanted him desperately. Wanted his body, wanted more than his body—she wanted to know *him*, who he was. She wanted him to care that he had her, Martha, in his arms, not the ghost of his dead wife.

Because wasn't that what this was all about? Charlotte Mae. The woman he'd loved more than a man should love a woman, according to Birdie.

Martha felt tears rise again but angrily brushed them away. She walked out of the bathroom. The room was empty. She noticed that his jacket was gone, and she knew what that meant. He hadn't gone down for a newspaper. He'd left. He'd gone for a walk. Or a drive. He might be back soon. He might not be back at all.

She didn't care. Besides, what was the big deal? So what if they didn't make love—have sex, she reminded herself—on their wedding night? A week and a half ago, neither of them had known they'd be in this situation. It took getting used to, for her and, obviously, for him. She could wait. She'd waited a long time for this opportunity to have a child of her own. She wasn't going to jeopardize everything by being ridiculous now.

She slipped off her robe and stood for a moment before the floor-length mirrors, arms half-raised in the dim light. *You're no raving beauty,* Martha Virginia. *You've always known that. You're too tall and you're too plain. Good sturdy stock, Welsh miners and Danish farmers.* She looked at her palms, then turned them over and looked at the gold band, brand-new and shiny, on her left hand.

She pulled back the coverlet on one of the beds and climbed in. It was nearly midnight. She turned off the bedside light and drew the blanket up over her shoulders. She felt cold. She felt sad. She felt lonelier than she'd ever felt in her entire life.

Amazingly she slept. How long, she wasn't sure at

first, but she awoke suddenly, very aware that she was no longer alone in the room. She wrinkled her nose. What was that smell?

She heard a dull thud and a low curse and then a heavy thump as a chair fell over. Fraser was back. At least she hoped it was Fraser.

Martha lay there, barely daring to breathe. There was another low curse, then the sound of someone walking heavily toward the bed in stocking feet. He stopped. Martha dared to open her eyes a crack. Yes, it was Fraser. He had his shirt off and his hands at the fastening of his trousers. What in the...?

Then he lurched forward and half fell, half kneeled beside the bed. Before she could think what was happening, he had his mouth on hers and was kissing her. She tasted stale whiskey and cigar smoke. Cigars? He didn't even smoke.

"Yech!" She pushed him, twisting her head away and feeling the heat of his bare skin under her hands. "What do you think you're doing?" she whispered fiercely, although why she felt she ought to whisper she didn't know.

"Kissing you, sweet Martha," he whispered back, blasting her with alcohol fumes. "Making love to my new wife, tha's what."

"You're crazy!" She rolled away from him, but he'd managed to heave himself fully onto the bed, and his upper torso pinned her down. He was heavy. His mouth sought and found hers again. He kissed her, over and over, with a naked hunger that fanned the embers of what she'd felt earlier. When they'd danced. Despite herself, despite her disgust at the condition he was in, she found herself tempted to kiss him back. Despite everything, she found this man attractive, desirable...sexy.

Lost for a few seconds, she quickly came to her senses when his hand encountered her breast. "Stop that!"

"Why, sweetheart?" he mumbled. "You want me, don't you?"

"Yes...no—"

"Just like I want you, dammit, and you know it," he growled, and muffled her protests with his mouth. She struggled, then found one traitorous hand reaching up to slide into his hair, to hold him closer. Her body, defying all good judgment, strained against his, only the thin fabric of her nightgown and the sheet between them.

As though sharing her thoughts, Fraser rolled to one side and ripped away the sheet and fumbled with the front of her nightie. "Oh, sweet, sweet Martha," he whispered hoarsely. "You're driving me mad, you know that? Crazy!" Then he swore. "How the hell do I get into this thing?"

"Buttons," she heard herself whispering urgently. "Three buttons at the front..." Why was she doing this? Why was she helping him? He was drunk. Did he have to go out and get drunk to find the courage to make love to her? Was it as bad as that?

"Hell!" He ripped the buttons from her nightgown and slid his hand under the fabric, unerringly finding and cupping her breast. She gasped, couldn't help herself.

He groaned her name, then dipped his head to find

her nipple, tight and aching. He took it in his mouth, and she thought she'd die. Flames shot through her veins, scorched every vital organ, turned her muscles limp, her mind to jelly. *"Fraser!"*

"Darlin'?" he mumbled, his hands finding secret places, wicked pleasures, hidden delights. He didn't stop.

This was insane! She didn't want her wedding night to end like this. She didn't want her first time with Fraser to be some quick furtive midnight coupling that one of them, at least, would have no memory of in the morning. She twisted from under him with every shred of energy she could summon, and somehow, suddenly, he was off her. She felt an icy chill at her bare wet breast. But he hadn't let go of her, and before she knew what was happening, he'd twisted, too, and now she was on top of him and he was laughing softly and running his hands along the length of her back, her bare back, under the skirt of her nightie. "Gotcha!"

"Fraser! For God's sake—"

"Whassamatter?"

"You're drunk!"

"You talk too much, d'you know that, darlin'?" He pulled her head down to him with one large hand, the other clamping her hips against his. She felt the urgent swell of his flesh beneath the half-opened zipper, pressing against her bare thigh. The sensation excited her unbearably.

Then—she wasn't sure exactly how it had happened—she was alone on the bed, lying there panting, one breast still exposed, nightie pushed up to her hips.

Fraser had fallen off, taking most of the sheet with him.

She wanted to laugh, sudden hysteria seizing her middle. She didn't dare. She knew if she laughed she'd never stop. Not to mention what it might to do the much-vaunted male ego. She lay there, her mind ablaze, her body on fire, only half-curious as to what might happen next.

Beyond a grunt and a curse, she hadn't heard anything from Fraser. Then she did. The unmistakable sound of snoring reached her ears. She sat up. *"I don't believe this!"*

She scrambled to the side of the bed. It was true. Her husband of just over fourteen hours was flat on his back on the carpet, arms sprawled, sheet half covering his bare chest, which rose and fell rhythmically. He was sound asleep.

CHAPTER THIRTEEN

FRASER AWOKE stiff and sore on the floor beside the bed. He had a hell of a headache, his mouth tasted like the bottom of a roadhouse ashtray, and all he had on was a pair of half-zipped pants and a twisted sheet. Martha, mercifully, was nowhere to be seen.

He wiped the steam off the bathroom mirror after his shower and took a good look. God, he didn't blame her for leaving. He needed a shave and a decent night's sleep—not on the floor of some hotel room, either.

How had he ended up there, anyway? Whatever had happened, it wasn't going to reflect too favorably on him, he was pretty sure of that. All he knew was he'd run into a couple of buddies last night and wound up celebrating old times. Old times, hell! What kind of man went out and got drunk with a couple of buddies on his wedding night?

Wedding night. Fraser stared at himself in the mirror and didn't much like what he saw. He frowned. He had a vague memory of walking back to the hotel last night. and a few sweet sinful shreds of recollection—getting into bed with her, kissing her...

Then what?

He tracked Martha down on the slopes just after

lunch. When he spotted her at the bottom of one of the intermediate runs, slim and swift in her pale green ski gear, laughing at something the good-looking guy with her had said, he felt himself bristle immediately. The depth of his reaction surprised him, but he didn't take time to think about it.

Her smile cooled when she noticed him, and that hurt, but she introduced him politely enough. Turned out the guy was some dentist from Cody, skiing with his teenage son.

"Thanks for looking after my wife," Fraser said, regretting his words when he saw the stormy look on Martha's face. What a dope. Just the kind of thing she needed to hear. Why had he made a dumb comment like that, anyway? Only to wipe off the other guy's smirk. Testosterone talking.

The dentist had been pleasant enough, simply waved and glided off with his pimply-faced son. Martha hadn't said a word yet, beyond her terse greeting. Could he blame her?

"You want to go up again?" he asked, feeling he had to say something. Somebody did.

"Sure." She shrugged and skied toward the lift.

Then they were on the chair lift, swinging thirty feet above the pine trees. His stomach felt queasy, his head was killing him, the glittering snow made his eyes throb, even with goggles on. If he'd known of a bear den nearby with a single occupant holed up for the winter, he might have crawled in to keep him company.

It'd no doubt beat what he had to face with Martha.

"I might be your wife," she finally said icily, "but

I sure as heck don't need anybody looking after me. Thank goodness.''

"Sorry." He winced. "It was a stupid thing to say." There was no way he was going to argue with her, not after what had happened last night. What *had* happened? He wished he could say for sure.

The chair lift swung wildly, then stopped. Great. Now some novice had to get tangled up in his ski poles somewhere and stop the lift. He wanted off. He wanted to sleep this whole thing off somewhere dead quiet, then he wanted to saddle up Banjo and ride hell-for-leather up into the mountains. Alone. In the fall After roundup. Maybe ten years ago, when he was pushing thirty, not forty.

"I thought you told me you weren't a drinking man," she said, still not looking at him. "When we first met."

"I'm not—"

"Really?" she snapped. "Could've fooled me last night."

"Not generally, I mean." He wanted to ask her what had happened last night, but he didn't dare. "I told you, I pay like hell for it the next day."

"So do other people," she said quietly. Just then the lift started again with a lurch, and he automatically tightened his arm on the back of the chair to steady her. She stiffened.

"Dammit, Martha." He pushed up his goggles. The light stabbed through his head. "Look at me."

After a few mutinous seconds, she turned to him. He could see the sheen of tears in her eyes. He'd felt like a jerk before, now he felt worse. "I'm sorry." He raised his hand. "That's all I can say—I'm sorry."

She nodded tightly.

"I...I don't know what got into me last night. I just...I just had to get some air all of a sudden. Had to get out of there. It was all too—" he shook his head, struggling to find the right words "—too intense or something."

"What you mean is, you had to get drunk before you could bring yourself to touch me."

He stared at her. He couldn't believe what he'd just heard. Was *that* what she thought?

"God, Martha." She held his gaze, chin up firmly, eyes unwavering. He could see the hurt deep beneath the blue, hurt she was trying desperately to hide. How could she get it so wrong? What she must think of him, what she must think of herself...

"Why don't you just admit it!"

"Because it's not true," he said. "It's not true. You want to know the truth? You want to know the real reason I went out and got hammered last night?"

She nodded. They were nearing the top of the mountain. Suddenly he was angry that she was forcing him to say what he didn't want to admit, not even to himself. "I went out and got drunk *because I felt too damn much, that's why.*"

He glided off the lift and replaced his goggles. In a way, he hoped she'd just leave him to ski down by himself. But she glided up and stopped in front of him. She adjusted her gloves, then seated her hands firmly in the straps of her poles.

"So why'd you come back then and try to make

love to me later? Have sex, I mean. Why'd you even bother?''

Try to make love…

"You just won't let it alone, will you, Martha?" He wondered if she could see his expression behind the colored plastic of his goggles. He hoped not.

She shook her head.

"Okay." He was angry now, definitely angry. "Because that's part of our deal. And when I make a deal, I keep my end of it."

She turned abruptly and skied away—and didn't look back even once to see whether he followed.

Damn. Why had he hurt her like that? On purpose. It wasn't even true, none of it.

What *was* true?

A TWO-HUNDRED-MILE road trip in the dead of winter to deliver a trailer full of frisky ram lambs gave a man plenty of time to reflect on what kind of an ass he'd been.

Fraser released his grip on the steering wheel. Another thirty miles and he'd reach the Blackwell ranch. He planned to stay overnight, then head back tomorrow. It was getting too late to even think about starting back tonight. Besides, he could use an evening with Dave. And Jeannie. He liked Dave's wife and their three boys. He and Dave had grown up together in the Wind Rivers, then the Blackwells had moved away when he was twelve and Dave was thirteen, about the age of Dave's youngest son now. They'd seen each other maybe once, twice a year since then. But they were still best buddies. Friends stayed friends.

Dave didn't need these young rams yet, Fraser knew; they wouldn't do for breeding until next fall. But as he and Martha had driven into the ranch yard yesterday, after the tense trip home from Jackson, something had made him decide to take the lambs to Utah right away. *Running away, that's what it's called, McKenna.* He ignored the voice inside him.

The girls wouldn't be back until the next day, Monday. That meant another evening—and night—alone with Martha. They'd spent the previous night in separate beds at the hotel in Jackson. They hadn't made love—had sex, as she called it. She hadn't said anything. But he felt like a complete fool. She didn't deserve this—no woman did. What in hell did he plan to do about it?

It was a problem he had to work out on his own. It wasn't that he didn't want her. The truth was, he wanted her too much. But the thought of making love to her not using anything, knowing she might get pregnant…

The thought of another baby, his baby, growing in a woman's body, his wife's body, made his blood run cold. He felt trapped, as he had the night he'd run out on her, their wedding night. He'd had to get out, get some fresh air, had to *think*. And then he'd run into Sam Garrett, a guy he'd cowboyed with many years before on the Broken Bar M, and then Sam had told him Brent Chisholm was in town, and before he knew it, they were toasting old times in Chuck Higgins' steak house. He hadn't even told them he'd gotten married again. Why? It wasn't as though this whole thing was going to go away, blow over like a piece of bad weather.

Begin as you mean to go on, or so the expression went. Well, he didn't intend to go on this way. Question was, just what was he going to do?

"WHAT'D YOU BRING these little fellas over for? I was thinking of coming up after Christmas to get them. Bringing you a little mare I think you'll like. Little vacation for me and Jeannie." Dave held up his gloved hand to guide Fraser, who was backing the truck and trailer. "You've got another two and a half feet, Fraser..." He held up both hands. "Whoa!"

Fraser stopped the truck and swung out of the cab. He clapped his hands together. Damn, it was cold. And if it was cold down here in the flat country, what was it like back home? The Blue River area registered some of the lowest temperatures in Wyoming. He never should have left Martha and the girls. Anything could go wrong. Electricity lines could go down, fuel lines could freeze. Tom was there, but he couldn't count on Tom to take over for him. He couldn't count on anyone; it was a hard-learned lesson, one he'd never forget.

"Good to see you, buddy." Dave smiled. "You know you're always welcome here. We'll let Ben unload these critters and go on up to the house. Jeannie'll be surprised to see you."

Fraser looked over at Ben, Dave's oldest son, tall, gangly, maybe sixteen. He'd unfastened the stock-trailer gate and was expertly checking the young rams before taking them into pens in the barn. Something grabbed at Fraser's insides as he watched the silent teenager straighten and settle his shoulder-length hair under his ball cap.

I should have sons that age. And daughters.

Sometimes he felt so old. "So, what's new down here on the flatlands?" Fraser fell into step with his friend.

"Nothing much. Ben made the high school basketball team, and Jeannie's got her eye on a new loom. How 'bout you?"

"Got married."

"Danny's pretty disappointed he never made the team this year, but he's only—" Dave stopped dead and grabbed his friend's sleeve. "You got married? What the hell you talking about?"

"Just what I said."

"When?"

"Couple days ago." Had it only been a couple of days since his life had turned upside down?

"Who? Jeez, Fraser, wait'll Jeannie hears this. She'll be mad you never invited us to the wedding."

"Not much of a wedding. It was…kinda sudden. You don't know her, Dave. Martha Thomas." *McKenna now,* he had to keep reminding himself. "From Wisconsin."

His friend stared at him, then gave a low whistle. "Kinda sudden, huh?"

Fraser didn't like the look on his friend's face. "Not what you think, Dave. You know me better than that."

Dave nodded; the reference was clear. Fraser had made no secret of how he felt about fathering another child. For the past two years, he'd even avoided anything in the way of a real relationship. But there'd been a time…

He'd been pretty wild, and Dave knew all about it. The first year after Charlotte died, Fraser had grieved and holed up on the ranch, the second year he'd tried to kill the pain with booze and women. Dave had hauled him out of more than one bad situation.

But Dave's words now, and the imputation—slight as it was—to Martha's good name, riled him. Then the fact that it riled him made him mad. Hell, the whole point of this marriage was that neither of them cared that much about the other! So why was he all of a sudden so prickly about everything that had to do with her?

Dave clapped him on the shoulder and laughed. "Any more news, buddy? Although I'll admit I'm kinda scared to ask." They'd almost reached the house, a neat two-story affair with lilac hedges, bare now, and a deserted snow-swept garden to the side. White-painted, picket fence, two-car garage.

"Brenda Langston died—you remember her?" Fraser stomped the snow off his boots on the frozen sidewalk.

Dave nodded. "Skinny little kid? Mousy blond?"

"Yeah. Got herself killed in a car accident down in Alabama somewhere. Hell of a thing. I was taking care of her two kids at the time." He hesitated. "I'm adopting them, Dave. Me and Martha."

"Legally?"

Fraser nodded.

"That's a big step, buddy." Dave looked worried. "You sure?"

"I'm sure." *Probably thinks I'm crazy,* Fraser thought. Married, adopting a couple of girls, new wife dying to get herself pregnant—of course, Dave doesn't know that part. "It's what I want to do, Dave. What I have to do."

His friend didn't have time to say anything more.

"Fraser!" Dave's wife threw her arms around him as they opened the door. "I wondered who was driving up here this time of night. Come on in. I've got the coffeepot on, and I can warm you up something to eat in a minute."

Fraser gave her a big hug, then released her and bent to take off his boots. "You're looking great, Jeannie." She always did. Today she had on one of her hand-woven skirts and a big multicolored sweater. Hand-spun, no doubt. Her prematurely graying hair was tied up in some loose attractive style. Her smile was wide and warm.

"You're not looking so bad yourself, Fraser. For an ornery old bachelor," she teased.

"Where you been, honey?" Dave tossed his hat onto a peg and turned to her with a grin. "Fraser's hitched again. Married some sweet-talkin' little lady from Wisconsin."

"No!"

"Yessir. Couple days ago. And he tells me he's all set to adopt a couple of kids. Any way you look at it, Jeannie, I'd say this here ornery bachelor has turned into a one-hundred-percent family man. Wouldn't you?"

ONE-HUNDRED-PERCENT family man.

Maybe Dave was right. And if he was, it was time

to put the past behind him, square up to the future. It wasn't just him anymore. There were the girls to consider.

But number one was making it up to Martha. If she'd accept his apologies and if she'd believe him when he said he wanted to start over again.

He felt himself getting more wound up the closer he got to Blue River. He'd left the Blackwell place late, after sitting up half the night talking with Dave and Jeannie, and then the weather had been worse than he'd expected. He'd had to take it slow with the trailer. He'd brought back the mare Dave had traded him for the lambs. He'd give her to Martha. A wedding present.

He remembered that time he'd come home in a snowstorm just like this, the night of Ted's wedding. How he'd come in the door, dog-tired and seen Martha standing there, her flannel nightgown sticking out below that exotic-looking red dressing gown she always wore, flip-flop slippers peeking out beneath. He remembered the hunger he'd felt for her then and there, despite the long drive and the events of the day.

He felt that hunger now, just remembering. Only now he could do something about it. Now she wasn't his employee or a guest in his house. She was his wife.

Fraser turned the mare into a big box stall in the barn and made sure she had feed and water. He ran his hand down her withers critically. She'd make a good saddle horse. A little on the small side, but Dave had told him she had some Arabian in her. You could see it in the shape of her head. He didn't even know if Martha rode. Showed how much he knew about the woman he'd married.

That would have to change.

The house was quiet and there were no lights on even in the bunkhouse. After all, it was past midnight. Fraser showered in the small bathroom off the kitchen. Then, towel hitched around his middle, he looked at himself in the mirror. He could use a decent haircut. He ran his hands quickly through his hair and made a mental note to get one next time he went to town. Then he ran one hand appraisingly over his jaw. Better shave. All the while he shaved, he couldn't get his mind off Martha, lying somewhere in this house—his bed, he hoped—sound asleep.

On his way down the hall, he gently pushed open the door to the girls' room. They were both asleep, sprawled in characteristic postures on their beds. Daisy held her new stuffed lamb close to her cheek. Fraser felt his heart swell almost to the point of hurting. It was a visceral feeling, unlike anything he'd ever felt before. They were his children now; he'd move heaven and earth to make sure of that. His to love, his to protect. He closed the door quietly.

At the entrance to his bedroom he took a deep breath, then pushed open the door. She wasn't there. Nothing had changed in this room since he'd left it yesterday. The shirt he'd tossed off then still hung over the footboard.

What did he expect? That she'd be lying here waiting for him in a sexy negligee? He had to woo her back; he had to bring her to his bed. He had to establish new terms with her. A new partnership.

Fraser's breath escaped with a whoosh, and, scooping up the dirty shirt in one hand and discarding it, along with the towel he wore, in the laundry basket, he stalked to the closet. He grabbed the dressing gown he rarely used and put it on. He wasn't exactly sure of the reception he was going to get, and there was no sense scaring her half to death, showing up wearing nothing but a towel in the middle of the night.

As he left his room, walking quietly, he thought about the many times he'd dreamed of making this trip down the hall. To Martha's room. How he'd dreamed of lying down beside her, taking her into his arms, kissing her...

This was no dream.

Martha lay on her back, head to the side, one hand tucked under her pillow. She'd pulled the old quilt up to her shoulders to ward off the chill. He could see her clearly in the reflected light from the moon, which had come out now that the snow had stopped falling. He crossed to the window and stood there for a moment.

The Wind River Mountains, familiar and eternal, rough and ragged, rose behind the ranch. He'd grown up here, and he'd never wanted to live anywhere else. Charlotte was up there on the ridge. The ashes of his wife. And the ashes of the child-that-never-was. Dead. Brenda was gone, and the girls' grandparents. Dead. Gone forever.

He was alive, and these girls were alive. Blossom Anne and Daisy. And this woman, Martha, this stranger who'd come to live with them. This woman he'd married. It was up to them—all of them—to take hold of the future.

Fraser took a deep slow breath and turned away from the window toward the sleeping woman.

His heart beat heavily, his blood swelled thickly in his veins, he felt his desire for her as keen and deep and fundamental as it had ever been. He moved closer to the bed.

He bent down. He touched her cheek with the back of his hand, softly. She opened her eyes. He saw the lightning flash of surprise, then saw it vanish. She knew why he'd come.

He didn't kiss her, although he longed to kiss her. He pulled back the quilt. Yes, she wore that flannel nightgown, flower-sprigged, hiked up nearly to her hips, but she made no move to cover herself. He bent and slipped one arm beneath her shoulders, one beneath her knees, and stood with her in his arms. She wasn't as heavy as he'd thought she'd be. He felt very strong, unnaturally strong, as though he could take her anywhere—over mountains, across rivers—and never let her fall.

She curved an arm around his shoulders. She knew they were going to make love. Now. Tonight. For the first time. Her eyes were a pool of waiting, of wanting. He felt himself tremble. He didn't know if he could wait to touch her, to kiss her, until he'd brought her to his bed.

Somehow he managed, pushing the door closed with his shoulder. He let her slide slowly to the floor.

"Fraser..."

"Shh." He put his thumb to her lips, rubbed them

lightly and felt her shudder run through the fire of his own body. "Don't say anything," he whispered. "I want us to start over. I want to begin again with you."

She nodded, holding her breath. He felt the tension in her.

"Let me touch you, Martha."

"Oh, Fraser...*yes*." Her voice was shaky, nervous.

Carefully he unfastened the row of buttons down the front of her flannel nightgown and pushed the fabric to the smooth rounded warmth of her shoulders. Holding her gaze, he let the fabric fall to the floor. She gasped slightly and he saw tiny goose bumps rise on her flesh, saw the tightness of her nipples, proud and erect. He knew it wasn't only the sudden chill.

Her breasts were small and perfect, her waist smooth and taut, her legs long and slender. He ran his hands lightly over her breasts, over the tender curve of her belly, over the warm swell of her hips. He kissed the side of her throat, once, twice, three times, tasting, absorbing the delicate sweetness of her skin.

She shuddered violently and grabbed his upper arm with one hand. "Fraser...please!"

Her plea was his undoing. She couldn't wait; nor could he. With a sudden uncontrolled movement he swept her into his arms again and took two steps, bringing her to his bed. *Their* bed. He laid her down and looked at her. God, she was beautiful. God, how he wanted her. Nothing else mattered. Nothing at all.

Eyes still on hers, he unfastened the belt that had loosely secured his dressing gown. He pulled it off and tossed it to the floor. He felt her gaze on his naked body like a flame trailing over his skin, scorching him wherever it touched. He looked down at her, saw himself between them, swollen, urgent. She could not possibly mistake how much he wanted her.

Then he was beside her, feeling the heat of her skin against his, the satiny length of her body pressed against him, her breasts warm and soft flattened against his chest. It was heaven. It was what he'd dreamed of, what he'd wanted for so long.

He kissed her throat, her shoulders, lowered his mouth to her breasts. She moaned. He couldn't kiss her mouth, didn't dare; couldn't risk the complete loss of control he knew kissing her would bring. Then, somehow, she was beneath him, her thighs welcoming him, her softness, her heat, her wetness driving every rational thought from his head. Every cell ached for completion.

He wanted her, he wanted to bury himself inside her, he wanted to flood her with pleasure and with his seed, his scent. He wanted to make her his woman. It was raw instinct. It was an urge much older than thought, as old as time.

It could not be denied.

He entered her slowly. She gasped and he forced himself to stop. To freeze. To think.

"Martha—" his muscles, his nerves, his very blood protested the interruption "—you okay? Am I hurting you?"

"No." Her hips rocked, rose to meet his. He nearly died. "You're not hurting me."

With a groan that came from beyond his soul, he met the rise of her hips. Far, far beyond reason, he plunged into her, again and again, going on pure instinct, knowing only the need to mate, to connect, reveling in the ancient rhythm that had only one goal—completion. Release.

Too late, Fraser realized that the control he'd prayed for had deserted him. Nothing mattered—not her pleasure, not his. Only physical release. Release from this exquisite torture.

Then release came, shimmering, pulsing, ascending, descending. Glorious. He fell, spent, against her neck, his breath hot on her hair. He twisted slightly to one side as he collapsed, so that she wouldn't have to support all his weight. She trembled in his arms.

Damn. You didn't get it right, McKenna. You lost it.

He lay there, panting, feeling the pooling heat of sweet release in every muscle, every nerve, every cell. How long? He had no idea.

Then sense returned. His own sweat felt cold on his back. He raised himself on one arm and looked down at her. She was smiling slightly, eyes warm, questioning. He saw the wet track of tears on her cheeks. He shook his head and bent to kiss her mouth gently. Her taste was sweet and salt and perfect. Her mouth was soft. He felt her hands on his back, stroking his damp skin, small, fluttering strokes that soothed and excited at the same time.

"Sorry," he muttered, kissing her cheeks, her jaw, her mouth lightly.

"Sorry?" she whispered, eyes wide. "About what?"

"Well, hell." He gave her a wry smile. "I guess

you could say I got carried away. I couldn't hold back. Not the sort of thing a guy's too proud of, you know.''

She simply smiled.

"It can't have been too good for you. I'm sorry."

"It was perfect, Fraser James McKenna," she whispered, still smiling. "Absolutely perfect. Don't you dare apologize."

To his dismay, he felt himself stir and swell inside her. He still wanted her. It wasn't just physical. It wasn't just that he owed her or that they had a deal. He wanted to please her, to give her pleasure. To please himself.

He rocked his hips slightly, and she opened her eyes wider. "I'll make it up to you, Martha," he promised with a smile he couldn't suppress, a smile he could only hope didn't look too ridiculously macho.

She didn't answer, simply pulled his head down with both hands to join her mouth to his, to fan the fire that still burned inside him. He welcomed the fire, let it roll over him, sear him, consume him. He had the terrible feeling that this—what he felt right now, with Martha—would never end. Ever.

It wasn't supposed to be this way.

CHAPTER FOURTEEN

PERHAPS HER DREAM had already come true.

Perhaps the baby she'd longed for had already begun to grow deep inside her body, tiny cells dividing, growing, becoming more than a possibility. Martha felt herself blush as she thought of exactly how that possibility had been realized. *If* it had.

Could she be right? She frowned, trying to recall for a moment when she'd had her last period. Offhand, she couldn't say. There hadn't been a reason to remember, and so much had happened since then.

Who cared? She intended to get pregnant. *That's what this is all about, isn't it?*

She stretched deliciously, welcoming every ache and tenderness. Could she have forgotten how wonderful it was to make love? It had been three years at least, nearly four, since she'd been in a physical relationship with a man, but a woman didn't forget that kind of thing. Unless the man had been pretty forgettable, and she had to admit most of the men she'd dated had been.

Fraser was gone. Somehow she'd known he wouldn't be there when she woke up. Waking up together, pillow talk—that wasn't part of the bargain. To get along as best they could, to hammer out some-

thing that would work for both of them... But what
had happened last night hadn't been a dream. It had
been completely, gloriously real.

He'd lost control.

He'd made it up to her, as he'd said he would, and
it was remembering *that* that made her blush. But the
fact remained—he'd lost control that first time, and
the knowledge allowed her to feel that they might, just
might, have a real future.

Possibilities.

It meant he wanted her. *Really* wanted her. He'd
wanted her so much, physically at least, that he hadn't
been able to hold back. He'd admitted it. He'd been
embarrassed by it. That one simple fact told her that
bringing her to his bed meant more to him than simply
fulfilling an obligation.

Perhaps his obligation had already been fulfilled.
What would that mean to this part of their relationship? Martha frowned again. She didn't want to think
about that.

Heavens! What time was it? She looked for a clock
by Fraser's bed and didn't see one. What she did see
was a nearly cold mug of coffee. The house was quiet.
Fraser must have brought her the coffee and then
taken Daisy and Anne to meet the school bus. Her
job. But it wasn't her job anymore, just her responsibility. And her privilege.

She saw her nightgown in a heap on the floor and
reached over to retrieve it, shaking out the folds. Re-
calling just how it had ended up there, she pulled it
on, feeling ridiculously modest all of a sudden. There

was nothing about her that Fraser hadn't seen. Or touched. Or kissed.

Swinging her legs over the side of the bed, she stood and walked to the window, absently fastening the buttons at her throat. One was missing. The image of Fraser tearing at those buttons last night, kissing her throat, hurriedly pushing the flannel from her shoulders, sent heat flooding through her body again. She closed her eyes.

He was wonderful, incredibly tender and passionate. The lover most women met only in their dreams. And he was her husband. Her legal husband.

Martha opened her eyes again. The morning sun was brilliant on the new snow. A fresh clean world. Not even tracks from the dogs yet, or the children. Smoke rose straight from the bunkhouse chimney. Clear sky, no wind—it must be very cold outside. A weather change. Christmas coming, barely three weeks away now. She'd call her mother this morning, invite her to spend Christmas with them, get to know her new family....

Martha stepped closer to the glass and traced the delicate lace of frost on the window. Last night's storm had swept the house violently, and she'd worried about Fraser driving in such weather. Now, thank heaven, he was home. So much had changed in the past few days.

Martha walked to the chest where the photograph of Fraser's first wife stood, its silver frame bright in the morning sun. Charlotte Mae. She studied the image, wondering at the sadness she felt as she looked at the young woman's smiling face.

Then she reached for the frame and rubbed her sleeve over the glass. What a tragedy. Young, in love, about to become a mother… With a shaky breath Martha returned the photograph to its place. Charlotte was part of Fraser's life, part of his past, and how could she feel jealous of a dead woman? A ghost? *A woman Fraser had loved more than a man ought to love a woman…*

Martha heard the growl of the truck's engine and felt her heart jump. She wasn't even dressed yet. She heard the door slam and Daisy's yell. Without thinking, she jumped back into bed and grabbed her coffee.

Yech! It was ice cold.

"Martha!" Daisy raced into the room, kangaroo clutched in one hand, hair flying. "Guess who's here? *Guess!* Fraser!"

She jumped onto the end of the bed with a shriek.

"Whoa, Daisy. Slow down." Martha laughed, then set the coffee cup down and gathered the little girl into her arms. "I know he's back, munchkin. He came back last night when you were sleeping."

"Hey!" Daisy turned to look at her fully, eyes wide. "You're in his bed."

Martha felt her face flood with heat. Good heavens! She hadn't thought of dealing with this just yet. "Er, yes, I—"

"I guess it's 'cause you're married now, huh?" Daisy nestled closer to Martha. "Anne says moms and dads always sleep together in the same bed without their jammies on, and now you're gonna be kinda like our mom, aren't you?" Daisy's eyes had never been bigger or bluer. "And Fraser's gonna be kinda like our dad, 'cept Anne says we don't have to call him Dad. She says it'd just 'barrass him.''

Martha hugged the warm little body. "I'm sure Fraser won't mind what you call him." She kissed the child's golden flyaway hair. Some sound, perhaps the scrape of a boot heel, had her looking, startled, toward the door.

Fraser stood there watching them. He leaned against the frame, hands supporting him on both sides—Martha had a flash of what he'd looked like the first time she'd ever seen him, only then he'd been half-dressed and hung over. Now he was wearing faded jeans and a red-and-blue-plaid work shirt, open at the throat. She could see the dark hair low in the V of his shirt, and felt every inch of her skin tingle as she remembered the feel of his hard hair-roughened chest against her bare breasts.

He said nothing, and his face gave nothing away, but Martha could feel the heat from his dark gaze burning right through her. She shivered.

"What's 'barrass mean, Martha?" Daisy asked solemnly, gazing up at her. Martha quickly looked at the child, away from Fraser's half smile. "Anne always uses big words on me, just to show off 'cause she goes to school," Daisy complained. "It's so ag-ger-vatin'."

Martha smiled. "Embarrass means…oh, you know, to feel kind of silly. Or rattled." She glanced up to meet Fraser's grin. The child's mimicry of Birdie's favorite expression was spot on.

"Come on, Daisy. Let's give Martha a chance to get dressed." His eyes held hers—she wasn't imagining the heat. "I think we might be, uh, embarrassing her."

Whooping, Daisy bounced off the bed, ducked under Fraser's arm and ran into the hall. With a slow smile and an even slower appraisal, Fraser reached for the doorknob. "I see you found your nightgown," was all he said before closing the door gently.

Just after lunch, Martha placed a call to California. Her mother's enthusiasm the previous week when Martha had called about her sudden decision to marry Fraser had surprised and pleased her. She hadn't realized her thoroughly modern completely unflappable mother had been so concerned, in her quiet way, about Martha's single status. Or—heaven forbid—was it the possibility of grandchildren on the horizon that had Ullie Thomas so sentimental?

"When can I meet him, dear? Your sheep farmer?"

Martha grinned. Her mother sounded as enthusiastic this week as she had been last. A good sign. And she was glad her mother hadn't asked too many questions. Deep down, for reasons she wasn't clear about herself, she wanted her mother to believe this marriage was a love match. "How about coming and spending Christmas with us?"

"Oh, that would be wonderful, a white Christmas, just like in Wisconsin. I'll bring Harry with me, if you don't mind, and—" who the heck was Harry? "—send me the sizes of those two darling girls you're looking after."

"We've decided to adopt them, Mom."

"Adopt them!" After a brief pause, Martha's mother continued, "Well, you just tell them to go ahead and call me Grandma right away. Oh, Martha, this is *such* good news!''

That afternoon, after Fraser and Tom had come up to the house for coffee—a time during which Martha kept herself overbusy peeling too many vegetables for supper, aware of Fraser's eyes on her as she worked— he asked her to come down to the barn with him. Said he had something to show her.

''Me?'' Daisy had chirped. ''Me, too?'' Fraser nodded, and she raced off to find Anne, who'd been reading and eating sunflower seeds in the sunny bay window ever since she'd come home from school.

The barn was relatively warm after the crispness of the winter air, and rich with the scents of animals and fodder. Horses nickered in the dimness as the little group entered, and Martha could hear bleating from the big sheep enclosures that adjoined the barn. At the machine shed Tom left them to fire up the tractor fitted out with a blade to clear snow from the yards.

Daisy and Anne immediately ran off to find the kittens. The litter was over six weeks old, and the girls often discovered the kittens exploring at their end of the barn, rarely in the nest where they'd been born. Daisy had—wisely, Martha thought—opted to have as many kittens as she wanted in the barn, rather than one in the house. Not that it would have mattered if she'd brought one up to the house, but perhaps Spook might have objected.

She glanced down at the lopsided little dog trotting importantly at Fraser's side, glaring up at her from time to time, as if to ask just what she thought *she* was doing here.

Martha stopped to pat Banjo's nose, the big roan gelding that Fraser often rode. The horse snorted and nibbled at her sleeve.

"Sorry, big fella," she said, scratching the side of his jaw, "nothing for you today. Maybe tomorrow."

Fraser waited patiently beside her, and when she turned to him with a smile, ready to move on, his expression surprised her. Intense, serious…nervous? What was there to be nervous about?

"Come down here on this side," he said, leading the way. They walked past two other box stalls, then Fraser paused in front of the next one.

"Oh, isn't she pretty?" Martha exclaimed, stepping forward. The small bay mare inside stretched out her neck, sniffing tentatively. Martha extended her hand, and gradually the animal moved forward until she was close enough for Martha to run a hand down her crooked blaze and pat her neck. She had a delicate head, well-defined, with large, luminous, melting brown eyes.

"Like her?"

"She's lovely, Fraser!" Martha dug in the pocket of her jacket. Maybe she did have something left from a previous visit to the barn, a wrinkled carrot, a crust of bread. "Is she new?"

Fraser looked at Martha. "Yeah. I brought her back from Utah with me. She's not quite three years old."

Martha cast Fraser a quick glance. There was something odd about his voice, as though he wanted to tell her something, yet was holding back.

"What's her name?"

"Strange name. Mercredi. Dave got her from a

Frenchman over in Elko.'' Fraser paused. ''But you can change her name if you want.''

''Me?'' Puzzled, Martha turned to him.

''She's yours.''

''Mine?'' Martha felt like a rather unimpressive echo. ''Why?''

Fraser looked at her for a few long seconds without speaking. Martha held her breath.

''Because you took the chance and married me,'' he said finally. Every word sent shivers down her spine. ''Because you're my wife. Because I didn't treat you right the day we got married and I should have, and now I want to start over again. Start out right. I want to put what happened in Jackson behind us.''

A wedding gift. Martha felt her heart hammer in her chest. Her throat felt dry. Something prickled in her throat. Hay dust, probably. ''You're giving her to *me?*'' she whispered.

''If you want her.'' Fraser looked away for an instant and then looked back, a wry smile twisting his handsome mouth. ''I don't even know if you like horses, or if you ride. I don't know much about you, Martha.'' He laughed, a harsh sound. ''Some husband I am.''

She put her hand on his arm. He froze, gazing down at her, the pain in his eyes tearing her apart. ''I think you're a wonderful man, Fraser. I think you're a wonderful husband.''

''You wouldn't know.'' He turned and pulled her gently closer to him, one hand on her waist, the other brushing back a lock of hair that had fallen from her

wool cap. ''Helluva start we've had, huh? Besides—''
he grinned ''—I'm the only husband you've ever had.
Right?''

''That's true,'' she admitted, aware that he was
teasing her, flirting with her. ''But a woman knows
these things deep down—''

He stopped her words with a kiss, his mouth covering hers warmly, gently at first, and then with growing urgency. She welcomed him, eager to explore his
mouth as he explored hers. Her heart pounded and she
felt her blood turn to flame. She'd never grow tired
of this man's kisses, never.

He drew back and stared down at her, his eyes
glowing. ''Martha, Martha,'' he said softly. She let
her head fall back against his arm. ''You know something, Martha?''

''Mmm?'' She loved the sound of her name when
he said it.

''If the girls weren't here, and if Tom wasn't about
to drive that tractor back into the shed and come looking for me at just the wrong moment, I think I'd take
you up in the hayloft and...'' He growled and nibbled
on her earlobe. She shivered.

''And what?''

''You know what.'' He buried his face in her neck,
sending little ripples of delight all the way to her toes.
''You'll be the end of me, Martha.''

''Why?''

''Because I want you so much,'' he said, his voice
rough. ''Too much. Last night was—'' He stopped,
looked at her, then kissed her again, only to wrench
his mouth from hers a moment later. ''Last night was

heaven, and I just can't believe it's true. I can't believe you married me inside of a week the way you did. That you wanted to do this with me.''

"This?" She raised her eyebrows.

"Adopt the girls, live out here way the hell and gone with all of us—"

"Even a cranky dog?"

He grinned. "Even a damn cranky three-legged dog."

"Don't forget I have my reasons," she said softly, thinking only to tease.

And felt him stiffen. Freeze.

"Yes," he said finally, and his voice was different, flatter, grimmer. "You're right. We both have our reasons. I haven't forgotten."

He held her then, continued to hold her, but the passion was gone. Still, she reveled in the sensation of closeness, too new, felt his body strong and warm, his arms tight around her. Felt the comfort of leaning against him, knowing she could trust him with her life. He was that kind of man. But she also realized that despite last night, despite their wanting each other physically—good sex or no good sex—he hadn't really come to terms with her reasons for wanting to marry him. Not where it counted, not deep inside.

Perhaps he never would.

For the first time, Martha felt a flicker of fear, real fear, across her skin. What had they done, the two of them?

CHRISTMAS AT WESTBANK Ranch was not normally a lavish affair. Or so it seemed when Martha dug through the attic hunting for decorations. It was time they got a tree up. *Surely* someone had once stored Christmas decorations up here. A grandmother, a great-aunt...?

With Anne's help, she found one ancient cardboard box that contained hand-painted glass baubles, mostly broken, and a bedraggled white porcelain treetop angel, with patchy hair and only one glass eye.

"That does it!" Martha got to her feet and clapped the dust from her hands. "We'll have to make a special trip into town to buy some decorations."

"Yay! Yippee!"

"I can see you two are really upset about that," she teased.

Anne smiled, the shy sweet smile Martha had come to know and love these past few weeks. Daisy, who'd been on the other side of the attic, twirled before them, holding up her skirts. "Look at me!" She wore a big navy blue hat with a tiny veil and a red-and-white-striped linen dress, floor-length on her.

Spook barked hopefully from the bottom of the ladder, as he'd done for the past half hour. Daisy had wanted him to come to the attic, too; Anne, with better judgment, had refused to carry him up. Of course, he wouldn't let Martha anywhere near him.

"What have you been into?"

Martha made her way to the other side of the attic, stepping carefully on the wide boards that spanned the ceiling joists. Anne was ahead of her. "All these dress-up clothes," Daisy said. "Look!" The little girl plunged both hands into a metal steamer trunk, a relatively new model, that stood open beside her. There were purses and silk scarves and shoes and skirts and even a fur jacket. Was it mink? Martha wasn't up on furs. Size eight, everything appeared to be.

Charlotte Mae.

Had these things belonged to her? Had Fraser stored them up here to be out of sight, out of mind?

"Let's get changed, girls," Martha said, glancing at her watch. "If we hurry, we can go into town and be back before supper."

The lure of town—each girl had twenty dollars to spend on Christmas gifts—was stronger than the lure of the mysterious trunk. Daisy tossed the clothes back in and Martha gently lowered the lid. She saw the handwritten label on top—Miss C. M. Racey and a San Francisco address. The sight of it chilled her heart. The feeling she'd had, many times, of a female presence besides hers and the girls' in this house, came back full force. Now, seeing all these clothes here...

She shook her head. *How perfectly ridiculous, Martha Virginia. Ghosts.* What would Gran Thomas say? "Vapors, lass, nothing but vapors"—she could hear her grandmother's abrupt dismissal now. Gran Thomas had had no patience for what she considered excessive female whimsy.

Gran Thomas. That made Martha think of her mother. Fraser had handed her a letter the day before that informed her of her mother's travel arrangements and that, yes, she was bringing Harry and mountains of gifts for everyone, including some decent coffee, which she was positive Martha couldn't get up there in God-Knows-Where, Wyoming. She sounded absolutely delighted to have been asked to share their Christmas celebrations. Martha was amazed. She'd really had no idea that her mother had even one tiny ribbon of sentimentality in her no-nonsense pragmatic Danish character, let alone a streak a yard wide.

Fraser had seemed…well, if not pleased with the news of the Christmas festivities Martha was planning, at least resigned to playing host. Martha had made it clear right from the beginning that she intended to make a big deal of Christmas and Santa. The girls' lives had been too grim and dreary for too long.

Fraser.

Martha's heart melted when she thought of him these days. The passion he brought to their bed at night more than made up for the distant self-contained man he was during the day. It was as though she'd married two men—a silent nighttime man who loved her deeply and passionately, and a reserved daytime man, always polite, who rarely touched her. Sometimes Martha longed for a word, a gesture that showed her he cared.

When it happened—such as that one afternoon in the barn or the evening he pulled her into his arms after she'd checked on the sleeping girls—it was always a surprise. He'd chanced upon her in the hall and kissed her so hungrily she nearly fainted. That time, he'd come close to taking her right there on the cold bare floorboards, before he'd smiled and said he was too damn old for that sort of thing and had gathered her into his arms and brought her to their bed.

Or the time he'd come back from an auction late one night—only a few days before—to find her at midnight still in the living room, knee-deep in paper, scissors and ribbon, wrapping up a few last gifts for the girls, things she'd ordered from a friend back in Wisconsin.

Fraser had made love to her in front of the roaring fire, surrounded by the domestic debris of her afternoon with the children—crushed paper lanterns and popcorn chains, plates of clumsily decorated sugar cookies, half-filled mugs of cold chocolate. She didn't think she could have dreamed up anything more romantic.

Afterward, snuggled against his chest, listening to the now familiar sound of his heart, Martha had felt a few fat tears leak through her closed lids. She was sure she'd never, ever had a happier moment. And then he'd turned to her and spoken, and she knew she'd been wrong.

"Martha," he'd said softly, stroking her hair. He looked so serious in the firelight. "I want to thank you for everything you're doing for the girls. For me. I..." He'd paused, then after an eternity, gone on, his voice rough, "I never dreamed you'd bring us so much joy."

Then she'd wept. And couldn't explain to her mystified husband exactly why she wept. Everything struck her that way these days. Everything was truer, crisper, more deeply felt. She didn't understand any of it; only that she was happy.

Happier than she'd ever thought possible.

CHAPTER FIFTEEN

WHISPERS AND MUTED giggles woke Martha Christmas morning. For a few moments she just lay there, as she often did in the morning, reveling in the sensation of Fraser's large warm body next to hers. His right arm was outflung, his face turned toward hers, unshaven, relaxed and handsome. Still, apparently, sound asleep. For a long moment she studied the face of the man she'd married, then feeling warm and happy inside, she slipped out of bed and pulled on her robe. Then she tiptoed out to see what all the giggling was about.

Anne and Daisy were huddled near the tree. One of them had plugged in the lights, and the sight that greeted Martha took her breath away. The girls in their pajamas, slipperless, hair awry, and their sweet shining faces—Martha thought she'd never seen anything so truly moving.

"Did Santa really bring us all this?" Daisy whispered, hugging her tattered kangaroo to her side, eyes big and round.

Martha nodded. "I guess so," she whispered back. She took a comb from the pocket of her robe and went to work on the worst of Daisy's tangles. "Let's make you all pretty before Grandma and Harry get up,'' she said, smiling.

Anne grinned and made a hesitant gesture toward the gift-laden tree. ''For us?'' Martha nodded again.

''Can we open up one of *these?*'' Daisy asked in a wondering voice, touching one of the gaily wrapped packages. Martha's eyes filled. She was remembering the excitement of her own childhood Christmases—and how she'd wished for a brother or sister to share it with.

''Can we?'' Daisy asked again.

''Why not?'' came the quiet gruff voice from the doorway.

''Fraser!'' Both girls rushed over to grab him by the hands and pull him into the room. Fraser looked sheepishly at Martha. ''Hated to miss all the fun,'' he said with a slow smile. Martha felt her heart turn over. He was wearing a dark plaid robe and—she was quite sure—not much else.

''Okay. One gift before the others get up,'' Martha said, and sat down to watch the girls. Santa had brought Anne a complete illustrated set of the *Anne* books, which she regarded with awe. For Daisy, there was a beautiful doll with long brown hair and socks and shoes and a dress that could come off—which it promptly did—and there was even a doll-size pajama set and a tiny brush and comb to go with it. Martha noticed that the kangaroo was quickly put to one side while Daisy examined her new doll in minute detail.

''For me?'' Martha asked foolishly as Fraser handed her a wrapped gift she hadn't noticed under the tree the night before.

''For you,'' he said with a smile Martha felt all the way to her toes.

It was an exquisitely carved leather box. Inside, resting on dark blue velvet, was a single shiny horseshoe nail. *Mercredi*. A precious memento of the day he'd given her the mare, the day her marriage had really begun.

''Oh, Fraser!'' Martha felt tears close to the surface. He reached over and pulled her into his arms.

''Like it?'' he murmured. ''I'm afraid I'm not too good at this stuff.''

''It's perfect,'' she breathed, and grew bold enough to kiss him right in front of the girls, both of whom giggled.

Martha gave him her gift then, a pair of fur-lined leather driving gloves that she'd had a friend in Wisconsin send her. Luckily they fit perfectly. Martha blushed when he returned her gesture and kissed her boldly. This time, to her dismay, both girls clapped their hands and shouted, ''Yay!''

Which must have roused her mother and Harry, who came in smiling a few minutes later. After Martha managed to convince everyone that they should wait till she put on a pot of coffee, they got down to the serious business of unwrapping the remainder of the gifts. There was smoked salmon and Starbucks coffee beans from Harry, matching sweaters and caps for the girls from her mother, more toys and oodles of other things, including more books for Anne and more doll clothes for Daisy, clothes that miraculously fit her new doll perfectly.

Harry turned out to be sleek, silver-haired and an

occasional pipe smoker. He was also a successful semiretired real-estate broker, five or six years younger than Martha's mother, and deeply in love. That was clear to anyone who spent any time in the same room with the two of them.

Her mother, Martha discovered later, had no intention of doing anything about it.

"Marriage! Whatever for, darling?" she said later that morning, helping prepare the goose she'd always insisted go along with the turkey. It was a Danish custom, and she'd followed it for as long as Martha could remember. "I was married for thirty-seven years to a dear and decent man who provided me with enough to live on, thank goodness. I've made a few good investments. I work two days a week at the library. I golf. I play bridge whenever I want to. Do I need to start cleaning some man's toilets again at my age?" Ullie Thomas was seventy-one.

"Don't get me wrong, dear. Marriage is great for you young people when you've got a family to worry about. Those two sweet girls." She patted Martha's hand and smiled. "And probably a dear little baby to take care of soon."

Martha smiled, too. *The sooner the better.* If her mother only knew. "But what about companionship, Mom? Don't you miss having someone around?"

"You mean sex, dear?" Ullie made a dismissive gesture. "Heavens, you can get all the sex you want without getting married, Martha. You should know that at your age."

"*Mother!*" Martha was glad the girls weren't in the kitchen with them.

Ullie looked at her daughter. "Honestly." She shook her head. "You young people are so old-fashioned sometimes. Where do you keep your skewers, Martha?" She pawed through drawers until Martha located them in a cupboard and handed them to her.

Martha felt so tired. She'd felt that way yesterday, too, She wasn't used to so much activity, she decided. The extra heat in the kitchen didn't help, either. With plans to cook both birds for Christmas dinner, Fraser had fired up the old wood-burning range, which they used in addition to the propane range.

Or perhaps it was the excitement. She'd even sneaked an afternoon nap the day before Christmas Eve, when Fraser had taken the girls to meet Harry and her mother at the Pine Ridge airport. She'd never napped in her life!

There were more Christmas visitors coming, besides Harry and her mother and Tom. Fraser had heard from a younger brother, one of the twins, who was planning to stop by in a few days on his way to a ski holiday with his girlfriend. The LeBlancs were arriving later this afternoon with some of their grandchildren, who'd been invited to join Daisy and Anne on the sleigh ride that Tom had promised as a Christmas gift. They were bringing their newest granddaughter, just three weeks old, to show off to the neighbors.

"I wonder when Fraser will be back," Martha mused aloud. He'd gone to check on the sheep and help Tom harness the horses before the LeBlancs arrived. The two women were readying a tray of sweets to serve with coffee later. Ullie had brought a supply of Martha's favorite homemade *brune kager,* the crisp brown clove-laced cookies Martha remembered from her own childhood Christmases.

"He's a wonderful man, Martha, your Fraser." Her mother's blue eyes were bright. "At your age…well, I thought you were married to your career. You're lucky some other woman hasn't snapped up a man like that by this time. Of course," she added, laughing, "he's lucky to get you!"

Then she shook her head again. "But I have to admit I thought it was too much to hope that you'd make me a grandmother one day. I'm glad it's all worked out for you, dear," she finished softly. "Since you lost your job and all."

Has it? Martha felt a deep pang. It was far too early to tell. "That's the doorbell, Mom," she said, wiping her hands on a kitchen towel. "I'll get it."

Probably the LeBlancs. Comfortable people to be with. But Martha was nervous about meeting Fraser's brother and his girlfriend later in the week. She'd face that when the time came. She felt she was on display. His family must have wondered at the speed with which she and Fraser had married. She was sure her own mother had. But her mother, thank goodness, had asked no questions.

As she expected, the LeBlancs had arrived.

"Here, you hold her," Birdie said, and thrust her newest grandchild at Martha. Martha took the baby, although there wasn't much baby to see, wrapped up as she was in quilted bunting bag and blanket.

"Hugh's right behind me," Birdie said, bending to unfasten her boots. "He's gettin' some stuff out of the trunk. And Verna and Patrick decided they'd go on the sleigh Tom's got rigged up.'' She glanced at Martha, eyes bright. ''The girls wanted them to go. Fraser's out there, too. I told Verna we'd keep an eye on the baby.''

''What a sweetie she is, aren't you?'' Martha cooed to the bundle in her arms. It hurt, it literally hurt, to have this tiny infant in her arms, knowing that soon— she hoped and prayed—she'd be holding her own child. Hers and Fraser's.

The baby waved one hand as Martha freed her from her cozy prison. She set the baby down on the sofa and gently untangled the blanket. Then she undid the zip on the bunting bag. The other tiny hand popped free, and the baby stared up at her, eyes wide, rosebud mouth pursed.

Martha felt her heart squeeze. Her mother came into the room and Martha introduced her to Birdie.

''Ah, your little granddaughter?'' Ullie smiled at Birdie, then the baby. ''What a darling!''

''Isn't she?'' Birdie leaned down to pull the baby's legs free of the bunting bag. Martha smiled helplessly. The baby wore red fuzzy sleepers with a candy cane stitched on each leg. Her little legs churned, and she waved her arms at them.

''She's beautiful,'' Martha said, stilling her speeding pulse. How could Fraser be so set against having a child of his own? Surely, when he saw a healthy happy baby like this… ''Is Verna nursing her?''

''Heavens yes,'' Birdie replied. ''She fed her just before we left, though, so she won't be hungry yet. I hope!'' She bent and made clucking noises at her granddaughter. "Will you, sweetie? Here." She picked up the baby and handed her to Martha again.

Martha took her carefully. "What's her name?"

"Elizabeth. They'll probably call her Betsy, Verna says."

The door opened. Hugh was there, his arms full of packages. And so was Fraser.

Martha thought her heart had stopped. The look on Fraser's face made her blood freeze. His eyes burned into hers, his face pale beneath the tan, his jaw grim.

"Here, Hugh," Fraser said quickly, his voice strangled. "Let me get those." He stooped to retrieve several packages Hugh had dropped. Birdie bustled over to help her husband, leaving Martha standing in the center of the room with the child in her arms. Fraser straightened, and again his eyes went straight to hers. She'd never seen such pain, such bleakness on a man's face.

"I—I thought you were out with the girls," Martha stammered. She had to say something—anything—to fill the dreadful silence.

"Tom had a full load."

Birdie glanced from Fraser to Martha, then stepped forward and scooped up the baby.

"Fraser!" she cried, apparently oblivious to the undertones in the room. "Look who's here. You haven't seen Verna and Patrick's latest, have you?" She thrust the child right under Fraser's nose. "Isn't she a doll?"

He stood back as though he'd been branded. His eyes were black with emotion. Anger, too. "She... she's great, Birdie."

Martha suddenly realized that Birdie would know

exactly what had happened with Fraser's first wife. Since she knew, why was she doing this?

"You take her, Fraser." Birdie handed him the baby. "There, just hold her like that for a minute. I'm going to help Hugh get these packages straightened out and stick some of them under the tree. You can help me, Ullie. We brought parcels for the kids, and some of my mincemeat tarts, although they're not so good this year as last, Hugh says. Umpteen things for the kids to play with…" She scurried around the room, arms loaded with packages.

Martha heard Birdie's voice through a haze, like wind rattling dead leaves in a storm. She couldn't take her eyes off Fraser. She thought he was going to be sick. He held the baby as though she were made of the most delicate crystal, as though she'd break if he dared to breathe. He wouldn't look at the child's face, and when he looked at Martha, his eyes were desperate. "Take her, Martha, dammit," he muttered, seemingly frozen in place. *"Take her!"*

Martha stepped forward and took the baby. She noticed his hands were shaking. With another oath, he turned on his heel and disappeared into the kitchen. She didn't dare follow.

She didn't have much time to think about what had happened. A few minutes later, Birdie took the baby from her with a quick shake of her head. "I thought he'd have changed since he married you, Martha," she said sadly. "I thought it'd be different now." She clucked and sent Martha's mother an enigmatic look, but didn't explain.

Refusing to be outdone in the grandmother department, Martha's mother cooed and fussed over the baby, too, until Verna returned twenty minutes later, rosy-cheeked and laughing from the sleigh ride. "Patrick's still out there with the kids. They're going to take another turn down to the road and back."

Half an hour later, all had returned, and Fraser quietly rejoined them. He said nothing, although Martha noticed he somehow managed to avoid whichever part of the room the baby was in—all the children wanted a turn holding her—and whenever Martha managed to catch his eye, his expression was bland.

Daisy and Anne opened the gifts the LeBlancs had brought, accompanied by squeals of excitement, at least from Daisy. Anne was quieter, but her shining face told Martha she was having a wonderful time. And when she stood at the kitchen counter making hot chocolate and Anne came up shyly and slipped an arm around her waist, resting her head gently, briefly, against her side, Martha felt her own heart spill over with joy. All of this—*everything*—was worth it, just to see these children's happy faces, after what they'd been through.

Later Martha sat by the fire and sipped her cup of tea. The trays of sandwiches and sweets they'd set out earlier had largely disappeared, and Verna had gathered up the plates and the children's sticky hot-chocolate mugs and joined Ullie in the kitchen to wash up. Patrick leafed through a stock magazine beside his youngest daughter, who lay on the sofa. From time to time he glanced at her and smiled and said something Martha couldn't hear. The baby's legs kicked vigorously in response to her father's words.

Anne was curled up in the window seat, curtain half-drawn for privacy, nose buried in one of her new books. Tom and Hugh traded lazy insults over a game of cribbage, and Martha could hear the faint sporadic "Fifteen two, fifteen four..." as though from a great distance.

This was so pleasant. She could smell the roasting turkey and goose, and the pungent scent of the crackling wood fire. She closed her eyes and leaned against the brick of the fireplace, hands clasped around one knee. The velvet of her new skirt felt warm and soft. Thank goodness her Sears order had arrived just before Christmas, or she wouldn't have had a thing to wear.

She opened her eyes. There was Harry, frowning in the easy chair in the corner as he drew on an unlit pipe and perused the old copy of the *Los Angeles Times* he'd brought with him. Two of the smallest LeBlancs lay on their backs, whispering, heads under the Christmas tree, which, Martha noted approvingly, had turned out better than expected, considering their limited resources. Even the battered angel looked positively angelic beaming down at them all from the top of the tree.

She gazed slowly around the rest of the room. Fraser was lying on his back near the tree, pretending to ignore the efforts of Daisy and Jenny to tie him up with discarded ribbon from the gifts they'd just opened. They were enraptured, giggling and panting as they tried to secure a floppy arm here, a large wool-stockinged foot there.

By sheer chance, Martha happened to catch Fraser's

amused glance. Suddenly she felt as though she was seeing everything in the room from the wrong end of a telescope. She felt the blood drain from her face. Her fingers tightened around the handle of her cup so much they hurt.

She loved Fraser. She was in love with him. This was all there was, really—family and love and laughter. This was what she'd dreamed of, and it had been in front of her nose all this time. A man worth loving, dear children who needed her, friends, good neighbors... A charming woman she was only beginning to get to know again, her own mother. After all this time.

Dazed, she realized Fraser was watching her. He frowned, his dark eyes concerned. Her heart melted with the knowledge she'd just received. *She loved her husband, Fraser McKenna. It wasn't part of the bargain—in fact, it went specifically against the bargain—but it had happened.* With a small gesture she let him know she was fine. Yes, she'd be all right. In a minute.

But would she? Would she ever be all right again?

That night Fraser made love to her with an intensity that nearly frightened her. Afterward, lying in his arms, she felt a desperate need to express what was in her heart.

She knew he wasn't asleep, but simply held her quietly. She knew he was thinking, as she was, too, of the baby they'd both held that day. She wished he'd say something so that she would have the opportunity to tell him she understood his pain.

But did she? Could anyone really feel another's

pain? Wasn't it one of the worst forms of arrogance to think so?

Still, if she couldn't tell him she loved him, she wanted to comfort him somehow, let him know that what he thought and felt mattered to her. She wanted to give him back something of what he'd given her since she'd been here, make him understand that she supported him, no matter what. But he wasn't a man who would allow it. He wasn't a man who would admit he needed that comfort. Not from her, not from anyone.

She realized it was impossible now to tell him she loved him. They'd ensured that with their bargain, sealed in law; she'd ensured it by spelling out her terms, that he must give her a child of her own.

But it was equally impossible not to tell him. She had to find the way.

Two weeks after Christmas, Martha flew to Wisconsin to tie up loose ends and bring back some of her clothes and the personal possessions she wanted to keep. The trip, she'd decided, marked her commitment to the future, the letting go of the bits and pieces that held her to the past.

Besides, she needed time to think.

Fraser and Anne drove her and Daisy to the small airport in Pine Ridge. They were changing in Cheyenne, and then going on to Madison, where Martha planned to stay with the friend who had her cat, Mr. Herbert. Daisy was excited, dressed all in green, a new coat and hat and leggings Martha had bought her for

the trip. Anne was philosophical about being left behind since she had to go to school.

On the way, Fraser filled Martha in briefly about
the trip he'd made to government offices in Rock
Springs three days before. Thanks to Anne's boom
box in the back seat, the children couldn't hear what
they had to discuss. Fraser and she had agreed it was
better not to get the girls' hopes up until the adoption
looked pretty secure.

Martha nodded but wondered if she'd remember
what he was saying.

"A meeting on the twenty-third? For us both?" she
asked nervously.

He gave her a long amused look. "The third, Martha," he said. "Of February."

"Okay, okay." Martha checked in her handbag for
the tenth time to make sure her and Daisy's tickets
were there. They were, just as they'd been the other
nine times. Why was she so rattled? She knew. She
was going to miss Anne. She was even going to miss
Spook.

And she was going to miss Fraser. She didn't know
if she'd be able to get to sleep alone in a bed anymore.
They'd made love nearly every night since they'd
been married. She'd grown used to knowing she could
reach out in the dark and find him there beside her
always. It was nerve-racking how a person's life could
change so much in such a short time.

At the airport, she tried to keep her mind on the
details. Did she have a snack in her bag for Daisy?
What about motion-sickness tablets?

Then they were at airport security.

Martha kissed Anne, who shrugged, slightly embarrassed. "Bye," she said nonchalantly, then promptly reburied her nose in the new *Archie* comic she'd bought.

"Hey, you!" Fraser scooped up Daisy, who flung her arms around his neck. "Take care of Martha, darlin'," he said, grinning at Martha over Daisy's shoulder and winking. "I think she could use some looking after. She's getting pretty forgetful these days."

"I will, Fraser," Daisy promised, blue eyes round and serious. "Don't you worry one little bit."

"Well, bye for now," Martha said hesitantly when Fraser put Daisy down. She felt absolutely foolish. Should she offer him her gloved hand? A formal goodbye to the man who knew her naked body more completely, more intimately, than any man ever had, ever would?

"So long, Martha." Fraser took a step forward and crushed her in his arms.

"Oh!" she gasped. His mouth met hers, hard, demanding, and oh-so-utterly delicious. For a few wonderful seconds she allowed herself to forget all her worries, to allow her senses to swim in the familiarity, the wonder.

Then he held her away from him, his dark gaze drifting admiringly over her face. Her very pink-cheeked face, she was certain. "For now," he repeated. Quietly, gruffly.

She nodded. "Yes."

"You're coming back," he said. It wasn't a question.

She nodded again, biting her lip. "Of course I am," she said, barely trusting her voice.

Then they were gone, the tall man guiding the black-haired girl who turned pages as she walked. And not long afterward, she and Daisy were buckled into seat belts and watching the snowy peaks and wind-swept fields recede beneath them.

Daisy colored happily in a book the flight attendant had given her, humming to herself. Martha kept her gaze on the window, the darkening sky, the fluffy gold-tinged clouds.

How could she do this to the man she loved? How could she put him through the hell of remembering, every single day for nine long months, what had happened before, to Charlotte? She realized now that he'd never even said if the baby had been a boy or a girl. That chest in the attic—he'd tried in every way to forget.

Did it matter so much anymore what *she* wanted? When she had Daisy to love, and Anne? When she knew beyond a scrap of doubt that she was in love with a man she'd married more or less by accident? That he was the husband she'd dreamed of? Even if he didn't love her now—and she knew he didn't—it wasn't impossible that he might learn to love her sometime in the future. It could happen; there was a chance.

For if Martha had even a shred of doubt in her mind as to how deep and real Fraser's pain was, it had vanished when she'd seen him hold little Betsy. She'd seen the horror he couldn't hide, the long-buried grief...

In the glass, Martha saw the slash of reflected tears on her cheeks. She knew she wouldn't be able to stop them even if she tried.

She had to release Fraser. She had to let go of her own dream. She had to let it go, so that a larger dream might have a chance to be born.

CHAPTER SIXTEEN

THIS WAS SOMETHING he had to do himself.

With Martha and Daisy arriving tomorrow—*coming home,* something inside him kept saying, *coming home*—with Anne still at school and Birdie finally gone after the thorough cleaning she'd insisted on doing before Martha's return, there was no putting it off any longer.

Fraser pushed back his chair with a scrape and deposited his mug in the kitchen sink. Then, jaw set, he moved toward the back staircase that led to the attic.

Topaz. She'd always worn it, even here in the backwoods of Wyoming. Wisps of her perfume came to him the instant he opened the trunk he'd wrestled up here the day after he'd come home from the hospital alone. He'd never opened it before now, had only wanted it out of his sight. He'd been afraid of the secrets it might hide, of the life she'd had that she'd never shown him. Nor had he wanted to know then.

Now he did. Now he wanted to make the fresh start that he knew Martha was making by going back to Madison. Put the past behind him, too. He owed it to Martha and to the girls. He owed it to the future they just might be able to patch together for themselves. It was ironic, really. The family he'd never wanted—an out-of-work Wisconsin tourist passing through and a couple of orphans. That family now seemed to mean more to him each day.

Life was crazy. There was no figuring it out.

You're afraid you'll find letters—to Weston, to some other lover. You're afraid you'll find out why she came up here on the run, pregnant and alone. Needing you.

She needed me, yes, Fraser told himself grimly, staring at the contents of the trunk but not touching anything. *But she loved me, too. And I loved her. And it wasn't her lover's child that killed her—it was mine.*

Why, there was nothing but clothes in here. Fraser gathered up a handful, wincing at the memories kindled by the perfume. The clothes themselves meant nothing to him. These were city clothes he'd seldom seen her wear. And hats! Heck, he'd never even seen her wear a hat. Not this kind, anyway. Idly he twirled one on his thumb. It was of finest palest Panama weave with a navy blue ribbon band. He let it fall back into the chest and sat down heavily on a dusty wooden chair with the back spindles missing.

He looked around, at the long rusty nails poking through the lumber sheathing of the roof, at the cobwebby beams, at the batts of fiberglass insulation that had been added between the floor joists—he remembered the year his father had decided to insulate the place. He'd been about sixteen, and had helped wrestle the scratchy pink bales up into the attic.

There was his grandmother's dressmaker's dummy. Someone had propped an old hat at a rakish angle on the headless neck. At first he almost smiled, then he shuddered and turned away.

There were piles of his father's leather-bound books, old ledgers that went back to before Will McKenna's time, to the days of his grandfather, Fraser—for whom he'd been named—and his great-grandfather, John, who'd settled the land. He hadn't remembered the ledgers were here. Sometime he ought to take a few down and have a look through them. Might be interesting to see what the price of oats was back then, or what a fellow could get for a hundredweight of grass-fed beef.

All around him were bits and pieces, scrapings of the lives that had gone on under this roof. His grandmother's curtains in a dusty pile under the eaves. No doubt full of spiders' nests and mouse tunnels by now. He remembered the roses on them. Cabbage roses, his mother had called them. She'd hated them and had taken them down as soon as there was spare money for new fabric and put up some of her own choosing. Some kind of scenic thing, as he recalled, that hadn't seemed a great improvement at the time.

Of course, he reflected, it wasn't that one set of curtains was really any better than the other, just that they were his mother's choice. She'd wanted to make her mark on the place. Did Martha feel the same way now that she was living here? Under this roof? Charlotte hadn't seemed to care and hadn't done much beyond a coat of paint here and a few new bits of furniture there, although he'd told her she could do what she wanted.

Suddenly Fraser felt lighter, easier in his mind.

He'd come up here with the idea that he'd drag Charlotte's chest downstairs and load it onto his pickup and take it to the Goodwill store in Pine Ridge. Get rid of it once and for all.

But now, looking around him, he realized that it might as well stay here. After all, it was only a pile of old clothes. Perhaps Daisy and Anne might like to play with the hats and shoes. They could have anything else they wanted up here, too. There wasn't much. Mostly junk.

Fraser bent to toss some of the clothes onto the floor. There were others, carefully folded, under the top layer. Then a shoe box, tied with a ribbon, which he lifted slowly. He felt his heart quicken, then stop. *Letters.*

He opened the box. There were envelopes inside, carefully slit open, the whole lot tied up with other ribbons. He replaced the lid of the shoe box, his heart pounding. He retied the ribbon around the box, fumbling in his haste, and thrust it back down into the depths of the chest.

That was Charlotte Mae. That was private. It wasn't for him. His first impulse, to take the box down and burn it in the kitchen stove, passed. That kind of violent aggressive action didn't mean a thing. Rubbing out any personal trace of the woman he'd married didn't take away the fact that he'd lost her. That she'd died and left him behind with his grief. And his guilt. He couldn't erase that. He could only accept it and hope that his new life with Martha and the girls would help push the memory from his mind.

He rummaged in the bottom of the chest. There was

another package there, a wide flat box, fairly heavy. Cautiously Fraser pulled out the box, then set it on his knee and opened the heavy pasteboard top.

It was filled to the brim with carefully folded baby clothes. Little white cotton shirts, leggings, and tiny knitted sweaters. A satin-edged blanket. Fraser felt the sweat run down his sides, although, if anything, it was chilly in the attic. He fought the image that sprang to his mind, of a miniature dusky blue thing with legs, arms and tiny perfect ears. He fought the roaring in his head and won.

She'd never told him she'd been collecting these things. *You never asked,* a voice inside him said. She'd been preparing for the birth of a child that never came. Perhaps, the thought struck him, she'd gathered these clothes for the first one, the one she'd lost, the one she'd wept for at night for so many months when she thought he was asleep.

Perhaps.

He'd never know. He replaced the lid and put her box gently back on the floor of the chest. He replaced the clothing, the shoes, the hats, the scarves that still whispered her scent. He refastened the metal catches on the trunk, took a deep breath and stood.

He was going to leave everything just as he'd found it. These few scraps that marked Charlotte's life were going to stay here, just as his grandmother's curtains remained, just as his father's ledgers and old-fashioned riding boots remained. Nothing was going to change. Maybe someday he'd come back and deal with those letters; maybe the contents weren't something the girls should accidentally discover. Maybe. He'd decide another time.

For now, all he wanted to think about was Martha. Martha Virginia. The woman he'd married just over a month ago. The honey brown of her hair, so shiny, the fresh scent of her skin, the way she felt in his arms—willing, eager…alive.

Martha and the girls.

Martha coming home.

"I'VE CHANGED MY MIND, Fraser."

Fraser stared at her. Her face was pale, but her voice was determined. He'd noticed since he'd picked them up from the airport this afternoon that Martha seemed quieter than usual, preoccupied. All he'd wanted to do when he'd seen her get off the plane was bring her home and make love to her. It frightened him—the intensity of what he'd felt, the desire. The sheer overwhelming lust he felt for her body. She'd bewitched him. It had taken her absence to make him realize just how completely.

But when he'd reached for her hand at the ranch, she'd smiled and busied herself with the children—and that bad-tempered excuse for a cat she'd brought back—and said she had something she wanted to discuss with him after the children were in bed. Something important.

That was all right with him. It was foolish even to think she might have missed him—physically—as much as he'd missed her.

Still, her words, her serious expression…

Something inside him chilled. "You haven't

changed your mind, Martha? About staying here with…us." He'd nearly said, "with me."

"No!" She looked surprised. "Of course not. I wouldn't dream of changing my mind about that. I love the girls. I want this adoption to work out as much as you do."

"Okay." He even managed a slight grin. "So what have you changed your mind about?"

"About our agreement." Her eyes were very round. She was nervous; her fingers pleated and repleated the edge of her T-shirt. "About my part of it, that is."

He frowned. What was she getting at?

She stared at him for a long time. "I don't want to have a baby anymore," she burst out. "That's what I'm trying to say."

Fraser couldn't believe his ears. And he hated himself for the relief he felt, for the crazy surge of joy. Surely to God she didn't mean it…

"I've thought it over, and I—" She bit her lip, which Fraser suddenly realized was trembling, and he wanted to step forward and take her in his arms. "I guess I didn't realize just how much you hated the idea, *really* hated it, until I saw you with Verna and Patrick's baby. At Christmas."

She took a deep breath, and he saw how hard this was, how painful she found it. He cursed himself silently for the relief he felt at the sacrifice of her dream. A dream, she'd told him, that meant everything to her. A dream that was why she'd become tangled up in this backward, mixed-up, crazy marriage in the first place.

"Look, I don't think you should be too hasty about

this, Martha,'' he began lamely, hating himself for the lie. ''Heck, I've had a chance to get used to the idea over the past while and—''

''That's not true,'' she broke in fiercely. ''I saw you that day. I saw how much it hurt you to touch that baby, little Betsy, and I—I just thought I'd die if I thought for a minute you might feel the same way about our baby, if we had one. And I decided, well, considering my age and all and the fact that I feel like Anne and Daisy are nearly my daughters now, my family—''

He moved toward her and caught her in his arms. ''Martha.'' Her body felt so good against his. *That she would do this for him!* He wanted to touch her and kiss her and carry her upstairs to their bed and make sweet love to her all night long. He didn't want to hear her words, or the pain behind them. He didn't want to think that he'd traded his pain for hers. ''You don't have to do this. I swear to God you don't.'' He paused. *How could he say that? How could he stand here and lie to her? What kind of an excuse for a man was he?*

''Yes, I do, Fraser,'' she said. ''I've made up my mind. And as soon as I can get an appointment with the doctor, I'm going to go into Pine Ridge and take care of...of birth control or whatever.''

He couldn't stand it any longer. He leaned over and covered her mouth with his. He didn't love her, but he could treat her the way a fine caring woman deserved to be treated. He could do his best to make her life here happy, make the rest of her dreams come true.

He felt her arms tighten around his neck and felt her relax in his arms as she kissed him back. Her mouth tasted so clean and sweet and good. How he'd missed her! He felt his body stir and relished the tiny moan she made deep in her throat when he rocked gently against her hips. He held her tight against him, savoring the feel of her body. Her small breasts—were they fuller, lusher than he'd remembered?—pressed softly against the thin cotton of his shirt. He wanted to rip his clothes off, rip hers off, take her right here on the kitchen floor, the way he'd wanted to one other time. So long ago. When she'd accused him of not knowing what was in his own heart.

Perhaps she'd been right. Perhaps if she'd never confronted him, he would never have found the courage to do the right thing by Brenda's girls. Then he'd have been a lonely man in a lonely house tonight, instead of a man for whom suddenly everything seemed to be going right. But at what price? he thought with a stab of guilt.

Martha pulled back. "Fraser—"

"I've missed you, Martha," he muttered, tasting the soft skin of her throat. "I've missed you so much." Instead of that lonely man he'd been, he was a new husband, about to take his wife up to the privacy of their bedroom. About to do all the things a man longed to do with his wife.

"We can't...we can't do this," she whispered. Her face was pink.

"Do what, Martha?" He couldn't resist teasing her.

"You know, make love."

"Why not?" He nibbled at an earlobe, his blood surging at her shiver of response.

"Because, well— Fraser!" She pushed at his chest and he allowed her to look up at him. "We can't take any chances, now that I've made up my mind."

"I see." He smiled. "I think I could rustle up something in the bottom of a drawer somewhere. For now."

"Oh!" She blushed again as she caught his meaning. Her eyes shone as he lifted her in his arms.

"Any more objections?" He grinned down into her flustered face.

She wrapped her arms around his neck and reached up to kiss him on the side of his jaw. He growled his response and she laughed. "I can't think of a single one."

THIS WASN'T LOVE. But it was enough. In fact, it was all he wanted anymore. At his age, at his time in life.

To touch her and watch her eyes darken. To strip the clothing from her body, piece by piece, to kiss and taste every inch of her skin. To be barely able to restrain himself as she did the same, as she pulled off his shirt, as she unbuckled his belt. To put his hand on her breast boldly, to draw the soft flesh into his mouth and to feel her tense beneath him as the pleasure of it shot through her body.

Pleasure he brought her.

To hear her gasp and whisper his name and to sink deeper, deeper into her body. To feel her welcome him, draw him ever closer. To have her cling to him and cry out as he brought her the same endless boundless pleasure she brought him. To feel the greatness of his sheer physical power over her, tempered by the richness of his feelings, his need to give her everything it was possible to give. Physically.

That was enough.

And to feel his body tense, then arch to find—always, unerringly—the kind of exquisite agonizing release he'd never felt with any woman before. *Ever*. That was his secret.

And to know that she chose to be here with him this way, freely, that he need never be alone again.

It was enough.

IT SHOULDN'T HAVE BEEN this easy, Martha thought, impatiently flipping the pages of an old *People* magazine in the doctor's office three days later. The decision felt right—when she clamped down on the terrible dismay that occasionally welled up when she thought of never having a child of her own. Not now.

But then she'd think of the man she'd married and how badly she wanted this marriage to work. She thought of the fire she'd seen in his eyes when he'd met them at the airport, and the joy she felt when he touched her, when they made love. She remembered how she'd noticed the moment she'd walked into their bedroom that the silver-framed photograph of Charlotte was gone from the place where it had always stood. Hope had leapt in her heart.

She loved him more than she'd ever thought possible—and she knew she'd done the right thing. No matter how much it hurt now, in the end, it *was* the right decision.

This way, they had a chance. The other way…well, perhaps eventually Fraser's pain would prove too much. When the bloom wore off their physical relationship—if it ever did—perhaps he'd resent her or, worse, their child. She had Anne and Daisy, she reminded herself for the thousandth time. Her children of the heart. Her ready-made family. And she'd had two weeks already to get used to the idea that she'd never give birth herself.

"Mrs. McKenna?"

Martha stood.

"The doctor will see you now."

The doctor was a woman in her fifties, with a friendly smile and iron gray hair. She was matter-of-fact about Martha's request and asked her a few straightforward questions about her medical background and family situation.

"You've discussed it with your husband?"

"Oh, yes," Martha said. "We've decided to, uh—" somehow, despite everything, she couldn't bear to state the utter finality of her decision "—wait a while. We've only been married a couple of months."

"I see. There's your age to consider, of course." The doctor raised one eyebrow.

"Yes, I know," Martha blurted. *Wasn't that what had gotten her into this in the first place, the fact that she was thirty-five and had no time to waste?* "We know we can't afford to put it off too long," she added. Not exactly true, but did it matter?

"Okay. When did you have your last period?"

My God. Martha thought back—when *had* she had

her last period? She might have known the doctor would ask. "Gosh," she said nervously, smiling. "This is so dumb. I can't really remember, but I don't think it was that long ago..."

"Maybe we'd better do a test before we get you set up with anything."

"Fine," Martha readily agreed. She'd always been careless at keeping track of her dates—there wasn't much point to it most of the time, was there? And she was quite sure she'd had some sort of period just after Christmas. She mentioned it to the doctor.

"Well, you're probably right. But it wouldn't hurt just to make sure."

Martha had a few nervous moments while she waited after providing the doctor with a sample. But it was crazy to worry. Mentally she ticked off some of the other symptoms of pregnancy. Besides missing a period, what were they?

The doctor came back into the room and Martha automatically stood.

"Sit down, Mrs. McKenna," the doctor said cheerfully, patting her arm.

"Congratulations. You're pregnant."

CHAPTER SEVENTEEN

PREGNANT!

Martha practically fell off her chair. "But…but what about…?"

"The period you thought you had? It's quite common. Many women have a little monthly spotting throughout their entire pregnancies." The doctor paused and gave her a serious look. "Is this unwelcome news, Mrs. McKenna?"

"Unwelcome?" Martha felt dazed. As though she'd been on a roller coaster that had suddenly stopped dead at the top of the track. Any minute now, the world would swoop out from beneath her again. "No. No," she repeated, her voice embarrassingly weepy. "It's *wonderful* news!"

"Good," the doctor said bluntly. "Now, let's check your blood pressure and get you undressed so we can do a proper examination."

An hour later, after a stop for coffee, which Martha felt she needed desperately but which she changed at the last moment to some rather insipid herbal tea, figuring it was better for the baby, she was on her way back to Westbank Ranch.

The baby! She had a tiny precious baby growing

inside her, Fraser's baby, this very minute, this very second.

My God, what was she going to tell him? He'd think she'd known all along. But she hadn't, she swore to God she hadn't. How could she have known that the tiredness she'd been feeling, the sensitive breasts, were early symptoms of pregnancy? She'd never been pregnant before. Dr. Pictou thought she was about six weeks along. That would mean she'd conceived shortly after their marriage. Maybe even that first time, the night Fraser had come back from Utah and come to her bed in the middle of the night. The night he'd apologized for his rotten behavior on their so-called honeymoon and sworn he'd make it up to her. Martha felt her cheeks warm as she remembered.

He'd made it up to her all right. He'd given her a baby. Martha's fingers gripped the steering wheel even tighter. One minute she wanted to stop the Bronco and dance around in the snow, shouting her joy to the crows in the frozen treetops; the next she wanted to pull off the highway and burst into tears.

Dear God in heaven, what was Fraser going to say?

SHE FOUND HIM in the barn. He'd been helping Tom and one of the hands nail together the hinged wooden panels they used for portable lambing pens. Fraser had told her that a few lambs would arrive as early as mid-February, although most were born in March and April.

He watched her walk toward the area where they were working. Her heart banged in her chest. He looked so tall, so handsome. *This man was the father of her baby.* She hoped her face wouldn't give her away.

"Fraser?"

He stepped toward the railing. Did he guess? His eyes were narrowed, his face serious. But no more serious than usual.

"Problem?"

She licked her lips. "I need to speak to you. Privately."

His eyes flared briefly, then he looked away and set down the hammer he carried, calmly balancing it on the top rail of the pen. "Sure."

"Where's Daisy?" Anne, she knew, was still in school.

"She's playing down by the east door with the kittens. She's..." His voice trailed off. "Martha. Is something wrong?"

She couldn't meet his eyes; didn't dare. "No, nothing's wrong. But I need to talk to you."

"I'll tell Tom." He gestured toward the back of the barn. "Why don't you go and say hello to Mercredi? I'll be there in a couple of minutes."

Martha hurried down the wide aisle that separated two rows of box stalls. The mare greeted her with a friendly nicker. Usually, Martha remembered to bring a carrot or a piece of apple when she came to the barn. Mercredi nuzzled her pockets.

"Sorry, sweetheart," Martha said, shocked to realize how shaky her voice was. "Nothing today." She stroked the animal's glossy neck and suddenly found herself on the verge of tears. *Stop this,* she said to herself fiercely. *Stop this sniveling, for Pete's sake.*

"Martha." Fraser opened the door of the stall and walked inside. "What happened? You okay? What did the doctor say?" His eyes raked her face.

Martha stared up at him. "She said I was pregnant." She bit her lip to stop the trembling. He'd gone pale under his tan, and his eyes... Dear God, she never wanted to see his eyes look like that again.

"I'm going to have a baby, Fraser," she repeated weakly. He still said nothing. Why didn't he say something?

Finally, after a silence that seemed to last an eternity, he spoke. "How far along?"

"About six weeks, the doctor thought."

"Six weeks," he repeated heavily.

Suddenly he slammed his fist into the wall of the stall. Martha screamed. The mare half reared and snorted, her nostrils distended, her eyes glowing eerily in the dim light.

He hit the side of the stall again and swore violently. Then he went to the mare and ran his hand down her neck and withers and muttered to her in a low tone, calming her. His back was to Martha.

"Fraser." She stepped closer to him, needing to touch him. She could feel the pain and anger oozing from his body. Before she could touch him, he whirled.

He lunged forward and grabbed her arm so hard it hurt, right through her jacket. "You should be happy," he bit out, eyes blazing.

"I am." She lifted her chin. Why shouldn't she be? And he knew she wanted a baby; had always wanted a baby.

"Why did you tell me you'd changed your mind the other day? All that song and dance about being too old, about having the girls for a family. You must have known—"

"I *had* changed my mind. I didn't know I was pregnant. I had no idea. It was a total shock to me."

He laughed, a curt derisive laugh, and let go of her arm. "Sure. There's usually a sign or two that goes along with the condition, sweetheart."

"*You* probably know more about it than me!" she snapped, not caring how much she hurt him. "*I've* never been pregnant before."

She'd hurt him all right; his face was ashen. Martha bitterly regretted her outburst. Of course this was a terrible shock to him. It had been a shock to her, but at least a welcome shock. Still, he must have known it was a possibility. A good possibility, considering how often they'd made love.

"I'm sorry, Fraser," she whispered. "I shouldn't have said that. I know you don't—" she could hardly bring herself to say it "—want this baby."

He moved closer and grabbed her again, this time by the shoulders. "You're right. I *don't* want this baby." His eyes, black as midnight, devoured her. She couldn't have looked away if her life had depended on it. "But there is something I *do* want." His voice made her shiver. *"You!"*

He clamped his mouth on hers so hard she tasted blood. She pushed at his chest, but it was like iron, and so was his grip on her shoulders. He lowered one arm to her waist and hauled her roughly against him. He smelled of hard work and the barn. He hadn't

shaved this morning and his beard scraped her skin.
She twisted and clawed at his shirt, pummeled the
broad width of his back with her fist, what she could
reach. It was no use; he was far stronger than she. She
was angry, but she wasn't afraid.

Then he shifted and she was up against the rough-
hewn boards of the stall, his body hard on hers, his
mouth seeking, punishing. Somehow she understood
that he had to do this—that she was the enemy. That
the life she carried inside her, a life he'd had as much
to do with creating as she had, had robbed him of
something he'd never thought he would ever have to
lose again.

She didn't know what it was; she didn't know what
made him the way he was deep down where it
counted. Perhaps she'd never know. She didn't care.
She only knew she loved him. She only knew that
they had to get beyond this. That if they didn't, they
were doomed.

Fraser's hands tore at her clothing and she shuddered. She heard his faint curse as he stumbled, tried
to maintain his balance with her in his arms, then fell.
She landed on him heavily and he rolled her over,
pinning her beneath him. Then he was on her and her
head was pressed into the straw and she discovered
she was kissing him back. Her hands, which had
fought him, now twined around his neck and her body
arched into his.

They were in a heap on the soft straw along one
side of the box stall. She could barely breathe. Fraser's
mouth was hungry on hers, probing, demanding. With
one hand he opened her jacket and swept her blouse

aside—she heard buttons rip—to expose one breast to the cold winter air. He abandoned her mouth then to move to her breast, his mouth hot and hungry.

"My God, Fraser," she gasped. Her face was wet with tears she hadn't realized had spilled over. She pushed at him weakly. "What in the world do you think you're doing?"

He didn't answer; simply covered her mouth with his again, as much to shut her up, she was sure, as to kiss her. He'd managed to slide one hand under the waistband of her jeans, and she felt his callused palm against her bare skin, his searching fingers, felt him pull her against him, so that she could feel his unmistakable arousal.

Then, as abruptly as he'd begun his assault, he stopped. He lay absolutely still for a moment. Groaning, he raised his head and rolled off her. The mare stretched down a long muzzle to sniff tentatively at them, and Martha thought she'd scream. The sudden stupid comedy of the situation almost overwhelmed her. But she knew if she started to laugh she'd never stop.

"God, Martha." Fraser flicked a piece of hay from her hair. They stared at each other. "I'm sorry."

Martha heard the sound of their breathing coming quick and hard together in the relative quiet of the stall. Mercredi reached to snatch a mouthful from her hay rack, losing interest. In the distance Martha heard male laughter and the ring of hammers on wood and metal as Tom and the hand continued their work.

Fraser ran one finger down her face, tracing the curve of her cheek, then her jaw to her earlobe. His fingers were gentle as they slipped beneath the hair at her nape. She shivered violently. "I—I didn't mean to hurt you."

She nodded. She didn't trust herself to speak. Not yet.

He got up and crossed to the door of the stall. Then he leaned against the wooden upright for a long time, his back to her. She watched him, fumbling blindly to rearrange her clothing. She barely dared to breathe.

"Dammit, Martha," he said without turning. "I don't want to hurt you." Finally he turned toward her and raised one hand briefly, then let it fall to his side.

"It's just that..." He stopped, and Martha wasn't sure he'd go on. When he did, his voice was bleak. "I never told you, but somewhere in the back of my mind I always remembered that it took over three years before Charlotte got pregnant the second time." He glanced at her, then away. "I thought maybe it was my fault, that maybe you wouldn't get pregnant at all."

She was bewildered. "Why'd you...? Our agreement..."

"Because I'm a coward, Martha," he said savagely. "*A coward!* I wanted what you could do for me." He turned away. "And, God help me, I wanted you."

Something began to glow and burn deep in Martha's soul. He'd *never* said he wanted her, not like that.

"I wanted you," he repeated simply, looking down the dark aisle of the barn, away from her. "Nothing's changed. I still want you." His words echoed in her head. *I want you, I want you.*

Then he turned again and took a step toward her. He smiled, a smile that broke her heart.

"Hell, it's just that..." His voice was rough with emotion. "I guess I figured it'd just be the two of us for a while longer. Just me, just you." He moved closer and offered her his hand. She took it and he helped her to her feet.

"I know this is what you want, Martha." He reached up to pluck another wisp of hay from her hair, his eyes dark with pain.

She smiled weakly through her tears. "I do." Her voice trembled. "Oh God, Fraser...I do."

"I know, I know." He smoothed a tangle of hair from her face. "I wish I could say I'm happy for you. For your sake. I can try to convince myself I am—" he took a deep breath "—but they're just words. I can't feel it, Martha. I just can't feel it."

HE WAS A SECOND SON. He'd never been first, or biggest or strongest.

But he always knew his time would come. And he thought it had when Charlotte came back from California and wanted to marry him.

She'd carried another man's baby deep in her belly, but it hadn't mattered. He'd wanted her too much to care. Her child would be his. But then later he'd lost her, and the child of his own flesh. Of his own making.

Now he was in the process of adopting someone else's children. Two girls. And Martha only wanted him for what he could give her.

Sometimes, in his dreams, he wished he'd be first. Just once.

IT COULD HAVE BEEN worse; at least he didn't love her.

That was what Fraser told himself through February, when he did the work of three men, anything to keep from spending time in the house. That was what he told himself while he and Martha attended seemingly endless interviews with state authorities regarding the adoption. On his more cynical days, he wondered what all the fuss was about. He knew the state authorities were enormously relieved that someone wanted to take the girls off their hands. Foster homes were hard enough to come by, and no one wanted to adopt two half-grown half-wild Wind River Mountain sisters.

Of course no bureaucrat would admit as much, and Fraser resigned himself to going through all the usual hoops. But he wished there was one thing in his life he knew he could count on. Possibly April, they'd said at the end of February, after they'd made contact with Brenda's sole surviving relative, her sister in Alabama. That gave Fraser a turn for a few moments; then he remembered the letter. No way Louise was going to put up any fuss. Nothing that cold hard cash couldn't take care of, anyway.

He'd stopped sleeping with Martha when he realized that it was impossible to lie there beside her in the same bed and not touch her. But he just didn't *feel* the same, and he couldn't pretend. The fact that he knew she had a baby growing inside her killed his desire as quickly as it arose. Even though Martha said he was being silly and the specialist they'd gone to in Rock Springs for a consultation in early March had told him the same, it didn't matter. He couldn't put aside the idea that if he made love with her, he might hurt her baby. That he might cause something terrible to happen to Martha's baby, just as had happened to Charlotte's baby.

Martha's baby. Not his baby. Not his and Martha's. *Martha's* baby.

Sleeping in the same room with her—he'd moved in a cot—was killing him. Night after night he'd lie awake, listening to the soft sound of her breathing from the other side of the room, wishing he had the courage to go to her. Night after night he'd try to wrap his mind around what was happening—what *had* happened—without getting anywhere. He'd fathered another child, and now he had to live with that. He'd been stupid to pretend to himself that she might not conceive. But now he'd fulfilled the letter of their bargain, hadn't he?

Yet, it could have been worse, he told himself over and over. At least he didn't love her.

March was busy with lambing, and April was even worse. Many long nights Fraser spent in the lambing pens with Tom and a couple of hired shepherds, helping bring hundreds of Westbank lambs into the world. Many times, as Fraser dabbed a ewe's nose with vanilla so she wouldn't be able to smell the orphan he was trying to get her to accept, or quickly skinned out a dead lamb so he could fasten the hide to another orphan to try to fool the mother with her own lamb's scent, he'd think about just what he was trying to get a handle on.

Motherhood. Mothering ability was what he called

it in his purebreds. Brenda sure as hell hadn't had it, and she'd had two kids. Martha seemed to have it in spades, and she'd never borne a child.

And it was during lambing season that Fraser realized how much he'd come to depend on Martha. She'd appear unexpectedly in the middle of the night with hot coffee and sandwiches for the tired crew when she should have been sleeping herself. He always chewed her out about it, but she simply smiled and disregarded him.

Once she even insisted on helping him with a delivery he'd nearly given up on. Obeying Tom's precise instructions, she'd managed to disentangle hooves and legs and noses with her much smaller hand and burst into tears when the ewe had then delivered healthy twins. Tom had cheered, the silly old fool.

Fraser had pulled her into his arms, his heart breaking for her, wishing he could help her, not hurt her the way he'd done. The way he kept doing. She didn't deserve to be saddled with a man like him. She deserved a whole man, a man who could share her joy, who would help make this the happy time of life it should be for her.

He wasn't that man. She'd had the plain bad luck to marry the wrong man.

Still, all through that spring, as her pregnancy began to show, as he saw the inevitable unfolding of new life before him, he thanked his lucky stars that he was on the outside looking in. At least he didn't love her.

Then, late in May, when the pussy willows had turned to tenderest green and the Canada geese had long flown north and the Blue was filled past its banks with meltwater, Fraser realized that he was wrong, that his worst nightmare was yet before him.

It had just begun.

AFTER MUCH GOOD-NATURED grumbling, Anne had put down her book and gone off with Daisy and Spook to explore the ancient orchard below the house where their grandparents had lived. The old homestead was falling down already, the veranda rotted and the roof caved in and gaping. And Old Man Langston had only been dead four or five years.

Just went to show you, thought Fraser, stretching out under a ponderosa pine, what could happen if a man didn't keep a hold on things. Stay on top.

He was feeling good. He had a bellyful of cold herb-roasted chicken and potato salad and apple cider and Martha's oatmeal-and-raisin cookies. He was glad he'd gone along with Martha's suggestion yesterday that they come up to the old Langston place for a Sunday picnic. The girls had settled right down these past few months. The adoption looked like it was pretty well set to go through. His lamb crop this year was almost ten percent better than last year's, and he had some prime stock coming along ready for the summer fairs. No getting away from it, he was just about as content as a man in his particular situation could ever expect to be.

Then he glanced over at Martha.

She had just settled herself on a slight knoll at the base of another pine tree ten or twelve feet away and was smoothing down the fabric of her dress over her tucked-up knees. Some thin flower-sprigged kind of cloth. She smiled that secret smile he'd seen before when she thought no one was looking and then smoothed the fabric over the gentle hummock of her belly. Over and over, she ran the flat of her hand over her belly.

She was half-turned from him, watching the girls in the distance. She'd tied her hair up loosely with a blue scarf, an unutterably feminine look. He could hear Anne ordering Daisy to do something in the distance and Daisy's shrill reply and Spook barking a couple of times. Martha's smile became one of tenderness and love. Anne had climbed high into an ancient apple tree, and Fraser saw Martha frown. He sensed her slight tension. But she didn't call out; she didn't stop Anne from climbing so high.

Fraser turned away and closed his eyes against the stab he felt in his gut. It didn't help. Something inside him burned and crushed and plowed a path through him, right through his heart, right through his soul. The truth. A juggernaut. Unstoppable.

He was in love with this woman. He loved the woman who carried his child so close to her heart. His child.

Silently, not breathing, afraid of attracting her attention, Fraser lay back on the soft bed of old pine needles under the tree. He felt his spine connect with the solidity of the earth—a few inches of leaf mold beneath him and then the solid rock of the mountains. Right down to the center of the planet.

He stared up through the whorl of branches to the blue, blue sky above. Some of the branches were soft with new green growth, some were dead and twisted

and still clinging to the gnarled trunk, others were
swathed with the lichen they'd called old man's beard
as boys. Boys growing up on this land…

The Blue River McKenna boys. He and Wes and
the twins. And always a few cousins around. Where
was Weston now? At Christmas, Cullen had said he'd
had a postcard from Bangkok. And Jack? He hadn't
seen his baby brother, younger than Cullen by fifteen
minutes, for years.

Why hadn't he made the effort? Why had he let it
all slip away?

He turned his head slightly. Martha was quietly
folding the napkins she'd brought in the picnic basket,
cotton napkins she'd helped Anne sew. By chance she
looked at him and their glances caught and held.

Fraser forced himself not to look away. Every instinct told him to run. But he was through running.

Martha's eyes widened slightly. She must have seen
something of the war raging in him. He could feel the
sweat on his back, on his chest. He could feel the
blood roaring in his veins, thundering in his ears. Still,
he didn't turn away.

Martha smiled a little uncertainly and turned back
to watch the girls. Fraser closed his eyes again. He
reached deep, deeper into himself and found the pain
that had lived there for so many years. It didn't disappear, but at least now he could face it for what it
was.

After an eternity—which was probably no more
than a few moments—Fraser raised himself onto one
elbow. Then he sat for a moment with his forearms
balanced across his knees. At last he stood and slowly

walked toward Martha, and as she looked up, a question in her eyes, eyes that matched the sky above, he sat down beside her. Not touching, not at first. He felt his heart hammer in his throat. Did he have the courage to tell her?

"Martha," he began, his voice sounding hoarse and strained. He took her hand, then turned it over in his, studying it. It was so soft, so pale, the fingernails trimmed sensibly short. "Martha," he repeated.

"What is it, Fraser?" Her reply was no more than a whisper.

"I want to tell you that I…" He could get no further. He closed his eyes and swallowed. Then he opened his eyes and managed a sort of half smile. He didn't want to frighten her. With her hand in his, he placed their two hands together on her abdomen. Her eyes widened. Surprise, growing wonder…

"You want to touch the baby?"

"Yes." It was a lie, but he allowed her to take his hand then, to guide it. He felt the tiniest flutter against his palm and fought the instinct to pull his hand away, to run, to hide somewhere dark and safe and secret.

"Martha," he began again, when he could trust his voice, "I, uh…" Again everything inside him seized up. He cast about wildly, searching, searching…

"I want to come back to your bed, Martha," he said finally. "I want to hold you again and touch you. If you'll have me."

"Yes, Fraser," she said, her face suddenly wet with tears. With her free hand she reached up and put her palm against his face. She pulled him down to her and brought her lips softly to his. "Oh, *yes!*"

THAT NIGHT he came to her bed and took her in his arms and allowed himself to touch her. He stroked the smooth skin of her back and hips, kissed her everywhere, tasted her everywhere. He learned the new contours of her hard and swollen belly, the new lushness of her blue-veined breasts, the new softness of her hips and thighs. And when she begged him to come to her, he brought her pleasure every other way he knew, refusing the ultimate act.

He wanted to worship her, wanted to please her and pleasure her. And then he let her touch him, let her bring him the deep shuddering release he craved.

Later he held her close, not sleeping. He cradled her in his arms as she cradled their child in her body. He couldn't bear to close his eyes. He was afraid to sleep, afraid to waste one moment of this new awareness, this new feeling—his love for the woman who slept in his arms.

Afraid, too, of the demons that still walked in the dark.

CHAPTER EIGHTEEN

"FRASER...FRASER!"

Fraser straightened and tilted his head back to shade his eyes with the brim of his hat. Lord, it was hot! He wiped the sweat from his upper lip with his bare forearm and squinted into the sunshine. Who the hell was that?

He could see a puff of dust in the distance, too small for a vehicle. For a few seconds he thought he'd only imagined hearing someone call his name. He watched as the puff of dust got a little closer. Looked like one of the kids—on a bike.

And she was pedaling hell-for-leather.

Fraser suddenly felt cold despite the August heat. *Martha.* Something had gone wrong. Something had gone terribly wrong. And, goddammit, he'd practically begged her to move into town, where she'd be close to the hospital. Next week, she'd said. Always next week.

Fraser threw down his gloves and ran to the fence, quartering the distance between him and the girl. Anne. It had to be. Daisy couldn't pedal that fast, not over the rough dirt lane that led to the hay field.

Daisy. What if something had happened to her? Fraser cursed. He felt his heart squeeze. This was what happened when a man let himself feel again. *This was what love did to a person.*

"Fraser!"

"Anne!" He vaulted the fence and strode up to where she'd wobbled to a halt on the dusty track. *Careful, McKenna. Don't frighten her.* He stopped himself from grabbing her. "What's going on, darlin'?"

"Birdie sent me," Anne panted, her hand on her thin chest. Her eyes were bright, her face flushed.

"Birdie?" What was she doing down at the ranch?

"Yep." Anne's eyes were dancing. "You're supposed to come home right away. Birdie says."

He could have shaken the girl. "Why? What else did Birdie say?"

"It's Martha. She's having her baby."

Fraser's blood turned to ice in his veins. He grabbed Anne by the shoulders, hard. "What?" *Dear God, please let her be wrong. It was too early. Nearly a month too early.*

"Birdie says not to worry," Anne said, eyes wide. "C'mon, Fraser. Let's go. I don't want to miss seeing the new baby come out."

God almighty, I do, Fraser thought. *There's nothing on earth I want to see less.*

Why had he run to the fence? Stupidest damn move he'd made. Now he had to run back to get his pickup, parked in the field.

"Wait here," he ordered. Anne nodded.

The next few minutes passed in a haze. He wasn't sure exactly what he'd done, except he'd moved fast. He was in the pickup, his foot to the floor, Anne's bike bouncing around in the back and the girl clinging to the passenger seat. *Slow down, slow down.*

Fraser let his foot off the accelerator. No sense scaring the kid half to death. "When'd Birdie get there?"

"Martha phoned her. She said she was going to have the baby and she wanted Birdie."

"She call a doctor? An ambulance?"

"I don't know."

"Where's Daisy?"

"Daisy's home. She said she was going to see the new baby before I did, and it ain't fair, Fraser! Birdie made me come get you 'cause I'm oldest." Anne scowled. "It just ain't fair."

"Nobody's going to see the baby before you," Fraser said flatly. "Babies don't get born that fast." He hoped to God he was right. "She's going to have that baby in Pine Ridge," he said through gritted teeth. "I'm going to get her to the hospital if I have to drive a hundred miles an hour."

Anne started to wail. "You mean we ain't going to get to see the baby right away? Me *or* Daisy?"

"That's right." Fraser was trying hard not to think about Charlotte. But he couldn't help it. All he could see was Martha, her face superimposed on Charlotte's, weak, pleading, desperate. *And the baby…*

In a way, he was glad he had Anne in the truck with him. There was no telling what he'd've done if he'd been on his own. This way, at least he had to appear strong, for Anne's sake.

He rounded the last corner before the ranch house. He saw the Bronco sitting there. And Birdie's car. And an unfamiliar one, a red station wagon with North

Dakota plates. Fraser slammed on the brakes and leapt from the truck.

"Hey, what about me?"

"Hurry up," he yelled back, not even looking at the girl.

He had to see Martha. He had to hold her, had to tell her what was in his mind before it was too late. What was in his heart.

He burst through the screen door. "Where is she?"

"Hold on." Birdie grabbed his sleeve. "You're going to scare her if you go in there looking like some kind of crazy man."

"Where is she, Birdie?" He couldn't ask the question he wanted to ask. *"Where is she?"*

"She's in the bedroom—"

He tried to bolt for the room, but Birdie had him firmly by the sleeve.

"Sit down. I've made some tea for the doctor. You better have a cup before you go in."

Fraser sank into the chair Birdie led him to, then her words registered. "Doctor?"

"You know the people who bought the old Strummond place? Well, she's a doctor. Lucky she was home when I called, and she came right over."

"Birdie…" Fraser's voice was strangled. He half rose from his chair. He felt like he was going crazy. *Martha.* He had to see Martha.

"Where's the new baby?" Anne came in, trailed by Spook.

"There's no baby yet," Birdie said. "Here, you take this cookie tin, young lady, and you go be with your sister. She's in the living room. Git!" Birdie shooed the child from the kitchen and came back to put a steaming cup of tea on the table. She stirred in a heaping spoonful of sugar.

Fraser pushed it away. "I can't drink this." He put both his hands in front of his face. He felt his breath coming too quickly, his heart beating too fast. His body was drenched with sweat, and it wasn't from the work he'd been doing before Anne arrived.

You're scared, McKenna. You've never been so goddamn scared in your life.

"The ambulance is on the way, Fraser. Everything's under control."

He looked at her. Ambulance? "Dammit, Birdie, is she all right?" He could barely get the words out.

"Just a precaution. The two of them might need to be checked over at the hospital later. Depends what the doctor says."

Birdie patted his hand, and he saw her blink rapidly. "Martha's going to be fine, Fraser. She's strong and she's healthy and she's got a doctor with her. And I'm an old nurse, don't forget!" She paused, then added, "It isn't going to be like last time, Fraser."

"I love her, Birdie," he burst out. *"I love her!"*

"I know you do," she said softly.

Fraser stood suddenly, almost upsetting his chair. "I'd better go and see her." He ran his hands through his hair. "What do you think, Birdie? Should I?"

His neighbor smiled at him, her bright eyes blinking rapidly again. "Of course you should, Fraser. It's your baby, too."

His baby, too. Dear God, he'd done this to her. He was the one responsible for putting her through this.

He didn't give a damn about the baby. He wanted Martha to be all right. He took a deep breath and put his hand on the door that led to the hall. At that exact moment, he heard an angry piercing cry and Birdie made an odd little sound behind him.

He whirled to face her. *"What in hell's that noise?"*

She was beaming. "That's your baby, you idiot. That's your new son or daughter."

WHEN HE WALKED into the bedroom, all he could see was Martha. Pale cheeks streaked with tears. Smiling. Wordlessly she held out her arms when she saw him, and he went to her. He held her for an eternity, whispering things he couldn't even remember, kissing the top of her head, kissing her face, letting her weep into his shoulder. Why was she crying?

"Shh. It's all right sweetheart. Don't cry. It's all over now. You're fine."

"The baby?" she whispered.

"The baby's fine." *The baby?* Dear God! He looked around him wildly. He had a baby, he and Martha—

"Your son." Beaming, Birdie handed him a tiny bundle wrapped up in something that resembled a tablecloth. He took it, caught a glimpse of dark fathomless eyes, black hair pasted to a tiny skull smudged with traces of blood and what looked like too much suntan lotion, and passed the bundle to Martha.

Martha took the baby in her arms and smiled. Even with her face streaked with perspiration and her hair a mess, she'd never looked more beautiful to him. She bared her breast, and his son began to nurse lustily. *His son.*

"My God, Martha," he said, his voice full. He felt like he'd just gone twelve rounds with George Foreman in his prime. "That's ours, yours and mine?"

She laughed through her tears. "Isn't he beautiful? I want to call him William. After your father. William Fraser McKenna."

"William Fraser," he repeated foolishly, liking the sound of it. "That's fine." Then he stretched out one finger to the tiny baby in Martha's arms, and his son grabbed hold. Tight. Tiny wrinkled fingers with sharp translucent nails. Hanging on for dear life. Fraser felt his eyes fill with what could only be tears. *That's the way to do it, son. Hang on tight.*

He cleared his throat. "I love you, Martha," he said roughly. "Dammit, I love you."

"Oh, Fraser." Martha reached up with both hands. Tears streamed down her face. Birdie snatched up the protesting baby, muttering about foolish women and aggravating men.

"I don't care if it's part of the bargain or not—" he began, but she placed a finger over his mouth.

"I love you, too, Fraser. I've been afraid to tell you. I've been hoping… Oh, Fraser…" Anything else she'd been about to say was lost as he pulled her into his arms with a hoarse cry.

"Uh, excuse me," the doctor said a moment later, laughing. "Could we break it up, you two? Just for a minute?"

Fraser ignored her. He was kissing his wife. He had a lot of catching up to do.

THEY'D DONE EVERYTHING backward—first they found a family, then they got married, then they fell in love. But by God, they'd finally got it right.

Now they had a child of their own flesh and blood. *He had a second son.*

Fraser walked through the house with his son in his arms, the girls trailing behind, squabbling over who got to hold him next. Willow, they'd christened him immediately when they heard his name. Blossom, Daisy and, now, Willow. Fraser and Martha had shared a secret smile over the heads of the excited girls. They were expecting the final adoption papers any day. Then their crazy mixed-up family would be truly complete.

He was in a daze. He showed his new son every room of the old McKenna house, then stood for a few moments at the kitchen window, looking up at the mountains behind the ranch. Where Charlotte lay, and the child she'd wanted so much. *His first son.* He took a deep breath that pushed back what was left of the pain, maybe forever.

The ridge where he'd placed their ashes looked sun-baked and brilliant in the late-afternoon sunshine. He felt at peace for the first time in a very long time.

"Here, hand me that baby," Birdie said, taking William from him. He gave him up gladly. Now that he'd had a chance to meet his son, he wanted to be with his wife. By now the doctor would have finished with her.

"Time I gave him his first bath, although I don't know if Martha's got anything to put on him," Birdie muttered. Despite her usual no-nonsense manner, she hadn't stopped smiling once. "You girls can help me. Anne, you find a nice big towel we can wrap him in."

"Yay!" Both girls ran off to look for a towel.

Fraser paused at the narrow door that led to the attic above the kitchen, then opened it and climbed the dusty stairs. When he came back down, he set the box of baby clothes on the kitchen table. "Here," he said gruffly, "Maybe you can find what you need in here."

Then he went to find his wife.

EPILOGUE

"GRILLED CHEESE on brown and a glass of milk," Martha called to the man behind the counter. She smiled at Fraser across the scarred Formica tabletop and raised one eyebrow.

"A burger for me and a side of fries. Coffee." He leaned toward her and took her hands in his. "Martha, what are we doing in here?" he asked in a low voice. Martha had insisted they stop for lunch at this particular diner.

Anne was reading a novel in the next booth, at nearly fourteen appalled by the thought of sitting with her parents. Daisy was devotedly following William around as he explored the diner on his chubby legs.

They were on their way to Sheridan to take Anne to a summer music camp for two weeks. Then they were leaving Daisy and William with her mother and Harry, who'd rented a cabin for the summer near Cody. And after that, they were going for a holiday of their own. Just the two of them. Although what good was it going to be—Martha glanced down ruefully at her swollen waist—since Fraser was being as stubborn about making love with her during this pregnancy as he'd been the first time? Oh, well, she had two weeks to change his mind.

"This is where it all started, Fraser," she answered mysteriously, squeezing his hands.

"*What* started?"

"You and me. The girls." She smiled again. "I had lunch here and saw your ad in the paper."

"No kidding." He looked around in surprise.

Martha glanced around, too. The same TV blared in the corner, only there was a baseball game on, instead of hockey. The same bored man waited tables and apparently did the cooking. And there was still no sign of "Mom."

And Fraser's burger, when it came, was underdone—just the way he liked it, he said—and came with plenty of half-fried onions and ballpark mustard stuck to the bun.

But this time her grilled cheese came on brown.

"What's that smile all about?" Fraser asked with a grin. If anything, he looked younger, handsomer, even more wonderful than he had three years ago when she'd married him. That was what happiness could do to a person. Her happiness and his.

"Never mind," she said with another smile. "I don't think I could begin to explain it."

TO LASSO A LADY
Renee Roszel

CHAPTER ONE

THE tall stranger exploded through the entrance of the country store, accompanied by a wail of cold wind and battering snow. Even after he shoved the door shut behind him, a foreboding chill seemed to linger in the air.

His stance was rigid, waiting, somehow angry. His arms were poised away from his body, as though it were high noon in the Old West and he expected to have to shoot it out at any second.

Amy had enough problems and needed to decide what to do quickly, but she couldn't resist an urge to scan the man's face and see if it went with the tough-as-nails image of his Western gear. Even though the small grocery store was flooded with stark, fluorescent light, she was disappointed to find his features shaded by a black Stetson. Still, the bright lights provided a spectacular show. The melting snow along the shoulders of his split-hide rancher's jacket and wide-brimmed hat glittered and winked like washed diamonds.

Now this man, she mused without hesitation, *is a real guts-and-leather cattleman.* He wasn't one of the citified pretenders who frequented the Chicago cowboy bar where she'd been a cocktail waitress for the past four years. This man, in his scuffed boots and well-worn jeans, was the real thing, and her heart fluttered with feminine appreciation.

He yanked off his hat and slapped it impatiently against a leg. Amy followed the motion, noting jeans so close fitting she could see saddle muscles bulge and flex in his outer thighs. She had no idea where she'd heard that term—saddle muscles. Probably somebody at the bar had mentioned how you could tell a real cowboy from a fake. A real cowboy's thighs were overdeveloped from long hours in the saddle. She swallowed hard at the stimulating sight, unable to recall seeing a pair of male legs quite that nicely contoured—except maybe in Olympic events—especially considering this cowboy's thighs were swathed in a layer of denim.

When he plowed a gloved hand through his mane of black hair, her glance followed, and she was startled to discover his eyes were aimed her way.

His glare was bold, defiant, the flinty blue of the wintry sky outside. Before she could react to the hostility in his stare, he'd snapped his wide shoulders around and was intent on searching the throng restlessly milling in the store.

Most of the stranded bus passengers were lined up at the establishment's only pay phone, scrambling to make arrangements for emergency lodging or calling relatives to say they'd be delayed. Roads north and west had been closed by the Highway Patrol because of a snowstorm.

Amy heard the crunch of boots on the gritty wood floor and realized the cowboy was stalking off, ap-

parently having located his prey. She watched him
round a rack of paperback books, heading toward the
line of travelers gathered before the phone. He moved
with solid grace, a man in total control of himself and
his world. But she could tell he was reining in his
emotions with difficulty, for his square jaw was working, his nostrils flaring. She pitied the person who'd
put him in his rabid state.

Dragging her attention from him to her watch, she
nervously began to chew her lower lip. Ira was a half
hour late, and he'd left no message that he'd been
delayed. She wondered if Diablo Butte was affected
by the snowstorm and if she should try to get a room
at the local motel—if there was a local motel. Though
this western Wyoming community was called Big Elk,
the only thing that seemed very big about it was its
name. From the bus window, she'd seen no buildings
for miles except for this clapboard general store and
the gas station across the street.

She supposed it didn't really matter if Big Elk had
a motel. She was low on funds, with exactly seven
dollars and thirty-three cents in her purse. That wasn't
enough for a cheap room in a ghost town, let alone in
a tiny dot-on-the-map community jammed with pan-
icky people whose options were shrinking as a nearby
snowstorm held them hostage.

The bus driver had given the passengers the choice
of going back with him to Kemmerer to get a room
there, then resume their journeys when the storm
passed and the next bus came through. Or, if their
destinations allowed it, they could take a more south-
erly bus route out of Kemmerer. He'd said he'd wait

another thirty minutes for anybody who wanted to go back with him.

Amy didn't know if the bus company would charge for taking them back to Kemmerer, considering this was an emergency. Probably. The storm wasn't the bus line's fault. If they did, she couldn't afford it. Besides, this was *her* stop. Ira was to have picked her up here to take her on west to Diablo Butte, her new home where she planned to build a new life as a rancher's bride.

She peered at the fidgety people waiting for the phone, wishing she'd tried to call Ira earlier. From the number still lined up to make calls, it would be another half hour before she'd even get the chance.

She noticed the tall stranger again as he edged up beside a stack of soft-drink cases. Perched cross-legged atop the stack was one of the passengers who'd been on the bus with her. Amy didn't know the woman's name, but had found out quite a bit about her, even so. She'd occupied a seat directly behind Amy and had spent almost every waking minute since she'd gotten on the bus, bumming cigarettes and talking to anybody who'd listen about her budding career as an exotic dancer, and how she was on her way to fame and fortune in Hollywood.

Amy wondered what this lanky, tough-as-rawhide cowboy had in common with a woman whose nostril was pierced, whose bleached hair was cut so short she could be in the Marines—except for one blue ponytail protruding above her right temple. She was wearing a stretch, zebra-striped bodysuit, white patent leather boots and a fake-fur leopard coat. They were as unlikely a pair as Madonna and John Wayne. Amy wondered if the cowboy had a kinky streak and if he picked up women this way very often.

The Madonna look-alike blew smoke out her nose and shook her head, causing her blue ponytail to wag back and forth across one heavily made-up eye. The cowboy nodded and turned away, his hooded gaze sweeping the store again. *Well*, Amy reflected, *either the woman isn't into gorgeous cowboys, or he'd asked her some other kind of question*. She had a feeling, if he'd actually been trying to pick her up, she'd be walking out of the store clinging to his coat sleeve right now. Evidently she hadn't been his quarry after all.

Amy told herself the cowboy wasn't her business. She had to figure out what to do. Ira was probably on his way, but she really should call his ranch and make sure everything was okay. She only hoped it wasn't long distance, for that would eat up too much of her dwindling funds.

She didn't feel as though she ought to call him collect. That was a silly idea, she supposed, since Ira *was* her fiancé. Naturally, he'd accept her call without hesitation. And he was certainly wealthy enough.

She balled her hands, hesitating. She absolutely didn't want Ira to believe she was marrying him for his money. He'd admitted he'd had bad luck that way in the past. No. She wanted to prove to him she was sincere in her desire to be a rancher's wife, and that when she took the vows, they would be forever. And she wasn't his wife yet. Wouldn't be until Valentine's Day, three days from now.

Since that was the case, somehow even a collect call seemed grasping. She wanted to prove herself first. Show her earnest desire to make their marriage a solid, honorable partnership before she started accepting material things from him, even small things—like collect calls.

She glanced hopefully out the store's window, hoping she'd see her cheerful fiancé—a man in his late fifties, yet charmingly young at heart—ambling toward the door. Her hopes faded. All she saw beyond the dingy glass was snow and more snow, swirling and dancing in the late-afternoon gloom. *Well*, she mused unhappily, knowing she had little choice now, *there was always the chance that Diablo Butte was a local call—*

"You must be Miss Vale," came a deep observation at her back.

Startled to hear her name, especially spoken in such a churlish tone, she spun around. For one instant, she had the bizarre notion she was expected to apologize for who she was. *How crazy!* Clearly she needed sleep.

The first thing she registered was a black bandanna, tied below a deeply cleft chin. In a square-cut jaw, a muscle flexed furiously. The broad shoulders of a split-leather coat were familiar, and realization hit like a club. Her gaze shot upward, clashing with eyes that were deep blue and as angry as when he'd first entered—maybe more so. Amy couldn't understand what this furious cowboy might want with her.

"Why—why, yes, I'm Amy Vale," she said, her voice peculiarly weak.

The eyes flashed with some caustic emotion, but it was quickly squelched. With a half smile that was far from friendly, he said, "I've been sent to fetch you for Ira. He's snowbound."

Amy experienced a rush of disappointment, but wasn't really surprised. Her whole trip west had seemed to portend nothing but disaster, with rain and snow dogging the entire route. Though she'd tried to push the thought aside, that very fear had nagged at her since she'd arrived here and her fiancé was nowhere to be found. "Well..." She exhaled tiredly. "I—I appreciate your offer, but I couldn't accept, Mr.—Mr...."

He settled his Stetson on his head, adjusting the brim low on his brow as he looked around. "Where are your bags?" he asked, apparently not registering her refusal.

"Excuse me, but I said I couldn't accept—"

"I heard you." His belligerent gaze snagged hers again. "Lady, I don't like this any more than you do. But Ira asked me to pick you up, so I'm picking you up. It'll take us nearly an hour to get to my ranch headquarters, even if the snow doesn't get worse. So where are your bags?"

She heard a muffled "thunk" and became aware that she'd stumbled backward into a shelf of canned goods, knocking one off in her defensive retreat. She flattened herself against the display, gaping at him, utterly confused. He was towering there too closely, invading her space. His obvious animosity and threatening nearness alarmed her. Everything about him radiated dislike, even disgust. There was *nothing* mixed in that signal. This cowboy didn't like her. Not one bit.

Amy had been born and bred in the big city, and like any large municipality it could sometimes be heartless and unfeeling to a young woman trying to make it on her own. She'd deflected the unwelcome advances of her share of jerks over the years. But faced with the cold fury in this cowboy's eyes, it took her more than one attempt to find her voice. "I—I'm going to give you five seconds to back off, mister," she warned unevenly. "Or I'll—I'll scream."

A dark brow arched, and for a moment he examined her with mistrust. He peered around, and Amy guessed he was deciding that even as big as he was, he'd have trouble fighting off ten or twelve rescuers who were already in a bad mood.

Clearing his throat, he took a step away from her and crossed his arms over his chest. "Look, Miss Vale," he stated less curtly, apparently concluding that his "I'm the bull and this is my grassland" attitude wasn't going to work with her, "I'm not the neighborhood kidnapper. I have a ranch west of here, and Ira asked me to put you up for a few days until the roads open." He pursed his lips, clearly an attempt to bridle his temper. "I'm pleased to do it for him," he finished thinly.

She didn't relax. His cordial act wasn't fooling her, but she had no idea how to react. Screaming didn't seem quite right any longer.

"Now, ma'am," he drawled, placing a finger to the brim of his hat in a gesture that was more mocking than gentlemanly, "if you'll show me your bags, we have a long drive ahead of us. If that storm turns our way, we may have more than our share of problems getting home.''

She continued to eye him with suspicion. In her job, she'd seen lots of overbearing, manipulative types, but this guy was in a class by himself. Just because he *said* he wasn't the neighborhood kidnapper didn't mean a thing. ''Just a second.'' Having made her decision, she spun away. A few steps had her at the cash register where a paunchy, balding man in a green flannel shirt was grinning ear to ear, overdosing in delight at the flurry of junk-food and cigarette sales he was making to the stranded wayfarers. ''Excuse me, sir?'' She waved to get his attention over the dull roar of voices.

When he aimed his protuberant eyes her way, she gestured toward the cowboy. ''Do you know this person?''

The proprietor's glance swung to the tall, range-rugged man and back to Amy. ''Beau?'' he asked, looking puzzled. ''Sure.''

''Then he does own a ranch around here?''

The man's grin widened, displaying big white teeth that would have been more at home in a horse's mouth. ''I'd say so, miss. If ya call eight hundred thousand acres a ranch.''

She blinked at the size. She assumed the proprietor was being sarcastic, but, even if he wasn't, eight hundred thousand acres sounded big to her. Nevertheless, the vastness of a ranch wasn't exactly a character reference. ''Is he trustworthy?'' she asked, beginning to feel silly. It was clear this uncivil rancher was known in the community. And it was laughably apparent to anyone who cared to take a casual glance at him that he was gorgeous enough to have women falling all over themselves to give him whatever he might want. If he ever chose to be the slightest bit charming, he wouldn't need to resort to force. Still, his manner was so—so—menacing. It was better to be safe than sorry.

The storekeeper looked once more at the cowboy, who had ambled up beside her. She could detect his after-shave—wood smoke and pine. Nice.

With a guttural laugh, the proprietor rang up a couple of candy bars for another customer, then kidded, "I guess to answer your question, miss, I ain't never heard no complainin' about ol' Beau." He winked in the cowboy's direction. "Especially not no *women*."

Beau grunted, appearing more annoyed than amused by the good-old-boy compliment. "Miss Vale," he ground out, drawing her unenthusiastic gaze. She stiffened, hoping the heat in her cheeks didn't denote a blush, but afraid it did. She was embarrassed beyond words at what the proprietor had implied about this stranger and his prowess with the ladies. Her glance skittered across his handsome face, but she avoided his eyes, apprehensive that she'd see something more bothersome in their depths than anger—very probably amusement at her expense. "What?" she finally asked, studying her nails and noticing her hands were trembling. She jammed them into her parka pockets.

"We don't have time for games." His tone was grim. "As I said, I'm doing Ira a favor."

"Pretty reluctantly, I'd say."

"Very reluctantly, Miss Vale."

Disconcerted by his bluntness, she jerked to stare at him. He was observing her through shuttered eyes. "By the way, the name's Diablo. Beau Diablo."

She couldn't have been more shocked if he'd tossed a handful of sand in her face. "*You're* related to Ira?"

"Yeah." He worriedly scanned the plate-glass window as a burst of wind-driven snow battered the panes.

She was dumbfounded by the news. This man was nothing like the fun-loving, jovial gentleman she'd met in Chicago. Yet, even as different as the two were, surely Ira wouldn't entrust her with anyone dangerous. "Mr. Diablo, why didn't you tell me—"

"*Dammit!*" He shifted to pin her with a threatening stare. "Miss Vale, you have five seconds to show me your bags, or we're leaving without them."

As Amy huddled in the warm cab of Beau Diablo's pickup truck, she felt as though she'd been sentenced to an eternity in The-Purgatory-of-the-Perpetually-Angry-and-Silent. She had no idea how much time had passed since they'd left Big Elk, but she prayed the trip would soon be over. She was getting a cramp from pressing herself against her door.

She'd relegated herself to a small section of the truck cab for two deeply disturbing reasons. First, she preferred to put as much distance as she could between herself and her ill-tempered host. Secondly, Beau's wide shoulders rudely took up more than their share of space, and she had no intention of being thrown against him every time they hit a bad spot in the road.

Trying to calm her frazzled nerves, she stared out the side window at the passing scenery of rolling hills. They were glazed with several inches of snow, punctured occasionally by statuesque stands of firs and pines. The blowing flakes seemed more lovely, cleaner, out here in this primitive Wyoming splendor than they did from the window of her tiny apartment over the pawnshop in Chicago—or from Mary's sterile-smelling hospital room.

Poor, dear Mary. She forced back a growing depression. Her little sister was recovering from surgery—hopefully her last—and the convalescent home was very nice. As soon as Mary was well enough, and the bills were paid, she would join Amy and her new husband on Diablo Butte.

Mary was so courageous. Amy already missed her spunky smile. A melancholy sigh escaped her throat and she cast a sidelong glance at Beau, wondering if he'd heard. His intent expression didn't indicate that he had, so she shifted to look away.

She supposed she could scream, clutch her chest and collapse into a lump on the floorboards and he wouldn't react. In all the time since they'd left Big Elk, he'd said nothing, hardly moved. He'd just sat behind the wheel, staring into the gathering darkness, eyeing the gravel road between labored swipes of the windshield wipers. Every so often he flexed his gloved hands as though he were gripping the wheel too tightly and his fingers were cramping.

She heard the sounds again of leather clenching and

unclenching, and peered at his profile. He'd deposited his hat into the storage area behind the seat along with her suitcase, for he was too tall to wear it inside the truck's cab. His hair was slightly mussed. A wisp brushed his forehead, softening the frown that seemed to permanently reside there.

He had a strong face, she mused, with cheekbones straight out of the ''Bone Structures For The Rich and Famous'' catalogue. She scanned his eyes and wondered why she'd always thought of long, curling lashes to be the sole domain of high-fashion models. Beau Diablo proved that notion false, for his thick sweep of lashes in no way diminished the masculine allure of his face. And the five-o'clock shadow of dark whiskers along his tense jaw completed a sinfully handsome picture.

Life wasn't fair, she brooded. Why did such an arrogant, bossy man have to be so appealing? He didn't deserve to be, but he no doubt used his good looks to their full potential when it suited him—which clearly *wasn't* now.

Irritated by the turn of her thoughts, she shifted in her leather seat, restlessly smoothing her beige twill slacks. For the first time, she realized how wrinkled and dingy they looked after the two-day bus ride. Even worse, her tan parka was spotted with dark stains where one of her bus seatmates had sloshed coffee on her somewhere in the middle of Iowa.

Casting her companion a hesitant look, she fought an internal battle. The last thing she wanted to do was broach any subject at all, let alone ask him a favor. She knew she'd have to do it sooner or later, so with a deep breath she plunged. "Do—do you suppose I could wash some clothes while I'm staying at your place?"

Barely turning his head, he flicked her an aggravated look but didn't speak.

Exasperated, she rolled her eyes toward the roof of the truck. "Look, Mr. Diablo, I suppose it's your business what sort of manners you cultivate—or *don't* cultivate. And if being a disagreeable pain in the neck works for you, it's none of my business. But I think Ira would at least expect you to be *civil*."

He surprised her with a chuckle, though it was the most bitter excuse for laughter she'd ever heard. "Miss Vale, Ira expects me to keep you from freezing to death. That's all."

She bounced around to glower at him. "If you hate the idea of a houseguest so much, why didn't you say *no*?"

He pursed his lips, then to her surprise, actually glanced her way, his gaze raking her face. "Because he threatened me."

"Oh, right," she scoffed, picturing her kindly, middle-aged fiancé threatening this powerful young stud. "What did Ira threaten to do? *Shoot* you?"

"No." He turned back to maneuver around a curve in the slick road. "Visit me."

Amy was taken off guard by his wry answer. She knew it was a ludicrous reaction, but she almost smiled. "Very funny." She snapped away to watch the wipers dispose of accumulating snow. "Okay, I may not be the brightest person in the world, but I can tell that you and Ira aren't close. What are you, some sort of distant, black-sheep cousin or something?''

He flexed his fingers, a sure indicator the question bothered him. ''Not exactly.''

When he didn't reveal more, she glared his way, determined to get a straight answer out of him, or die trying. ''Please, don't make it easy for me. I've got nothing better to do. I'll just *guess*. Let's see, you're a cattle-rustling nephew?'' Pretending to be deep in thought, she shook her head. ''No—no, it's coming to me. Could you be his dipsomaniac uncle? No. That's not quite right. Let me think....'' She tapped her cheek as though this was an earth-shattering dilemma she was bound to solve. ''I have it. You're his transsexual *sister*-in-law!'' She eyed him narrowly. She could keep up this foolishness if he could, darn him. ''Nope. Nope. Nope,'' she babbled on, ''now that I see your earlobes up close, I'll bet you're his demented half brother out on bail for the ax murder of—''

''I'm his son, Miss Vale.''

He'd spoken so quietly she wasn't sure she'd heard right. For a long minute, all she could do was stare at his forbidding profile. Finally, she managed, ''You're his *what*?''

The truck slowed as he braked. When they came to a stop, he faced her. Resting one arm on the back of his seat, he leaned across the console, looming very close, too close. Though his bracing scent beckoned, his eyes were as hard and cutting as steel. ''We're home—*Mom*.'' Scorn twisted his lips. ''What's for dinner?''

CHAPTER TWO

THERE was nothing physically threatening about Beau's closeness, but somewhere deep inside herself, Amy grew fearful. Something she couldn't even guess at seemed suddenly very wrong.

Though his revelation about being Ira's son shook her, she managed to scramble from the truck before he could open her door for her. She had no intention of causing him one more second of inconvenience than she already had. But she was too late to get her suitcase; he'd grabbed it up when he retrieved his Stetson.

As he came around the truck, he planted his hat on his head. His rough-cut features were solemn yet extremely engaging—too engaging for a future stepson. She forced her glance away and focused on the house. Snow was drifting down around them and dusk had fallen, but the brass lantern lighting the porch gave her a muted view of his rustic and rambling home. Made of logs and set picturesquely amid a copse of snow-mantled hemlocks, it was more enchanting than she'd imagined a remote ranch house could be.

The roof was gabled with deep overhangs. A wide porch was supported by heavy columns of whole tree trunks, bark and all, making the house seem to blend magically with the towering evergreens that embraced it. Amid the falling snow and haloed porch light, the place had an unexpectedly warm appeal, paradoxical considering the coldness of the man who owned it.

There was a grip at her elbow, and Amy came out of her trance, allowing herself to be towed along a meandering stone path, then up three steps to the long porch. "I'll leave you with Cookie," he muttered over the hollow thud of his boots on the wood planking. Swinging open the rough-hewn door, he deposited her suitcase in the entry. "Go on in," he said, as a tall, thin woman in jeans, boots and bright wool shirt hurried along a side hall toward them.

"I'll take her from here, boss." The woman smiled and waved, as though she knew he was in a hurry. "She'll be fine. Don't you worry."

Before Amy knew what was happening, the woman had scooped up her hand. "Come along, honey." She grinned. "I figure you'll want to clean up and change before you eat. So I won't waste no time with prattle, now. We'll talk later, over stew and biscuits."

Amy didn't know what she'd expected, but it certainly hadn't been anyone quite so friendly and breezy. "Why—thank you. I do feel pretty grubby."

The woman laughed, a croaking, happy sound. "You look as fine as them mail-order catalogue gals, but I know how traveling can tucker a body out. We'll take care of that in no time." She squeezed Amy's hand. "I'm Cookie. I pretty much take care of Mr. Beau's house. You'll meet Archie, my mister. Best cook in the state—to hear him tell it." She croaked out another splintery chuckle. "He does fry up the best mountain oysters in the state, if I do say so. But don't never let him hear I said it. He's hard enough to live with as it is, the ol' coot.''

Amy had no idea what mountain oysters might be, but the woman was chattering nonstop, giving her no opening to ask. Besides, Western dishes were the least of her worries right now. She stared at the animated woman beside her, gray hair pulled up in an untidy knot. Her face was long, nut brown and seamed from wind and sun. The creases around her small violet eyes and thin lips hinted at a perpetually sunny disposition, and she wondered at how difficult that must be, working for Mr. Picklepuss.

They'd walked through the entry hall and descended two steps into the living room where a massive stone fireplace dominated. She swept her gaze around in awe, noting rough beams and rafters, earth tones and furnishings hewn straight from the forest.

As Cookie chitchatted about what a shame it was the bad weather had stranded Ira on Diablo Butte, they exited the living room and went along a hall where a striking Navajo blanket dominated the log wall. After a right turn, Cookie announced, ''Here's your room, hon.'' She deposited the suitcase by the door, and the sound it made scraping the cottonwood planks was the first time Amy realized the woman had picked it up. Embarrassed, she said, ''Oh, I'm sorry. I didn't think about my bag.''

Cookie appeared puzzled. ''Your bag?''

She indicated her suitcase. ''I—I didn't mean to make work for you.''

Cookie's laughter rang out again. ''Hon...'' She

shook that head full of flyaway gray. "Takin' care of houseguests is my job." She stepped back from the room's entrance and nodded toward an interior door. "That there's the bathroom. It opens on the hallway, too, so take care to lock that outside door if you don't want no surprise company." She put a hand on the doorknob. "Now you get in there and take a relaxing bath. Supper'll be ready for you when you're ready for it."

The door clicked shut and Cookie was gone. Amy scanned her surroundings—homespun and service-able. The bed's headboard was ingeniously simple, fashioned out of three curved branches. On the far side of the bed was a modest writing desk, and the chair that sat beside it was formed with more branches, the seat and back covered with cowhide.

The window curtains were of coarse linen, match-ing the bedspread, and throw rugs were woven from colorful rags. A knotty, peeled stump served as a bed-side table, and the reading lamp was fashioned from an old-time wagon-wheel hub.

This place was a far cry from the steel-and-Plexiglas world of Chicago. Yet, even as sparsely dec-orated as Beau's home was, it had a dignity and strength, a sense of self, that was all its own. She was impressed—*completely against her will*—since it so obviously reflected the distinctive taste and indepen-dent spirit of her antisocial host. And since he was so unimpressed by her, she had no desire to be impressed by anything about him.

Amy looked up from her book, thinking she'd heard someone enter the living room. Apprehension tingled

along her spine when she realized it was her host. His
hair, damp from a shower, glimmered in the fire's
flicker and she noticed that same unruly wisp that had
been out of place in the pickup was trailing across his
forehead, giving the false image that he was nonchalant and friendly.

She wondered if he did that on purpose to attract
unsuspecting women into a night of wild debauchery
before they really got to *know* him, or if his hair was
as obstinate as he was, and he couldn't quite control
it. She smiled inwardly, hoping that was it. She'd like
to think this ill-tempered cattleman didn't have control
over *something* in his world, and that, maybe, he lived
every day of his life tromping around in coiffure hell.

His footfalls resounded as he crossed the polished
floor, but grew muffled on the massive Southwestern
rug that anchored the seating area before the hearth.
Amy swallowed nervously, wondering if he was going
to take a seat beside her on the couch.

He passed by without a glance, picking up a fireplace poker and nudging the burning logs into height-
ened frenzy. When he ran his fingers through his damp
mane, sweeping the wayward lock into place, Amy's
buoyant mood vanished. So much for her wicked fantasy life.

She opened her mouth to speak, but couldn't seem
to find her voice. She swallowed several times, wondering at herself. Why was she so nervous? He turned
away to pull a log from an arched alcove in the stone
wall, and she surreptitiously scanned him, wondering
why his every move drew her interest. He had a rotten

disposition and a hateful attitude, and he didn't deserve one second of her attention.

His damp hair gleamed in the firelight, and she grew irritated at how attractive he looked in the flame's glow. He'd cleaned up and changed into fresh clothes. The bulky white turtleneck he was wearing only served to accent the thickness and breadth of his shoulders. His jeans were freshly creased, yet every bit as snug against his thighs as those he'd worn earlier. His boots were different, too. Polished and light tan, they looked as soft as glove leather. She bet they were custom-made and more comfortable than the furry slippers she was wearing.

She hadn't heard him come into the house, and was startled to find him joining her at this late hour. She knew it was after ten, for the mantel clock had chimed a few moments ago. Of course, it was *his* living room. He had every right to enjoy his own fire any time he pleased. She should have stayed in her room if she'd wanted to dodge his company. Unfortunately for her, the scent of wood smoke had beckoned so strongly she'd weakened and come in to curl up on the thick, slubby cushions of the pine couch.

After a delicious dinner of elk stew, she'd spent a peaceful couple of hours before the fire, reading the book she'd brought with her. She had to admit, Beau Diablo's home was an absolute dream, with all the warm, honey-golden wood—until *he* walked into a room with that ever-present anger in his eyes and turned it into a smoldering nightmare.

He hadn't seemed surprised to find her here, but didn't smile in greeting when their eyes met. She was getting used to that glower by now so she tried not to let it get under her skin. For the past couple of hours, she'd tried to convince herself that her host wasn't such a bad guy. Both Cookie and Archie seemed quite fond of the man. So she reaffirmed her vow to give him the benefit of the doubt. Maybe he didn't dislike her at all. Quite possibly he had a really bad hangnail that was making him cranky, or he'd just been informed he was being audited by the IRS. Everybody had bad days. She'd probably met him at an unfortunate time, that was all. She would try to hold on to that thought no matter how hard he glowered at her.

After replacing the poker beside the other fireplace tools, he took a seat in one of the matching, rust-colored armchairs that sprawled on the opposite side of a unique coffee table. Amy had admired it when she'd come into the room. Constructed of twisted, fossilized wood supporting a square slab of thick glass, it was more like artwork than mere furniture. She'd thought the table had been enormous, but when Beau stretched out his lanky legs, crossing his ankles beneath the glass, the massive barrier seemed puny.

"Evening," he said minimally as he settled in, his darkly sensuous gaze roving over her.

"Good evening." She smiled, trying to mean it. For some reason, his piercing stare made her feel under-dressed, though that was ridiculous. She was perfectly respectable in her navy, velour warm-up. She was proud of the outfit, as a matter of fact. Nobody would ever be able to tell she'd bought it for practically nothing at a secondhand store, for she'd mended the rip in the leg so carefully it wasn't detectable. She had nothing to be ashamed of. Still, as he perused her from the tips of her fuzzy slippers to her straight hair, freshly washed and pulled back in a loose ponytail, she felt as though she should run to her room and put on a coat.

When she realized he wasn't going to say anything more, she pondered what she should do. He turned away to glare into the fire, making it clear he wasn't in the mood for idle chatter, so she tried to go back to her reading. After five minutes of scanning the same sentence, she was frustrated to discover she had no idea what it said. *Where was her mind?*

The fire crackled and popped, a restful sound that should have eased her nervousness. It wasn't working. She didn't have any idea she'd slid her glance back to Beau's face until she became conscious of the fact that he was watching her. With a surge of discomfort, she decided she had to try to chip away at his bad mood. She'd always had a knack of coaxing people into a smile. Maybe Mr. Diablo just needed to get his mind off whatever was bothering him. She cleared her throat. "You have a lovely home."

Fixing an elbow on one knotty chair arm, he rested his chin on a fist. His frown didn't waver and he didn't respond.

She fidgeted, unprepared for such rudeness. In her job, she'd dealt with bad manners and knew there were a few people in the world who were terminally uncivilized, and there was little that could be done about them. Still, she decided not to give up quite yet. After all, she was his houseguest. "Oh, thank you, Amy," she quipped, as though he were responding to her comment. "I built it all by myself. I'm such a *manly* man." She spread her arms as if to show off the room. "I didn't chop down these trees, you know. I chewed them with my strong, manly teeth!"

He cocked his head, squinting slightly. She couldn't tell if he thought she'd gone insane and he should call a mental hospital, or if he'd found what she'd said barely entertaining. Whatever he might have thought, he made no comment.

With a rankled sigh, she decided Mr. Diablo might be one of those terminally rude people. Readjusting her book, she tried to read again. The words blurred, seemed somehow foreign and unintelligible. She started a paragraph several times, but it was no good. Her mind was simply not on reading.

The fire hissed and snapped and the wood smoke invaded her senses like a kindly old friend. Inhaling deeply to compose herself, she caught another scent. It was subtle, a clean smell. She breathed it in, trying to guess what it was. After a second deep sniff, she decided it must be Beau's fresh-from-the-shower scent. Wincing, she rubbed her eyes. She didn't need this.

He was so quiet for so long, she couldn't stand it. As far as she could tell, she had three choices. She could either try again to engage him in conversation, leap up and scream "Are you trying to drive me crazy?"—or simply leave. The idea of leaving seemed best, but she didn't think rudeness on her part would solve anything. With a heartening inhale, she opted to try one last time to draw him into civil communication. After all, even beasts of the jungles and forests had been domesticated over the centuries. Why not this glowering brute?

She met those stormy eyes with reluctance. "I— I've been reading about Wyoming," she began, trying for a topic she hoped might spark his interest. "And I was surprised to read that the first women's suffrage legislation was passed here in 1869, and that Wyoming had the first woman governor in the United States." She paused to take a breath, praying he'd respond.

His gaze went on impaling her. "Uh…" She cast about mentally to find anything to fill the awkward breach. "The Equality State, right? I mean—that's what Wyoming's called. Sounds like this is a great place for women." She tried to maintain a pleasant facade, but her mind was shrieking, *Apparently, boorish stinkers are in the minority in Wyoming! Just my luck I'd be stuck with one!*

His eyes narrowed suspiciously, as though he was reading her thoughts, but he didn't speak. Aggravated, she eyed heaven. "I'm impressed, Amy," she chirped, answering for him again. "Did you read all that on the bus? You've got quite a strong constitution. I usually get carsick and barf when I try to read on a bus." She uncurled from the couch, sitting forward as though in animated conversation. "How enchanting, Mr. Diablo. I had no idea you were a bus-barfer. And people say you're not a sparkling conversationalist."

He sat back, running a hand across his mouth, then simply watched her again with eyes that were shuttered and unreadable.

Feeling about as foolish as she ever intended to feel,

she slid her gaze away toward the fire. *That was it!*
Nobody could say she hadn't tried! "You know," she
muttered more to herself than to him, "in some radical
segments of our society, people actually *answer* other
people. It's considered polite."

"But you were doing so well all by yourself."

She jumped at the sound of his voice. After the
silent treatment, she'd resigned herself to expect nothing but a closemouthed glare from him for her entire
captivity.

She had a feeling her expression must be almost
cringing, which was certainly an overreaction. After
all, he'd made a simple statement—however mocking.
He was Ira's son, not a deranged maniac with knives
for fingernails. "W-what?" she asked, sorry the question had come out in a high-pitched squeak.

He placed his elbows on the chair arms, templing
his fingers before him. "Bus-barfer, Miss Vale?" His
eyes were hooded, and his tone gave away nothing.
She couldn't tell if he was amused or irritated.

She shrugged. "Sorry. I'm new at talking for everybody in a room. Maybe if I stay here long enough,
I'll get better."

"It's good to have goals," he taunted quietly. Lowering his hands, he sat slightly forward. "I understand
my father called you this evening."

She was startled by the abrupt change of subject,
and for some reason his choice of topics made her
restless. On the plus side, at least he was speaking to
her. She nodded. "Y-yes. He said he was up to his
ears in snow, but he was his usual cheerful self."

"I'm sure," Beau muttered. "And I assume you told him I was the perfect host?"

She could detect his sarcasm, but didn't rise to the bait. "Of course that's what I told him." It wasn't her habit to speak badly of people who did her a favor, however grudgingly.

He lifted a skeptical brow. "And did he seem surprised?"

Actually, Ira had called her a sweet little liar, but she didn't want to make matters worse by admitting that, so she shook her head. "Not a bit," she lied.

His lips quirked. "Don't ever play poker, Miss Vale. You'd lose your shirt."

She dropped her gaze to the rug of bright maize and chocolate brown, with splashes of rust. It was a striking floor covering, but she was too uncomfortable to appreciate the decor right now. He was right. She didn't lie well. She could hardly deny what must be apparent in her troubled features.

Unhappy with the current subject, she leaped to a new, safer one that had been on her mind. She glanced at him. Well, not quite at him, more past his shoulder toward the wall of windows some distance away. There was nothing but a black void beyond the glass. "I—was wondering," she began tentatively. "Doesn't Beau mean 'handsome' in French, and Diablo mean 'devil' in Spanish? And if that's true, doesn't that make your name Handsome Devil?"

"Does it?" An eyebrow rose inquiringly. "I wonder why no one's ever pointed that out to me before."

His mocking tone made it clear his quixotic name had caused him no end of trouble over the years. And

watching him in the flickering firelight, she had to
admit that no matter how much inconvenience his
name had caused him, it couldn't be closer to the
truth. *He was a handsome devil.*

Now that she'd studied him closely, she could see
that he was every bit his father's son, similarly handsome, only more so. Taller, darker, with the long-
limbed, muscular build of a man who lived a life that
required much from him physically.

She was surprised at herself for feeling any affinity
for him at all, considering how unfriendly he'd been.
Unsettled by her contrary emotions, she looked away,
gritting her teeth.

"Where did my father meet you, Miss Vale?"

The question was completely unanticipated. She assumed Ira had at least told Beau that much. Apparently they never talked to each other, and she wondered what had caused such a rift between father and
son.

She heard a flutter-flap, flutter-flap, flutter-flap, and
noticed she was anxiously fanning the pages of her
book. The mention of her job occasionally caused eyebrows to rise. It didn't happen much, but it happened
enough to make her self-conscious.

She sat up straighter and closed the book, placing
it beside her. She had nothing to be ashamed of and
made unflinching eye contact. "I was a cocktail waitress in a Chicago cowboy bar. Ira went there every
night for the two weeks he was at that cattlemen's
conference last December."

Beau made no comment, but he pursed his lips, a
cool inference that she was guilty of something. She

bristled. *That was the look she hated*! She'd met people like Beau Diablo before—intolerant, judgmental types who believed that just because a woman worked in a bar she was cheap and easy.

The truth was, the tips were good, and with her parents' insurance money gone and her sister's medical bills mounting, she needed all the cash she could scrape together. So, she made a living serving drinks to pseudocowboys who liked to shuffle around the dance floor doing the "Cotton-Eyed Joe" and the "Boot-Scootin' Boogie." That was hardly evil.

Indignation bubbled inside her, but she tried to keep her affront from showing. Her mind tumbled back to when she'd first seen Beau Diablo in the little grocery store that afternoon. He'd been furious, and he'd gone straight to the exotic dancer. She began to think the two things might be connected, and asked, "Since you didn't know anything about me when you came to pick me up, I'm curious about why you asked the woman with the blue hair if she was me?"

He half grinned, but there was no humor in the expression. "Because she looked the most like Ira's last three wives."

His revelation stung. "Ira told me he'd had some bad luck in the past with wives, but that's over!"

His gaze narrowed, and Amy had a feeling he didn't buy that for a minute. "Whatever," he muttered. "When Ira described you to me, he said you'd be wearing your hair in a ponytail, so—"

"So you naturally assumed it would be *blue*?"

He grunted out a chuckle, clearly surprised to find her able to make a witty remark. "Ira also mentioned you had brown eyes and blond hair. The woman with the nose ring matched that description." He casually crossed his arms before him. "Your hair isn't that blond, Miss Vale."

It was now painfully clear why he'd been so hostile. It hadn't been a stomachache or stopped-up sinuses or anything of the sort. He just plain didn't like her, or what he perceived her to be. The fact that Ira's son could be so narrow-minded came as a blow. She pointedly turned away. "Sorry if I don't *exactly* fit your stereotype of a bloodsucking bimbo."

There was a drawn-out pause. "Ira also told me you were beautiful," he added flatly.

She swallowed with difficulty, her throat dust dry. *So naturally you decided to talk to every other blonde in the store before you came to me*! she fumed silently.

She couldn't understand why this stranger's opinion bothered her, but it did. Tired from lack of sleep, she was quickly reaching the end of her rope. "Just for the record, Mr. Diablo, your thoughts on the subject of my *looks* don't interest me in the least. I detest men like you, who put people into neat little heaps—nice girls here, bad girls there, computer nerds behind the sleazy lawyers! You didn't have to meet me or get to know me. You'd already made your decision about the kind of person I am." She hated the fact that she'd let him get to her. She hardly ever lost her temper this way, but she couldn't seem to stop the angry words from pouring out. "As far as you're concerned, I'm a trampy bubblehead grabbing a meal ticket! Well, you're one hundred percent wrong, Mr. Diablo. *One hundred percent*!"

Though her motives for marrying Ira were far different from what Beau believed, the fact that she didn't love her fiancé would only make any explanation she might give seem as contemptible as if she really were becoming his wife for his money. In truth, she intended to make a lasting commitment to Ira, but she had no plans to explain herself to this insolent man.

She had no desire to go into her reasons for getting married, or of explaining that, after Ira had gone to the cowboy bar every night for the two weeks he was in Chicago, he'd stunned her with a proposal of marriage. Of course, she'd thought he'd been kidding, but he'd been so sincere, so refreshingly chivalrous, she'd finally believed him.

It had seemed like the answer to a prayer for both her and Mary. And as Amy and Ira exchanged one chaste kiss, he'd promised he would never ask anything of her that would make her uncomfortable with her decision to marry him. He'd said he'd learned from his past mistakes and was looking for companionship, pure and simple.

Amy was looking for someone nice to spend her life with, someone honest who could make her smile. She'd never been in love, and wasn't even sure such an emotion existed. Passion, as far as she was concerned, was highly overrated. It was a solid, trusting partnership that counted and that's what she wanted. Ira had even offered to pay for Mary's convalescence, promising she could join them when she was well enough. Amy could almost say she loved Ira for that act of kindness alone.

So, let Beau think whatever he wanted—he would anyway. Why waste her breath telling him her marriage to his father was to be a platonic match? It was her business and Ira's business how they planned to live their lives, not Beau's! "I've already told your father, and now I'm telling you." She jumped up. "I plan to be the *best* rancher's wife in Wyoming. Any other plans Ira and I have are none of your business!" She grabbed up her book, then threw him an odious glare, deciding it was time he got a taste of his own medicine.

He didn't seem chastised by her outburst, and that made her even angrier. Was there no way to get to this man?

"The best rancher's wife in Wyoming?" A sardonic grin tugged at the corners of his mouth. "Who are you trying to convince, Miss Vale? Me—or you?"

The query was as hurtful as a slap, and she gasped. "Your father is completely different from you. He's so—so accepting."

Beau pushed himself up to stand before her. Even from the far side of the coffee table he seemed dangerously tall, ominously close. "If you mean he accepts every woman he meets in a bar as his bride, then I have to agree with you."

She was so horrified she couldn't respond. How crude! How rude he was! In all her twenty-four years she'd never met a man as unredeemably loathsome as Beau Diablo.

"I apologize if I seem severe," he said, his tone far from repentant. "My father is a grown man, and you're obviously a grown woman. And you're quite right, your plans are none of my business. You're welcome here as long as necessary.'' With a slow, unsmiling nod, he pivoted away, murmuring, ''Evening.''

She stared speechless as he ambled away. When he reached the hall, he turned back, thrusting his hands into his pockets. His stance looked elegantly casual, but she wasn't fooled. His disdain for her was as hot and palpable as the fire that raged in the hearth. She lifted a belligerent chin, positive he would be astute enough to detect her dislike for him, too.

He chuckled, and the sound was harsh in her ears. Yes, he'd received her message loud and clear, and it hadn't even fazed him. ''Miss Vale,'' he drawled, ''John Ruskin once said the most beautiful things in the world are the most useless.'' He paused, and she watched as a muscle flexed in his lean cheek. ''Just for the record, I think you're very beautiful.''

A heartbeat later he was gone. Amy stood there feeling like she'd been dashed with a bucket of ice water. His eyes had glittered with such utter contempt, she couldn't move. The man had told her she was beautiful, yet she'd never felt so insulted in her life. Even standing before the blazing fire, she found herself shivering uncontrollably.

Amy was awakened by a tapping on her door. She rubbed her eyes and yawned. It was so dark she couldn't see a thing. ''Yes?'' she called sleepily.

''Hon?'' Amy thought she heard a tinge of pity in the female voice, and couldn't imagine why. ''Mr.

Beau said to wake you. Seems he thinks you have a hankerin' to help with the haying and chopping ice.''

Amy rose up on an elbow, confused. She had no idea what either of those things were. ''He—did?''

The door clicked open a crack, and in the yellow light from the hallway, she could see the flyaway-gray head of the housekeeper. ''There's hot coffee, buckwheat cakes, steak and eggs for breakfast.''

Amy couldn't imagine anyone eating that much food, especially in the middle of the night. Yawning again, she wriggled up to sit. ''What time is it?'' she asked, brushing hair from her face.

''Five, or there'bouts.''

Making a pained face, Amy squinted at the luminous dial on her travel clock to make sure she'd heard right. Five-o-three, to be exact. Shaking her head, she tried to clear the cobwebs from her brain. The last time she'd looked at that clock it had been four-thirty. She hadn't slept well, her inability to settle down probably due to the fact that she was used to getting off work at two o'clock in the morning. It was close to four many mornings before she crawled into bed. At least that's what she hoped the reason was. She didn't like to think Beau Diablo had invaded her dreams, making her restless and upset even in sleep.

She stifled another yawn. She would rather spend another evening in front of a fire being glared at by her host than get up now. But she had a sneaking suspicion why he was doing this. She'd told him she wanted to be the best rancher's wife in Wyoming, so he was giving her a taste of what ranch life was like.

The underhanded sneak! "Okay—sure." She rubbed her eyes. "How long do I have?"

"Mr. Beau wants to be in the truck and movin' by five-fifteen."

She was sliding her feet over the side of the bed and into her slippers, but she stopped dead. *He was giving her ten minutes to dress and eat*! Keeping any negative thoughts to herself, she nodded. "I'll hurry."

"Hon," Cookie said, "have you got some nice, warm longhandles?"

Amy exhaled wearily. "What kind of handles?"

The door opened wider. "Didn't figure you knew about those. Here. I got plenty. You take these. And I brung you some heavy socks and other warm gear. You need to layer up in this cold."

The housekeeper seemed concerned, not her smiling self, and Amy took pity on her. "Don't worry about me, Cookie." Putting on a brave face, she threw off her covers. "If Mr. Diablo wants to give me a feel for ranch life, then I'm thrilled about it. Honestly." She shuffled to the door and took the bundle of clothes. "I'll be ready for breakfast in five minutes."

Cookie nodded and smiled, but a trace of pity lingered in her expression. "I don't rightly know what's going through Mr. Beau's head, Miss Amy. That ain't no work for a little city gal like you."

She smiled wanly. "Cookie, I have a feeling that's exactly his point."

CHAPTER THREE

FOUR minutes later, Amy was at the kitchen door, her head held high. She was not going to give Mr. Beau Diablo a single thing to fault her about. When she pushed through into the brightly lit room, she was surprised to find Cookie sipping coffee all alone before a stone fireplace. Disconcerted, she asked, "Am I late? Have they already left?"

The housekeeper smiled. "Shucks, no, hon." She put her mug on the long table and hurried toward the kitchen's back door to retrieve a battered old field coat from a hook. "They're in the cook house. Mr. Beau usually eats breakfast with the hands, bein' a bachelor and all." She took down Amy's freshly washed parka and beckoned for her to follow. "I'll show you the way."

Once Amy was bundled against the cold, she and Cookie stepped out into the dawning day. The cold was so bitter, it staggered her. Her step faltered. "How cold is it?" she asked, watching her breath freeze in the air.

"Oh, 'bout fifteen below."

"Below? *Freezing*?"

Cookie let out one of her splintery laughs. "Zero, hon. Not a bad day. No wind." They trudged along a gentle slope away from the ranch house in about three inches of snow. "If the sun comes out, it'll get up near zero."

Amy swallowed. "That's nice." It got cold in Chicago, too. But she didn't spend her days out in it. Her stinging ears reminded her to pull up her parka hood. Fifteen below zero! She clutched her hands together apprehensively.

The view was hazy with falling snow, making the cloudy dawn seem to be brushstroked by an artist's hand. And the silence. How could a place so vast be so quiet? Amy took a deep breath. Though her lungs froze, she delighted in the smell. Sweet, pure, cold. It was a refreshing change from the city's exhaust and pollution, even if it was a little on the deathly cold side.

Though much of the landscape still lay in relative darkness, the fallen snow provided luminescence, and she could see a scattering of buildings silhouetting the landscape. Farther away, behind wooden pens and a log barn, the rolling hills were forested with stands of pines.

Cookie touched her elbow. "This is me and Archie's place." She waved toward a quaint log cabin not far from the main house. "On the other side's the cook house and then the bunkhouse."

Amy noticed that all of them were of the same pine-log construction, their roofs blanketed by an icing of snow. Smoke curled from each chimney, and she could smell it. The whole experience was wonderful. Like a scratch-and-sniff Currier and Ives painting.

"You go on in the cook house, hon. I've gotta stop

by my place for some cleanin' supplies. It's that plank door, there.''

Amy nodded her thanks and tromped along the path of footprints already marring the pristine snow. With every step her stomach knotted tighter. She looked down at her running shoes and shook her head. If her feet didn't freeze off today, it would be a miracle. They were already numb.

She heard a general hum and rumble of male voices when she got to the door, but the instant she stepped inside, the room went still, ten pairs of male eyes turning in her direction.

Amy stumbled to a halt, embarrassed to be the center of attention. She felt like a bug that had just appeared in the middle of somebody's birthday cake. Surprise seemed to be the expression of the day, except for Archie-the-cook's squinty old gray eyes smiling at her. She didn't see Beau, and it was clear that her unwanted presence on his ranch hadn't been passed on to the hired help. She wondered where he was.

The cook house was long and rustic. Devoid of frills like curtains or seat cushions, it seemed perfectly fitted out for brawny cowboys. The ten-foot table, made of pine planks, was flanked by two long benches, and sat before a soot-blackened rock fireplace. The fire flickered warmly amid delicious mingled scents of homemade bread, hotcakes, strong coffee, scrambled eggs and steaks. Beyond the table where the cowhands gathered were the kitchen appliances—two industrial-size ovens, cooktops and refrigerators—tucked neatly in and around the rough log walls.

Amy heard someone clear his throat; it sounded like crushed rock banging down a metal chute. Her gaze swung to the table. The scene there was almost comical. Denim-and-flannel-clad cowboys sat or stood in a frozen tableau, halted in the act of swabbing up the last dab of maple syrup with a crust of bread, or gulping down a final swig of coffee.

The throat-clearing sound came again, more loudly this time. Amy saw movement, then, as Archie went on pouring coffee into one leathery-faced cowpoke's mug, she heard him say, "Mornin', Miss Amy." He grinned in his bashful way. "Come on over here and get yourself some hot coffee."

She smiled at the weathered cook, but before she could take a step, there was a thunderous scraping sound as the benches were pushed back and the hands abruptly stood. A couple of men who'd donned their ten-gallon hats in anticipation of leaving, grabbed them off and crushed them respectfully to their chests.

"Men. This is Miss Amy Vale," came a deep voice that she recognized as her host's. She heard another scrape of wood on wood and saw Beau as he rose from a hard-backed chair in a dim corner. "Miss Vale will be staying with us until the roads west are clear."

Amy smiled as the men timidly grinned and mumbled guttural greetings.

"Now that the pleasantries are over," he cut in, "Marv, you, Homer and Willie get those extra round bales to the north pasture. J.C. and Snapper, you do a ride-through to check for cattle that need doctoring.

Buddy and Chick, make sure the creek water's open.
Ed. You come with Miss Vale and me in the old
pickup.''

Amy watched Beau as he barked out orders, slipping a black down vest on over his black wool shirt.
It jolted her when Archie shoved a thermos into one
hand and a small brown sack into the other. ''I fixed
you a scrambled egg sandwich. And the coffee'll
warm your innards.'' He grinned, and his sun-dried
face crinkled like withered leaves.

''Thanks,'' she whispered. Tucking the thermos under her arm, she gave his callused paw a squeeze, then
noticed the ranch hands were clomping out the far
door. ''I'd better go. I think I'm expected in the
pickup.''

''It seems so.'' Archie crossed his arms over a stout
belly, giving his boss a dubious squint as Beau planted
his Stetson on his brow. When he turned to face them,
his eyes were shadowed, but there was no masking
the spark of antagonism that hovered there. ''Are you
ready, Miss Vale?'' he asked, his tone less a question
than a dare.

Though she'd been scared and unsure of herself
when she'd walked in, his challenge turned her into a
rock of determination. Did he think a little Wild West
browbeating would frighten her off? Not likely! She'd
been living on her own and caring for her invalid sister for the past five years. If he thought she couldn't
handle cold weather and a few disagreeable chores, he
was nuts.

She marched across the room to where he was
standing beside the wooden coat hooks. ''I thought

you'd *never* ask, Mr. Diablo.'' Her smile was as sweet as she could coerce it to be. With barely a glance in his direction, she breezed out the door.

As soon as she was outside, a blast of knife-sharp wind hit her, spattering her face with needles of snow. She was so shocked by it, she stumbled to a halt, which was a mistake, for she found herself slammed into a very immovable object at her back. The unexpectedness of the impact made her tumble forward in the slick snow. Almost as quickly as it had begun, her forward motion ended as something strong encircled her middle.

''What in the—''

Hearing that growl near her ear, it only took her a split second to realize she'd run into Beau Diablo, and when she'd toppled forward, he'd caught her against him to keep her from falling. His arms held her tightly. His breath was coffee warm against her cheek, his legs and hips fitting familiarly against her.

''Miss Vale, don't people who live in Chicago know how to walk in snow?''

She yanked away from both his intimate hold and the unsettling feel of his body against hers. Turning to face him, she objected, ''Surely you didn't expect someone as useless and beautiful as I am to be able to *walk*, too!'' She didn't enjoy sarcasm, but, considering he'd only given her time to throw her hair into a quick ponytail and brush her teeth, no one in his right mind could call her beautiful this morning. It had to be obvious that she'd slipped on an icy spot. Anybody could slip. Even *he* had to obey the laws of gravity.

He frowned at her, his glance sliding to her jogging shoes. "What the hell are those?"

She followed his gaze. "In Chicago we call them shoes. What's the matter with them?"

He muttered something unintelligible and pivoted away to reenter the cook house. In a few seconds he returned, carrying something. Stooping, he grasped one of her ankles. "Lift your foot."

"I'll fall."

"Hold on to my shoulders, and lift your damn foot."

She could see now that he'd brought out a pair of fleece-lined rubber boots. Deciding he'd only snap her head off if she objected, she juggled her thermos and sack and placed a hand on his shoulder to balance herself while she lifted her foot. He quickly shoved on the boot. It was too big and swallowed her leg all the way up to her knee, but it was toasty warm. "Now the other one."

She mutely obeyed, feeling like a four-year-old child needing help getting dressed. When the other boot slid into place, she complained, "I've dressed myself for years, Mr. Diablo."

He straightened. "We can discuss your hobbies some other time. Right now, we have cold, hungry cattle to feed." Taking her by the arm, he aimed her toward a waiting pickup. It wasn't the one he'd driven to Big Elk. This one was older, battered, and a cowhand was stacking square bales of hay in the back.

A few minutes later, Amy found herself wedged between the two men, bouncing along a snowy path. Except for barbed-wire fences that ran along on both sides of them, she would never have guessed this was a road. They hadn't gone far when the fence grew to ten feet high, with slats of wood running vertically from the ground up. "What's that for?" She didn't realize she'd verbalized her question until she heard her voice break the silence.

Her query was followed by even more silence, until finally the cowhand named Ed turned their way and glanced skittishly at his boss, apparently assuming he'd answer. Amy looked at the cowboy, knowing full well her host didn't speak to her unless he had something he wanted to shout. She smiled at the cowboy and was startled to see a flush darken his already-boot-brown face. He fingered his droopy mustache, which was dripping melted snow. "Them's snow fences, ma'am. Helps keep the roads clear of snow in spots where there's a lot of blowin' wind."

Amy nodded. "My goodness. You must get some pretty high drifts here."

He fingered his mustache again, and Amy realized he was nervous. She was puzzled. She could think of no earthly reason she should make him nervous. "Sometimes six foot and more, ma'am."

She shook her head in disbelief. "Look, Ed, since we'll be working together, I wish you'd call me Amy."

His squinty black eyes widened, and he gave another peek at his boss. But when there was no overt objection, he looked back at Amy and grinned. "Sure—Miss Amy. I'd be pleased."

She laughed. "Amy, Ed. Just Amy."

She heard the squeak of leather and shifted to see

Beau's hands flex on the wheel. "Ed. Get the gate," he muttered.

Almost before the words were spoken, the hired hand jumped from the truck and was sloughing through the snow to swing a metal gate out of their way.

Amy couldn't stand the suspense any longer and shifted to face Beau. "What, exactly, are we going to do?"

He stepped on the gas and they bounced through the gate. When Ed opened his door, Beau said, "You drive. Miss Vale and I'll pitch the hay."

Ed's eyes widened again, and he stood there speechless for a second before he found his voice. "Uh—boss? I can pitch it jes' fine." He was frowning, clearly aghast that the young woman was expected to do such a demanding, bone-chilling chore.

"You drive, Ed. The lady wants to learn about ranch life." Beau climbed out of the cab, making it clear he didn't intend to argue the matter. "Come with me, Miss Vale."

Amy smiled at the cowboy. "I really do want to learn." She only hoped she meant it.

He swallowed, and she could see his prominent Adam's apple bob up and down. "If you get too chilly, you let the boss know, now," he cautioned, his grimace never easing.

Fairly sure "the boss" wouldn't care if she turned into a female Popsicle before his eyes, she merely nodded and slid out Beau's side of the cab. When she got around to the back of the pickup, he was squatting in the truck bed snipping the wire from around a bale of hay. The snow had already dusted his shoulders and the brim of his hat and had left a light coating on the bales.

Amy heard a bawling sound and turned toward it. For the first time, she could see dark splotches over the rise. Hundreds of milling, meandering blotches vaguely shaped like cows. "Wow," she breathed. "There are so many—"

"Miss Vale?"

She spun back to see that he was now standing on the tailgate. Apparently the loose hay had muffled his approach. "Yes?" She took an involuntary step back.

He reached down. "Let me give you a hand."

"No thanks." Presenting him with her back, she sidestepped him and boosted herself up on the tailgate, then pushed up to stand. "Okay." She slapped her hands together to knock straw from her knit gloves, purposely scanning the stacked bales to avoid facing those stern eyes. "What do I do?"

She could hear him move, but refused to turn.

"Take this pitchfork, and as Ed drives along the draw, you pitch the hay out on the snow."

She plucked the pitchfork from his hand, again evading eye contact. "No problem."

"I'll be breaking up the bales for you."

"Lucky me." She hefted the pitchfork gingerly, trying to get a feel for it. "Do I start now?"

"Just a minute." He leaned over the side. "Okay, Ed. Start moving."

The truck lurched, but Amy was ready. She hadn't ridden the "L" train in Chicago for all those years without learning how to brace herself for staggering starts and stops. She had an urge to give Beau a smug smile but decided against it. The less eye contact they shared, the better she felt about it, and he no doubt felt the same way.

The truck went down an incline toward the roving clumps of cattle. Amy shivered just watching them. The poor things were huffing and puffing frozen air, looking pretty miserable.

"You can start any time," he said from behind her, and she realized she'd gotten lost in her thoughts. The first few pitches netted her only a strand or two of straw. She cringed, knowing Beau was back there scowling at her ineptness. Any second he'd say something like, "That's fine, Miss Vale. Those cows need to go on a diet anyway."

After a few attempts, she figured out how to keep most of the hay on the pitchfork, and then get it over the end of the truck and actually onto the snow.

Cattle were ambling up, ready to eat. She found herself pitching and pitching, faster and faster, worried sick that the cattle get enough food.

"Miss Vale, the stock at the far end of the draw are going to be irritated with you if they don't get any feed."

She inhaled, feeling oddly light-headed. Leaning on her pitchfork, she cast him a direct glance for the first time since she'd climbed into the back of the truck. "Don't be shy, Mr. Diablo. Be sure and tell me if I do anything *right*."

His expression was unreadable, and she turned quickly away, cursing herself for forgetting her own rule of ignoring him at all costs.

She tried to switch her thoughts to more pleasant things. The morning sky, though heavily overcast, gave off a pearlescent glow, and the snow was puffy and chaste on a sloping hillside dotted with spruce and winter-bare cottonwood. It was beautiful. Even under these less than perfect circumstances, Amy was falling in love with Wyoming, and it made her smile.

Digging out a forkful of straw, she thoughtlessly glanced in Beau's direction and her smile faded. It wasn't particularly bad lighting for him, either. Somehow his expression seemed almost agreeable, his eyes less antagonistic out here. Gritting her teeth against the foolish notion, she pitched the hay into the air, hoping both her technique and her speed were closer to his exacting standards.

"That's better," he said after a time.

She caught her breath, but tried not to display her shock in her body language. She took another forkful of hay and pitched it off the back of the truck, never uttering a word. Off in the distance, she saw a couple of cowboys on horseback picking their way through the milling cattle, and wondered if they were the ones Beau had told to check to see if any of the cows were sick. As far as she was concerned, they should be suffering from bad cases of pneumonia if they had any sense at all.

For a long time, she didn't hear anything but the lowing cattle, the twang of the wires Beau cut, and the crunchy sound of cold hay being broken up. Once or twice she was startled to see an entire bale fly over the side of the truck and break up when it hit the snow. Apparently her cow-feeding speed had dropped below

Mr. Diablo's standards again, but she didn't intend to give him the satisfaction of knowing she'd even noticed he'd done anything. Though she was exhausted and a little dizzy, she picked up her pitching speed a little and tried to ignore the fact that he existed on the face of the earth.

"After we finish here, we need to chop ice off the pond."

With shrieking muscles, she pitched again, grateful he couldn't see her face. Chopping ice off a pond didn't sound like a warm thing to do, and she was freezing. Her arms were killing her, and she was getting more and more light-headed from hunger. But she would have to faint dead away and have her nose crack off and drop into his lap before she'd admit that.

"Are you tired?"

"No," she wheezed, watching her icy breath dissipate in the air as the truck moved forward.

"Are you cold?"

"Why should—I be cold?" She blanched. The sentence had been long enough for him to detect the gap where she'd had to take a gasping breath. And worse, her voice had *quivered*.

She heard a banging, and spun around before she remembered she wasn't going to look at him. She had to catch herself, and shook her head. Why was she so dizzy?

Beau pounded on the cab's back window, giving Ed the signal to stop. When he did, she stumbled again, but caught herself.

Before she had time to absorb what was going on, Beau had leaped over the side of the truck and moved around to the back. "Come on." He lifted his arms as if he expected her to leap gratefully into them.

She laid the pitchfork against the remainder of the bales. There were only seven or eight, and it surprised her that she'd distributed so much hay. There had been at least twenty when they'd begun.

When she turned back, she eyed his uplifted arms with hauteur, then shook her head. "I have a feeling you wouldn't help Ed down. Don't do me any favors." She dropped to one knee, but before she could slide off, he took her around the waist and lifted her down.

"Ed's accustomed to being at seven thousand feet. You look a little unsteady. Besides, it's time for a coffee break." His hands lingered on her for a second longer before he released her and took a step back. "Are you too dizzy to walk?"

She blinked at him, puzzled by the lack of hostility in his tone. Every fiber of her body was revved up for a fight, and she was in a belligerent mood. He'd worked her like an ox for the past hour, treated her like an indentured servant, and suddenly he was being—what? What was he being? *Nice*? "I—I can walk." She eyed him with high suspicion. "So, do you want me to hike back to the cook house for coffee cups?"

His lips twitched. "If you prefer. But I thought we could share the thermos lid."

A flush heated her frigid cheeks. The idea of sharing anything so intimate as a cup of coffee with this man troubled her.

"And you can eat your breakfast."

She was even more surprised that he remembered she hadn't eaten. He led her around to his door and opened it. "Slide in."

Ed had already shifted to the passenger side, so she did as he asked without argument. If she'd been forced to admit it, she didn't know how much longer she could have gone on without food. She was pretty shaky. She supposed the altitude was part of her problem, but she had a feeling she was more hungry than she was disoriented from thin air.

"Ed, get back there and finish haying."

The cowman was already half out of the cab. "Yessir, boss," he shouted, closing the door behind him.

Beau took off his Stetson and placed it behind the seat, then motioned toward the glove compartment. "Your breakfast's in there."

As Amy ate, Beau drove along the valley while Ed finished breaking up the hay and pitching it. She turned around to watch what he was doing. The cowboy was much better at the chore than she'd been. "This isn't Ed's first day of haying."

Beau grunted out a chuckle. "How can you tell?"

"He has a great wrist twist that looks like it might be hard to master." She shrugged, turning back. "Oh, well, I'll learn. Coffee?" With a start, she realized she'd spoken to Beau in a pleasant voice. Where had *that* come from? Most likely it was because she felt better having eaten.

"I'd love some," he said, without glancing her way.

She couldn't unscrew the thermos lid with her

gloves on, so she slipped one off. She'd begun to thaw out, and once her skin was exposed to the warmth of the cab, she felt the sting of the blister she'd worn on her palm. She must have made a sound of dismay when she uncovered the raw flesh, for Beau glanced at her.

She flipped her hand over, not wanting him to think she couldn't handle what he was dishing out. Trying not to wince with pain, she went about her task.

"Damn useless city gloves," he groused under his breath.

"Yes, but don't you think they're *beautiful*?" she joked, then immediately wondered why she'd blurted that, of all things?

His thick-lashed eyes touched hers, and for the briefest instant, honest amusement seemed to glimmer between them. The intensity of the experience stunned her. Was there more in his glance than humor? Before she could be sure of all she'd seen, a frown rode his features again. With nostrils flaring, he shifted his attention back to his driving. "There's a first-aid kit behind your seat. You'd better see to that hand."

Swallowing thickly, she twisted away to stare out the window, but saw none of the snowy scene before her. An irritation spiced with uneasiness engulfed her. Something intense had flared behind those dusky eyes. Or had it? Her breathing was suddenly labored and her pulse quickened. Had she actually seen masculine attraction there? Surely not. *Definitely not*! It was crazy. The man didn't like her. And she certainly didn't like him.

More importantly, she reminded herself, she was engaged to his *father*.

Amy sighed, squeezing warm water over her breasts as she relaxed in a hot bath. Even the act of squeezing the washcloth hurt. She was sore all over from the hard, physical work she'd done today.

Opening her eyes, she inhaled the steamy, rose-scented water. Even with all the hard work, she was surprised to find she was basking in a glow of satisfaction. She'd kept up, and she'd discovered she enjoyed the exhilarating outdoor life—something, being a city kid, she'd never experienced.

Lifting her right hand, she looked at her red badge of courage. That's what she called her blister. It stung, but it wasn't too bad. Beau had bandaged it for her. He'd had a surprisingly gentle touch. Then he'd insisted she wear his fur-lined leather gloves the rest of the day. She didn't know how his fingers kept from dropping off in the cold, but she noticed a couple of the other cowhands were gloveless, too.

Sighing again, she shook her head. Maybe Wyoming cowboys' skin had mutated over the centuries to endure ice-age temperatures. That was the only answer she could come up with that seemed plausible to explain why those men hadn't left broken-off bits of fingers littering the pastures where they'd spent the day chopping ice from the pond, haying and doctoring the cattle for foot rot and some other revolting virus she couldn't recall.

Her eyelids began to droop, and she was amazed at how tired she was. Dipping her head beneath the water for one last rinse, she came up wringing out her wet hair. It wasn't even ten o'clock, but she had a feeling she'd fall asleep the instant her head hit the pillow. With both the physical work and the emotional battering her nearness to Beau Diablo had caused her, she didn't have an ounce of energy left.

Stepping out of the tub and grabbing a towel, she exhaled despondently. Her close proximity to Beau for so many hours had been a distracting experience—the smoky-pine scent of his after-shave, the warmth of his breath on her face every time he'd turned to talk to Ed, and worst of all, the feel of his torso crushed hard against her as the three of them bounced along on that fiendish bench seat that insisted on sloping in Beau's direction. By the end of the day, she'd been a worn-out, nervous wreck.

Beau, on the other hand, had been in total control, all business, never tiring. Unlike the other cowhands—who watched her, insisting on helping if she appeared confused or cold—Beau hardly seemed to notice she was alive, except when he shouted orders in her direction.

She toweled her hair more fiercely than she'd intended, muttering, "I'll show you who's useless, Mr. Beau Diablo!"

She heard a sound and looked up in time to see the hall door swing open. Hastily, she pressed her towel to her breasts to preserve her modesty as her eyes clashed with an all-too-familiar sultry gaze.

"What do you think you're doing?" she demanded, her voice a breathy whisper.

Beau had come to an abrupt halt. His eyes widening slightly, he mouthed an oath.

"I locked that door!" She fumbled to better cover herself.

"Sometimes the latch doesn't catch." He frowned. "I thought you'd gone to bed."

She gave him a look that made it plain she didn't believe him.

His expression altered from apologetic to annoyed. "I don't have to burst in on naked women to get sexual gratification, Miss Vale."

Amy didn't follow her urge to avoid the severity in his glare, and eyed him levelly. She was unstrung to her soul, standing there practically naked and totally vulnerable before him. But she was angry, too. How dare he loiter there debating with her.

She already knew he disliked her, but she hadn't missed the look in his eyes when he'd first stepped through the door. He might not care for her as a person, but he had *definitely* reacted to her as a woman, whether he'd meant to walk in on her or not. She wanted to get back at him for his hurtful remark the night before, and for his ungentlemanly behavior now. Her voice chilled and scathing, she challenged, "Who are *you* trying to convince, Mr. Diablo? Me—or you?"

His face and body grew rigid, and he frightened her by stalking farther into the bathroom rather than hurriedly leaving as she'd expected. Taking a protective step away, she found herself pinned against the tub. "What—what are you going to do?"

He paused, his flinty eyes raking her face. "Why, ravage you, of course."

Before she could protest, he'd scooped up several pairs of leather gloves that had been drying on a rack above the heater. He pivoted away, and a second later the bathroom door closed behind him.

Amy stared after him, her breathing shallow, a tight, mortified ache in her stomach. Why in the world had she intimated he was sexually attracted to her? Even though she'd been positive at the time she'd seen lust in his eyes, now she was afraid it might have been nothing more than a trick of light playing on his startled features.

Moaning aloud, she slumped to the tub's rim. Who did she think she was anyway? Sharon Stone's sexier sister? Dismay slid through her. *How could she ever face the man again*?

CHAPTER FOUR

AMY woke with a start from a nightmare where huge, howling wolves were using battering rams to break into her room. She rubbed her eyes and sat up, growing wary, afraid. Even though she was awake, she could still hear the wolves and their bloodcurdling howls as they clawed and slammed into the walls and roof.

Terror clutched her by the throat, but before a scream could escape, she had grown alert enough to understand it wasn't an attack of rabid, giant wolves after all. It was the blizzard they'd been both expecting and dreading. It had finally turned south and was here, beating down on them with violent, frigid wings.

Instinctively, she jumped from the bed and threw on some jeans and a heavy wool shirt and raced to the kitchen. As she expected, no one was there. Biting her lip, she peered out the back door's window. A bawling wind shrieked beyond the frosted glass, blinding snow in its breath. As she stared in awe at the raw power nature could unleash, it slashed madly at the windowpane, a ferocious beast bent on getting at her and ripping her to shreds.

She stumbled a step backward in the face of such wild, yet dazzling savagery, but only for a second. She dared not dwell on it or she would lose her courage. Determinedly, she grabbed her parka and pushed open the door, forcing her fears aside. The wind pressed against the door, nearly throwing her to the floor, but she held on, finally managing to extract herself from the kitchen as the door slammed at her back.

Turning into the flesh-cutting snow, she pulled her parka hood close around her face and bent into the wind, heading for the cook house where she sensed she would find activity, and hopefully, something she could do to help.

The wind ripped at her and shoved her sideways and backward, twice knocking her to her knees, but at last she made it to the cook-house door. Once inside, she fell backward against the thick planks, using all her strength to get it closed.

After the raging storm, the relative silence of the cook house was almost deafening. She glanced round to see Cookie and Archie scurrying around the kitchen area while three of the cowhands sat at the table slugging down coffee and sandwiches.

"What in land's sake are you doing here, hon?" Cookie hurried over to take hold of stinging hands she'd foolishly forgotten to protect. "Why, you shouldn't be running around in this heller of a storm!"

"I—I wanted to help," she managed, still breathing heavily.

"Well, that's mighty good of you." Cookie smiled, rubbing life back into her cold fingers. "Me and Archie could use another pair of hands, truth be told. But I don't know if Mr. Beau'd want his guest workin'."

Amy smiled and removed her fingers from the com-

passionate woman's ministrations. "I'm sure he'd expect me to help." Numbly, she fumbled to untie her
hood. Her fingers tingled painfully and so did her
cheeks and nose. She wasn't used to the sort of cold
Wyoming could dish out, and decided she'd better
take more care to bundle up from now on. This kind
of cold could kill very quickly. "What—what do you
want me to do?"

"Maybe make us another big pot of strong coffee?"
Cookie suggested.

"How strong?" Amy followed the older woman to
the kitchen area, where a big, stainless-steel urn stood
in a corner, emitting fragrant steam.

Cookie laughed. "That's easy. Just make it strong
enough to haul a broke-down pickup, hon, and it'll be
dandy."

Amy nodded, unsure how strong that might be, but
deciding it was probably a million times stronger than
she'd ever *considered* making coffee. "Tow-truck
strength it is." She headed for the coffee urn, determined not to mess up her first emergency assignment.
They might have to eat it with a fork, but if nothing
else, her coffee would be *strong*.

The hours blurred. If she wasn't shoveling coffee
into the urn, she was slicing beef or smearing bread
with mustard, piling on lettuce, pickles, cheese, or
washing ton after ton of dishes, as the cowboys took
shifts breaking ice and feeding the three thousand
head of cattle that were wintering there.

She'd overheard a couple of the hands talking about
ten young cows that were having babies during the
blizzard—calving, they'd called it. Even though they

were in the relative warmth of the barn, she had a feeling this wasn't the most ideal night for little baby cows to come into the world. She wished the little guys and their mommies luck. She supposed cows were no luckier than humans when it came to timing a baby's birth. Didn't it always seem like babies were born in the worst possible circumstances? In taxis or storms or theater lobbies?

She didn't have time to dwell on the miracle of birth happening nearby. She had cold, hungry men to feed. Hours ago, she'd slipped into her cocktail-waitress mentality and was moving automatically amid the chaos and noise, smiling, serving, cleaning up, smiling, serving.

Along about dawn, she laid a plate loaded down with two roast beef sandwiches and a mound of bar-becued beans before yet another cowboy. Noticing the pitcher of cream was empty, she reached across to pick it up, intent on refilling it, but felt a hand grip her wrist. "What the hell are you doing?" came her host's accusatory voice.

She stared down into critical eyes, startled to discover she'd just served Beau without realizing it. She must be more woozy from lack of sleep than she'd thought. Had it only been last night when he'd ambled into her bathroom, humiliated her beyond repair, then grabbed up some gloves and promptly forgotten about her? So much for her fears of how she'd ever face him again. He was his old, disagreeable self.

She jerked from his grasp. "I'm dancing *Swan Lake*! What does it look like I'm doing?" Startled to hear herself so uncharacteristically snappish, she sighed wearily. "I'm sorry. I guess I'm just tired. Do you want coffee?"

His eyes narrowed, and he continued to watch her for another few seconds. She noticed he looked fatigued around his eyes, his hair was wet and mussed and his striking features were snowburned. She swallowed at the sight. He and his men were fighting a rough battle against blinding, freezing elements she'd only spent a few seconds struggling against. What must they be suffering in an effort to save their cattle? Against her better judgment, her heart went out to him. She was about to wish him luck when he nodded curtly in answer to her question about coffee, then, without further comment, lowered his gaze to his plate to continue eating.

Aware that she'd been summarily dismissed, she spun away, her ire sparking again. "You're welcome, Mr. Diablo. Happy to help!" she grumbled, heading for the coffee urn.

She was tired, but not so tired that she didn't notice Beau leaving in a billow of windblown snow. She hadn't realized she'd stopped what she was doing until the cowman, Ed, touched her arm. "Miss Amy," he asked tentatively, "is them sandwiches for me?"

She snapped back to reality, grinned down at him and handed him his refilled plate. "Coffee coming up," she said as cheerfully as she could, then spun away to refill his mug.

The blizzard raged on and on, abusing the little cook house from all sides as wind-driven snow swirled and ranted and shrieked outside. Amy was accustomed to the cook-house door opening and closing every fifteen minutes or so with a new batch of ravenous, snow-covered cowhands coming and going. But when the door suddenly burst wide open with an explosive bang, she lurched around in shock and fear, almost depositing a pile of hot barbecued beans in Marv's lap. The cowhand caught the tipping plate, but Amy hardly noticed as Beau surged into the room, a bandanna covering his nose and mouth and his coat collar turned up. He looked like an Old West bandit, and Amy's pulse accelerated against her will. He was loaded down with a large bundle clutched in his arms, a couple of gangly brown legs and hoofed feet protruding from the horse blanket he carried.

As she stared, he stalked to the fireplace and spread the blanket over the oval rag rug, displaying a spindling newborn calf, all brown with a precious white face and the biggest black eyes. The poor little thing seemed so weak it was barely able to lift its head. "We need to warm this one up," Beau shouted, yanking down his bandanna. "*Cookie*!" he called.

"Boss, it'll be a minute." She held up flour-coated hands. "I'm in the middle of a batch of biscuits."

Amy was standing a few feet from where Beau was kneeling and rubbing the calf with a gloved hand. Setting the plate in front of Marv, she turned toward the sickly animal sprawled before the fire, and her heart twisted with concern. "I—can I help?" Having always lived in apartments in the city, she'd never even owned a dog, so she wasn't sure what to do with a sick calf. But it looked so pitiful and sweet, with those big, sorrowful eyes aimed her way. She had to do something.

She was on her knees beside the shivering calf before Beau had time to respond. When she placed a
hand on the baby's thin rib cage and began to mimic
Beau's stroking movements, she could hear him shift
to look at her. For a minute, she didn't look back, just
continued to stroke along the calf's silky, damp fur.
"Like this?" When he didn't immediately answer, she
reluctantly met his gaze.

His glare drilled through her. "What the hell sort
of game are you playing, Miss Vale?"

Hurt by his continued antagonism, she grew defiant.
"It's obviously too alien an idea for you to grasp, Mr.
Diablo. But just so you'll recognize it in the future,
it's called *trying to help*. Now, am I doing this right
or not?"

They stared at each other, the sparks of their mutual
hostility almost visible in the air around them. A weak
bawling sound brought them back, and Beau snapped
his attention away to look at the calf, automatically
patting it. When his hand brushed hers, Amy drew
away from his touch, but continued to stroke the shiv-
ery animal.

"Try to get her to take some milk." He retrieved
a baby bottle from beneath his coat and thrust it toward her. "I'll be back in a couple of hours to check
on her." When she took the bottle, he stood, half pivoted away, then stopped.

Amy looked up at him, prepared for another outburst of bad temper. When she met his eyes, she was
startled to see something else mingled with the antip-
athy glimmering there. What was it? Guarded civility?
Possibly even gratitude? His jaw shifted from side to

side, and his nostrils flared. She stiffened, waiting, but for what she didn't know.

Yanking off his hat, he dragged a hand through his hair and spun to leave. As he did, she thought she heard him mutter something. Whatever it had been, it was more growled than spoken, but she was almost sure he'd uttered one small but significant word—*Thanks*.

She stared after him as he tromped off and swung open the door, exiting in a riot of storm-tossed snow.

Bewildered, she shifted back to her trembly charge. Scooting closer, she supported its wobbly head in her lap. "Did he really say that, little one?" She rubbed its scrawny neck. "Or am I so exhausted I'm having fits of delirium?"

Amy felt warm and cozy, except for a little crick in her neck. The bed seemed hard, and her pillow was missing. But she was so tired she didn't mind. It was nice just getting the chance to sleep.

She heard an odd shushing sound, then a scrape of wood against wood, followed quickly by what sounded like a masculine murmur. She stretched and sighed. Probably just the wind—the everlasting, pummeling blizzard.

A cough registered in her sleep-hazed brain. *Wind didn't cough, did it*? She stirred again, her eyes fluttering open a crack. She saw what seemed like the flicker of firelight, then closed her eyes. It was so toasty and welcome against her face she didn't want to wake up and find it was only a dream. She turned slightly, her hand coming to rest on something furry—

and moving? She slid her fingers over it, perplexed. Why did her sheets feel as if they were covered in hair—and breathing?

Her eyes came wide open, and she looked around, hoping she was wrong about where she was. Unfortunately, the first thing her glance came to rest on was a pair of familiar black cowboy boots. Her glance surged up to take in the man lounging not far away at the cook-house table.

She swallowed, forcing her gaze upward to his face, indistinct beneath the wide brim of a cowboy hat. Even though she couldn't see his features well, she had a terrible feeling a pair of hypercritical eyes were trained on her.

"Good morning, Miss Vale," Beau drawled, pushing the wide brim back with his thumb. "Sleep well?" She could see his face now and was startled to note that he was less grim than she'd imagined he would be. But she wasn't relieved, for what she did see was worse. His eyes held the glitter of wry amusement. No doubt he found her inability to keep up during a blizzard highly satisfying. He seemed to be silently saying "I told you so," and that hurt! *The superior bum*! But she had to admit, she *had* failed—even in her own eyes. Abashed, she lowered her perusal to the sleeping calf and nervously stroked its rib cage.

She heard a few throats being cleared and her gaze flew back up. For the first time, she became aware that most of the cowhands were gathered around the long table, quietly eating. Apparently they'd tried to be quiet in deference to their sleeping guest.

Feeling like a complete fool, she struggled to sit,

drawing a drowsy moo from her sleepy charge, its head still nestled in her lap. "What time is it?" she asked, brushing a stray wisp of hair from her face.

"Around ten. Blizzard's letting up." Cookie hurried over with a mug of steaming coffee. "You ought to go back to bed, hon. Archie and me can handle things from here on."

She gratefully took the mug and sipped, grimacing at the bitter taste. "No—no, I'm fine," she lied.

"The calf doing okay?" Beau queried, even though he was fully aware that Amy's attention had not been riveted on the animal lately.

Her cheeks went fiery at his continued taunting, but she worked at ignoring it. "Well—she had a couple of bottles of milk after she quit shivering. Then she settled down and slept." Unable to meet his gaze, she asked, "Doesn't she look better to you?"

He got up from the bench to kneel beside her. "I think she can go back to her mother now."

He gathered the blanket around the calf, but when he began to lift her, Amy put a restraining hand on his arm. "Are you sure that's a good idea?"

He looked at her, then at her hand resting on his arm. When he looked back, his features had eased into a contrary grin. "I'm fairly sure it's a good idea, Miss Vale, even though I've only had thirty-five years of ranching experience."

She didn't doubt that he knew his business, but she couldn't help the way she felt. She'd bonded with this little creature and was unhappy with the idea of it going out in such bitter cold. "What if she gets chilled?"

"Her mother can take care of her now."

Amy frowned as he lifted the baby in his arms. "You're not going to kill her and eat her, are you?"

He shifted to stare at her, his brows knitting. "You're going to make a *fine* rancher's wife."

"Are you?"

He shrugged, readjusting his bundle, its big black eyes on her. "She'll grow up and have babies of her own, Miss Vale. Feel better?"

She inhaled deeply, surprised she'd been holding her breath. Scrambling up, she patted the calf between its eyes. "See you later, Desiree," she whispered.

"Desiree?" Beau echoed incredulously.

"I named her that." She squared her shoulders mutinously. "She looks like a Desiree to me. What does she look like to you?"

"Pretty much like a cow."

There were a couple of snickers from his men. "I think she looks like a Desiree, boss," Ed piped up.

"Heck, yeah," Marv interjected. "If I said it once today, I said it a thousand times. Now that little heifer is a *Desiree* if I ever seen one!"

Beau frowned at his men. "You're all very funny. Maybe you should give up ranching and go on the comedy-club circuit."

Laughter abounded and Amy blinked in surprise. She looked back and forth from Beau to his men, surprised to discover that they liked him well enough to kid with him. Oddly, he didn't seem upset. His lips quirked in what looked very much like the beginnings of a grin. "Bye, *Desiree,* sweetheart," she ventured cautiously, offering a small smile as she stroked its soft forehead. "I'll come visit you."

As if in answer, the cow gave out a loud bawl and licked her hand.

"Lord," Beau muttered, turning to go amid wry calls from his cowhands of "So long, Desiree" and "Keep warm, little Desiree."

Amy couldn't stifle a giggle. For once, he was on the receiving end of the teasing, and she was tickled to witness it.

Even amid the jovial chatter, she had a feeling he heard her laugh, for at the door he paused. His gaze veered her way, and she froze, stunned and more disconcerted now than she'd been since she first met Beau Diablo. She thought he would stare daggers at her, but he didn't. His striking blue eyes held the flicker of grudging humor, and somehow, that disturbed her more than his fury ever had.

Wyoming was a white wonderland to Amy. Everything was half-buried in snowdrifts three to five feet deep, and trenches crisscrossed the land where cowhands on horseback trekked from buildings to barns to equipment sheds to pastures, and where they continuously had to break up ice on the creek and ponds and feed and doctor the cattle.

She'd grabbed a quick shower, but was back in the cook house in time to help Cookie and Archie serve beef stew and biscuits for lunch. Now, she was sitting in the back of a sleigh wagon full of hay bales, snow falling gently around her. The two husky horses drawing the wagon were high-stepping through the snow, huffing and puffing clouds of white in the frigid, over-cast afternoon.

Ed was driving the team and Marv was nearby, cut-ting wire from around the bales in preparation for dis-tributing the hay when they reached the low pasture where hungry cattle lowed and loitered.

The wagon topped a rise and she could see the cat-tle. Hundreds and hundreds roamed the valley, some tan, some black, some white with blotches of brown. Sitting tall in the saddle, roaming among them, she spied the unmistakable form of Beau Diablo. He was motioning, shouting orders to his men, but he was too far away for Amy to distinguish what he was saying.

She turned to Marv, the bearded bear of a man who spoke rarely, but when he did, it was bound to be witty. "Marv," she asked, drawing his squinty gaze, "what are they doing?" She gestured toward Beau.

Marv shifted his ceaseless squint toward his boss just as Beau began to spin a rope above his head. Before Amy could register what was happening, he'd dropped the lasso over a nearby steer. The animal didn't seem thrilled at being roped around the neck, and tried to scamper away. As he kicked and strug-gled, another cowboy lassoed his hind legs and yanked, toppling the cow on its side. As it fell, Beau dismounted and ran to the squirming beast. A third cowhand joined his boss, holding the cow still.

"He's playin' doctor today, ma'am." Making a pained face, Marv shook his shaggy head. "I can't stomach watchin' him stick them cows with a needle. Passed clean out a couple of times. So I get hayin' duty. Which is fine by me."

Amy watched as Beau kneeled beside the steer's rump. Though he was too far away for her to discern details, she could tell by his movements that he was giving the poor thing a shot. "Why's he doing it?" she asked, feeling queasy.

"That yearling's got pinkeye. After the boss sticks it, he'll spray his bad eye with medicine. Leastways that's what I hear. Never seen it myself, 'cause once I see that needle, I'm suckin' sod."

Amy swallowed spasmodically. She glanced away, noticing the man still in his saddle was straining on his rope, working to keep the animal immobile. After a minute, Beau moved to the cow's head and treated the infected eye with an aerosol spray. The cowboy who had been holding the steer stroked its exposed side with some kind of stick. "What's he doing now?"

"Paint stick," Marv explained minimally. "Ol' Homer paints 'em with the date, so the boss knows when that steer's been doctored and can check it in a couple of days."

"Oh…" Amy wondered if giving cows shots would become part of her job one day. She didn't like shots much, and cringed at the idea that she'd humiliate herself by ending up fainting, too. Trying to quell a growing discomfort in her stomach, she took a couple of deep breaths. Her gaze drifted back to Beau as he retrieved his rope and pulled himself into his saddle with a masculine grace that bordered on criminal. Turning abruptly away from the stimulating sight, she called to Ed, "Uh—let me know when to start forking this stuff out to them."

He leaned around to smile at her, his droopy mustache frosty and stiff. "You sure you don't want to drive the team, Miss Amy? Me and Marv can pitch the hay."

She smiled back. "I'd drive us into a tree."

"I could teach you real quick," he offered, his Adam's apple bobbing nervously.

Amy sensed that he had a bit of a crush on her. Though he was trying to hide it, he wasn't doing very well. Not wanting to encourage him, she shook her head. "Maybe someday after I get *really* good at haying—"

"Your optimism is admirable, Miss Vale."

Amy jerked around to find Beau astride his black stallion, trotting up behind them. Surprised by his relatively pleasant response, she said, "Why—thanks."

He grinned, a dashing, crooked show of teeth that brought out a roguish dimple in one cheek. She had no idea why, but the out-of-character charm sent a tingle of unease along her spine. "On the other hand," he drawled, "it's been said that an optimist is someone who hasn't had enough experience."

That did it! She'd taken all the ridicule from this man she could stand. Bristling, she cried, "I'd rather be an optimistic *fool* than an arrogant tyrant!" Her anger drove her to her feet. "I've tried to think well of you, Mr. Diablo, but I've had enough of your disapproving attitude. As far as I'm concerned, you're a bitter, suspicious man, and I feel sorry for you!"

Without having to look, she knew Ed and Marv were staring in horror. The wagon had stopped, and it seemed as though the whole world had gone starkly silent. She hadn't known her host long, but one thing she was sure of. Beau Diablo was not a man who allowed himself to be insulted in public and then granted pardon easily. She had a feeling that if the roads weren't still closed west of them, she'd soon be standing waist-deep in snow, thumbing a ride to Diablo Butte. From the glower on his face, she had a sinking feeling she might be anyway, closed roads or no closed roads.

His jaw worked for what seemed like an eternity. It was agonizingly clear he was reining in his temper and finding the job difficult. "Marv!" He shifted his sparking gaze to the bearded cowboy squatting motionless amid the bales. "You and Ed finish the haying. I'm shorthanded at the creek. I thought Miss Vale could help over there." Urging his mount up beside the wagon, he held out a hand to her. "Slip onto the saddle in front of me. It's too far to walk."

Now it was Amy's turn to stare in horror. She had no intention—no desire whatsoever—to be *that* close to him. Besides, she'd never ridden a horse in her life. "On—on that?" she squeaked.

"I'm fresh out of sports cars at the moment." He lifted a sardonic brow. "The *best* rancher's wife in Wyoming would be able to ride a horse."

That was a dare if she'd ever heard one. She could tell from the steely hardness of his eyes that he'd like nothing better than to have her decline, admit she couldn't take it. She'd be *darned* if she'd give him the satisfaction.

Even as determined as she was, she hesitated. There was no room on the saddle for her. She'd be in his *lap*! "But—but I won't be riding the horse, I'll be riding—" She clamped her lips closed, avoiding his eyes. More quietly, she asked, "Couldn't I please have my own horse?"

His exhale was born of aggravation. "The cattle don't have time for you to indulge in a charade of modesty, Miss Vale. We have work to do."

She hated to admit it, but he was right. It would take an hour for him to go back to the ranch headquarters and get her a horse. And she couldn't plod around in three feet of snow for very long without dropping out of sight from exhaustion and freezing to death—since he'd eat his fancy boots before he'd send out a search party.

Reluctantly handing her pitchfork to Marv, she took hold of the wagon's rail and lifted one boot over the edge. The black stallion whinnied, but was otherwise very still. She was grateful for that, but paused, not quite sure how to go about settling onto Beau's thighs. It wasn't so much that she wasn't sure how to do it; gravity would take care of getting on. It was more that she was trying to figure out how to best do it without *touching* him.

"Dammit, I'm not a nest of rattlesnakes." She felt herself being grasped by the waist and set squarely on his hard thighs. She didn't know if it was the landing or the unsettling location, but her breath caught in her chest and she couldn't speak.

They'd traveled some distance from the wagon when she found her voice, but she didn't know what to say. Hysteria was bubbling up inside her, and she had to fight an urge to burst into tears. Whether her emotional turmoil was because of pure exhaustion, Beau's incessant rudeness or his unwelcome intimacy, she couldn't fathom.

She knew she'd overreacted back on the wagon. She knew she was overreacting now. But knowing it didn't seem to help, not with Beau's thighs warm against her hips, making her crazy. And *that* realization made her angry. She didn't know if she was angrier at herself or at him. She couldn't think straight. Whatever it was, she simply couldn't stop herself from hissing, "I've met a lot of jerks in my work, but I've never met a man I despised so completely as I despise you!"

A chuckle near her ear astounded her. After that outburst, she'd expected him to toss her into a snowbank and leave her to be devoured by buzzards after the spring thaw. "Well, well," he whispered. "Maybe it would do you good to work off some of that healthy hatred wielding a sledgehammer."

She sagged with defeat. What was with this man? It was almost as if he was *trying* to make her hate him, pushing her away with taunts and sarcasm. She had no idea why anyone would deliberately do such a thing, but if that was Beau's aim, he was succeeding beautifully. "You have a charming way of motivating people, Mr. Diablo."

Another chuckle rumbled through her as his exhilarating aroma invaded her senses. Blanching, she clutched the saddle horn, leaning as far away from his chest as possible. Unfortunately, there was no escaping the manly feel of him beneath her as they bounced through the snowy meadow. It mortified her to discover how stirring his closeness was, even now, after she'd made it very clear she felt *nothing* for him but contempt.

CHAPTER FIVE

CAPTIVITY in Beau's arms was a disconcerting experience. She'd been so cold for so long, she found his radiating warmth to be every bit as inviting as his attitude was offensive. She bit the inside of her cheek, frustrated by her warring emotions. Cuddled there, his hands on the reins only inches from her breasts, his warm breath caressing her cheek, she was having difficulty keeping her loathing for him worked up to a frenzy.

He projected an energy, an exotic power that drew her against her will. She'd never experienced anything like it before with any man. Even when he was growling at her, her pulse raced and her throat went dry. She didn't like the helplessness of the feeling his nearness caused, didn't like the way he derailed her logical thinking and made her mind career down disgraceful paths.

"Have you spoken with Ira today?" he murmured near her ear.

"*Who*?" She jumped, trying to gather her wayward thoughts.

"Ira?" he coaxed. "Your fiancé and my father?" Readjusting the reins, he brushed her breast with his arm. Even through her parka, she registered the touch and her flesh tingled. Pulling her lips between her teeth, she inhaled to calm herself. Seconds ticked by, long seconds, but she couldn't find her voice.

"Would you like to start with a simpler question?"

She winced at his sarcasm. "The phone lines are down. I—I heard it on the radio when I went to my room to take a shower."

"I see."

Her heart hammered in her ears. What was her problem, and why did he seem to have the power to reduce her to acting like a complete dolt? This couldn't go on. *She had to get out of here.* "When do you think the roads will be clear?" she asked, upset by the frantic edge in her voice.

"Around here, they'll be bulldozed by tonight."

"Then I should be able to get to Diablo Butte tonight?"

"I said, around here." He gave his stallion a signal with his legs and his muscles flexed seductively beneath her. It was all she could do to keep from screaming. "High winds through Diablo Pass will prevent the dozers from clearing the road for another day or two. That is, *if* we don't get more bad weather."

"Oh—no…"

Another bothersome chuckle sent a shiver through her, and it startled her to discover she was leaning against him. When had that happened?

"I'd love to sit here and bask in your enthusiasm, Miss Vale, but we're here." Before the words were out of his mouth, he'd somehow managed to dismount, leaving her in his saddle. "Grab my shoulders." He lifted his arms to help her down.

"Grab your *own* shoulders." She swung her leg over the saddle horn to the opposite side, intent on dismounting as far away from him as possible. She slid to the ground, delighted with herself for her smooth escape. Unfortunately, the soft snow was deeper than she'd anticipated, and she couldn't find her footing. With a surprised squeal, she sprawled face first in the pillowy drift.

Beau's stallion snorted and pranced with surprise, and she wondered if her rashness was about to get her trampled to death. As quickly as she could, she rolled away, clearing snow from her eyes. When she righted herself, the first sight she saw was Beau, towering above her, his lips quirked in wry amusement.

"Okay, go ahead," she charged. "Tell me the best rancher's wife in Wyoming would have been able to get *more* snow down her blouse!"

Lifting a brow, he warned softly, "Don't do that again, Miss Vale." He affectionately stroked his stallion's neck. "Not many horses take surprises as well as Sovereign."

She grew fidgety under his close observation and dropped her glance to the spot where the big stallion was pawing impatiently at the snow. She couldn't think of a single argument in her defense. Probably because she had none.

"Want a hand up?"

"*No!*" She shoved against the snow in an attempt to stand, but once again couldn't find a solid hold. Her arm sank deeper, and she plummeted back downward, tasting snow again. "Don't you—*dare* say anything!" she sputtered.

She found herself being lifted. While she cleared her vision, she was carried several strides away. About the time she could see, he said, "Empty your mind, Miss Vale. Try to visualize standing upright."

She glared at him. "You're so cute!"

"People will say we're in love." His tormenting grin made her senses leap foolishly. Before she could think of a sharp retort, he dumped her unceremoniously on her feet. This time, she managed to remain standing, for he'd deposited her in an area beneath a tree where the snow had been trampled by his men. He indicated an ax and a sledgehammer leaning against the cottonwood trunk. "If you're not too exhausted from your little Indiana Jones quest to stand up, go take J.C.'s place chopping ice. Tell him to use the snowmobile and scout for broken fence and cattle that might have drifted during the storm."

Incensed at his belittling attitude, she stiffened. "Oh, right! Make *me* chop ice and let one of your big, strong hands ride around in a snowmobile." She fairly shivered with rage. "Some people would say that's not a wise use of manpower."

Irritation flickered across his face. "How many of your ribs are cracked?"

She blinked, startled by the question. "Uh—why—none."

"I see. Well, J.C. has three cracked ribs, and he's hurting, but he won't admit it and he won't take any time off." She was taken aback and must have looked it, for he chuckled ruefully. "From your expression I assume you haven't nominated me for sainthood." He crossed his arms at his chest. "No matter what you think, Miss Vale, everyone has some good traits. Even me. I assume you have some, too.''

That remark tweaked her pride. ''But so far you haven't seen *any*?'' she demanded.

He didn't respond immediately, merely watched her. After a strained silence, his lips twisted ruefully. ''I'll give you credit for one thing. You take more punishment than I thought you would.''

She eyed him with pure abhorrence. ''Your sentiment is so enchanting I think I'll have it embroidered on a pillow!''

The squeak of leather was her only answer as he mounted his stallion.

Upset that he could remain so dispassionate while forcing her to the brink of hysteria, she said, ''For your information, I'll relieve J.C. and I'll break up your darned ice as well as any man.''

He'd nudged Sovereign into a turn, but when she spoke, he halted his mount and looked at her, his expression preoccupied. ''Did you say something?''

Wanting to get a rise out of him and not sure why such a crazy need was so strong in her, she lied, ''I said your name suits you, Mr. *Diablo*. I'm sure you'd be right at home in Hades!''

Though his flexing jaw told her she'd hit a nerve, she didn't feel vindicated. As she stared up at him, an emotion more distressing than anger held her in its grip. He was an imposing, self-confident presence on his big stallion. His magnetism was riveting, almost overpowering. She'd intended to spin disdainfully away, but faced with his lean good looks and his hooded stare, she had to compel herself to break eye contact. Her spin, when she finally made it, was more regretful than adamant.

Unclenching a fist she had no idea she'd clenched, she grabbed for the sledgehammer. It made her stumble when it didn't budge. She hadn't realized how heavy a sledgehammer was.

"It appears your hatred of me isn't as strong as you thought, Miss Vale," he taunted. "I'd work on it. Meanwhile, use the ax."

Before she could spin around and suggest that he might rethink giving deadly weapons to women who despised him, she heard the muffled sound of hooves plowing through deep snow as Beau spurred his stallion back to work.

Amy was surprised at how warm she was. Even though the wind had picked up and the pewter sky was spitting new snow, she wasn't cold. The exercise of slamming an ax into ice for the past hour had kept her blood flowing all the way to the tips of her fingers. But warm or not, her muscles were crying out that they were going to stop functioning altogether if she didn't take a break.

"Miss Amy? Want some coffee?"

She shifted toward the young cowboy about her age, called Snapper. His face was long and bony and red from the cold. An unlit cigarette hung from a corner of his wide mouth because, as he'd told her, he was trying to quit but couldn't give up the feel of it dangling there.

She straightened from her crouched position, grateful for the respite. She accepted the thermos lid with a smile. "Thanks, Snapper." Now she understood why coffee out here was so strong. The caffeine kept these men pumped up with the energy they needed for the intense cold and physical labor. In her case, it was keeping her awake after days of little or no sleep.

"Take a breather, Miss Amy," he said. "This is mighty hard work, especially for a city gal."

She took a sip of the strong brew, beginning to wonder if her mind was that easy to read. Still, she didn't dare take a rest. All she needed was to have Beau ride up and find her sitting around doing nothing.

"See, the rule is," Snapper went on, "fifteen minutes off every hour. Ain't it, Willie?"

The fortyish wrangler with a scar where his right eye should be and a graying braid hanging to his waist, stopped shoveling ice. Leaning on the shovel handle, he nodded. "You betcha, ma'am." He winked his good eye. "Take your time with that java. Have yourself another cup. Me and Snapper'll be fine."

She sighed, unable to deny she needed a rest. Taking another sip, she nodded her thanks and set her ax down near the thermos and Snapper's sledgehammer. "I think I will."

"Take a good, long spell." Snapper hefted the sledge. "You done your share and more already."

She savored another taste of the hot coffee and scanned the creek where they'd already broken the surface ice. Cattle contentedly lapped at the water, oblivious to the fact that they were being waited on hand and foot. She shook her head, murmuring toward the cattle, "A thank-you would be nice, guys."

She grinned and turned to examine the frozen stream as it undulated along the draw. About fifty feet on down, it disappeared into a lush thicket. How lovely. There was a quaint little fence made from branches on this side of the thicket. It didn't seem to be holding anything, had no gate. It was just a little circle of fence about ten feet across, curving along the landscape. Snow mantled and rustic, it made a tranquil scene.

She wished she had a camera. Every direction she faced, she was confronted by a fantasyland of snow, juxtaposed against the stark beauty of denuded limbs, twisted trunks and dramatic rock outcroppings. Or she would delight in the grace of scampering jackrabbits, spy a shy deer peeping at her from a copse of pines, or gasp at the majesty of big horned elk off in the distance, silhouetted against sparkling whiteness. There was so much untamed, unpretentious beauty here. Every day, almost hourly, she found this dazzling wilderness more and more thrilling. After experiencing Wyoming in winter, she knew she could never be contented in a big city again.

"Miss Vale! *Stop!*"

Amy almost spilled her coffee when she heard Beau's stern command, and she gritted her teeth with consternation. He *would* show up just when she was taking her break. She'd reached the little fence and bent to step through the rails. As she did, she turned and shouted, "I don't take well to intimidation, Mr. Diablo!"

"Come back here!"

"*Make me*, Mr. Big Shot!" After stepping through

the fence, she straightened and trudged away, vowing to ignore him. There was a nice-size rock on the far side of the little pen where she could sit and lean against the fence to finish her coffee. Beau Diablo had no right to shout at her and treat her like a two-year-old. She'd been *told* she could take a break and she planned take it. If he wanted to browbeat her, he could just wait until she finished her coffee.

"Dammit! *Amy*!"

Her first clue that anything was wrong was when she watched the thermos lid go flying into the air, tumbling end over end as it flung its dark contents to the wind. Before she could imagine what caused it, she was jerked backward as something cinched her around the waist. It was as though a sea monster had reached out with a tentacle and snatched her off her feet. The only problem with that scenario was that she wasn't twenty thousand leagues under the sea. She stumbled once, but finally lost her battle with gravity and fell with a cry.

As soon as she was sprawled on her back, she came up flailing defensively. She focused her struggles on the tentacle gripping her waist, fearful she'd become the captive of some sort of Wyoming killer snow snake intent on squeezing the life out of her. But when she saw what clutched her, she was astounded to discover it was nothing more lethal than a length of rope.

Rope? Her mind was so clouded by fear it took her a second or two for that fact to register. But when it did, she grew livid. Rope? As in *lasso*?

"Beau Diablo!" she growled. "You did this, you controlling *swine*!" How dare he use physical force to get his way. It was then that she noticed the sound of horses' hooves thundering her way and she scrambled around, struggling to stand. She grappled to free herself, but Beau was keeping the rope taut and she found herself yanked against the fence. To keep from tumbling over it, she clamped her hands on the wood and glared at him. He was walking his stallion now, gathering his rope as he came, leaving her no slack.

She threw him a reproachful glare. "Who do you think you are, the Sundance Kid? I'm going to—I hope you know I plan to—" She swallowed, so furious she couldn't think of a threat horrible enough to fling at him. She tried again. "You—you bullying snake! I—I—*Don't come near me!*"

He climbed down from his horse and continued to imprison her against the fence while he looped the excess rope in his other hand. When he reached the fence, he startled her by straddling it and stepping over. He was only inches away now, and she couldn't escape him.

He said her name but she cut him off. "Let me go!" Punctuating her demand, she pummeled his chest. "I'm going to have you arrested for kidnapping and—and mugging and—and—illegal use of a *lasso*, and—"

"Amy!" He took her by the arms and gave her a shake. "Shut up."

"I won't shut up! I—I..." She frowned when he shifted toward the fence. Incensed that he would ignore her in the face of her fury, her glower followed his movements to find out what he was up to. "What are you doing? Why are you tying me to the fence?"

"So you can't get into any more trouble." He yanked the knot tight. "Now, be still and watch."

She yanked on the rope, but when it didn't give, she twirled toward him, intent on giving him another piece of her mind. Though she'd opened her mouth to shout at him, she stopped before any more recriminations could tumble out. As she glared, he kicked aside some snow and located a boulder about the size of a bowling ball and picked it up. She stared, perplexed. What was he planning to do? "Do you intend to hit me with that?"

"It's a thought," he grumbled without turning her way. "You'd be less trouble unconscious." He tossed the heavy rock about two feet in front of him, just beyond where she'd been before he'd jerked her back with his lasso.

To her surprise, the rock promptly disappeared. When it did, the disturbed snow around the hole also began to fall away a chunk at a time. The thermos lid toppled sideways and dropped out of sight. After a few seconds, the hole had opened up to about three feet in diameter. Straining on the rope, she peered into the chasm. There was nothing but a black void beyond the snowy crust. "What—what is it?" she whispered.

"Sinkhole." He came to her and bent to untie her from the fence. "Next time, listen to me," he admonished softly.

She watched speechless as more snow lost its precarious grasp on the grasses that were bowed over the hole, disguising the crater from those who weren't aware of it.

"How—how deep is it?"

"Deep enough to break your neck."

When realization hit, she went weak and had to grab the rail to keep from sinking to her knees. "That's why there's a fence?"

As the rope went slack at her waist, his sultry tang invaded her senses, for he'd drawn very close to relieve her of her bonds. "That's why there's a fence," he repeated, lifting his gaze to hers.

When he did, their lips were barely a handsbreadth apart, his glorious blue eyes so close his lashes brushed her brow. She squeezed the railing, suddenly recklessly conscious of his sexual appeal. His stare was bold, lazily sensual, and she found herself battling an urge to move the short distance that separated them and press her lips to his. The idea jolted her, took her breath away.

She heard a muffled curse as Beau abruptly straightened. She wondered if something about the experience had bothered him, too, but didn't have the time to dwell on it, for he barked, "You can step out of the rope now, Miss Vale."

Something was wrong with her brain. She was moving in a drugged slow motion, and it took her several seconds to pull her gaze from his troubled eyes. With great effort, she managed to look down at her rubber boots. His lasso lay in a perfect circle in the snow. "Oh, right..." Before she moved, however, her glance lifted on its own to meet his again. What did she expect to see? What did she want to see? His eyes were shuttered now, giving away nothing.

In a self-protective impulse, she bent and stepped between the fence rails, putting distance between them. Supporting herself against the wood, she clutched her hands together. "Thank you, Mr. Diablo," she whispered, her eyes downcast, "for saving my life."

"You're welcome." There was movement as he crossed the fence. "And I'm sorry for the way I had to do that. I hope I didn't hurt you."

Not expecting an apology, she shifted toward him, but he was already gathering up his rope and heading toward his horse. "I'm okay—and I apologize, too." She hadn't been aware she was going to say that until the words were out of her mouth.

He was poised with one boot in the stirrup, but when she spoke he stopped, glancing at her. "For what?"

She shrugged, embarrassed. "For hitting you. I hope I didn't hurt you, either."

A faint sparkle lit his blue eyes. "I may never recover."

"And—and for the name-calling, too. I'm sorry—but—" she had to add in her defense "—you shout at me all the time, so how was I to know..." She let the sentence die.

"Good point," he acknowledged, going sober. "From now on, if I call you Amy, you're in danger. Deal?"

She nodded glumly. "You must have an interesting life, if every woman you call by her given name is in danger." He suddenly grinned, showing that slashing dimple in his cheek. Her heart turned over at the sight—so sexy yet at the same time so alarming. It belatedly occurred to her that her remark had another meaning, one she hadn't intended—that his female companions were in danger of succumbing to his masculine charisma. Heavens! Maybe he even mistakenly believed that *she* was affected that way. Her cheeks grew hot with mortification. "Wait a second. I hope you don't think—"

"Afternoon, Miss Vale," he drawled, cutting off her denial. With a finger to the brim of his hat, he bounded into his saddle and rode away.

She toyed with her lower lip as she headed back to Snapper and Willie and her ax. While she shuffled along, she began to have a nagging suspicion that Beau should have called her Amy when he'd smiled just then. Forcing the notion aside, she rebuked herself. *How foolish! What could be dangerous about a smile?*

Valentine's Day was passing swiftly. The roads west were still closed due to high winds and blowing snow, and the phone lines were still down for the same reason. Amy had spent the day just like she'd spent the previous two, and she felt pretty good about herself. She could break ice on a creek and toss hay from a pitchfork as well as any city-born-and-bred woman in America. At least any with three days' experience. Maybe she was grasping at straws for things to feel good about, but she had to try to feel positive about something. Today was supposed to have been her wedding day. Instead she was being worked like an indentured servant from dawn until dark in subzero temperatures by a glowering host.

At least there was one positive thing about today.

She was going to get to experience a real live barn dance. Cookie had chattered happily about it as Amy had helped scramble eggs for breakfast. A neighboring rancher and his wife were celebrating their fiftieth wedding anniversary, and they were hosting an old-fashioned, down-home barn dance.

She smiled and patted Desiree's forehead. "So, I guess I'd better go, honey. You run back to your mama." Leaning through the fence of the pen behind the calving barn where the new calves were housed, she gave Desiree a hug. The cow bawled and nudged her cheek affectionately. "I love you, too. See you tomorrow."

Her bright mood faded with every step she took toward the ranch house. She hoped a barn dance would take her mind off her situation. Maybe, if she was lucky, Beau would be too busy to go. He hadn't left with the off-duty cowhands as they'd clambered into the newer pickup. The five wranglers who'd lost the draw to ride in the warm cab had crammed themselves into the truck bed along with insulated containers full of hot food. They hadn't seemed too unhappy with their fate, and had ridden away an hour ago, laughing and hooting, clearly planning to enjoy the distraction of an evening off.

She hadn't gotten far from the barn when she heard the jingling of bells. Pausing, she peered around to find the source of the sound. Out of the darkness, she spotted a pair of harnessed horses. They were drawing a wagon. No. As she looked closer, she could see it wasn't a wagon, but the most charming sleigh she'd

ever seen. It was painted silver, its back seat and front
seat made of red tufted leather.

She'd never seen a sleigh except in old romantic
movies or on holiday greeting cards with Santa at the
reins, but this had to be as charming as any she could
imagine. Draped over the horses' backs were leather
strips lined with silver bells, jingling and jangling as
the horses pranced through the snow.

"Thought we'd come get you, Miss Amy," Archie
called as he halted the team beside her.

He was sitting in the front seat. Cookie was in the
back, a woolen lap blanket drawn up to her throat.
"Slip that robe up there around your legs, hon,"
Cookie called. "It's gonna be about a forty-minute
ride, so you'll welcome it before we get there."

Amy was so charmed by the idea of going on a
sleigh ride, she didn't know what to say. Her spirits
soared as she climbed up beside Archie and pulled the
throw over her. She'd opted to wear a long, broom-
stick skirt tonight, and though she had on a slip, tights,
lace-up boots and heavy socks, the throw was going
to help. "This is exciting!" She shifted to smile at
Cookie. "I thought we were going in the old truck."

"That old sweetheart's been dying on me the past
couple of days." Archie shook his head, the tassel of
his red wool cap bobbing to and fro. "Since we had
this little rig in the machine shed, I decided why not
use her. There's nothing in this world as dependable
as *real* horsepower."

Amy sat back, breathing in the crisp night air. "Oh,
it's just so wonderful. I never imagined—"

"What the *hell* is this?"

Amy jerked up, startled to hear Beau's irritated question. She could just make him out, stalking toward them from the direction of the ranch house.

"Howdy, boss." Archie waved, seemingly unconcerned by the dire tone in Beau's voice. "I was jes' explainin' to Miss Amy about the pickup dyin' on me the past couple of days. Don't think we better chance it tonight. Could get stranded and that wouldn't be no fun."

Amy watched her host from beneath lowered lids. The floodlight above the barn door held him in its stark grasp, illuminating his wide-brimmed hat, his sternly sensual lips and the imposing width of his shoulders swathed in his split-cowhide coat. He stood not far away, his muscular legs braced wide. The tensing of his jaw betrayed high annoyance.

"Besides, boss," Cookie chimed in, "you know if we go cross-country we can cut twenty minutes off the trip. And we're late as it is."

Amy hoped the "we" she was talking about didn't include her host. Unfortunately, just as that hope sprang full bloom in her heart, Archie slid away from her. When she turned to see what he was doing, he'd already swung around to clamber into the back seat. "Hope you don't mind driving, Mr. Beau, but my bursitis is acting up on me in this cold."

Her hope died a silent, sickly death when Beau said nothing further. Scowling at his cook, he pulled himself up beside Amy and took the reins.

Cookie and Archie immediately became immersed in a lively discussion about how many years they'd been married. It had been going on all day and didn't sound as though it was near an end. "You're crazy, you old coot." Cookie laughed. "It'll be thirty-five years a week from today, and you know what the thirty-fifth anniversary gift is."

"Like I been tryin' to tell you, it ain't thirty-five, it's thirty-three. Do the math, old woman. Do the math."

As the couple behind them calculated aloud, chuckling and playfully grousing, Beau's thigh brushed hers and Amy swallowed hard. She shifted away as he signaled the team to move and they slid into motion. Amy remembered the lap blanket and knew she ought to do the polite thing. Nervously, she offered, "Uh— would you like a piece of my lap?"

Archie and Cookie continued to debate additions and subtractions at the top of their lungs as Beau canted his head in her direction. "Would I like a piece of your *lap*?" His gruffness seemed muted by curiosity. "Does this mean you care?"

She was horrified by her bizarre slip of the tongue. "Er—lap *blanket*!" She held up a corner of the wool for clarification. "I meant to say *blanket*."

"Did you?" His lips twisted as he held her gaze with shrewd, sparkling eyes. "Miss Vale, don't pretend you think, because you're engaged to my father, I wouldn't take you up on your proposition. We can share a blanket any time you say."

His challenge stunned her and she flung herself as far away from him as possible, which wasn't nearly far enough. "If I thought you *meant* that, Mr. Diablo, I'd slap your insolent face!" she warned under her breath. "For all I care, feel free to turn into Rudolph-the-red-nose *icicle*!"

CHAPTER SIX

THE Jones farm was all but hidden in a rugged, timbered valley. It was a quaint little spread out there in the middle of nowhere. The venerable barn looked like something out of an Old West movie. The first story was made of round pine logs while the top half was rough-sawn planks.

From atop the ridge where they were gliding along, Amy could see the front of the structure with its big double doors, bright light seeping out the cracks outlining it. Near the peak of the roof was a diamond-shaped window from which spilled more golden light. It was so picturesque she couldn't wait to get there—and leave a certain bothersome rancher's side.

Long before she'd been able to see any sign of civilization, she'd heard far-off Western music lilting across the frosty air. For most of the trip, the only sound she'd heard had been the jingling of bells on the horses' harness as they crunched through the sparkling, moonlit snow. Not long after they'd left the ranch, Cookie and Archie had lapsed into naps, and at the moment, neither was snoring. Beau, typically, had opted not to speak to her at all.

The melody wafting across the air was lively, and Amy found her foot tapping as she tried to recall the name of the piece the band was playing. It was a classic Western tune, but she couldn't quite think of the title.

She chanced a glimpse at Beau, silently handling the reins, leading the horses down into the valley. His expression was closed and he appeared to be concentrating on what he was doing as he led the team through the scattering of pines, heavy with twinkling snow.

She wondered if he noticed the beauty of the night or heard the far-off melody? Was he seeing the brightly lit barn? Did he detect the distant laughter that burst onto the night air every so often? On what dark trail did his thoughts dwell? She wondered, too, if he was cold. After his lewd remark earlier, she'd huddled alone in the blanket, trying to keep from noticeably shivering as the chill seeped through to her bones.

He didn't appear to be affected by the frigid temperature. She sighed, relatively sure she'd bitten off her own nose to spite her face. If she'd shared the lap blanket with him, she would be warmer now.

"What's that—s-song?" she asked, deciding since they were almost there, she might as well start getting into the spirit. Besides, talking would take her mind off freezing to death.

He turned his intense gaze on her. "Are you cold?"

Chafing beneath his regard, she wished she hadn't spoken at all. Defiantly, she shook her head. "I don't think that's the name of the tune. S-something about Texas, isn't it?"

His brows drew together in a fierce frown before he

turned away. "It's 'Yellow Rose of Texas'," he muttered. "Miss Vale, if you were cold, you should have
told me."

"Oh? What w-would you have done about it?"

"I would have kept you warm."

The quiet way he said it sent a quiver down her
spine that had nothing to do with the weather. "I'd
rather freeze," she retorted, hoping she meant it.

He considered her silently for a minute before he
shifted away to guide the team to a protected area
behind the barn where several other sleighs waited.

Amy compelled herself to take in the scene and to
attempt to forget about Beau. She noticed a number
of pickup trucks parked in the clearing before the
barn, along with a half-dozen four-wheel-drive vehi-
cles. There was a handful of saddled horses tied to a
nearby hitching post, as well as a few snowmobiles
scattered here and there. She shook her head, doubting
she'd ever see this many different modes of transpor-
tation parked outside any Chicago party.

"The Yellow Rose of Texas" had ended and another tune began. Amy remembered hearing this one
at the cowboy bar. It was something she liked by
George Jones. She couldn't recall the name, and didn't
intend to ask Beau. Hearing rustling behind her, she
noticed that Cookie and Archie had awakened. "We
here?" Cookie yawned loudly.

"Musta dropped off," Archie chimed in, sounding
groggy.

Amy felt the sleigh bob and realized Beau had
climbed down and was helping Cookie from the back.
Gritting her teeth, she tossed the blanket aside and

jumped down on her side. Intent on a swift escape, she took a step toward the barn, but found herself unable to move. She winced. Her skirt was caught on something, exposing most of her legs.

When she turned back to free herself, she caught Beau glancing her way.

"Problem?" he asked.

She couldn't see what her skirt was hooked on in the shadowy sleigh, but she had no plans to accept his help. "Nothing I can't handle." She fumbled in the darkness, but wasn't able to loosen her skirt from whatever was holding it.

"Sure?"

She cast him a defiant look. "I'm *fine*."

With a dubious lift of his brow, he turned to help Archie lumber down.

"Better get on in, hon," Cookie called as she and her husband hustled toward a side door. "Cold out here."

"I'll—b-be right there." She smiled bravely, waving them off.

"Skirt caught?" came a soft question nearby.

Darn the man! She couldn't turn her back on him for one minute or he'd sneak up on her! "A little," she admitted. "But I have it under control." Unaccountably jittery, she tugged harder than she'd intended and couldn't miss the ripping noise.

"Sounds like it."

She exhaled, exasperated with herself for letting him get to her. She fumbled, but could hardly get her hands to work. It wasn't until then that she faced the fact that she was numb from the tip of her head to her toes. Her hands were like chunks of ice and her fingers would hardly obey her. The ripping noise came again.

Her fingers were brushed away and her skirt was abruptly freed from a loose nail. "You're welcome," he muttered, taking her arm and towing her toward the barn.

"I a-almost had it!"

"Out here, that's what we chisel on tombstones of the terminally stubborn."

She yanked on his hold. "Would you at least let me check my dress to see if I'm decent?"

"I'll do it."

She managed to free herself with one mighty jerk. "Oh, no, you won't!"

His eyes twinkled with such masculine appeal she couldn't find her voice for a minute. "But it's all in the family, isn't it—Mom?"

"That's *not* funny!" Flustered, she spun away to scrutinize her skirt, fearful of finding a bad rip.

"It's right there." He knelt to lift her hem. "You tore the bottom ruffle away for a couple of inches. Nobody will see it."

"Thank you, Calvin Klein!" She snatched the fabric from his hand and bent to inspect it. Sure enough, he was right. No real harm done. She could restitch it easily enough.

Hearing the squeak of hinges, she glanced up. Beau was holding the door for her.

"Coming?" he asked, once again his serious self.

"I suppose." She straightened and brushed at her skirt more from uneasiness than anything else.

"I'll introduce you around." Extending his arm, he wordlessly offered to escort her inside.

She brushed past him, carefully avoiding his touch. He didn't force the issue, just followed her in. Though she was unwilling to admit it, she supposed it was only right that Beau introduce her to her future neighbors. After all, he was Ira's son.

Pasting on a smile, she vowed to have a nice time, even though Beau Diablo would be under the same roof. That's why she didn't object when he helped her out of her parka and hung it on a harness peg. It was far harder to keep her pleasant facade when he took her arm and began guiding her from person to person, which was no easy task. The barn was one hundred feet by thirty, lined with stacks and stacks of hay bales that served as bleacher seats to accommodate the guests while they ate or rested from dancing.

For what seemed like an eternity, Beau helped her up and down, around and over bales and reclining people, introducing her to most everyone in the barn. Though she didn't think anyone else could tell, she was painfully aware that Beau's dashing grin was every bit as counterfeit as hers.

A deep, shadowy hayloft stretched across the back half of the barn. A number of people had clambered up to find spots to nap, smooch, clap along with the music, or simply get a better view of the dance floor, strewn with hay and clogged with high-spirited cowboys and their ladies. Along one side of the lower level was a row of stalls. No longer used for calving, they were now filled with coolers and boxes of extra food and drink. In front of the stalls stretched a row of tables heaped high with steaming barbecued ribs, potato salad, baked beans, pies, cakes, spiced apple cider, coffee and soft drinks. Near the back, a butane stove was putting out plenty of welcome heat.

On the other side of the barn, the band dominated on a platform made of hay bales and plywood. Between the two sides, couples two-stepped and waltzed around the floor, hooting and laughing, feet thudding in time-honored country rhythms on the worn pine floorboards. With the women outnumbered by the men, Amy had spent little time cooling her heels as a wallflower. She'd gotten to know every cowboy in the county almost as well as every crack and worn spot in the floor.

A few minutes ago, she'd declined several invitations to dance so she could take a breather. Perched on the end of a row of bales about halfway up the bleachers, she was enjoying her view of the dancefloor. She hadn't seen Beau for a while and assumed he was reacquainting himself with several of the local ladies—possibly up in a dark corner of the hayloft. It wasn't a particularly outlandish idea, considering how popular he seemed to be with the local women.

Unfortunately, even against her will, she'd taken notice of him from time to time on the dance floor as one pretty girl after another took a turn around the floor in his arms. But she *wasn't* counting and she *wasn't* watching and she *didn't* care where he was.

"Having fun?"

She almost shrieked with surprise, but stopped herself, wondering what was wrong with her nerves lately. Though she governed her features to remain unruffled, she couldn't quite meet his face. Instead she pretended to watch the dancers. "I don't know when I've had this much fun," she said truthfully, managing the beginnings of a real smile. "The cowboy bar can't hold a candle to this."

He didn't speak, and her curiosity made her turn toward him. When she did, she was startled to see that his face was very close to her own. She hadn't realized her elevated position would place her in such intimate proximity to eyes that were such a pure blue—unwavering and direct. Her smile faded, but she refreshed it quickly. "And—and everybody's nice, too."

"Yes, they are nice."

His lips were close. Too close. And even though his expression was serious, something in his eyes seemed far from dispassionate. "Would you like to dance?"

No! her mind cried. "I—yes..." She blanched. Who had said *that*?

As he took her hand and helped her down, she had the oddest feeling she was standing on the sidelines watching some idiot who bore a strong resemblance to herself slipping into Beau Diablo's arms. She wondered who the look-alike fool could be?

A new tune began, and Amy recognized it as one of the most popular requests at the cowboy bar. It was called "Shut Up and Kiss Me!" a lively, two-step. She was so startled when Beau pulled her against him, she stopped breathing. At the bar, she'd seen the really good two-steppers dance close like this. But if you weren't good at it, your legs could get tangled and you could trip your partner. Her heart thudded, with a vivid mental picture of herself toppling them both and ending up sprawled on the floor.

Why couldn't the band have opted to play the "Cotton-Eyed Joe"? Men didn't slide women into their embrace during the "Cotton-Eyed Joe". And she didn't need to be pressed against his hard torso the way she was, didn't need to feel his warm fingers splayed across the small of her back. She didn't need that at all.

"You're a good dancer," he murmured.

She met his eyes with difficulty. "Every once in a while, somebody in the bar would get drunk enough to pull me out onto the floor while I was trying to clean off a table. After four years, I've picked up most of the dances." She added honestly, "I'm surprised I can dance with somebody who's sober."

He grinned, displaying his bothersome dimple. "That explains why you stagger and weave more than most of my partners."

She giggled at his wit and was startled by her amused reaction. Quickly controlling herself, she lowered her gaze and found herself wanting to put distance between them—at least emotionally—since she was clasped so securely to his body. "It upset me a little that you introduced me to everyone as a family friend instead of Ira's fiancé."

He quirked a brow. "Not many people around here marry more than once, Miss Vale." Though he maintained his outward affability, there was a hardening in his tone. "Since you're to be Ira's fifth wife, let's just say I decided to spare you some embarrassment. At least for a while.''

The cynicism of his remark grated on her. "That's very gallant of you, I'm sure."

"It's the least I could do as your host," he said, his tone equally caustic.

She wanted to slap his face and run away, but she endured the torture of his embrace, deciding it would be worse to make a scene. For a long time, they two-stepped around the floor without speaking, the lead singer whispering his husky "Shut up and kiss me!" all too often for Amy's state of mind.

She could feel the weight of Beau's gaze on her. When she could stand it no longer, she forced herself to meet it. His stare was insolent and assessing, but he didn't speak, didn't acknowledge the fact that she was staring at him, too. He merely held her against him, moving her expertly around the floor, watching her with that narrowed, penetrating look.

The long, silent observation preyed on her nerves, yet she was also filled with heady anticipation. She became all too aware of the warmth of his flesh, of his hand massaging her back through her cotton sweater. His scent was stimulating, and she couldn't avoid breathing deeply of him.

The composure she'd managed to maintain was quickly crumbling. Though his eyes glittered with resentment, she had the oddest sensation that mingled with all that passionate dislike there was a flicker of attraction, that his gaze was echoing the erotic lyrics of the song. "Shut up and kiss me!" "Shut up and kiss me!" "Shut up and kiss me, *Amy*....''

She stumbled, going faint at the very idea. *Could he possibly be saying he wanted to kiss her? And horror of horrors—did she have the remotest desire to kiss him back?*

Noting her unsteadiness, he gathered her more securely against him. "Maybe I should have a few beers," he said softly. "I'd be more what you're used to."

She found herself shyly smiling and wondering at herself. Before she could make any sense of the seesawing of her emotions, the song ended and a drumroll sounded.

There was a fraction of a second hesitation before Beau released her so that she could face the platform. When she was set free, she separated herself to a safer distance and focused her attention on Mr. Jones, their host. He stood before the five-piece band and beamed down at his guests. A wiry man with a strong, angular face, Al Jones was dressed in jeans, brown roper boots and a green-and-yellow plaid shirt. He sported a thick shock of silver hair, keen black eyes, a blade-sharp nose and affectionate smile that reminded her of Ira. Her mood darkened, and she had no idea why.

"Folks," Al began, raising his hands for silence, "I don't mean to spoil the fun with a lot of jabberin', but I figure since it's my barn, I can speak my mind." He wagged thick gray brows and grinned as his guests chortled. He lifted his hands for quiet. "It's time I said my piece about why Edna and I invited you all over here on this cold Valentine's Day."

Amy experienced a stab at the reminder of what

day it was, and that she was supposed to have been married today.

"Come on up here, sugar." Al gestured for his wife to join him. In her starched jeans, fancy boots and red ruffled shirt, Edna clambered up the wobbly bales. She was a spry, narrow-waisted, wide-hipped woman with rosy cheeks and a cap of curly gray hair. Though she wasn't classically pretty, her sweetness shone so brightly in her button-brown eyes, she seemed striking. What a dear couple they made. And they seemed so in love.

Al put an arm around his wife's waist and cleared his throat. "Edna and I are glad to be sharing our happiness with all our friends this evening. Getting to share fifty choice years with this woman is celebration enough for me, but, heck, a party's nice any time." He bent to kiss Edna's temple. "I'm the luckiest man on this crazy ol' earth, and I only hope every one of you sons of bucks in my barn here finds the same brand of love in your own lives. Makes this hard, back-country life worth the livin'."

Edna gave him a loving pat on the cheek, her face going an attractive crimson as she accepted his words of love. The two kissed amid sighs from the onlooking women and laughter and applause from the men. The couple became a blurry picture to Amy, and she discovered she was crying. Al Jones's statement had been far from flowery and as simple a declaration of devotion as she'd ever heard, yet it touched her deeply. Even frightened her, somehow. This sweet couple seemed to have found that elusive thing called love.

It was obvious, glimmering in their eyes, even after all these years.

She hugged herself, unsettled by the discovery. Could she be making a mistake by marrying Ira? Could there be someone out there she should wait for—her true love?

She tried to shake off the thought. Ira was a wonderful, kind man. After all, Amy's mother, Louise, had married a man she hardly knew. Louise's parents had arranged for her to marry a man much older than she was. Amy remembered her mother telling her that when Amy's grandfather had suffered a bad heart attack, he'd decided to find a stable home for his only daughter, Louise, and had chosen to marry her off to a family friend, Bill Vale. A high school teacher in Chicago, Bill Vale was twenty years Louise's senior.

Amy's mother had said her relationship with Bill had been platonic for nearly two years after their marriage, and that Amy's father had been a patient, compassionate man. Only after Louise had grown extremely fond of him had their marriage grown intimate.

Louise and Bill Vale had been a contented couple all Amy's life. She'd never heard her mother mention being head-over-heels in love with her father. Louise Vale had used words like "comfortable", and "compatible", and had seemed satisfied with her life. Until this minute, Amy had thought consideration and shared interests were what counted, not some intangible entity called "love".

She gave Al and Edna Jones another glance. They were arm in arm as Al helped his wife down from the platform. He kissed her lightly on the cheek, and they exchanged smiles as the band struck up a waltz. Couples came together and began to slow dance.

Unsettled, Amy sidled away, not daring to look at Beau. A thought nagged, upsetting her further. Could he possibly be right about her? Was she marrying Ira for his money? Would she have rushed into accepting his proposal if it hadn't been for Mary's situation and his offer to help?

No! she told herself. She *wasn't* a money-grubbing bimbo. She truly wanted to make a good life on Diablo Butte, to be Ira's wife—the best rancher's wife in Wyoming.

Feeling queasy, she swallowed several times. The welcome warmth of the barn had become stifling. Maybe she needed fresh air. Yes, that was it. All she needed was a little fresh air and she'd be fine.

Hurrying out the side door, she took in a knife-sharp breath and headed away from the barn. The snow crunched beneath her feet as she broke through the frozen crust, her skirt flirting with the surface as she dashed away.

She reached a pine tree, its lower branches cut away, and leaned against the trunk, huffing and puffing. Squeezing her eyes closed, she attempted to shut everything from her mind. She *was* doing the right thing, marrying Ira. Maybe Al and Edna had been matched up by their own parents fifty years ago. Lots of people came together in arranged marriages all over the world, and many worked out fine, didn't they? Most of them weren't in love in the beginning, were they?

Her teeth chattered as the cold began to penetrate. Pressing her hands to her cheeks, she was surprised to discover how hot they were. With a sigh, she sagged farther against the rough tree trunk, hardly registering that her body was raked by shivers.

"Are you nuts?"

She jerked around to see Beau stalking toward her. "Have you ever heard of hypothermia?"

She wasn't in the mood for his browbeating. "I d-don't know. Hum a few bars and maybe it'll c-come to me."

He shrugged out of his coat, putting it around her quaking shoulders. "From what I hear, suddenly gaining a sense of humor is one of the danger signs that you're freezing to death."

She sniffed disdainfully. "Well, *you're* obviously in n-no danger." His coat felt like sunlight itself, for it held the radiant warmth of his body.

"What are you doing out here?"

She deliberately faced away from him, restively tracing along the scabrous trunk in pretended nonchalance. "I wanted to think."

"Something wrong?"

He sounded almost interested, but it might be a trick of the cold on her frozen eardrums. She shook her head. "Go back inside. You'll get cold."

"Do you want to go home?"

Surprised by the question, she shifted to face him. "Wouldn't that spoil your fun? I mean, leaving all your devoted lady friends behind?"

He shrugged his hands into his jeans pockets and nearly smiled. "I'd be devastated."

His tone told her he didn't care one way or the other. "Then what about Cookie and Archie?"

"They have to get up early. They won't care."

"No." She toyed with her lower lip. "I'm fine. Really. I just needed some air."

"And to think," he added.

"Right." Her glance veered away. His dubious expression told her he knew something was wrong, but she had no intention of telling him what it was.

"Need more time to think?"

She didn't know if he was teasing her or not, but she decided to ignore it if he was. She was too emotionally spent to fight. "No, I'm all done." Avoiding eyes she feared might be glittering with wry amusement, she added, "Lucky I'm a fast thinker." Intent on going inside, she stepped away from the tree.

"I've been thinking, too."

Curious, she peered his way. She was afraid she'd regret it if she took the bait, but for some reason she couldn't help herself. "Thinking? All by yourself?" Now that she wasn't freezing anymore, she felt more sure of herself. Why not give him a taste of his own medicine?

He surprised her with one of his charming grins, and a tiny tingle raced through her at the sight. "Don't be bashful," he coaxed, lounging casually against the tree. "Tell me how you *really* feel." As he spoke, his breath clouded in the air. It was awfully cold, and even though he wore a heavy off-white sweater layered over a navy turtleneck, he had to be feeling it.

"Maybe we'd better go inside." She took a step in the direction of the barn.

He moved into her path. "Wouldn't you like to know what I've been thinking?"

His face was silhouetted against the soft moonlight, but even in the duskiness, his eyes riveted her to the spot. "Uh—actually, Mr. Diablo, I don't think I need to know—"

"I was thinking, since I won't be attending the wedding, maybe I'd better kiss the bride—now."

She blinked up at him, positive she'd misunderstood. But before she could ask him to repeat himself, his large hands were holding her face, his lips covering hers with a kiss that was disconcertingly tender. Amy realized for the first time that she'd imagined this man's kisses—hot, demanding, angry. But never gentle, never giving. This kiss was startlingly loving as his lips feather-touched hers in soft persuasion.

What was this? What did he think he was doing? If this was intended to be a chaste token between relatives, then he was sadly mistaken about the effect of his kisses. The tenderness of his lips sent sparks rushing through her veins, drugged her senses, and she found herself reaching up, clinging to him to keep from collapsing in a heap.

She heard herself moan as his mouth slanted across hers, caressing, lightly coaxing her lips apart. The subtle invitation was deliciously sensual and she responded by doing exactly what he'd slyly demanded, her lips parting joyfully.

He released her face and slipped his hands beneath the coat draped from her shoulders. Massaging her back, he moved his hands downward, delighting her flesh. She was stunned to find herself pressed wantonly against him, relishing his potent maleness, craving even more seductive stroking from his talented fingers. Her woman's intuition told her he would be a magnificent lover, and somewhere deep inside, a need awakened in her to know the full depth of his passion.

She felt luscious jolt after jolt as his tongue did wild, wonderful things to the sensitive recesses of her mouth. Some little voice in her brain was shrieking that this was scandalous. Wasn't this supposed to have been *her* wedding day? Didn't she plan to be Ira Diablo's wife? If so, then why was she kissing Beau Diablo so madly? *Why?*

The little voice was starting to penetrate through to her desire-numbed mind, and she grew mortified at what she'd allowed to happen. Her fingers were wound in the soft hair at Beau's nape, and she tried desperately to compel her hands to let go, push him away, but her limbs were simply not obeying.

Suddenly, he lifted his face from her throbbing lips, abruptly stepping away. Amy thought he staggered slightly, but she couldn't trust her own senses. Helpless, she slumped against the tree, holding on for dear life. Shamed, she hugged the trunk and leaned her fiery cheek against the cold, craggy bark.

"Dammit," Beau growled.

She tilted her face his way, breathing heavily. "You did that on purpose," she moaned, her words thick and sluggish.

He ran a hand through his hair without responding, but his jaw worked ferociously.

"That didn't prove I'm cheap!" she cried.

He gave her a malevolent look. "Who are you trying to convince, Miss Vale? Me—or you?"

"I've been kissed a few times, and you *meant* that one." She swallowed several times to clear the huskiness from her voice. "Don't tell me you didn't mean it!" She wasn't sure why she had to say that, but she did.

"What do you want from me? Sure, I meant it," he said, his voice hard. "I've already told you you're damn beautiful and I'd share a blanket with you any time. We'd be good in bed, and you know it."

Her heart stopped beating as he confirmed her worst fear. It would have been fine with him if he'd killed two birds with one stone—proved she had loose morals, and had an hour or so of meaningless sex in the process. It was all so cruelly calculated she wanted to scream. But something inside her was too broken apart for her to even stand without support. Closing her eyes, she turned away. "You don't think much of me, do you?"

"On the contrary," he said grimly, "I don't think of you at all."

When she looked at him again, her eyes were swimming with tears. "I've changed my mind. I'd like to go home." She was grateful the words came out as calmly as they did.

Nodding almost imperceptibly, he turned on his heel and headed toward the barn. She watched him go, watched his hard, powerful body, the same glorious body she'd so recently clutched and craved. Choking, she covered her mouth with her hands, fearing she would burst out sobbing if she didn't.

Before Beau entered the barn, he stopped and leaned a shoulder against the wall, apparently taking a restorative breath. He shocked her by turning her way, his expression grave as their eyes locked. Time seemed to slow, then stop as they stared across the shadowy stillness. Caught in the snare of his gaze, a painful irony engulfed her. Why had she never felt this connected to anyone else in her life—yet felt so completely alone?

CHAPTER SEVEN

WHEN Amy regained her senses, she realized she was being rude not to make her own goodbyes. She rushed inside and found Al and Edna Jones, then wished them fifty more happy years together. Then she shrugged out of Beau's coat and wordlessly handed it to him, tugging her own parka from his hand. She had no intention of allowing him to help her with it. She'd had enough fake gallantry for one evening.

Once they were loaded in the sleigh and bundled up, Beau headed away from the barn and out of the valley. Music resonated through the night for a long time after they left: happy, bright, spirited music, much like the rugged, hardworking people she'd met since coming to Wyoming. She'd become fond of the people very quickly, which only strengthened her original plans to make a good life for herself out here with Ira.

The only flaw in her plan was the fact that after her marriage she'd be related to Beau Diablo. The idea of seeing him, even on an occasional basis, was disturbing. His kiss had been a well-crafted act of sabotage. She didn't know why he'd bothered, since his relationship with his father wasn't close. Why should he care how many times his father got married? Maybe he just wanted to prove to himself that he was right, or demonstrate very graphically to her that she was no more honorable than Ira's other wives. So he'd used his subtle male expertise to catch her off guard and make her slip helplessly into his arms.

She glared in his direction as he lead the team along a moonlit trail that mocked her with its romantic beauty. Beau was very good at seduction. With every muscle, every fiber of her being, she wanted to leap up and shout that he had been ruthlessly unfair, kissing her the way he had. A few very select, very skillful men knew how to turn cold marble into molten lava with their kisses. That didn't mean the marble had been scheming to erupt into a fountain of sparks, ash and liquid rock, did it? So what if Beau Diablo was sexy. So what if he knew how to make a woman want him. That didn't mean she wasn't completely honest about her desire to make a good marriage to Ira.

She had an almost overpowering urge to scream, *"There should be a law against kissing like that! You should wear a warning label!"* She wondered how many poor, unsuspecting women had been led astray by those clever lips. Well, she didn't intend to be one of them. Her life's plan was made. She wouldn't be put on the defensive by his cold-blooded ploy; she wouldn't be made to feel guilty or wrong, darn him!

"Say, Amy, hon?" Cookie piped up, drawing her from her mental struggles.

"Yes?" Silently, she blessed the housekeeper for speaking. Any subject would be better than dwelling on Beau's kisses.

"You never said where your folks are. Do they live in Chicago, too?"

Sadness pricked her heart. "My parents passed away." She shifted to face Archie and Cookie, careful not to brush against Beau as she did. Their expressions were clear in the moonglow and she watched their smiles fade with her news. "A plane crash five years ago," she explained somberly. "I'd just graduated from high school and had been accepted at Northwestern on a scholarship. We were taking a trip to Florida as a combination celebration-vacation." She cleared her throat, surprised that after all these years it was still hard to talk about. "I was lucky. I just broke a leg. My sister—" She cut herself off. She hadn't meant to say anything about Mary.

"Oh, Lordy!" Cookie clutched her gloved hands to her breasts. "Please don't tell me you lost a sister in the crash, too."

Realizing it was too late to take back the admission, she shook her head, peeking at Beau. He was staring ahead, apparently disinterested in her chatter. "Mary's my sister's name. She was hurt badly, but the doctors think this last operation might finally help her walk again."

"How old is she?" Archie asked, his beefy face troubled.

"Sixteen." Amy smiled, thinking of her sister. "She's a great kid. Never complains. I know she'll walk again."

"Must be pretty expensive, those operations," Cookie said. "What about your schooling?"

Amy dropped her gaze to the hand she had draped

along the back of the seat. She was clinching it into
a fist and forced herself to relax, though the subject
was difficult to deal with. "Well, naturally, I couldn't
afford to go to college after my folks—died. But their
insurance helped pay for Mary's operations. At least
up until this last one. It's pretty much gone now."

"You poor kid." Cookie shook her head, tugging
her wool cap more tightly over her ears. "You've
been supporting yourself and your little sis all this
time—by yourself?"

Amy's cheeks flamed with embarrassment. She'd
never gotten used to the sound of pity in people's
voices, no matter how well-meaning they were. "I
found a job with pretty good tips." She shrugged it
off. "We've done okay."

"Where's your sister now?" Archie asked.

"A convalescent home in Chicago. As soon as
she's better, Ira said she can join us."

"That's dandy." Cookie's smile returned. "I always said, there's nothin' like fresh air to heal a person. She'll cure up fine once she gets out of that big,
dirty town."

Amy had to grin at Cookie's description of Chicago. Obviously, she didn't think much of city life.
"I hope you're right."

"The operation was a success?" Archie asked.

"The doctors thought the prognosis was good when
I left."

"Miss Vale," Beau interrupted brusquely, "don't
you care how your sister is doing now?"

She veered his way, breathing fire. "How dare you
ask me such a question?"

"Then why haven't you called her?"

Furious that he would suggest that she didn't care about Mary, she had difficulty keeping her rage under control. "Since I'm *obviously* a burden to you, I didn't want to trespass on your hospitality any more than I already have."

His jaw tightened. "Call your sister, dammit. Why would you think you couldn't?"

She heaved a groan. "You have the most irritating talent for making me feel wrong when I'm not!"

The stillness became oppressive, and Amy was mortified she'd let Cookie and Archie see the antagonism that simmered between her and their employer. She turned away, depressed. This Valentine's Day would go into her diary as one of her very worst— dead opposite from anything she'd imagined.

Hunching down in her blanket, she tried to absorb every ounce of warmth it had to offer. Though she would never admit it, she was uncomfortably cold. She didn't think she was freezing to death, for she'd read somewhere that freezing people started to feel nice and warm and drowsy. She was neither warm nor sleepy. She was cold and mad. Unfortunately, she was also quivering like a striptease dancer.

"Slide over, Miss Vale."

She glanced his way, then slid to the edge of the sleigh. "Far enough?"

"I meant toward me," he corrected, impatience in his tone. "Slip the blanket over my legs so my body heat can warm you."

She was so hostile to the idea, she found herself

hesitating even as another bone-jarring tremor shook
her body. "I—I find the brisk air invigorating."

"If you like shaking, you'll love pneumonia." He
grasped her wrist, drawing her close. "I told my father
I'd keep you from freezing to death. I keep my promises."

The next thing she knew, she was snuggled hip to
thigh against him, aggravated that their close proximity was so foolishly welcome in some primal, womanly part of her—the same foolish womanly place that
refused to let her forget his kiss.

The stillness was punctuated only by jingling bells
and the mingled snores of the couple in the back of
the sleigh, who apparently were able to drop off to
sleep at the speed of light. Amy would have preferred
that they remained awake and all joined in singing one
hundred rousing choruses of "Ninety-nine Bottles of
Beer on the Wall". She hated the grinding repet-
itiveness of the ditty and had heard it in the cowboy
bar more times than she cared to recall. But this forced
confinement beneath a shared blanket, wrapped in
Beau's warmth, brought unfamiliar senses to life inside her that were as disturbing as the touch of his
lips.

His arm slid around her shoulders, hugging her
against him, and she jumped in surprise.

"Getting warmer?" he queried softly, so as not to
awaken their sleeping passengers.

His chest was solid and inviting, his scent hypnotic.
If she were to tell him the whole, ugly truth, she'd
have to say she was sizzling, but she had a feeling he
was referring to the environment, not her libido.

"Yes—thank you," she mumbled, deciding there was no point in arguing. It would serve no purpose except to wake Archie and Cookie. She might as well accept his warmth humbly and remember to keep her distance from now on.

"Sleepy?"

"No."

"Go ahead and sleep, if you want. It'll be another half hour before we get home."

"I don't think so," she grumbled. Why did the Wyoming winter night have to be so wildly beautiful and the sleigh ride such an idyllic setting, with bells jangling and sturdy horses prancing through snow luminescent in the moonlight? Why did a bizarre feeling of having come home niggle at her brain?

"A nap would do you good." The statement came quietly, hardly discernible over the tinkling of the bells. "If you're worried, I don't attack unconscious women."

She shot him a sharp look and was sorry she did. His eyes glowed strangely in the dimness, and her throat constricted. After several ponderous seconds, she found her voice, rasping, "*Now* you tell me the rules!"

His lips quirked. "If you'd rather drive the sleigh, I'll sleep."

"Fine!" she retorted. "I just hope these horses are half bloodhound or we might end up in Japan."

He handed her the reins. "Good night, Miss Vale."

She stared, incredulous. "You can't mean it!"

"Hush. I'm trying to sleep." He leaned back, tugging his Stetson brim down over his eyes.

She held the reins warily, muttering under her breath, ''I *hate* you.''

He smiled, but otherwise didn't move. ''I gave you your chance to sleep.''

''I hope we *do* end up in Japan. I assume these horses are good swimmers, because sooner or later—''

''Just one question,'' he interrupted, prodding his hat brim up with a thumb and eyeing her speculatively. ''Do *you* attack unconscious men?''

She stared openmouthed. How dare he goad her so unmercifully? The egotistical bum! She thrust the reins into his lap. ''You know—the idea *is* appealing. It's just a shame I forgot my ax!''

His low chuckle warmed the chilly night.

Amy awoke at dawn to bad news. Snow was spinning and swirling outside her window. It wasn't a blizzard, but it was coming down hard enough to spell the end to her hopes of getting to Diablo Butte today.

Pushing up to sit, she brushed her hair back, dejection flooding through her. She shook her head in a physical effort to throw off her depression. ''Getting upset about it won't help, Amy. Work will take your mind off—everything. So get up and get busy.''

Ten minutes later, she was hanging her parka on a peg in the cook house, ready to help Archie and Cookie make breakfast. For a change, Archie was nowhere to be found and Cookie was measuring out flour for biscuits.

Amy plucked a dish towel from a drawer and tied a makeshift apron around her middle. ''What do I do?'' she asked. ''I'm getting pretty good at coffee and bacon. Maybe I ought to start there.'' She grinned at the older woman and headed to the nearest industrial-size refrigerator without waiting for a reply.

"Sounds good, hon,'' Cookie called over her shoulder as she worked at the room's center island work space. "We're startin' to make a pretty fair team.''

Amy laughed and grabbed the plastic container of thick-sliced bacon. "Sure. You and Archie do the cooking and I do the burning.''

Cookie chortled. "Now, that was jes' that one batch of biscuits. You're doing better'n Archie does most days, truth told.''

Amy started bacon frying, then measured out the coffee. "Speaking of Archie...'' She came over to Cookie's side. "Is he sleeping in this morning?''

Cookie grimaced and shook her head. "Bursitis has got him movin' slow, poor darlin'.''

That reminded Amy of something. "By the way, how many years have you and Archie been married? Did you ever figure it out?''

Cookie smirked. "Been married thirty-three years, but I got the old fool convinced it's thirty-five. So, next week about now, he's givin' me one of them relax-o-lounge chairs. You know, the kind that sits up or lays back.''

Amy nodded, having seen the commercials on TV. "So the thirty-fifth anniversary is the 'relax-o-lounge' anniversary?''

Cookie guffawed as she stirred the biscuit makings. "Heck if I know. But that's what I want, so that's what I told him.''

Amy had begun cracking eggs into a bowl but

stopped to grin at her companion. "What a sneak you are."

Cookie winked. "Hon, when you've been married as long as me, you'll know these men don't know a thing about shoppin', so you give 'em any good reason not to and they won't *have* to shop. They just buy what you say."

Amy lifted her brows, nodding sagely. "Sounds like a good plan."

The two woman were silent for a few minutes while Cookie got her first batch of biscuits into the oven. Amy dumped the eggs and other ingredients into a frying pan and was dutifully tending both eggs and bacon when she was startled to find Cookie lurking at her elbow. She turned, curious. "Anything wrong?" The housekeeper's normally jolly expression had gone somber. "Have I done something wrong?"

The housekeeper put a companionable hand on Amy's shoulder. "Not a drop, hon." She paused, appearing to vacillate about something. After a minute, she patted Amy's shoulder again, her decision made. "It's just that I figured you should know something, seeing how you're gettin' ready to marry into the Diablo family."

Amy grew apprehensive and fumbled with her cooking fork. "What is it?" she asked, not sure she wanted to know.

Cookie heaved a deep breath and removed her hand from Amy's shoulder to absently wipe it on her apron. "Well, it's like this." Her brows knit contemplatively. "I saw the way you and Mr. Beau was outa sorts with each other last night, and I figure it's because of what his daddy done these last years. You may already know, but they ain't real close.''

Amy nodded. "I gathered that."

Cookie shrugged. "Now, I ain't speaking bad of Mr. Ira. Every man's gotta live his own life. It's jes' that when he divorced Beau's ma, Mrs. Pamela, nine years ago, it tore her up pretty bad. Mrs. Pamela and Mr. Ira been married near thirty years. Poor Mrs. Pamela came to stay with her boy. Mr. Beau had to watch his mama waste away and die. She lived long enough to see her Ira cavort with one trashy woman after another, then marry that first one. That blow to her heart finished her, I figure.'' She plucked a checkered handkerchief from her hip pocket and noisily wiped at her nose. "Mr. Beau ain't never forgave his daddy for tossin' his mama off that cold way."

Cookie screwed up her face, clearly not wanting to say something else, but deciding she must. "This is nothin' against you, Miss Amy. You're a lady. I saw that the first day you worried 'bout me carryin' your bag for you. But Beau's heart was beat down when his mama died, and I don't figure he's seeing Ira's newest fiancée with such a clear eye as me. All them other women of Ira's was nothin' but a bunch of lowdown trash."

As Cookie stuffed the handkerchief away, Amy winced. Maybe it *had* been kinder of Beau not to introduce her as Ira's fiancée, if this was the reputation his previous wives had around here.

"No offense, hon. But that's the way it is." She took the cooking fork from Amy's slack hand. It was the first time she noticed she'd gone still. How sad for

Beau to have had to helplessly watch his mother die from grieving over her lost love. No wonder he didn't care much for his father or his string of young wives.

Cookie absently poked at the bacon. "So, if Mr. Beau acts like he's lookin' for a hog to kick, I was hoping you'd give him a little rope. He's a fair man. But if I say so myself, his papa's foolin' around made him miserable as a cowpoke ridin' night herd in freezing rain." With an encouraging grin, she added, "Jes' keep being the nice person I see, and one of these days he'll accept how different you are from them other gals. I swear he will."

There was a banging sound behind them, indicating the first of the hungry cowboys were gathering to eat. Amy's throat had closed, and she couldn't speak around the lump that had formed there. After what Cookie had said, she could hardly blame Beau for having a chip on his shoulder. Nodding mutely at the housekeeper, she took back the fork. "Thanks for telling me," she managed. As the older woman started to move away, Amy took her hand. "And, Cookie, I—I really believe Ira's seen his mistake. It'll work this time."

The housekeeper's eyes glimmered with compassion. Turning Amy's hand into her own callused one, she squeezed. "You're a fine person, hon. And for your sake, I'll pray it's true."

"*Coffee!*" bellowed one of the wranglers.

"You better have two broke feet, Willie Stumpet, shoutin' at me thata way," Cookie bellowed back. "Maybe you just got one good eye, but I figure you can see we're shorthanded here."

The weathered cowhand hee-hawed and ambled to the shelf where the coffee mugs were housed. "Miss Amy." He greeted her with a nod. "Don't let that bossy old stretch o' barbed wire teach you to be crusty and mean. You stay sweet and pretty like you are."

Amy felt a blush rush up her face, but before she could respond, Cookie retorted, "I'd watch the name-callin', you old slab of buzzard bait, or you'll be sorry the next time you want your grubby clothes washed."

Good-natured banter filled the room as more and more cowhands blew in with the frolicking snow. Amy busied herself filling plates. But as busy as she got, she couldn't stop thinking about Beau's mother and about Ira's treatment of her.

Though outwardly happy, she was far from it. Inwardly, she was eaten up with anxiety. Ira had admitted he'd done some stupid things in his past. He'd assured her he'd changed and learned the hard way what was important in life.

Surely that was true.

The day had been long and cold for everyone. Amy was tired and hungry, but she stopped by the pen that held the new calves to visit with Desiree. Her little chats with the calf had become the most enjoyable part of her day.

Once in the cook house, Archie had dinner ready, and when Amy began to help serve, he shooed her away. "No, you don't, Miss Amy. You work with them hands all day. I ain't lettin' you come back here and work in the kitchen, too. Have yourself a cup of coffee and relax there by the fire like the rest of them wranglers.''

Amy was too tired to argue. As she poured herself some of the strong stuff, she had to admit she could hardly lift the mug, let alone do much cooking. ''Something smells good,'' she said, taking a sip.

''That's a world-famous recipe of mine cookin'.''

Amy nodded. ''Smells like it must be famous.''

''Won first place ten years runnin' at the State Fair,'' Archie boasted, lifting the lid on a skillet to scan the contents. ''Now, you go sit yourself down. Supper's near done.''

She took a seat on the bench. Mysteriously, there'd been a spot left vacant in front of the fire. She knew that to be the most coveted location after a long, cold workday, and she had a feeling the men were being gallant, leaving it for her. Silently, she blessed every scraggly whisker on their faces. She was bone chilled, and the heat of that blaze meant more to her than a million-dollar diamond ever could.

The cowhands kept her laughing with hilarious ranching stories as their supper was served. Beau joined them late, taking a seat across from Amy just as she had her first taste of what she assumed to be chicken nuggets. It didn't taste quite like chicken nuggets, however. Trying to avoid eye contact with her host, she turned toward Snapper, sitting on her right. ''This doesn't taste like chicken, but it's good. What is it?''

Snapper had taken a mouthful of mashed potatoes, and tried spasmodically to swallow so he could respond.

"Mountain oysters," Beau said before Snapper could speak.

Her gaze drifted to his face with reluctance. "Mountain oysters?" she repeated, not sure she'd heard right. "I've never heard of them."

Beau's lips twitched and Amy noticed the other cowhands had stopped eating. She looked around, wondering why they were all so intent on her comment about the dinner. "Do you like them?" he asked.

Amy didn't trust the twinkle in his eyes. "They're fine." She started to worry. "Why do I have a feeling they're not oysters at all?"

A couple of the cowboys snickered and a tremor went up her spine.

Suddenly feeling a little sick, she placed her fork on her plate and stared at Beau. "It's something disgusting, isn't it—like rattlesnake patties or possum tongues?"

"We learned long ago not to waste anything out here, Miss Vale," Beau said, taking a bite.

She pulled her lips between her teeth, fairly sure she was turning green. "Oh, no—it's worse than I thought."

After finishing the mouthful, he went on, "Every spring when we castrate the calves, we toss the testicles in a bucket and—"

Amy's jaw dropped. "Oh—my—heaven!" She moaned, launching herself from the bench. "Oh—*dear*..." Nauseous, she lurched away from the table and grabbed her parka. She dashed out into the snow, hoping the slap of cold air would keep her from being sick.

She was leaning against the log wall, her eyes closed and inhaling deeply, when she heard the door open and close. Someone had come outside. She hoped it was Cookie checking on her, but she didn't dare open her eyes to be sure. Instead she just inhaled again, fighting nausea.

"The best rancher's wife in Wyoming wouldn't be your shade of green."

Her stomach reeled, but she held herself under control. "You enjoyed that, didn't you?" she mumbled between clenched teeth.

"Miss Vale," he said, sounding very close, "it's a prank we play on city people. If it makes you feel any better, most folks new to ranching areas react the way you did."

She opened one eye, feeling a little less like dying. "You people need to find some hobbies."

He grinned, lounging against the wall. "Don't tell me you wouldn't get a chuckle out of watching some hayseed trying to figure out how to eat his first lobster?"

She opened her other eye and lifted her chin. "It's not the same thing at all."

"How so?"

She wasn't sure her argument was on solid ground, but she refused to admit it. "Because—because a lobster is not an obscene part of a *cow*, that's how so!"

He chuckled. "I can't argue that."

She found herself smiling back and realized she didn't feel sick any longer. As a matter of fact, she felt a bit *too* good. It amazed her how quickly Beau's charisma could affect her. She didn't like that about herself, and she quickly sobered. "I—I hope I didn't hurt Archie's feelings."

"He'll live."

She eyed heaven, wanting to do the brave thing— go back in there and eat Archie's prizewinning mountain oysters, but she was highly doubtful that she could.

"Did you call your sister today?" he asked, startling her with the change of subject.

Wanting to avoid the troubles that came with looking at his handsome face, she stared past him. Snow danced through a shaft of golden light from one of the cook-house windows. "I—I thought I should wait until the rates went down in the evening."

"Go call her, Miss Vale," he commanded quietly. "Now."

She shifted her unwilling gaze to meet his. Several snowflakes had settled on his long black eyelashes. Melting with his body warmth, they sparkled like precious gems. Her heart skipped two consecutive beats at the sight, and the memory of his kiss came flooding back. Hurriedly, she moved away from his disconcerting nearness. "I think I will," she whispered, making a brisk escape toward the ranch house.

"By the way..."

She didn't want to stop, didn't want to turn back, but she forced herself, though she kept her glance focused no higher than his feet. "Yes?"

"Ira's been trying to call you on his shortwave radio." He continued to lounge against the wall, lifting one boot to rest against the wood. "Apparently our radio's been broken. I fixed it today."

Amy frowned, skeptical at the nonchalant tone. Why did she have the sneaking suspicion he'd purposely pulled out a wire or loosened a tube to keep her from talking to his father? What could he hope to gain, except maybe an opportunity to work her so hard she'd run screaming back to Chicago before Ira could talk her out of it? It would be just like Beau Diablo to pull such a dirty trick. "How did you discover it was broken?" she asked, the tightness in her voice revealing her distrust.

He shrugged, and it was the first time she became aware that she'd lifted her gaze. "Al Jones told me last night that Ira radioed him and asked if we were all dead out here."

A stinging accusation was on the tip of her tongue, and she wanted to shout, *"Lucky there was a party or your trickery would never have been found out!"* She didn't know if it was prudence or cowardice, but she decided not to blurt her indictment. Instead she began to back away. "Lucky there was a party, then."

"Lucky," he agreed with a shrug.

Her anger building, she halted, eyeing him narrowly. "So, how do I use this radio?"

"If you'd like, after dinner I'll radio Ira for you. You can speak to him then."

"If I'd *like*?" she echoed, incredulous. Spinning away, she tromped off. "Don't go to any trouble on *my* account, Mr. Diablo!"

"No trouble at all, Miss Vale," he assured her with infuriating politeness.

CHAPTER EIGHT

AMY had never been in the bunkhouse before, so she hadn't been aware Beau owned a shortwave radio. He'd sent her a message through Cookie to meet him there, and he would radio Ira for her. When she arrived, she entered to find a long, barrackslike room similar to the cook house, but without cooking facilities.

At the end where she entered, there were several easy chairs scattered around next to table lamps or standing lamps. A couple of wranglers looked up from books and smiled. J.C., the man with the cracked ribs, grinned at her through his chest-length beard, and continued to puff on a pipe that gave off a mellow cherry scent. She smiled back. "Mr. Diablo sent for me."

J.C. nodded his balding head. "Probably be right here, miss," he said, his teeth clenched around his pipe. She wanted to ask him how his ribs were, but decided he'd be embarrassed. Nodding, she turned away and scanned a bookcase, filled with dog-eared novels, that dominated the front wall. Colorful woven rugs dotted the plank floor giving the room its only touches of color—except for the colorfully clad cowhands.

In one corner sat a card table. Four folding chairs

stood away from the table as though they'd been left in haste—probably about the time the blizzard hit— and hadn't been used since.

Midway into the sparsely furnished room, there were six sets of bunk beds, three to a side, all neatly made. A couple of off-duty hands were dozing, oblivious to lights or conversation. Wooden lockers were fastened to the wall between the beds. The rear of the long room held a couple of doors. Amy assumed they led to the bath and shower.

There was no fireplace in the bunkhouse, but there were a couple of butane stoves, one in front and one in back. Even so, the room was a little cool for her tastes. She decided not to take off her parka or she'd have to huddle by one of the stoves. Besides, she wouldn't be here long. Since the shortwave radio was sitting right next to the card table, she had a feeling there would be absolutely no privacy, so the conversation would be short and discreet.

The door burst open, and Amy thought it was Beau, but instead she saw Snapper dash in, his face even more red than usual. "Come on, J.C." He darted to the bunks and swatted at the sleeping men to rouse them. "Marv! Ed! We got a cow down in the north pasture and the boss said to get her on the downer cow skid as quick as possible."

J.C. and the others were up and pulling on coats and gloves almost before Snapper's words were out. "Can I help?" she asked.

Snapper grinned shyly. "No, ma'am. We got it handled."

"What's wrong with the cow?"

"Slipped on ice. She'll be okay once we get her to solid ground. But right now she can't get her footin'."

"Poor thing," Amy mused as the men filed out into the cold night.

After the noise of tromping boots and the slamming door, the place seemed eerily quiet. She could hear the hiss of the nearby butane stove and the tick of a clock she hadn't yet spotted. Looking around, she spied it: a little cuckoo with painted alps and a mountain chalet above the clock face was nailed to the wall above one of the lower bunks. Its hands showed the time as a few minutes after seven. She'd just missed the birdie, or chalet owner, or whatever it might be, make his seven o'clock appearance.

The door squeaked again, and she stiffened. The authoritative tread on the floor had a disturbingly familiar sound. "Sorry to keep you waiting," he said, not sounding sorry at all.

She turned, her expression as stiff as her posture. "I just got here," she lied. For all she knew he'd been lurking outside and knew exactly how long he'd kept her cooling her heels. "Will that cow be okay?"

He'd slid out of his jacket and was hanging it on a peg. He frowned her way. "What cow?"

"The one that slipped on the ice."

He deposited his Stetson on a second hook. "It'll be fine, since Willie spotted it. If it'd been down all night, it could have frozen to death."

She bit her lip. "You deal with a lot of life and death things out here."

He scanned her face, his expression cool. "Nature can be cruel, Miss Vale."

She nodded. "Still, it must be hard some days...."

"Getting cold feet?" He headed toward the corner where the shortwave was housed.

"My feet have been cold for days, Mr. Diablo. But if you mean, am I changing my mind, the answer's no." She joined him as he sat down before the radio, and for some reason found herself tugging her coat more closely around her. His attitude was decidedly chilly this evening. Adding ice to her tone so it would match his, she asked, "Could we get on with the call?"

He leaned back and grabbed the nearest folding chair and drew it up beside him. "Here, sit down."

She didn't like the idea, but had no intention of letting him think he frightened her. She plopped into the chair and listened in stoic silence while he radioed Diablo Butte. It took several attempts before someone came on the transceiver at the other end. The voice was full of static and definitely not Ira's. After telling the employee to get his father, Beau handed Amy the microphone. "Press this talk switch when you're speaking. When you're finished, let go. Got it?"

She nodded, hoping she did, but she hid her insecurity. "No problem."

He stood, but instead of leaving, he lingered. Amy couldn't see his expression without turning and she didn't want him to know she was even aware that he hadn't disappeared in a puff of black smoke. But she was very aware of him, his scent taunted, his eyes burned into her. She shifted, crossed and uncrossed her legs, cleared her throat. Nothing worked to remove him from her consciousness.

"Did you talk to your sister?"

His curt question made her fumble with the mike in her hand. Getting hold of herself, she nodded. "She's doing fine." Unable to help it, she faced him and found herself smiling. It had been a real balm to her soul to have a nice visit with Mary.

He watched her, eyes brooding. "Call her tomorrow if you want." He pivoted away, apparently to give her privacy.

"Thank you," she murmured, truly meaning it. Though his brusque attitude dimmed her smile, she was more grateful for his permission to call Mary than she'd been for his food and shelter. She was sorry he disliked her so much that he couldn't accept her thanks with any friendliness.

He looked over his shoulder, clearly startled by her show of gratitude. He frowned, but before he could say anything, there was a squawk on the radio. Amy jumped as the jarring noise became Ira's voice. She turned toward the radio, straining to hear. "Is that you, little sweetheart?" came the cheery voice, sounding metallic.

Amy pressed the talk switch. "Hi, Ira. How are you?" She stopped, then belatedly remembered Beau's instructions and let go of the talk switch.

"I'm *lonely*, little one! But I bet you're having the worst of it, stuck there with my grouchy son." He laughed one of his melodious laughs she remembered so well, but she was surprised his joviality didn't lift her spirits. Far from it. She felt oddly distanced from him. Trying to shake off the feeling, sure it was pre-wedding jitters, she laughed back. "It's been an experience," she called into the microphone. "I've learned how to feed cattle and break up ice."

"The hell you say," Ira shouted back. "Well, don't worry about it, little one. Right after the wedding, I'm going to reward your patience about this damnable snow with a shopping spree in Paris. How does that sound?"

Amy was taken aback. "Oh—Ira. You never mentioned a honeymoon trip."

He laughed his big, happy laugh again. "Well, little one, to be honest, I can't leave the ranch right now. But I figured you'd want to get out of all this snow. And what's nicer than spending money in an exotic place to take your mind off lousy weather? You can stay until spring."

She stared at the microphone, far from thrilled with this news. Her plan had been to get to know her husband, learn about his ranch, become a real rancher's wife. Besides, she didn't want to be gone when Mary was ready to travel. "Ira—that's kind of you…" She stopped, grimacing. She didn't want to hurt his feelings, but she had to find a way to explain that she had no intention of chasing off to Europe.

"Sweetheart," he came back, and Amy realized she must have let go of the talk switch. "Cook's yelling at me to come to dinner or he'll toss it to the dogs. I'll talk to you tomorrow."

"Oh—okay…" She wanted more time to discuss this Paris trip with him, but was frustrated by the unnatural way she was having to do it. "Uh—goodbye, Ira."

There was nothing but static to answer her.

"Finished?"

She spun around. Beau was lounging against the far wall, certainly not far enough away to be out of earshot. She glared at him. "You should know if I'm finished or not. You could hear everything as well as I could."

He pushed away from the wall. "Sounds like these few days with a grouch are going to pay off royally."

His tone was so sarcastic, Amy found Cookie's request to give him a little rope an impossibility. How dare he eavesdrop and then make fun of her in the bargain. "Why, yes, it looks like it *is* going to pay off! I *adore* Paris. Enough to put up with the biggest grouch west of the Mississippi for an entire week!" Hopping up from the chair, she sailed past him, highly insulted. Most of what she blurted was a lie. But there was one part of her speech she meant. He *was* a grouch. Even his handsome face and sculptured body couldn't change that. "Good night, Mr. Diablo." She threw open the door and headed out into fluttering snow.

"*Au revoir, mademoiselle,*" he drawled, cold irony in his voice.

Amy didn't know if she was more irritated or more hungry. If pressed for the truth, she was fairly sure she knew what was bothering her, but she preferred to think she was tossing and turning because she hadn't eaten dinner. The other possibility was too unsettling to dwell on.

Tossing off the covers, she got out of bed and dressed. She couldn't bear lying there with nothing to do but think! Grabbing her parka, she tiptoed through the house and into the kitchen, where she threw together a cheese sandwich, then slipped out the kitchen door. Another inch of snow had fallen since she'd gone to bed several hours ago. She decided that trudging to the barn in this bitter cold was exactly what she needed to work off her pent-up energy.

She ate the sandwich as she walked, downing the last bite when she reached the pen where Desiree was housed. Climbing through the rails, she softly called her little friend. After a minute, she saw the spindly baby amble over and bawl with recognition. Perching on the bottom fence rail, she hugged the calf. It was nice to be offered a tidbit of unqualified love, even if it was from a dumb animal that probably couldn't tell her from any of the other humans on the place. But she didn't care. She just needed some comfort and warmth. "How are you doing, Desiree?" She rubbed the calf's neck affectionately. "If you've got some time, I need to talk—woman to woman."

Right on cue, the baby bawled again, and Amy smiled. "Thanks, sweetie. I'll do the same for you, any time."

For several minutes, she stroked Desiree's silky back. She wasn't hungry any longer, but she didn't feel better. She'd been afraid all along that it hadn't been hunger keeping her awake. She opened her mouth, but couldn't voice her apprehensions. She wasn't sure if it was because her thoughts were too muddled to put into words, or if they were too horrible to say out loud.

Restive and anxious, she stroked the calf. The conversation with Ira last evening had struck fear in her heart. Was he really interested in a true wife, a true home? What if she was just another girl-toy to him? She hugged Desiree's neck, suddenly frightened.

She couldn't stand the idea of such a sham of a life. What should she do? Should she pack up and go back to Chicago? Or was she overreacting? Maybe all she had to do was have a nice, private talk with Ira, convince him she didn't need trips to Paris to make her happy. All she wanted was a stable, secure home and family, like the one her parents had made together.

"Okay, Desiree. Since I don't seem to be able to talk about it out loud, how are you at mental telepathy?" The calf blinked and she smiled wanly. "That good? Wonderful." She pressed her cheek against the calf's neck, pondering what she should do. She supposed she shouldn't act rashly. Maybe Ira was overcompensating out of his concern for her happiness. If she explained how she felt, everything would probably be fine, wouldn't it?

A tear slid down her cheek and she had to stifle a sob. "Oh—Desiree." She shook her head to staunch the afflicted words from flowing out. Still, her mind cried, *"Why do I have the feeling it's not that easy?"*

The calf wiped a sloppy tongue across her chin, seeming to show compassion. Amy sat back on the rail and swiped at her eyes. "Thanks, sweetie." She began to absently stroke the animal's back again, staring up at the sky. There were no stars and hardly any illumination, and she felt very alone. She kept stroking Desiree's back, contemplating why it seemed like nothing in life was easy. She liked Ira, she really did, but...

Biting down hard on the inside of her cheek, she struggled to force back a thought that kept trying to break into her consciousness. Fisting her hands at her cheeks, she squeezed her eyes tight. She was *not* falling in love with Beau Diablo! She was not! His kiss had *not* meant the moon and the stars to her! Besides, his contempt for her was so palpable, she was surprised she didn't keep hitting it head-on, like an invisible shield, whenever she got within ten feet of the man.

She was crazy to allow such a ludicrous idea to intrude on her thoughts, spoiling her sleep. It didn't matter that she melted when she saw him, that her heart tripped over itself at the sound of his voice. It didn't mean anything that even his grim expression thrilled her more than Ira's friendly laugh and ingratiating charm. Beau made it clear with every look, every word he spoke, that he didn't like her, and she was determined to keep that feeling completely mutual.

Deep inside her brain, a little voice nagged, *"Who are you trying to convince, Amy? Me—or you?"* The mental query shook her.

"What do you think, Desiree?" she whispered shakily. "Any answers?" She shook her head at herself. Here she was seeking advice from a three-day-old calf, in weather that would gleefully turn her to an ice sculpture in an hour's time. Was she going crazy or was she just lonely and nervous about getting married?

She remembered her mother confiding how frightened she'd been before her wedding, and how she'd almost run screaming into the street. But she hadn't, and years later she'd been able to smile at her daughter and say that she was glad she hadn't.

Taking a breath of icy air, she stood, giving the calf one last hug. "Thanks, honey. I think you're right." This quiet time out here with an accepting companion had helped clear her mind. What she needed to do was get to Diablo Butte and see Ira face-to-face. Have that talk. And if by some chance she felt he wasn't willing to try to make a real marriage, then she wouldn't go through with it.

If it came to that, she would figure out a way to deal with Mary's money problems. She knew, without a miracle, their medical debts were becoming insurmountable, but she wouldn't consider marrying someone for his money. If she did, she'd be as bad as Beau believed her to be.

Stepping back between the railing, she patted the calf's cheek. "You're a good little listener. Now get some sleep." The calf bawled and scooted up to stick its face through the fence, big eyes wistful. Amy gave in and hugged her again. "I guess you deserve a little extra loving, being awakened at three o'clock in the morning that way."

After kissing the calf on the top of its furry head, she hurried toward the ranch house. She was so cold she felt like a block of ice, and was grateful there would be coffee in the kitchen pot. Cookie always left some warming on winter nights for what she called "frost-bit cowboys".

After removing her parka, she checked the wall clock. It was just past three-thirty. Pouring herself a cup, she sat down before the kitchen fire. It didn't provide much warmth, and when she looked at it, she discovered there was nothing left but embers.

Resolved to find heat somewhere, she stood and pushed through the kitchen door, heading around the corner. Flickering light in the living room caught her eye, and she smiled. How nice. She could thaw out before a real fire. Silently blessing the person who'd put on logs too large to burn quickly away, she headed for the fireplace, settling on the wide stone lip of the outer hearth.

She sniffed the strong coffee, then sipped. It warmed her insides as the blaze caressed her back. Inhaling deeply, she savored the smell of the wood fire mingled with the coffee. She was learning to like this brawny Wyoming brew, and she was discovering she enjoyed spending quiet time like this. She only wished she didn't have such troublesome thoughts milling around in her brain, driving her insane with worry. Trying to push from her mind all her fears about Ira's motives and her uninvited attraction to Beau, she muttered, "I really, really *hate* this!"

"I'm sorry our coffee isn't up to your standards, Miss Vale."

Amy's head snapped up and she scanned the darkness. He wasn't on the couch or the nearby chairs. She could see them too well in the fire's glow. Hearing movement, she veered around to stare into the blackness at the back of the room. He must have been standing before the window wall, watching the night.

Now she could see him, a vague silhouette, slightly blacker than the blackness of the shadowy world beyond. He was moving, coming nearer.

She set her mug aside, for it had begun to shake so violently she was afraid she'd drop it if she didn't. "D-don't you sleep?" Why did he—*of all people*—have to show up?

"Apparently I get as much sleep as you do." He came so close their boots almost touched. When he stopped, he shrugged his hands into his jeans pockets. "What are you doing prowling around at this hour?"

She couldn't tell if he was accusing her of anything or not. His tone gave nothing away. Presenting a cavalier attitude she didn't feel, she smirked. "I was casing the joint for pawnable stuff. You know, sterling silverware, gold jewelry, big wheels of cheese. The usual loot *bimbos* steal."

An ironic smile tugged at one corner of his mouth. "And you decided to take a break from stealing cheese and have some coffee?"

She shifted away from his bothersome good looks. Drawing her legs up onto the hearth, she wrapped her knees with her arms. "You know what they say—all work and no play…"

"Excited about your trip?"

"What trip?" She turned, confused. His features were highlighted by the golden flicker, his hair radiant with amber highlights. Those blue eyes were pure fire, making her pulse jump and leap awkwardly.

"To France."

The reminder was like a slap, but she worked at keeping her expression bland. "Aren't you clever to

guess it. My fabulous trip to Paris has been keeping
me awake, I'm so hot to buy, buy, buy!''

He startled her by joining her on the hearth, his arm
brushing her back as he sat down. Reflexively, she
dropped her feet to the floor and scooted away from
him.

When she peered at his face, he was scanning her
critically. ''Am I crowding you?''

''It's your fire.'' Her teeth worried her lower lip.
He was too close, observing her too thoroughly. As
much out of nervousness as to restore warmth to her
body, she rubbed her arms.

''Are you cold?''

Deciding her little trek in the snow was none of his
business, she shrugged. ''The atmosphere's been
pretty chilly around here.'' He didn't respond, and his
continued silent regard began to wear on her. If it
weren't that the blaze felt so good, she would have
vaulted up and fled. But since she was chilled to the
bone, she refused to allow his stare to intimidate her
into flight—at least not as long as her feet were numb.
Concluding that conversation had to be better than this
strained quiet, she asked, ''So—what are you doing
up?''

''Thinking about you.''

The softly spoken admission shot through her like
liquid fire, staggering her. She couldn't believe she'd
heard right and twisted his way. ''Thinking about
what?''

''You,'' he repeated, and the world teetered
slightly. ''I've been wondering what makes you tick.''

She was unable to move or think. She could only

stare at him as firelight danced along his ruggedly handsome features. She didn't dare look into his eyes for fear she would see something undeniable there, something that would draw her into his dangerous arms again. "It—wouldn't matter what I told you," she managed weakly. "You have your mind made up about me."

"You mean the fact that I think you're a shallow party girl?"

His harsh portrayal hurt, but she wouldn't allow him to see her pain. "Is that what you really think I am?" she countered. "Or is it what you *want* me to be?"

There was a change in his eyes, an ominous change, and a hardening around his jaw, but she refused to cower beneath his glare. Her heart was pounding so hard she didn't know if her rib cage would survive the battering. Weary of fighting her fascination for him, and fearing she was about to lose the battle, she decided drastic measures had become necessary.

Her plan came to her in a rush, fully formed and brutal out of necessity and self-preservation. She had to make him so enraged at her he would have nothing to do with her for the rest of her time here. She must fling some hard truths at him, make him furious enough to keep his distance.

"I think you—you *want* me, Mr. Diablo." She eyed him directly, using all her willpower to keep her voice from cracking. "I think it irritates you that your father is marrying me—because—because you're hot for me and you can't have me!" She had no idea if what she was saying would truly make him mad or if he'd

merely laugh at her and mock her the way he had so
many times before. But she'd started this, so she had
to plunge on, intent on making him despise the sight
of her. "I think you want to kiss me right now, but
you're trying to manipulate me—*the shallow party
girl*—to start things for you so you don't have to betray your father. You want me to betray him for you.
Well, I'm *not* the conniving snake here. You are. So,
if you want a piece of my—my action, buddy, you
have to do your own dirty work. And I don't believe
even an egotistical jerk like you would sink that low."
She clamped her jaws together and jumped to her feet.
There! *If that didn't make him want to throw her off
a cliff, she didn't know what would*!

She had only taken a step away from him when she
found herself caught by the wrist. He was suddenly
standing, growling out an oath. "*Dammit*!" He
dragged her to face him, his features fierce. "You're
right, Amy. I do want you. But you're wrong about
my father." Taking her by the shoulders, he tugged
her against him. "I don't give a damn about betraying
him. He *invented* the word."

Amy's eyes stung with tears at his savage tone, but
she blinked them back. "Let me go!"

"You don't want that. You want me as much as I
want you."

She was dizzy with longing, but she tried to deny
the truth. She opened her lips, but no angry rejection
came. Suddenly, they were clinging together in a rush
of wayward desire. Claiming her lips hungrily, he
crushed her to him. The sensual ravishment of her
mouth sent spirals of delight through her and she stood

on tiptoe, hugging him, hating herself, but unable to push away. What he'd told her had been agonizingly on target. She wanted him as badly as he wanted her. His slightest touch set her aflame, burning away all her good intentions.

Moaning with desire, she returned his kisses with careless abandon, her hands searching, exploring his broad back. He felt so thrillingly male, his scent an aphrodisiac as his hands massaged an exciting message she couldn't ignore.

The demanding mastery of his kisses made her feel faint, and when his lips moved along her jaw and began to nip gently at her throat, she grew so light-headed with need she feared she would lose her ability to stand.

Just when she knew she would surely sink to the floor, he lifted her in his arms. "You're so beautiful." He kissed her temple. "I knew we'd be good together."

Drugged by his lovemaking, she allowed herself to be eased onto the couch. How welcome Beau's hard warmth was as he slid over her. She sighed, pressing her open lips to his, quivering with the hot intimacy of his kiss. Gathered against his firm torso, her body cried out for a deeper intimacy. As he inflamed her passion, she could feel his arousal grow and her senses reeled.

"You'll never marry my father," Beau muttered against her mouth.

Something in his ragged assertion caused the reasoning part of her brain to click on, setting off an alarm. Was there a tinge of satisfaction in his voice?

What was going on here? What was she doing? How could she lose herself the way she had—like some mindless, amoral twit?

She was acting just the way Beau had expected her to act! A horrible idea struck. Was this seduction planned to pay his father back—betrayal for betrayal? Of course it was. Beau didn't even *like* her. What had possessed her to dare him with her own foolish lips? Did she really believe he wouldn't take her up on it? *She'd played right into his hands.* Now he would take satisfaction in reporting to Ira that his shallow, party-girl fiancée had cheated on him only days before the wedding—with his own son.

She moaned, sick at heart. Though her limbs were passion weakened and her body loath to comply, she slid her arms from around his neck and pressed impotently against his chest. "No…" she cried, but the only sound she heard was a fervent sigh. His hand was on her thigh, moving upward to breach the ribbing of her sweater. She gasped with involuntary delight as his seductive fingers dipped beneath the knit fabric to touch bare flesh. With all her flagging strength, she fought her hunger to surrender. "I—I'm not going to give you the satisfaction," she whimpered against his jaw. "Get off me!"

"Amy, you don't mean that." His hand had stilled, but he made no move to obey her. "Let me."

She closed her eyes, struggling for supremacy over her crazy need for him. "It's wrong. I wouldn't be able to forgive myself."

"Sex is natural." He caressed her throat with persuasive lips. "Don't fight it."

Every fiber in her body wanted those marvelous lips to dip lower but she resisted her craving, pushing hard. "Get—*up*!"

She thought she heard him groan, but she wasn't sure it was anything but a frustrated exhaling. "Amy—you don't love my father."

"That's between your father and me." She shoved harder against him. "Why should you care anyway?"

"I don't care." He lifted his face from hers, his jaw tight. But he didn't relinquish his intimate position. "I've told you I don't care."

"I think you do." She managed to conjure up a withering stare, though she felt drained, humiliated. "Oh—I don't mean you care about *me*. But I know you're full of rage about what your father did to your mother, and how he's lived his life since."

Beau's nostrils flared, and she thought she saw a flash of pain mix with the ire in his gaze.

Desperate to rid herself of the haunting feel of his kisses, she rubbed shaky fingers across her lips. It didn't help; the feeling lingered, torturing her. She was so miserable she had to strike back at him for his cruel, revengeful seduction. "You're so arrogant you think you know everything," she hissed. "Well, maybe you have a right to resent some things about Ira's past, but this time you're wrong. Your father has asked *nothing* of me but my companionship for as long as I want it that way."

For an endless moment, he watched her with sparking eyes. "Miss Vale," he finally ground out, "either you're very naive about what marriage is, or you think *I* am."

Before she could conjure up a scathing retort, he slid to her side. In a defensive move, she scrambled away. Far from steady on her feet, she leaned against the arm of the couch to collect herself.

He stood, too, every line of his body taut as if held still by ironfisted control. He shoved his hands into his pockets, and she had the feeling he would have grabbed her back into his arms if not for his conscious effort to resist. "You're still planning to go through with the marriage?" he asked.

"Of course!" Fury edged her words with ice, covering her breathlessness. She was so confused and hurt she didn't even stop to wonder if what she was saying was true anymore. Besides, Beau didn't deserve any open, honest admissions after what he'd done. "If your father still *wants* to marry me after you revenge yourself by reporting back what happened here tonight."

Fleetingly, a small, bitter smile twisted his lips. "I assume I don't have your vote for gentleman of the year, then?"

"What does that mean?"

His gaze slid to the fire as he clenched and unclenched his jaw. "Nothing happened here," he muttered.

Misery filled her heart at his gibe. It didn't matter that he was unaware of her love for him; it was just so hurtful that he could casually toss off what they'd shared as an unsuccessful means to an end.

Righteous indignation surged through her, strengthening her limbs and her resolve. "Why don't you go look at yourself in the mirror, Mr. Diablo?'' Fighting tears, she pivoted away. ''You might see some of the same imperfections you hate in your father in your *own* reflection!''

CHAPTER NINE

ONLY an inch of snow fell today, but the winds through Diablo Pass were howling up to forty miles an hour, piling more snow on the road and making visibility nonexistent. Beau had received reports that it would take at least two days of calm weather to clear the mounting drifts. This couldn't have been worse news for Amy.

She'd talked to Ira on the radio this evening after dinner. There were four cowhands in the bunkhouse at the time, as well as Beau's forbidding presence, so she could only chat about the weather, her newly acquired ranching skills and her growing affection for Wyoming. She didn't mention her blisters, her sore muscles or her scowling host. And once again, she was left with Ira's promise to repay her patience with that trip to France.

When she'd left the bunkhouse, she had a feeling everyone's eyes had been on her. She hadn't realized Beau's employees still didn't know she was Ira's fiancée and she sensed that they didn't think highly of the idea, though no one said anything. It was something in their eyes—a sort of disappointment in her—and it made her unaccountably sad. Clearly, Ira and his string of women weren't the most beloved people in this part of the state.

As she carried a pile of towels and clothes to the laundry room, she tried to shake off the realization. Work had always helped her forget her troubles before. So she decided to let work do its job again. Besides, she'd never liked the idea of Cookie waiting on her hand and foot, and had no intention of allowing the housekeeper to increase her work load on her account. Doing laundry seemed like a good way to be helpful and to take her mind off Beau—er—the unrelenting *snow*.

Heading into the kitchen with her bundle, she found her mind drifting to thoughts about what had happened between Beau and her last night. Even all her activity couldn't seem to keep those heated memories at bay. Pulling her lips between her teeth, she recalled his admonition about how naive she was. She didn't want to believe it, but she was starting to realize she'd been naive about a lot of things, things that—because of her sister's needs—had blinded her to certain troublesome facts.

Now that she'd had all day to stew on Beau's remark, she understood Ira would want more than simple companionship before too long. After all, he was only in his late fifties, a healthy man, with many good years left. And recently she'd discovered how very normal she was—with all the needs and desires of any woman. How ironic that she'd learned that truth from a man who disliked her so intensely.

She knew now, if she planned to keep her marriage to Ira platonic, she would ultimately be cheating them both. Besides, how could she offer him anything more than companionship after what she'd learned these past few days? She didn't love him. And having met his son, she feared she never could feel anything more for him than mild affection.

Mindlessly, she opened the door to the steamy laundry room where at least one of the washing machines and two commercial-size dryers were sloshing and whirring all day long. Loading up another of the washers with her things, she reluctantly let her mind roam along dark, worrisome paths she could no longer avoid.

What if Ira *had* been making empty promises, playing on her trusting nature and her weakness for Mary, just to get himself another young plaything? If so, it would be better this way, breaking it off before it got worse. On the other hand, could Beau be deliberately making trouble, manipulating her to doubt her own motives and Ira's? If that was the case, then she would be hurting Ira badly by breaking their engagement. She hated the thought. The last thing she wanted was to hurt anyone, but she really had no choice—not after tasting Beau's sizzling kisses.

She added bleach and soap and turned on the machine, hardly registering her actions. Her mind rebuked, *"How could you have gotten yourself into such a mess?"* She supposed her mental state when she'd met Ira had been greatly to blame. She'd been weary of the sleazy passes she received every night from drunks who thought they were God's gift to womankind. And she'd been worried sick about her sister's upcoming surgery and the ever-present bills. Ira had been so kind, such a respectful gentleman. And he'd made her laugh. When he'd proposed, it had seemed like the perfect answer to all her predicaments.

Beau was right. She had been naive. The only difference was, he'd made the remark sarcastically. He didn't truly believe she was naive. There was no doubt in her mind that he thought she was using Ira for his money and lying to Beau to appease him.

She left the kitchen and hurried through the living room, working to stave off mental images of what had happened there last night. Turning down the long hall that headed away from her room, she made for the linen closet to retrieve clean towels.

Her mind spiraled back to Mary, and she swiped at a tear. It was all so painfully clear now. She'd acted impetuously, not carefully considering what her marriage to Ira would be like. And adding guilt upon guilt, she finally had to admit to herself that her concern over Mary had been the major reason she'd so abruptly accepted Ira's proposal.

She felt vile about that. If that wasn't enough, she now knew she would be carrying around the memory of a pair of furious blue eyes for a very long time.

Reaching the linen-closet door, she made a vow to herself. She would keep a brave face until the weather cleared. Then she would travel to Ira's ranch and break off her engagement. She owed Ira the courtesy of telling him face-to-face. It would be unfair just to run away. The specter of Mary's medical bills rose before her like a threatening demon, and she shuddered with dismay. Still, she couldn't allow money to sway her any longer. She refused to believe she could be the sort of woman Beau thought she was.

Swinging open the door, she froze in a stunned tableau, her hands outstretched toward shelves that weren't there. Her lips parted in horror. Clearly, she'd opened the wrong door. Instead of a linen closet, she found herself standing in the entryway of a bathroom, a simple, well-lit cubicle, its foggy air fragrant with the scent of soap. A few scant steps in front of her, Beau stood, clad only in a towel.

Her heart stopped as he paused in the act of shaving, a straight razor hovering along his jaw. He was so striking, towering there in his near nudity. His well-muscled chest, silky with dark hair, glistened with moisture from his shower, and his long, sturdy legs were braced wide. The saddle muscles were clearly defined in his powerful thighs. She watched them flex as he shifted, and a tingle of excitement danced along her spine as she recalled how delightfully firm they'd felt beneath her hips.

For some reason, she couldn't back away and close the door. She just stood rooted there like a potted plant, gaping. With the lift of an inquiring brow, he canted his head her way. "Is this a come-on, or were you hoping to see me slit my throat?"

"*Oh!* I—I'm sorry," she stuttered. "I was looking for a towel...."

With a roguish twitch of his lips, he tucked a thumb inside the one tied at his waist and tugged. "If you need one that badly—take mine."

The flash of bare, taut hip knocked her out of her

paralysis. Fumbling for the knob, she managed to slam the door a second before his towel thudded against it.

Rich, mocking laughter chased her down the hall.

Snow, snow and more snow! The next day was an exhausting carbon copy of so many before, and Amy was tired. But before she fell into bed, she decided to look in on Desiree. The innocent little calf always lifted her spirits. And now that her future was so bleak and insecure, she found herself visiting Desiree more and more.

Though the cowboys were friendly and respectful, they seemed distant, knowing she was engaged to Ira. She felt bad about that. Even so, she didn't intend to defensively blurt out that she wasn't going to marry him after all. Ira deserved to hear it from her first.

After a quiet visit, she gave Desiree a melancholy hug. "Good night, sweetie. I promise, after I leave here, I'll write." She stood, then realized what she'd said and laughed at herself, even in her dour mood. "Well, maybe not *write*. But since we're so good at mental telepathy, I'll 'think' my love to you. Okay?"

The calf blinked and bawled.

"Then it's settled. After I leave, I'll think to you every day." Turning away, she waved at the calf, feeling a new surge of depression. She would have to leave her little pet behind when she returned to Chicago. She had a feeling her landlord's "no pets" rule probably included cows. "Get some sleep, sweetie." The sadness in her voice startled her. This place had gotten into her blood awfully quickly. *"Not just the place,"* her brain jeered. She bit down hard on her lip, hoping the pain would make her forget *who* had gotten into her blood since her coming out here.

She trudged around the calving barn toward the ranch house, noticing the snow had stopped and the wind that had blown insistently all day had died. She looked up. There were even a few brave stars twinkling down at her.

Off in the distance, she heard the crunch of hooves on frozen snow. Turning toward the sound, she squinted through the dimness, focusing on a stand of pines. In the dusk, she saw a man on horseback emerging from the woods.

Her heart lurched when she realized it was Beau astride his black stallion. As he drew nearer, she could see his brows were frosted silver and he was wearing a dark bandanna over his mouth and nose. For a split second, she was transported back in time—to a lawless era where even the best of men could be wild and dangerous if driven far enough. Right now, Amy couldn't think of any man, anywhere, more threatening to her peace of mind than the one before her now.

The horse stilled under Beau's wordless command, and for a long moment they watched each other. He reached up and yanked his kerchief down, revealing a grim smile that hid nothing of his smoldering antagonism. He startled her when he signaled his horse forward. She didn't move, and wasn't sure why she didn't, for he was heading directly at her.

Lifting her chin, she eyed him grudgingly. She didn't want to be spellbound, standing helplessly in the subzero night, breathless to see what he was planning. But for some reason, she couldn't bear the idea of leaving, never to know what was on his mind.

When he reached her, he brought the stallion to a halt and held out a gloved hand, as though there was no question that she'd accept it and allow herself to be lifted into his lap. *How audacious of him! How dare he?* Yet even as she mentally berated him, finding him the most arrogant, egotistical rogue in the world, she lifted her arms, welcoming his invitation.

In the wink of an eye, he swung her up into the saddle, her legs straddling his thighs. Though she snuggled against him, she was shocked at herself for allowing this to happen. It couldn't have been a worse time to discover she no longer had the strength to fight her attraction for him. These days and nights of imprisonment with him had broken her resolve until it was nothing more than tattered, useless threads.

He steered his stallion away from the light, leading them toward the darkened wood. For a long time, Sovereign walked among the snow-laden pine boughs, the only sounds his hoofbeats in the snow and the occasional creak of leather. Amy didn't know where they were going and didn't care. She inhaled the cold air, Beau's warm scent mingling with it, stirring the embers of her passion. She squeezed her eyes shut, praying she wouldn't betray herself tonight, but far from sure of anything anymore.

After a long, quiet ride, they emerged on a bluff overlooking a wide, open valley. After the darkness of the wood, the clearing night and luminous snow seemed almost as bright as day. Amy blinked, taking a slow sweep of the idyllic scene. In the valley's center, a teardrop lake glimmered like a dusky jewel. Within the depths of the frozen water winked reflected stars from the Wyoming heavens, like diamonds set in the lake floor.

Beau didn't say a word, just led his steed along the bluff above the Christmas-card lake. The setting was so charming and unspoiled, Amy couldn't speak even if she'd wanted to. They rode along in the white silence, and she found herself wishing she had the slightest urge to be anywhere else in the world. But, sadly, she didn't.

After a time, Beau reined in his horse, and she felt him move, tilt back his Stetson and gaze into the sky. She heard him inhale, but he said nothing. Unable to stand the suspense, she worked to gather the remnants of her wits. "Do you have some ice that needs chopping?" she asked, trying to make light of her loss of control. His chuckle tingled through her, giving her a guilty sense of pleasure. *This wasn't helping!* She tried again. "Is there a cow that's slipped on the ice and you need me to lift him up?"

"I didn't realize you could lift cows, Miss Vale."

His tone was teasing, and she tried to be affronted, but she wasn't in the mood to fight. Far from it. "Try me." She flinched. That challenge had come out more like a sexual invitation than a test of her cow-lifting skills. She had to get ahold of herself. Grabbing the saddle horn, she shifted forward. "Where are we going, then? Are you planning to murder me and dump me in that sinkhole?"

"Maybe later." His warm breath ruffled her hair. Using his free arm, he coaxed her back against him, cutting off her renewed vow to keep an emotional distance. She settled there, regretfully accepting the terrible knowledge that she was his—body and soul. Defeat shrouded her heart. She had no more strength to escape him, and tragically, she had no desire to.

With the boundless winter stillness as their companion, he led his steed farther into the storybook valley. "Take a deep breath," he murmured. "That's the perfume of snow on the sage."

She did as he asked, catching his stirring scent in the bargain. The combination was mellow and stimulating. Though she reacted inwardly with a wanton shiver, she managed to remain outwardly composed. Even so, words failed her.

"I wanted you to experience the Wyoming I love."

She sensed his scorn and frowned. "You really don't believe I could appreciate the beauty of all this?"

"I don't think you can appreciate anything but a dollar sign."

She stiffened, pulling away. "You can't mean that! Surely you've found out *that* much about me!"

"I think your motives are possibly less grasping than I'd first thought, but marrying someone because of medical bills doesn't take you out of the bimbo category, and you know it."

"So you've figured that out, have you?" she snapped, stung by his accusation. Struggling from his arms, she managed to jump from the saddle. "Congratulations, Inspector Clouseau! You've nabbed your bimbo!" She tumbled into the snow, floundering to her knees. "Just for the record, I love Wyoming, I love my sister and—"

"And what?" he demanded, suddenly there, his hands gripping her arms.

She grappled to keep him from helping her, but couldn't extricate herself from his grasp. Jamming her fists against him, she fought not only his sensual pull but her inner turmoil. She wasn't the cheap sort of woman he thought she was. But what could she do—blurt out her love for him? That would be quite a sight—his amused expression at the conquest of his father's fiancée. That would kill her soul.

"And *nothing*!" she retorted. "I keep telling you, what's between your father and me is none of your business!"

She tried to jerk from his hold, but only succeeded in falling on her back. His strength was too much for her and she couldn't evade him. They were lying in the snow, Beau above her. His mouth set, he demanded coldly, "Admit you're *not* in love."

Dismay washed through her. How could she admit that? She was in love—only *not* with Ira, but with a man who didn't trust her, didn't believe a word she said. "I can't admit that!" She told the sad truth contemptuously, in an effort to mask her heartbreak. "Because I *am* in love." Their breaths mingled in charged air. She wanted to hold him, kiss him, love him right here in the snow. But knowing it would be a fool's errand to start anything that could only lead to heartbreak, she grabbed at the snow to keep from taking him in her arms. With heavy sadness in her heart, she demanded, "*Happy* now?"

His gaze held all the warmth of a block of granite. "Ecstatic." Suddenly, he lowered angry lips to hers. She gasped at the blistering effect of his mouth against hers, and her resistance melted like a snowflake in a volcano. She moved to take him in her desperate embrace, to return fiery kiss for fiery kiss. But before she could even lift her arms, he cursed against her lips, flinging himself away.

Shaken and aching for more, she lay there staring up at him as he yanked off his Stetson and jerked a hand through his hair. She was astonished to discover he was gentleman enough to be ashamed of himself for kissing an engaged woman who'd just confessed she was in love—though he was wrong about *whom* she loved.

Oddly, she realized she was no longer ashamed of herself for wanting him to kiss her, or even angry with him for mistrusting her. On the contrary, lying here on her back in the snow, she felt thoroughly alive. How devious life could be.

He stood and swatted his hat against his jeans, dusting off snow in quick, angry strokes. Not sure why she wanted to communicate with him, but positive she must, she struggled up on an elbow. "For your information, I think Wyoming in winter is lovely, too. I'm not exactly the Wicked Witch of the West, you know."

He glanced at her. For an instant, his eyes seemed to flash with the rage and pain of a wounded animal, but the look was gone so quickly, Amy decided her dazed mind was playing tricks on her.

"Forget it," he growled. "Go live your life. I'll

stay out of it from now on.'' Stooping, he took her arm, hoisting her to her feet. ''I'll help you into the saddle.''

She stared at him. ''Aren't you—''

''I need to walk.''

After boosting her on his horse, he grabbed the reins, leading them back toward civilization. Taking a deep, unsteady breath, she watched him hike through the snow with long, irascible strides.

Strangling the saddle horn, she battled to keep from bursting into tears. Why did she have to discover love was real in this horrible way? And why did she have to learn that the soft emotion was not necessarily returned?

She loved Beau Diablo with all her heart—a man committed to his land, admired by his employees and friends and true to his word. She had a strong sense that when the right woman came along, he would be totally committed to her, too. Unfortunately, he thought Amy Vale was the most *wrong* female to ever walk the face of the earth.

She knew it would do no good to tell him how she felt. He would only laugh, unable to trust anything she said, unable to believe she could actually love him—not after coming out here to marry his father. He would simply think she'd discovered through idle ranch chatter that he was a wealthier—and therefore *better*—meal ticket.

She fought her need to slip from the saddle, run to him, pull him down in the snow and savor the full heat and depth of his passions, no matter how fleeting her joy might be. She was a coward and couldn't bear to witness his dry grin of vengeance once it was done. So she simply stared after him, hopeless longing shimmering in her eyes.

Two days passed as the weather gradually cleared. The phone lines to Diablo Butte were repaired, and the bulldozers were making headway clearing the pass. Amy's heart was torn with a need to leave Beau's ranch and a tormenting desire to stay—even if she had to endure blisters and angry glowers forever. She knew that was crazy and impractical. Ever since their rash tumble in the snow, Beau had kept a distance. Every time their eyes met, his glances were stormy and brooding.

Amy finished lunch in the cook house. So far today, she hadn't seen Beau, so it startled her when he called her name. She shifted toward the side door where he'd just entered. Before she could speak, he said, ''Ira's on the phone for you.''

A knot tightened in her stomach, but she stood, nodding.

''You can take it in my den.''

Refusing to meet his malevolent gaze, she grabbed her coat and darted outside.

As she rushed into the kitchen, she spied the wall phone and decided to take the call there. Everybody was in the cook house. And she didn't feel like facing Beau's den. She knew it was down the hall from his room, but entering his personal sanctuary would be more agonizing than worthwhile. She lifted the receiver and worked on sounding cheerful ''Hello, Ira.''

''Hello, little one,'' he bellowed through a laugh.

"You sound fine. I'm surprised. I thought you'd be sick with a cold after all the work my slave-driver son made you do."

She ducked her head, her gaze sliding to the floor. "No, I'm just fine." She wanted to say she'd enjoyed being out in the snow, laughing and joking with the men, warming her insides with coffee strong enough to support a cow all by itself. She liked the feeling of accomplishment at the end of the day. She'd certainly never felt fulfilled after a night at the bar.

"The road's almost cleared, little one. Boy, I can't wait to see you," he was saying. "I have a special dinner waiting. French champagne's on ice, too." Amy flinched. He sounded excited—like a bridegroom. "I figure we can get the preacher out here tomorrow and make it official."

"Official..." She echoed the word, a bad feeling creeping up her spine. Why did she sense that he was planning on starting the marriage *unofficially* tonight—in a very carnal way. "Uh—Ira—I need to talk to you about something that's very important—"

"Sure, little one. We can do anything you want."

She anxiously twisted the phone cord around a finger. He was appeasing her, not really listening. "Ira," she whispered, "I'm not quite packed. Maybe I'd better go finish."

"Great. Great." He laughed again. "Don't want to have you get here one second later than you have to."

"Okay. Well—bye."

"Love you, little one." He made a kissing sound in the phone. "Now get here as soon as you can."

"I—I will." She heard a click in her ear, signaling

that he'd hung up. Feeling suddenly very contaminated, she needed to talk to her sister and dialed the number for the convalescent home. It rang only two times before it was answered.

"Hello? This is Amy Vale. May I speak to my sister, please?"

The operator said the usual "One moment," before she was put on hold.

"Hello, Miss Vale?" came a nasal male voice.

"Yes?"

"This is Dr. Rampling."

He sounded jovial, so she assumed he must have left instructions to put her on for an update the next time she called. "Oh, hi, Dr. Rampling. Everything okay?"

"Splendid. I just wanted to let you know how much we appreciate the payment your fiancé made. It covers Mary's bills up to now, and includes an advance for next month. That should take her right up until time to travel."

The knot in Amy's stomach constricted, and she leaned weakly against the wall. "Oh? I—he didn't mention it."

"Well, I won't keep you talking. Mary is coming along very well. I believe with this last surgery, she'll be walking without a limp before too long."

Tears of joy welled in her eyes. "Oh, Doctor, I've waited five years to hear that. Thank you—" Her voice broke. "Thank you so much."

"It was your sister's courage that got her this far. Here, I'll transfer you to her room."

"Thank you, Doctor, and once again I want to—"

Before she could finish speaking, he was gone. She shook her head at his disinclination to accept thanks. When she heard Mary's voice, her spirits soared.

They talked for a quarter of an hour, and Mary's lightheartedness made Amy laugh several times. Yet deep in her heart she knew she had to tell her sister the truth. Finally, Mary asked, "What is it, Amy? You sound—funny."

Eyeing the ceiling, Amy sighed. She should have known. Mary didn't miss much. "Er—look, honey, I'm really sorry to have to tell you this, but I don't think I can go through with marrying Ira."

There was a pause of a few heartbeats before Mary said, "Good."

Amy was taken off guard. "Why good?"

"You didn't love him. Isn't that enough reason?"

Amy smiled wanly, feeling as though a weight had been lifted from her shoulders. "You knew?"

"Yeah. But I figured it was your business who you married."

"But Mom was happy, and she didn't love Dad when they got married."

"Ira isn't Dad."

Amy frowned, then realized Mary's simple statement had been terribly insightful. She laughed then. It wasn't much of a laugh, but it was a beginning. "You only talked to him on the phone one time. How did you get to be so wise?"

"I'm your sister, that's how," Mary insisted. "Now, come home as soon as you can. We'll make out. Why, in a month I'll be fine and I can get a job, too."

Amy's mood plummeted. "Don't you worry about getting a job, young lady. Just think about getting well."

"I love you, Amy. I can't wait to see you."

She heard a squeak and knew the kitchen door was opening. "I can't wait to see you either, honey. I love you. Bye."

She turned to hang up the receiver and was startled to see Beau, not Cookie, as she'd expected.

By some sort of ironic retribution, he appeared very much the same as he had the first moment she'd seen him—his Stetson brim pulled low over sparking eyes, that split-hide coat snug across wide shoulders. Anger curved his lips now, just as it had then. Only she hadn't been in love with him then—or maybe she had, even at that first crazy instant he'd stalked into the store.

"How is my father?" he asked.

Jarred from her dark musing, she realized he assumed she'd been on the phone with her fiancé all the time. "He's fine," she said minimally. What did it matter now? Soon she'd be on a bus to Chicago and she'd never see Beau again. "I—I was just about to finish packing."

"Good." He hung up his coat and tossed his hat onto one of the hooks. "The road to Diablo Butte is open."

Amy had the peculiar notion there was something behind the scorn in his words. Was it a touch of melancholy? Surely not. She shook off the fantasy. "I—guess I'd better get ready, then."

He nodded, his glance flicking her way for an instant. The quick, sharp look was like a knife in her soul. "When you're ready, Snapper will drive you."

Before she could say thank-you or even goodbye, he disappeared through the kitchen door. As his footsteps faded in the distance, her throat closed and she found it hard to catch her breath. The man she loved had just cavalierly walked away, making it brutally clear he didn't care to see her—ever again.

CHAPTER TEN

THE general store in Big Elk was brightly lit and practically empty. Ira's ranch hand who had given her a ride to the bus stop had dropped her off over an hour ago, and the bus wouldn't be arriving for another hour.

Amy turned the little book display, wishing she had enough money to buy a paperback novel. The trip back would be long and she desperately wished she had something to take her mind off this fateful trip out west.

In her mind's eye, she saw Ira's face when she'd told him she couldn't go through with the marriage. He'd pursed his lips and shaken his head, saying, "You can't be serious."

She had only been able to nod, fearful of how he would react when he realized she meant it. But he'd been civil, though he clearly wasn't happy. He'd even waved off her offer to pay him back for Mary's bills and insisted on giving her money for the bus. Still, she'd sworn she would repay him a little every month until the debt was settled.

She didn't blame him for leaving her to eat a silent, self-conscious dinner with his cowhands, and for assigning his testy old cook to show her to a guest room for the night. The same grumpy, toothless man had driven her to the bus stop this morning, grumbling to himself most of the way. Ira had come by this morning as she was eating breakfast and given an offhand wave, mouthing wishes that she have a good trip back; but he hadn't stopped to visit or ask how she'd slept. That hadn't surprised her. After all, he *had* been dumped. He probably felt he had a right to make her a little uncomfortable if he wanted to.

She had a feeling both his pride and his ego would soon heal, for the last thing he'd told her before he ambled out of the kitchen was that he planned to go to Houston, Texas in a couple of weeks for a cattlemen's meeting. She could already see plans for a new conquest gleaming in his eyes.

She browsed through the paperback novels, not really seeing the titles. The metal rack squawked as she turned it, the sound like a shriek in the empty store. She had her Wyoming textbook in her suitcase, but she couldn't stand the thought of reading about a place she'd grown to love but would never see again.

"Lady?"

Amy jumped at the unexpectedness of the store owner's voice. Since she was the only person in the place, he had to be speaking to her. "Yes?" She spun his way.

He grinned bashfully, and she remembered those big horse teeth. "I got some used books over here. These old *Star Trek* novels are only a dime each."

She colored. How did he know she couldn't afford a new book? She dropped her gaze to her suitcase, mortified. "No, thanks—I—I was just passing the time until the bus going east comes by."

"Sure—okay..." he mumbled, sounding embarrassed. She felt for him. He'd only been trying to do her a kindness. He probably kept old books under the counter for down-in-the-mouth wayfarers, charging a small price just to protect their pride.

The truth was, she didn't even have a dime to spare. Though she'd reluctantly accepted the ticket money from Ira, she'd refused to be indebted to him for a penny more. Edging away from the book rack, she self-consciously wound her hands together, trying to melt into the background. Bumping into a shelf below the front window, she decided to pass the time reading the sayings printed on the side of the souvenir mugs. Some of the phrases were off-color, but most were funny. She picked up one cup at a time, looking at each picture then reading its quotation. A few times, she almost smiled.

"Well, hon, I'm more surprised to see you than I would be to find a rattlesnake in my petticoats!"

Amy recognized Cookie's croaking voice and jerked around, nearly dropping the mug she was reading. "Oh...hello...." Apprehensive, she scanned the store to see if the housekeeper was alone. When she realized Beau wasn't with her, she let out a long breath, not sure if the sigh was one of relief or depression. Trying not to think about which it might be, she straightened her shoulders, working to appear casual.

"What in Sam Hill are you doing here?" Cookie absently handed the store owner a list. "Get me this stuff, will ya, Bud?" Before the portly man could respond, she'd turned back to Amy. "And when you find it all, go ahead and stick it in the back of the pickup. I want to gossip with my friend over here.''

''Are—are you alone?'' Amy asked, unable to help herself.

Cookie nodded, pulling off her knit cap, her fly-away hair popping out in all directions. She stuffed the cap in her coat pocket. ''The dang thing's warm, but it itches.'' She grinned, though her eyes held more inquisitiveness than pleasure. ''Now what are you doin' hanging around this ol' dump?'' She waved off the proprietor's objection with a laugh, adding, ''Is Mr. Ira dragging you in here to fetch supplies on your *honeymoon*?''

Amy shook her head, wondering why fate insisted on one more humiliation. Replacing the mug on the shelf, she stared out at the late-morning brightness. Sunshine glistened off the snow. Everything looked polished and gleaming and pure. How ironic that the most glorious day she'd experienced in Wyoming would not only be her last, but her saddest.

''Where is Mr. Ira anyway? Over at the gas station gabbing with Pete?''

''Cookie...'' She faltered, unable to meet the older woman's eyes. ''Ira and I aren't getting married after all.''

When Cookie didn't speak, she found she had to see her expression, and shifted her gaze. ''I'm afraid I made a mistake when I said I would marry him, and I decided it wouldn't work out.''

Cookie's eyes were as big as saucers. ''You told Mr. Ira *no*?''

Amy shrugged unhappily. ''I had to. I found out I

was—'' She stopped herself, thinking better of what she'd almost revealed. ''I guess I'm not cut out to be a rancher's wife after all.''

Cookie pursed her lips, frowning. ''Well, I can't say I'm sorry you ain't gonna marry Mr. Ira. That ol' maverick will find himself another filly soon enough.'' She put a friendly hand on Amy's arm. ''So, what are you going to do?''

''Go back to Chicago. The doctor said Mary will be fine in a month. We'll get by.''

Cookie nodded. ''I sure wish you all the luck, hon, but I think you're wrong about one thing. You'd make a good rancher's wife.''

Amy smiled sadly, then had a thought and her smile died. ''Look, Cookie—'' she took the housekeeper's arms in a pleading gesture ''—don't tell Beau. Promise?''

The older woman gave her such a piercing, thorough look Amy was afraid she might detect the awful truth in her eyes. Hurriedly releasing the woman, she turned away, pretending to hunt for just the right souvenir mug.

After a long, strained minute, Cookie said, ''Why would I tell that old grouch a thing?'' She sounded oddly chipper, and Amy couldn't imagine why. ''Mr. Beau ain't done nothin' but growl at everybody lately—like an ol' grizzly bear with a toothache.'' She harrumphed. ''Ain't never seen him so cantankerous. Near bit my head off last night, and all I did was ask him if he wanted me to send your gloves over to Diablo Butte with one of the cowpokes. He near jumped down my throat. Grabbed 'em up. Said he'd handle it. Sorry. If I'da known you was going to be here, I'da brought 'em.''

Amy unconsciously rubbed her cold hands together. The gloves had never entered her mind. "Don't worry about them—"

"Shucks, hon." She pulled off her worn leather gloves. "You take these. What if your bus got stuck. You could get mighty cold. Besides, I got me a ton of gloves.''

"No—"

"Shush now," she admonished, thrusting them into Amy's fingers. "Call it a thank-you gift for all your help this past week.''

Embarrassed, Amy accepted the gloves and slipped them on, silently vowing to mail them back after she got to Chicago. "Thanks. I appreciate it." She picked up a mug, feigning interest in it. "And you will promise you won't mention seeing me to Beau?''

"Sure, sure, hon. He won't hear nothin' from these lips.''

Amy lowered the mug, relieved. "Thanks." She faced the woman again. Unable to help herself, she hugged her. "I'll miss you.''

"Shucks," Cookie said gently. "A tough old piece of jerky like me?" She patted Amy's shoulder. "That's a real sweet lie, hon. Real sweet.''

"Got your stuff packed in the pickup," Bud called, his pudgy face florid from the chore. The women separated after one more affectionate squeeze. "Cookie, do you want me to put this load of supplies on Beau's bill or would you rather pay cash and close out your account? That way you can truck your grub in from someplace that ain't such a dump.''

Cookie guffawed. ''Send the bill to Mr. Beau the same as always, and quit lookin' so hangdog, you fool.'' She slung an arm about the man's slumped shoulders. ''Okay. What if my next trip in I bring you a pound of my pecan fudge? Will that square me with ya?''

His puckered features cleared. ''For your fudge, I'd forgive you if you burned down this dump.''

They both laughed. At the door, Cookie turned to Amy and gave her a wink. ''You know, hon, I have a real strong feelin' things are going to work out for you.''

Amy waved, forcing a smile. ''Goodbye, Cookie...'' Her voice broke with regret, and she couldn't say more. The door banged shut as Bud left with the housekeeper to escort her to the pickup.

The feeble rein Amy had on her emotions suddenly gave way and she sagged against the shelf. Her eyes were open but unseeing as a forlorn tear escaped down her cheek.

The bus was late, finally arriving at nearly one o'clock in the afternoon. Amy was tired and hungry, but she'd been tired and hungry before and she knew it wasn't fatal. One other passenger had arrived about fifteen minutes before the bus came, and Amy had the feeling Ira had been a bit vindictive, dropping her off so early. Apparently the bus was routinely late.

The motor coach was far from full, with plenty of empty seats, but the last thing she wanted was to be alone with her thoughts. She took a seat beside a young redhead about her age. The woman was extremely slender, with a sharp nose and big, wide-set hazel eyes, her lips full and wide. Amy decided with the right lighting and makeup, the thin woman could be a fashion model. The only flaw in the picture was the huge wad of gum she was chewing openmouthed. But Amy didn't care. The girl looked pleasant and might provide enough distraction to ease her aching heart.

"Hi," she said, after she'd stowed her suitcase on the overhead rack. "I hope you don't mind if I join you."

The redhead pulled a long, stringy ribbon of gum out of her mouth, then stuck it back, smiling all the while. "Hey, sit! I've been bored stiff." She shook out her red curls, running an emaciated hand through them. "I'm from Los Angeles. On my way to visit my boyfriend in Chicago. He's in graduate school there."

"I live there," Amy said, delighted she'd have a traveling companion for the entire trip.

"Cool." The girl snapped her gum, then held out her hand. "Name's Milly Koontz."

"Amy Vale." She accepted the girl's hand.

"Nice to meet you." She cast a glance out the window. "Pretty country around here."

Amy followed her gaze, feeling a wave of melancholy as she watched white-clad hills roll by. A knot formed in her throat. "Yes—it is...." she whispered.

"What were you doing out here? Visiting friends?"

Amy felt flushed and hoped she wasn't blushing

with distress. Forcing herself to relax, she lay back against the seat, avoiding her seatmate's eyes. "Sort of…" Wanting to change the subject, she asked, "Where's your boyfriend studying?"

"Northwestern."

She felt another pang. Attending Northwestern had been another dream she'd seen slip through her fingers. "It's a fine school," she murmured. "What's he studying?"

"*Giddyap, stud-a-rama!*"

Amy grimaced in confusion. What sort of graduate course was that? She shifted to look at Milly. "I've never heard of giddy—whatever. Is it a foreign language or something?" Milly seemed not to hear, something outside the bus having caught her attention. Nudging her seatmate, Amy asked, "What sort of graduate course is your boyfriend in?"

Milly came back with a start. "Huh? Oh, Vernon? He's a classical flautist, working on a master's degree in music. I was talking about that cowboy out there." She pointed toward the horizon, dotted with pine and fur trees. "Is he a total *stud* or what?"

Amy didn't see anyone from her vantage point, but when the bus chugged around a turn, she saw the object of Milly's admiration. A horseman atop a black stallion galloped along a ridge. The horse was throwing up great clouds of snow as it plunged across the range, its muscles pumping and straining, nostrils blowing frosty air.

"I wonder where he's racing?"

Amy watched the approaching cowboy with a sense

of disbelief. He looked awfully familiar, but of course that was impossible.

"He seems to be racing the bus," Milly said, echoing the conjecture of several other passengers who'd also spotted the rider's approach.

Something swelled in her throat, something she didn't even want to think of as hope. She tamped the emotion down. First of all, it couldn't possibly be Beau, and even if it was, it was a coincidence that he was here. He wasn't racing the bus, for heaven's sake.

"Wow," Milly whispered. "He's *gorgeous*."

Amy stared, afraid to even think. The bus had rounded another curve, and the cowboy was now heading straight for them. He'd taken off his black Stetson and was waving it at the driver.

"Stop the bus," a woman shouted. "That guy wants on."

"Not with no horse, he's not getting on," the driver complained.

"Maybe he's going to rob us!" a bespectacled woman whined. "I've heard of that sort of thing out here in the West."

"That was a hundred years ago, Mabel," the woman's portly husband rebuked. "The guy doesn't even have a gun."

"You don't know that. It could be hidden in his jeans!"

"I'll check for suspicious bulges," Milly cracked with a wicked chuckle.

"Stop the bus," another passenger shouted. Amy craned around to look at him. He was the middle-aged man wearing Western clothes who'd gotten on the bus with Amy, so he must be from the area. "That's Beau Diablo. Owns one of the biggest spreads in the state. He ain't gonna rob us. Maybe he needs help."

The argument went on, but Amy didn't hear it. Her mind was reeling with such a wild mixture of hope and dread, she couldn't think straight. What did Beau want with this bus? Surely he didn't need to get rid of her gloves so badly he'd race cross-country to personally toss them in her face.

"Anybody know why this man wants me to stop my bus?" the driver asked over his loudspeaker.

Amy swallowed hard, but couldn't answer.

"He's shouting something," Milly said, sliding her window open.

"*Dammit, Amy, tell him to stop the bus!*"

"*Amy?*" Milly asked, twirling to her new friend. "Is that you?"

"I—I'm not sure," she hedged.

Milly pulled up on her knees, sticking her head out the window. "Amy *who?*" she yelled.

"*Vale!*"

Milly plopped down in the seat, staring at Amy. "Is that gorgeous hunk the 'sort of' friend you were visiting? And if he is, why are you *leaving?*"

"He hates me," she mumbled. "He probably decided to give me a bill for my room and board, that's all."

"Stop the damn bus," shouted the man who'd recognized Beau. "If you don't, he's going to jump off that horse and kill himself trying to get on."

"Oh, let him jump!" Milly cried, her eyes alight. "I bet he can make it."

Amy hid her head in her hands, scandalized.

"Hell," the driver groused. "This ain't in the manual."

"He's going to do it! He's going to jump!" Mabel cried. "Speed up. He'll murder us all."

"Shut up, woman," her husband snapped. "No more caffeine for you. It makes you nuts."

Beau had moved up alongside the bus and was pounding on the door, demanding that it be opened. By now, the general chant was *"Stop the bus! Stop the bus!" The only people not joining in were Mabel and Amy.*

"*Crap!*" the driver groused. Pulling the lever, he opened the front door with a whoosh.

Amid gasps and applause, Beau leaped off his panting stallion and onto the vehicle.

"Stop this damned thing," Beau growled.

Milly groaned. "Shoot! I swallowed my gum!" But Amy hardly registered her choked complaint. She couldn't take her eyes off the furious man towering down the aisle in front of her, dwarfing the vehicle with his angry presence.

When his sparking eyes fell on his quarry, they narrowed dangerously. "One of your passengers took something of mine and I intend to get it back."

The initial shock of Beau's appearance was wearing off, and she found herself overcome by a wave of black, unreasoning anger. Why had Cookie broken her word? And what had she done that had been so unforgivable that would make Beau go to such lengths to disgrace her one final time?

Milly poked Amy's ribs. "What did you take from this guy, the Hope diamond?"

"I didn't take anything. He just hates me."

He stalked over to her and scooped her up, depositing her unceremoniously over a shoulder. She was so disoriented by being treated like a sack of feed, she didn't even struggle as he turned around and headed toward the door.

"Wow!" Milly heaved a breathy sigh. "When Tarzan's through hating you, tell him he can hate me!"

"You can't take that woman off the bus, mister!" the driver yelled.

Beau jerked around to scowl at the scrawny man. "Are *you* going to stop me?"

The driver's head seemed to shrink into his shoulders with Beau's intimidating stare. "Uh—well, I guess it's none of my business. Just get off with her quick. I got my schedule, you know."

Beau carted her down the steps to the roadside. Amy registered the fact that the bus's engines were revving up, and it snapped her out of her stupefaction. "I didn't take anything of yours! Let me down!" She pounded on his back. "That's my bus!"

"Not anymore, it's not."

She wriggled to get free, but without success. "You—you can't *kidnap* me!"

"Weren't you paying attention, Miss Vale?" He began to trudge toward his horse. "I just did."

"Yoooohooo!"

She veered toward the sound. Milly was wagging her suitcase outside the window, clearly not convinced her life was in jeopardy. "You might need this some-day."

Beau altered directions and plucked the suitcase from the girl with a nod of thanks.

"Hey, stud-muffin," Milly called after Beau, "you have any brothers?"

Beau chuckled, but if he responded, Amy couldn't hear, because the bus chose that minute to belch out a roaring backfire. A second later, it began to chug away—abandoning her alone in the wilderness with a crazy man.

She watched the vehicle grow smaller and smaller in the distance as she bounced along on her captor's shoulder. "Who—who do you think you are—Bronco Billy?"

"Shut up, Amy."

"*What*!"

"Which part of *shut up* don't you understand?"

"Don't tell me to shut up, you *snake*. The next bus doesn't come by for three days. What do you expect me to do?"

"I expect you to miss it."

She twisted around, rewarded only with a view of the back of his Stetson. "Put me down, you bully!" She grabbed his hat and swatted his thigh with it. "You'd better get your testosterone checked. I think you're *way* over your quota!" She abruptly found herself settled in his saddle. She blinked in surprise, but regained her senses quickly. "That's better. Now, before you go, point this thing at the nearest police station."

Retrieving his hat from her fingers, he planted it low on his brow. "Sit forward while I get mounted."

"I will not!"

He strapped her suitcase to the saddle, casting her a skeptical look. "I may be a little heavy for you, but if you insist." Placing a boot in the stirrup, he swung himself up. Panicked, she launched herself at the horse's neck. The stallion whinnied and shook his mane at the unexpected weight, but before she toppled head over heels into the snow, she found herself in Beau's lap.

"What's wrong with you?" she cried, wishing she didn't relish the feel of his body against hers. "Has the cold driven you berserk? You do realize it's against the law to hold a person hostage!"

"I thought you wanted to be a rancher's wife," he whispered near her ear.

"I changed my mind," she lied, nervous flutterings prickling her chest.

"Why? Don't you like ranch life?"

Wary of his tricks, she wrenched around to glower at him. "I—I *hate* ranch life."

A sardonic brow rose. "And I suppose you hate Wyoming, too?"

"I *do*. I hate Wyoming with all my heart." No longer able to look him in the eye, she spun away.

"Is there anything else you hate with all your heart?" he queried softly. "Or anyone?"

Her face burned with indignation. "What is this, one last humiliation for the road?"

"Don't change the subject." He aimed his stallion toward a stand of denuded cottonwoods and snow-heavy pines. "I asked if there was anything or anyone out here you hated with all your heart. Besides mountain oysters."

Rancor rose in her like a geyser. How dare he play with her this way. Feeling thwarted and lost, she snapped, "I hate *you* with all my heart!"

"That's too bad," he said, his tone lower, huskier. "Because there's something I have to tell you. Something that has to do with the way I feel about you."

She shifted to eye him suspiciously. "You've made your feelings pretty clear. You hate me."

His half grin was rueful. "No. Not you, Amy. Never you." His tone was gentle, almost apologetic, and her frown deepened with confusion. "I hated what I thought you were. I wanted to hate you, so I made your life miserable. But you tried so hard, I couldn't find anything about you to hate. I almost told you that night in the snow, but when you said you were in love, it made me—well..." His jaw worked. "I vowed to have nothing to do with you after that. But when Snapper rode out to tell me you were leaving on the bus—"

"Snapper told you?"

She was swaying awkwardly as the horse highstepped through the snow. He hugged her securely against him. "Apparently Cookie told Archie, and he told everybody else. I'd ridden out to check fence. It seems everyone on the damned ranch was looking for me to give me the news." He shifted the reins, altering their direction. "I guess they all hoped you and I would get together."

She couldn't stand it any longer, and swung one leg

over the saddle horn so she could more easily read his face. Riding sideways, she peered directly at him, asking hesitantly, "They wanted *us*...?" The revelation was so startling, she couldn't finish.

He nodded, his expression somber. "When I found out you were going away—not marrying Ira—I had to see you. Because if you love my father, I need to know why you're leaving without marrying him."

She saw something new in his eyes, a bright shimmer of vulnerability. The sight was so breathtaking everything inside her went still, and she knew at last her heart needed to be heard. "I don't love your father."

He hesitated, his eyes narrowing. "But I saw love in your eyes."

She shook her head, her lips lifting with melancholy. "You asked me if I was in love. And I was— I *am*. Only—not with your father."

He leaned forward, his lips very near hers. "Then who do you love, Amy?" he whispered.

She closed her eyes, unable to put her feelings into words. "I'm not sure kidnapping me off a bus gives you the right to ask."

"I do have that right," he said, his voice colored by urgency. Perplexed, her gaze shot to his. "Because I love you more than life itself, and I have to find out if you could ever give a damn about me." He brushed her lips with a gentle kiss. "I think I fell in love with you the moment I saw you in that store." He angled his face to the sky, exhaling tiredly. "I wanted you right there, but when I found out you were my father's fiancée, I went a little crazy.'' He shook his head. ''I'm sorry I took out my frustrations on you.''

She stared, hardly aware that they'd entered a secluded wood. High above them, bare cottonwood branches stirred and pine boughs bobbed, raining snow on their heads like cold little kisses.

He considered her quietly as they rode, concern etched on his handsome face. After a time, his lips lifted in a wary smile. ''I see now why the silent treatment can be torture.''

She lowered her gaze, unable to believe the magnitude of what he'd just told her. Trying to convince herself she wasn't dreaming, she drank in his marvelous, male scent, snuggled within his protective embrace. He was really here, really holding her, really whispering the words she'd lost all hope of hearing.

Lifting a shy glance, she was startled to see that his face was indistinct before her, and she blinked back tears of gladness. ''I—I love you....'' she whispered, fearing she would explode if she didn't finally say it aloud. ''I always have, Beau—and I always will.''

He dipped his head for a second, as though in thankful prayer, then gathered her more securely against him.

The way they fitted together was intoxicating, and hot desire sang in her veins. When he lowered his face to hers, she joyfully kissed the man for whom she had so long harbored a love more boundless than the Wyoming sky. From the first time she saw him—as angry, powerful and awe inspiring as the blizzard that brought them together—she had sensed it, but had been afraid to face the truth.

His lips were gentle, coaxing, more thrilling than anything they had shared before. Hugging him to her, she couldn't control her outcry of delight. "Oh, Beau..." she sighed against his lips, feeling a sense of completeness, a rightness. This was where she belonged. She knew she would always find a haven in Beau's arms, and he would find one in hers.

"I want you to marry me as soon as possible," he said, his voice a delicious rumble. "But if you'd rather, we can wait until Mary comes to live with us."

Amy lifted her face away to look at this most remarkable man. Her heart was so full of happiness, she couldn't help but tease, "Ah, but aren't you sending me to France?"

"Not a chance, sweetheart." His grin was so sexy it made her skin prickle with delight. "Someday, we'll go—with Mary *and* our children."

She accepted his kisses with the eager abandon of a woman who has finally found her true love and was no longer afraid to show the depth of her feelings.

Beau chuckled. "By the way, Desiree's been a pain since you left."

She traced his lips with her tongue, teasing, "I hear you were, too."

He laughed, then surprised her by slipping from the saddle and lifting her after him. "Have you ever made love in the snow?"

Her body grew hot with expectation as he shrugged off his coat and spread it in a sunny spot among the trees. "Won't we freeze?" she asked, her voice breathy with yearning.

"I won't let you get cold." He grinned that dimpled

grin that made her melt, and drew her onto the coat. "But we might cause an early thaw."

A soft giggle rose in her throat, and she lifted her arms around his neck, gazing into soft blue eyes so full of deep, sweet emotion the sight took her to a place of contentment she'd never known existed.

He gathered her in his arms, murmuring erotic promises. She closed her eyes, moaning luxuriously as his knowing hands began to pleasure and arouse, his touch almost unbearable in its tenderness.

On this Wyoming winter afternoon, Beau Diablo taught Amy very intimately what passionate commitment was. And Amy knew deep in her soul she would rejoice in the learning—today and forevermore....

Coming in January 2002 from Silhouette Books...

THE GREAT MONTANA COWBOY AUCTION
by
ANNE McALLISTER

With a neighbor's ranch at stake, Montana-cowboy-turned-Hollywood-heartthrob Sloan Gallagher agreed to take part in the Great Montana Cowboy Auction organized by Polly McMaster. Then, in order to avoid going home with an overly enthusiastic fan, he provided the money so that Polly could buy him and take him home for a weekend of playing house. But Polly had other ideas....

Also in the Code of the West

Available at your favorite retail outlet.

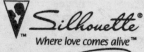

Silhouette®
Where love comes alive™

Visit Silhouette at www.eHarlequin.com

PSGMCA

Uncover the truth behind

CODE NAME: DANGER

in **Merline Lovelace's** thrilling duo

DANGEROUS TO HOLD

When tricky situations need a cool head, quick wits and a touch of ruthlessness, Adam Ridgeway, director of the top secret OMEGA agency, sends in his team. Lately, though, his agents have had romantic troubles of their own....

NIGHT OF THE JAGUAR
&
THE COWBOY AND THE COSSACK

And don't miss
HOT AS ICE (IM #1129, 2/02)
which features the newest OMEGA adventure!

DANGEROUS TO HOLD is available this February
at your local retail outlet!

Look for **DANGEROUS TO KNOW,** the second set of
stories in this collection, in July 2002.

Silhouette®

Where love comes alive™